The Evil in Asheville

The Evil in Asheville

Joshua P. Warren

Writers Club Press
San Jose New York Lincoln Shanghai

Writers Club Press
an imprint of iUniverse.com, Inc.

For information address:
iUniverse.com, Inc.
620 North 48th Street, Suite 201
Lincoln, NE 68504-3467
www.iuniverse.com

ISBN: 0-595-12226-4

Printed in the United States of America

For Mark-Ellis Bennett

I shall hunt him, the ghost and haunter of myself. I have lost the blood that fed me; I have died the hundred deaths that lead to life. By the slow thunder of the drums, the flare of dying cities, I have come to this dark place. And this is the true voyage, the good one, the best. And now prepare, my soul, for the beginning hunt. I will plumb seas stranger than those haunted by the Albatross.

Thomas Wolfe
Look Homeward, Angel

Prologue

ASHEVILLE, NORTH CAROLINA, is a good place for a man to come from—but *he* was from elsewhere. He had nearly glided into town beneath a veil of dark and hungry clouds that loomed above like a reflection of his own mystery. A strong and steely presence, the long gray coat that swirled about his frame gave him the air of a deadly night bird. He swept briskly down each sidewalk, and eyes shifted wearily in their sockets as passersby shuddered at the chill of his swift presence. He seemed to carry the weather with him, as an unsteady sky moved along at his dismal pace.

Since he had arrived, a week or so before, murmurs had followed his fleeting appearances throughout the city. And though he had inspired such clandestine gossip and mystique, superficially, there appeared nothing blatantly special about the man. He was tall and square-shoul-dered, clean cut and stern. A solid brow rested heavily above his deep and crystalline eyes, and his jaw seemed immovable, except to allow stirring words of brutal honesty to escape. There was a gloom about him, and a baggage of emotion and experience that was powerfully felt, yet mortally incomprehensible. Though not particularly old, there was a great oldness and wisdom in his somewhat prematurely weathered face—and that wisdom could be felt like a physical force around him, or projected with his intense, piercing eyes. He was the sort of man who could have shown brightly if he'd so chosen, but instead he seemed like a three-dimensional shadow, even taking the light *in* as he stepped into a room. In short, for better or worse, a man in his presence would surely declare that he stood in the presence of greatness.

Though no one seemed to know why he had appeared so suddenly, lurking about the streets of Asheville, no one dared ask. There was something unapproachable about him—something that would intimidate those wishing to pry into his arcane motives. It was seldom that someone even heard him speak, and those who had claimed his voice carried a solemn resonance that rumbled slightly from deep within his chest. He was a bold figure, great, dark, and tragic—a man of meaning and purpose. And it was easily felt and known by all that whatever mysteries he guarded, he would keep to himself for all time.

As his glinting eyes scanned the great and towering structures of Asheville, there was an ancient sense of kinship between the two. He looked upon the aged buildings and monuments as though they were his own silent sentinels; and the gargoyles, craning wickedly from above, as though they might be old and devilish friends. He shared a darkness with the town that reached deep below its surface and mangled with it below, like the roots of two great and ancient oaks which had twisted inseparably underground.

He was very much like Asheville. To an unseen eye, it might seem as though the two were worn and shaped by the same memories. For Asheville is a harbor of trapped memories. There is a beauty and enchantment which shines from its surface like a polished precious metal. It is that glowing aura of scenic ridges and blinding sunsets that adorns pamphlets and posters. But far below the superficial allure of the town lies the force which feeds its true magnetism. It is a somber river of souls and residues which is always drawing. It is a great and brooding strength that transcends the present, and reaches far into the ever-fleeting chasm of times lost. It is a black and hungry hole, feeding upon life, offering mystery and the ages' wisdom in return. He had so completely tapped into its immortal pipeline that he drew its knowledge into his own veins, and inhaled its emotions to the bottom of his soul.

There is an overwhelming darkness in Asheville that the more sensitive can readily feel, and perhaps he had come to seek it. Who knows from how far he had been drawn? There is a Native American legend about a curse placed on the mountains of Asheville long ago—a curse of which is seldom spoken. It is a spell, whispered by generations, that whosoever shall venture to Asheville must surely return. It is a curse meant to deliver those souls upon which the mountains must continue to feed. But the mountains would not feed upon him. No. For he would feed upon the mountains, and use them for the nourishment of his deeds. But his motive, like the ranges, was great, complex and secret. Upon a mere glance, an intuitive observer could see his intentions were surely of the highest good, or the deepest and most sinister of evils.

CHAPTER ONE

THERE ARE FEW things so morbid as the sunken features of a waxy corpse, and this one, rich or not, was certainly no different. For the first time in his life, Crawford Borley was rested and still. For at last he had ventured unto that shrouded valley from which nary a cold and final whisper escapes.

Let there be no mistaking, however, the exquisite nature of this corpse. It was displayed so beautifully at the head of the funeral parlor that there was no doubting the significance of the man. Standing upright, the coffin, open only at the top, shone a bold and gleaming silver. Intricate designs of lordly valor and prestige, alongside strong, straight lines of strength and definition, reflected the character of its eternal resident. At each side of the suited body, apart from the clutter of floral offerings, there stood two statues. Placed there by the virtue of Borley's final, written wishes, was an owl and a wolf. Like icy guardians, standing at three feet, each was carved from gray stone and possessed a sense of such life and detail that the sculptor, who remained unknown, had surely surrendered a piece of his soul to the idols.

It was a truly majestic sight, and at the center of it all, an enigmatic man, legendary in his stature, whose gaunt face would soon be seen by mortal eyes no more. But despite the fact the reclusive Borley had been rumored to rule his subordinates with a stern and unsympathetic hand, his face looked surprisingly kind, peaceful, and at ease.

His old and peppered hair was parted on the right side with a boyish delicacy. As always in life, his thin mustache was neatly trimmed upon

<1>

his lip. The ghost of a face with firm, dark lines remained—worn and weakened by relentless time. In the pale and ghastly light of the parlor, his flesh looked dull and artificial. The makeup applied to shield the discolorations of death cast a soft glow; a look of powdered plastic, too uniform and cold for flesh.

His lashes were long, black and thin. And though the rest of him possessed the feel of absence, his lashes still seemed alive. They looked as though a surge of thought might shoot into them, and spring them open any moment—like they might flutter and blink, as his glazed brown eyes adjusted to the gasps of the somber crowd. Perhaps he would then lift his head, as though having awoken from a bad dream, to show he wasn't dead after all.

But no. It was not to be. Any life his lashes contained would surely wither away, locked inside the coffin. Yes. Every part of this man was dead. Each wrinkle on his face was frozen stiff and hard. His lips, a faded plum, would never part again. He now appeared like an unreal sculpture, given all the shapes, contours and details of life, yet possessing none.

The first in line, a tall man in an ash-colored suit hovered over the body of his deceased father. He was J.C. Borley, dark and strong. His black, shiny eyes stared blankly onto the corpse of his elder. His wavy, black hair and mustache nearly mirrored the corpse before him; save the thickness of the hair beneath his nose. He was larger than his father, with broad shoulders and long, firm legs. The shadow he cast upon the body made the pale flesh glow like a mask of distant foxfire.

Rich and dismal piano music crept throughout the air as J.C. Borley reached down to bring his hand near his father's. He wanted to touch the flesh, and yet something made him hesitate. Tears streamed from the eyes of those in line behind him. After a few moments, he almost unwillingly placed his fingertips gently on the back of the old Borley's hand. The contact sent a chill up his arm. It was the utter emptiness that stunned him; it was the feeling of flesh like cold, hard rubber. Like all, he had come to think of hands as soft, warm things. He knew of flesh

<2>

like a tender elastic substance, tingling with life. But there was no life in this hand. This hand was a hard shell, completely different from the energy it once housed. It was like a warm and dripping sponge, dried out now into a hard, unfeeling brick.

His fingers sat there lightly for a moment. He waited for them to adjust to the eeriness of the appendage, but it was not to be. And so accepting that, he curled his thumb around to meet the palm of his father's dead hand. The arms of the old Borley were folded in the traditional way, and gripping the corpse's right hand uncomfortably, the middle-aged Borley lifted it a couple inches from the left. His action seemed born more of curiosity than macabre affection, and he immediately regretted the movement. Its fingers slightly bent, the wrinkly hand felt uncannily heavy, weighted down with the complete relaxation only death can bring. The weight, along with the coldness and hardness, solidified the hand as more of an object, than a body part. He lowered it once again.

J.C. Borley retracted his hand and exhaled, as though relieved his experiment was done. With that, a tear flowed from his left eye. He reached up and lightly stroked his father's hair, and then, he bent towards the cadaver in a loving manner, nearly resting his face against the corpse's. Bending his head a touch inward, he gave the old man a soft kiss on the cheek. He then closed his eyes, as if sharing a last moment of silence with his father. Dead man and live one both rested cheek to cheek, and then J.C. Borley slid his face slowly forward, until his own skin touched the silky insides of the coffin, and his lips were intimately next to his rich father's cold ears. "Now it's all mine, you ol' bastard," he whispered softly and wickedly, "now it's all mine."

When he arose, there was nary a dry eye in the parlor. It appeared a beautiful gesture, and though no one had heard his good-bye, they knew it must have been sweet and sacred. To J.C. Borley, it was.

The parlor, located on the west side of Asheville, was filled the most prestigious personalities of the city. Despite his old age, it came as a

<3>

shock to hear Crawford Borley had died. He was the sort of fellow who might have lived forever. His power and intensity had beamed with invincibility. He had lived his life having always gotten the upper hand; and now that he was gone, murmurs spilled throughout Asheville about the mysterious millionaire who lived hidden away in a secluded castle. Though his presence was scarce, his money was intermingled with the town. Most everyone was somehow tied to "Borley money," and this had afforded him great respect, as well as a name of fear.

As J.C. Borley took his seat, the long line of mourners moved tediously through the posh room. The rest of the Borley family followed behind him, and then the mayor, Gil Chesnick. Chesnick, a short, dashing, and artificial man, came from New York, and had only lived in Asheville a few years. It was Borley money that had assured his office, though. Behind him was the county District Attorney, the city Chief of Police, and a host of businessmen, doctors, lawyers, media personalities, and fellow millionaires. J.C. Borley eyed them all, his pupils gleaming devilishly. His father was dead, and he knew they had not come for the dead man, but for him. Now, the castle, the land, the influence—the money—was his.

Each personality, conforming superbly to the code of respect, approached J.C., now standing, to shake his golden hand, hug his mighty shoulders, and speak kind words to his remembering ears. He soaked them all up completely. He embraced his public with all the tenderness of a brand new rich man, and eyed each one innocently, with a smirk concealed below his mustache. He was certainly no stranger to this style. His entire life, he had lived in the leisurely way, traveling the world and sharing the castle with his father and the rest of his family. He had always hovered beneath the cloud of Borley power and protection. He had always worn his suit, combed his hair, minded his manners, and spoken with the eloquence of his breeding. And, most importantly, he had learned the raw greatness of money. But now, he

<4>

had broken through the Borley cloud to become its master. At long last, the labors of his father had truly delivered his own reward.

Standing to the right of J.C. Borley, ready to take a seat beside him, was his wife, Eileen. Short, firm, and with brown hair cropped just above her shoulders, she was a stern and arrogant woman. She was a "lady" of society, proud of her name and influence. The beauty of her youth had faded over the years, and turned more and more rugged as her inner nature seeped out like a destructive acid. An underprivileged child, her first taste of wealth had tainted her forever. It had opened her eyes like fruit from the forbidden tree, and inspired her, with evergrowing aggression, to chase it hungrily, scoffing at those not yet corrupted.

To the left of Borley stood a chunk of condescending muscle named Brock. A combination of fiber and hard fat, he was the prideful remnant of a high school football star. Big in every physical way, he stood as a symbol of intimidation to any fool who might question the power of J.C. Borley alone. Though Borley was a man capable of force in all ways, including physical, he was too rich to sweat. The very basic brain inside Brock's great, sloping cranium was not sharp enough to acquire wealth through mental strategy, but could nonetheless see an opportunity to seize in the company of riches. Introduced to the Borleys by his father, a realtor with whom the family had once dealt, he had served the Borleys faithfully for fifteen years. Like a cartoon gorilla, yet ruddy and clean cut with a chunky, gold school ring, he loomed, contained, at Borley's side. A mist of sweetly biting cologne hovered about him, conflicting strangely and adolescently with the hardness he projected. He was a form of parasite, like most everyone else around Borley. He was a man who had adopted Borley's stature as his own, simply because he was a grunt, confusing his job with that of a somewhat important confidant.

As the unending line of mourners laboriously continued by the old Borley, Brock's eyes routinely scanned the parlor. He was in the privately gleeful habit of eyeing all things suspiciously, like a secret service agent securing his president's perimeter. With a stiff lip and forced

<5>

brow, he searched the most innocent of scenes. But when his eyes passed the broad doorway to the room, his glance screeched to a halt and zoomed back to focus in.

There, partly leaning against the doorway, was the dark figure of the stranger in a long coat. The stranger's crystalline eyes immediately locked with the bulbous, brown pupils of the guard, and an instant tension was felt between the two. A rush of angry heat tingled in Brock's cheeks. For his easily bruised ego, a look in the eye was a threat of confrontation. Brock unlocked his gaze and placed his heavy arm softly on the back of his master. Borley leaned his ear close in the usual way, to hear Brock's observation.

"Do you know that guy in the doorway?" Brock whispered roughly. Both men glanced back slowly and deliberately.

"Where?" asked Borley. The doorway was empty once again.

"He's gone...he must've walked around the corner." His voice pitched slightly higher, Brock felt a tinge of insult by the disappearance of the stranger. "You want me to check it out?"

"What did he look like?" Borley inquired calmly, far less interested in the matter.

"Brown hair, long coat, real stern," Brock gestured as he spoke.

"Don't worry about it," ordered Borley, returning his full attention to the solemn spectacle at hand.

Brock looked to the doorway once again, waiting for another glimpse of the stranger. Borley commonly accused him of overdramatizing small peculiarities in his environment. Like many rich men, Borley felt supremely confident in his own immortality. It was Brock's job to be paranoid, and he sometimes loathed Borley's attitude of carelessness. He waited a full minute for another sign of the stranger's presence, feeling certain of his ominous significance. What Brock lacked in intuition, he compensated for in corruptly obese egotism. Though he was a man of little depth, he was always on guard for signs of confrontation in a likely opponent. In that brief exchange, he had

<6>

seen the steely stare of a predator. He gazed back to the doorway spo-
radically throughout the rest of the session, but there was no sign of
the stranger's imposing form again.

✳   ✳   ✳

The procession moving through Riverside Cemetery was black and
poetic. Against a surrealy-purpled horizon moved the dreary silhouettes of a hearse, and a legion of long, expensive automobiles moving
sadly across the landscape. The narrow roadway was filled with wealth
from side to side, as the silent string of mourners passed each stately
tree, and rounded each sloping curve of the hilly grounds.

The somber, grainy monoliths of Asheville's finest patrons welcomed
their newest tenant. From tall, exquisite angels, wings spread, arms
folded, and eyes closed tight in stony remembrance, to simple marble
slates half-hidden in the shiny grass, there was an air of distinction
greater than that of most cemeteries. Amongst the tombs and graves of
congressmen and visionaries, and accepted sons of the city like Thomas
Wolfe and O. Henry, there stood mausoleums sculpted with the passion
and precision of times lost. The place smelled as priceless as a museum,
and felt more dark and sacred than a cathedral of the highest order. It
represented that gray era of man when art, intellect, and taste merged to
create an unsure etiquette; when the old fashioned times were withering
like an autumn leaf, never to be truly found again, but cherished like a
religion in the unwavering walls of high society. It was the perfect bed
for Crawford Borley.

Like the phantom of one great, crawling organism, the procession
crept rhythmically as J.C. Borley, in black fedora, listened dreamily to
Mozart's *Requiem* within his limousine. He contributed to the bleak
atmosphere of death in every way. He felt it was his father's wish, and he
knew it was his own.

<7>

At last, the procession stopped before a lush plot of land veiled by the branches of a towering oak. All had anticipated the marker at the gravesite of Crawford Borley. Ebony and slick, tall, sharp and phallic with a massive, stone base, it truly met their expectations. "BORLEY" was etched deep and thickly on its face. The accompanying text was simple, direct, minimal, and powerful. In life, Borley had been a master of understatement, and so it was in death. For him, images were the greatest messengers.

After pouring slowly from their vehicles and gathering traditionally by the gravesite, the small ocean of mourners parted biblically to allow the casket passage to the grave. Those six carrying it, not including J.C. Borley, held it slightly higher than usual, despite their own discomfort. There was something so meaningful—historical almost—about the duty, or honor, that it compelled them to lift the fallen icon as far as possible from the infinite earth in which he would soon be entombed.

With a gray sky presiding, J.C. Borley, his wife, and Brock all stood close to the neatly dug pit beneath a tent. To look upon that voluminous rectangle conjured waves of philosophical conflict. There was something so basic and natural about a great, damp hole in the dirt, and yet the metal framing around it, there to facilitate the coffin's final decent, appeared so rigid, mechanical, and far from the sensitivities of death. There was no honor in its presence. As J.C. Borley stared blankly upon it, he felt a tinge of regret deep inside. It occurred to him that these same accessories had been used to bury filthy commoners, and he felt it nearly disgraceful to his father. Had he anticipated the necessity of such gear, he would have surely seen his father's body was treated more personally. That was how it had always been. Crawford Borley liked to humanize all things as much as possible. He never typed, but always scrawled elegantly with a fine pen; he never ate food from a chain— only meals prepared by a cook whose name he knew, and who would oversee its personal delivery.

<8>

As J.C. Borley retreated deeper and deeper into the vastness of his mind, he was startled by the sudden, small, but nearly violent tug on his sleeve. It came at a moment of least expectation, and its recognition was immediately followed by a sense of outrage. Borley shot his head around to face Brock. Brock's eyes were large, and his face looked both surprised and concerned. "Look!" he whispered, nodding behind them, "there he is again!"

Obviously displeased that Brock had disturbed him at such a time, Borley glanced back. What he saw however, immediately replaced his disapproval of the disruption with eerie fascination.

Across the road, and near the tree line that enclosed a section of the cemetery, sat the stranger. Like a sinister vulture, he was perched upon a brawny tombstone, his coat hanging down as though he might have long, concealing wings. His presence brought an unnatural shadow to the plots which surrounded him, and from his melancholy outpost, he was watching. He observed the festivities before him, his face unsympathetic, nearly defiant even, as he stared sternly and directly into the somewhat distant face of J.C. Borley.

Though such a display of disrespect would normally enrage the mighty Borley, he felt no such emotion mingled with his bewilderment. Brock turned quickly as though to storm off towards the stranger, feeling it surely unnecessary to even ask Borley's permission under such conditions. Borley however, grabbed his upper arm. "No," he said quietly, still staring at the bold intruder, "just calm down." Brock was shocked.

"But…?"

"No," Borley repeated a bit more firmly. "This isn't the time."

By this point, a few more people in the crowd had realized something strange was going on. Scattered faces quietly turned to investigate, just as puzzled at the sight of the observer. Borley turned back to the burial activities with the apparent desire, or duty, to ignore the dark watcher. Deep within his black eyes though, gears were cranking. He remained supremely cognizant of his peripheries, yet stayed focused on the final

<9>

glimpses of his father's container. He was physically calm and strong, as usual, despite Brock's restlessness beside him.

For the rest of the ceremony, Borley did not look back to the stranger. He felt, in a way, to acknowledge the watcher might grant him some dignity which Borley refused to give. Especially considering his ascent upon the old Borley's death, he was a man too powerful for any individual to be of concern. Upon the slightest notion of worry, he quickly reassured himself that there was nothing to fear. J.C. Borley knew all too well that his deepest power came not from the money, dignity, or contacts, but instead his pure lack of scruples. He was willing to take the low blows—to make that clandestine midnight phone call to the men who wore the gloves—and this methodology of subsystems gave him the greatest confidence of all. For him, subservience to codes of moral ethics was a weakness to be condemned. In his mind, a man of true power and greatness accepted no societal restriction as his master. In this world, it seemed he alone would master himself. At times of threat, great or subtle, he reminded himself of this in a piercing flash of thought.

When it came time to lower the coffin into the abyss, a hole of such finality that no one dared look within, the group adjourned to the outside perimeter of the gravesite. Once again, J.C. Borley allowed his eyes a casual pass by the tombstone where the stranger had been. As expected, he was gone. Even more so than his presence, his absence garnered an uneasiness deep in Borley's gut.

"You know that guy?" Brock asked anxiously, leaning down to bring his ear close to Borley as they walked away.

"What's going on, J.C.?" Eileen's words darted from her mouth, as she paced a bit swiftly at his side.

"Listen," said Borley, stopping and drawing the two close into a private triangle. "No. I don't know him. And frankly I don't care."

"Know who?" Eileen chimed, her mouth tight, and eyes scornful.

"Some guy watching the funeral over there," Borley waved his hand as though partially exasperated.

<10>

Brock spoke dutifully and professionally. "He looked suspicious, Mrs. Borley. I think he's been following us." Eileen looked back to Borley with a flash of concern.

"For God's sake, it was just a weirdo," Borley stated firmly, turning his attention away from the two to accept a hug from an elegant female patron of the Chamber of Commerce. Both Brock and Eileen could instantly identify the meaning of Borley's tone. He routinely ended conversations in such a way. It was Borley's way of emphasizing *the final word*. Accepting that, each quickly switched their attention to the distractions of the setting—mingling with the sympathetic crowd. Borley carried on in his usual, charismatic way, making no more mention of the strange occurrences. But secretly, a portion of his mind was pondering, carefully and thoroughly, the stranger. J.C. Borley was a man of great intuition, and deep inside he knew that he would see the dark watcher again.

✳   ✳   ✳

That night, the chilling freshness of October air filled the streets of Asheville. A hint of rich wood smoke drifted about in soothing wisps, and drying leaves scraped across the rough pavement in a gentle evening breeze. Suddenly, a patch of crisp leaves crunched beneath the firm footsteps of the stranger in the long coat. He walked briskly, with intent, as a clear full moon shone pale and bright above. The sky was a dark but glowing shade of blue, streaming down like a celestial cloak upon the city. The color of the moon speckled the textures of the town, enhancing some elements of the streets mystically, while burying others in the deepest tones of indigo.

As he made his way down Lexington Avenue, a street buzzing with night life, music, chatter, and traffic, merged into a hum of social activity, he eyed those he passed carefully. There were tattered hippies, toting tall,

<11>

twisted walking sticks, unkempt bushes of hair, filthy sandals, and reeking of freshly-smoked marijuana; there were new age gurus, from those simpletons who adhered stylishly to the trends of baggy clothes, exotic jewelry and ultra laid-back attitudes, to hard core patrons, wearing gowns, carrying drums and flutes, and sporting all from turbans to head dresses; there were punk rockers, with spiked, colored hair, black leather, dog collars, army boots, chains dangling from the attire, and piercings riddling the body's most bizarre places; there were preppy teenagers, and prospective "20-something" singles, well-groomed with stylish, trendy clothes, mingling about; there was a host of vagabonds, prostitutes, and drug pushers, as well as a strictly conservative, upright population of Christian youth, congregating in cafes. From God to Satan, all were represented—and most all had come together to drink coffee, smoke cigarettes, discuss their overly-philosophical, and certainly proprietary, perspectives, and be "unique" within their pseudo-macrocosm.

Navigating the peaceful, sometimes intoxicated, bystanders, the stranger passed through the broken, amber light spilling from windows and doorways, and disappeared momentarily within the darkness cast by each alley. It was evident he was searching. Those small groups of socialites gathering at lamp posts viewed him suspiciously, if but for an instant, as he blatantly ignored their presence and continued to weave about, spying those more ragged patrons, sitting hunched against a building, as though he might be shopping for an item at the local grocer's.

He entered an inviting wrought iron entrance, skillfully crafted between two brick buildings, to find an open veranda, upon which much of the young crowd sat smoking and conversing beneath the arms of weeping, carefully-planted trees. Constructed in levels of antiquated red tile, there were narrow, dark corridors leading off between a peculiar design of adjoining buildings. Some descended, or ascended, in a short flight of steps, off of which the main or back entrance to a shady new bar may reside. He explored the dirty, forgotten crevices, until two

<12>

gray, bulky forms, barely visible in the half-light, caught his eye. Cautiously, he approached them.

Two filthy, musty vagabonds sat side by side, carelessly and relaxed, with their heads slightly arched back against a concrete wall. One black and one white, they had each constructed a wardrobe from both whole pieces, like olive drab coats from the Salvation Army, and tattered remains of worn clothes. Despite the awkward buildup of unnecessary bulk, such tatters, in sufficient quantity, conglomerate into whole out-fits, unattractive to the eye but effective in shielding from the harrowing elements. The black one, scruffy, middle-aged, but prematurely weath-ered, wore a black toboggan pulled tight below his ears. The white one, much older, wore a ragged blue cap, from beneath which long locks of dirty white hair flowed. He wore a thick, well-formed beard, as white as his locks, but tainted with a slightly yellowish tint. Apart in their crevice, they were a strong contrast to the blossoming, exploring culture that dawdled around them. Their eyes beamed dully with the hard, glassy look of experience. These were men who had struggled fiercely and lengthily with life—and lost.

Though usually glad to see company, the two were overcome by a pang of dread when the large, erect form of the stranger obstructed the dim light in the walkway, blocking them inside. Instantly speechless and anxious, they both stared up impotently with large expectant eyes. The power of his presence dwarfed their worn and broken spirits. He stood quietly for a moment, examining the prospects. Seeing some desirable qualities, which only he could know, he spoke sternly.

"How would you gentlemen like to make some money?" The bums were surprised, but not yet relieved, by his introduction.

"Money?" the black one yelped. The two had often begged for money, but it was seldom offered. "Hell yeah."

"What're your names?"

"I'm Sergeant William Elkins Bromfield the Third," answered the black one with the prideful overenthusiasm typical of an obnoxious vagabond.

<13>

"You can just call me Fish," the old white one grinned. His teeth were rotted and yellow. Fish extended his hand, "So how much money we talkin' here buddy?"

The stranger made no attempt to shake hands, but stood firmly as a superior figure. "Come with me," he said.

✳   ✳   ✳

Despite its artistic beauty, many considered Riverside Cemetery an eerie place during the day—but most any sensible person considered it eerie in the gloom of night. For after the sun has dwindled and died behind the mountains, all those qualities of tranquillity and everlasting rest began to change. That sentimental era bridged by the history of the grounds came to life. There was a palpable sense of awareness in the place, as though the sleeping spirits yawned, and then seeped up to the surface to roam and interact. There was a swirling sense of life about the grounds—but not life as we know it; life in its full, dark magnitude, as only the dead can know. That noble smell of a museum, which floats upon the air in daytime, changed; smelling instead like the damp aroma of a cavern, teeming with unseen life. The unfamiliar shadows cast by tombstones and statues oozed along the ground and around the trees, soaking up the terrain as though a quiet, nocturnal creature, returning to reclaim its ground and feed. It was a time for the disembodied, and those carrying flesh were not welcomed.

On that October night, the dark life of the cemetery was startled by faint, orange illumination parting the growth outside the grounds. Having scaled the iron fence, the stranger and his two companions emerged. Upon entering the clearing, they stopped for a moment of observation.

"Man, I donno about this here," the Sergeant said, a slight whine below his softly panting breath.

<14>

"You just do as you're told if you want the rest of your money," the stranger reprimanded him. Each man held an old fashioned kerosene lantern, casting forth a ghastly glow. The two bums were loaded down with shovels, a crowbar, sledgehammer, wedge, and various other highly suspicious tools.

"Say," fish added, "how come we couldn't carry flashlights instead o' these old lanterns."

"Because flashlights throw a farther, brighter beam. We have all the light we need right here." The stranger examined each man to make sure none of the tools had been dropped or left behind. "All right," he said, "from now on, be quiet. The only one who needs to talk is me. Understand?" The two bums nodded in affirmation. "Okay, let's go."

The three figures started across the cemetery, choosing their steps carefully. Avoiding the dry fallen leaves proved tedious, and so they proceeded slowly, calmly, and strategically. The farther they walked, the more the bums feared the place. Old superstitions were embedded deeply in their skulls, and they could easily feel the dark life of the cemetery, breathing without breath, watching without sight. Thick, wispy clouds obscured the full moon, making the path outside the faint lantern light look black. The air was even more chilly, and they felt it more sensitively on their flesh, as their hearts pounded faster in their chests, and jitters in their empty stomachs fluttered into a wave of weakness that swept across their bodies.

Fish was suddenly overcome by instinct. "This don't feel right—I think we need to turn back."

The stranger halted with a flash of outrage, briskly drawing his index finger to his lips. "Shhh…Listen, you wanna go back? Fine. But you're going alone," he whispered.

"Man, I donno," the Sergeant chimed in quietly, "I gotta bad feelin' about this, too."

"Fine," the stranger resolved. "Give me my money back, and go on."

<15>

Only then did it occur to both bums that neither of them had the courage to separate from the stranger, even if they did so together. Although he, too, was aware of the magnitude of the place, he was convinced his mission was important. And though they didn't know him, his personal strength alone was their only fragment of security.

"You have nothing to fear from the dead," said the stranger, "but if you don't shut up and calm down, you might join them." The two vagabonds looked shocked at his words. "A caretaker's liable to put a bullet in you."

The two men took deep breaths, and the stranger nodded onward. They continued their trek near the edge of the grounds, towards the secluded plot where Crawford Borley had chosen to rest in peace. Tense and nervous, the vagabonds weren't sure what worried them more: the threat of ghosts, or the threat of humans. In any case, they stayed tight on the heels of the stranger, his head held high like a true leader, marching fearlessly into the heart of an enemy mine field. The Sergeant cringed as the stranger led them across graves. Despite the pattern of fallen leaves, he tried desperately to step over them, imagining the dark earth below him riddled with decaying corpses, and the grounds spread before him, a field of skeletons and death. The thought of what he would soon be doing made him even more uneasy.

The Sergeant suddenly shuddered. "I just got a cold chill man," he said.

The stranger suddenly stopped, and the men halted. Casting his eyes downward, the stranger nodded. The Sergeant was standing on hard soil, bizarrely enough, a blank headstone was mounted at its side.

"Perhaps you're standing on your own grave," said the stranger.

The Sergeant's eyes blossomed, and he rushed onward, the stranger chuckling behind him.

At last, they arrived. The lone monument of Crawford Borley looked even more potent as the warm lantern light cast a devilish aura on the stone. Black shadows reached up from below the etched letters, turning and stretching wickedly as the lights moved around them. A

<16>

breeze rustled the dry trees as the stranger grabbed a shovel which Fish held balanced on his left shoulder. Lifting it like a spear, he plunged it powerfully downward into the soft soil. It stuck deep with a muffled sound of impact. "Well," said the stranger, gazing down, "this is it."

With horror, Fish's eyes seemed to supernova. "Jesus Christ! We're gonna dig up Crawford Borley?!"

"Quiet!" the stranger exclaimed under his breath. "Now go on. You know what to do."

"I know our deal," said the Sergeant, shaking his head wearily, "but I think this is wrong, man."

"Listen," the stranger lowered his brow, looking the Sergeant directly in the eye, "you want the other twenty dollars, don't you?" The Sergeant hesitated, then nodded. "Besides, you said you were in the war. Right? A dead body's no big deal to you, eh?"

"Okay man, all right," the Sergeant agreed, setting down his tools and taking up the other shovel. "Let's get this over with."

Within the next few minutes, the bums were well within the straining task of digging up Crawford Borley. The sound of hard, flat metal being shoved into softly packed dirt filled the air, followed by the weighty pat of a clump hitting the ground. From time to time the stranger, standing on the sideline, arms crossed and watching intensely, would remind them to quieten down. It was a sight fit for an old thriller—two silhouettes, their surroundings basked by the soft orange fire light, digging up a grave beneath a partially-clad full moon; the ebony obelisk of a millionaire looming over them.

Stopping occasionally for breaks, and a near-mad guzzle from a water bottle, the two bums shined and dripped with sweat. Each had already stripped off his coat and shirt halfway through the task. As they disappeared farther and farther below the surface, it wasn't long before the two were standing down within the lightless pit, looking above occasionally to see the stranger hovering at the entrance to the hole, like a foreman in hell, peering down to oversee the hard labor of the

<17>

damned. He seemed so far above that it chilled them to look up. And it occurred to them, more than once, that they might be digging their own grave—having been lured by a demon to desecrate holy ground for wicked money.

It seemed a short eternity before the Sergeant's shovel clanked sharply against hard metal. The sound echoed from the pit and carried farther than any of the men expected. All motion suddenly halted as the stranger's eyes scanned the darkness, watching for the appearance of a new light. After a few moments of continued stillness, he motioned to the diggers that all was clear.

"Quiet," he said. "Now clear it off carefully."

The bums tossed the shovels to the surface in graceful, forceful arches. Then, dropping to their knees, they began clearing the dirt away. The dirt hissed across the surface of the metal as the bums wiped it aside. The Sergeant continued wiping while Fish used his stiffened fingers like spades, digging a trench along the side of the coffin where the latch might be. The process of clearing the coffin, and digging out its side for opening, seemed slower and more painstaking than burrowing to the casket. When its side was finally exposed enough for opening, Fish motioned to the stranger.

The stranger handed a lantern down to the Sergeant, his muscular arm outstretched almost painfully to accept it. Next, he handed down the crowbar. "I ain't openin' this damn thing," the Sergeant whispered, "I just said I'd help dig it up."

"You don't have to open it," replied the stranger, "just break the lock."

Maneuvering awkwardly in the pit, the two vagabonds tried to orient the crowbar properly. Once they had established a hold for the tool, they strained desperately on the lever to break the seal. The sole lock was positioned between the upper and lower halves of the casket, serving them both. Their arms weak from exertion, they couldn't budge the solid connection. "It's too hard," Fish called up softly.

<18>

"All right," said the stranger, as though accepting the two bums had done a good enough job. He reached down to the Sergeant. "Give me your hand." The Sergeant gladly complied. Embracing his sweaty fingers, the stranger pulled him, with surprisingly little effort, from the hole. Taking hold of the sledgehammer and wedge, the stranger himself, hopped down.

Once inside the morbid pit, he handed the wedge to Fish. "Stick this in the middle of the lock," he ordered.

"Ain't that gonna be awful loud?" Fish asked doubtfully.

"That's why we do it swift and hard," answered the stranger, as though experienced in the task. Fish didn't question him again, but placed the wedge at the lock as he'd been told. However, the space provided was not tight enough to hold it in.

"It won't stay," Fish said.

"Then hold it."

"Hold it!" Fish looked up, his brow furrowed at the absurdity of the statement. "You'll mash my fingers off."

"Hold it, I said," the stranger ordered firmly. With a great sigh, Fish lifted the wedge and held it firm in the hole, moving his fingers as far down as possible. The stranger lifted the sledgehammer. Both Fish, and Sergeant watching above, cringed. With a quick and mighty strike, the sledgehammer came down in a blur. It hit the top of the wedge squarely, and a burst of energy released with a powerful pop. The seal was broken.

Though his expression was unchanged, there was an air of satisfaction about the stranger. "Here," he said, retrieving the wedge and handing it, along with the sledgehammer, up to the Sergeant. The stranger knelt down to the coffin, and a new sense of seriousness and respect emanated from him. It was time to open the coffin.

"I don't know if I need to see this," Fish's voice trembled. The stranger ignored him, and reached for the top half of the coffin. Bothered by the scenario more than he would outwardly express, the stranger's fingers curled underneath the cold, heavy lip at the coffin's

<19>

edge, and a chill ran through him to see his fingers inside with the dead man. Without prolonging the suspense of the action, he lifted the unwieldy top half.

There, in the distorted light of the lantern, was exposed the head of a man. Though more object than human, its basic shape and form sent a surge of fear through all three men the very instant it was seen. The lantern was placed poorly, and the details of the face could not be plainly observed. The stranger lifted the lantern and brought it over the coffin. The soft amber light fell mysteriously on the empty, sallow face of Crawford Borley. There was complete silence amongst the men, as they stared at the lifeless visage and torso.

Borley's face wore the look of calmness and tranquillity that the stranger had seen at the funeral. His hair looked surprisingly natural, and the serenity of his features brought a strange calmness to the men. There was a look of peace as though the old millionaire had seen an angel at the moment his soul had slipped away tenderly. Fish was most impressed. He knew this was the only way he would ever come so close to the mythical titan. And from all the pictures he'd seen and stories he'd heard, he expected the corpse's face to be rigid and abhorrent. It was a near magical moment, as the two vagabonds, especially, felt an unexplainable bond with the man.

The stranger studied him carefully, shifting perspectives to see the corpse from several sides. Uplifting his nose and noble chin, peering down with a crinkled brow like a jeweler inspecting a rare gem, he looked in Borley's ears, up his nostrils, and down upon his crown. He never touched the corpse, though the bums, who could only speculate on the stranger's intent, could imagine him prodding it any time. Finally, feeling satisfied with his examination, he motioned for Fish to help him with the lower half of the casket.

Fish, and the stranger, slipped their fingers underneath, and then lifted the steely panel. Once open, and resting against the wall of the pit,

<20>

the stranger brought the lantern down for a look. Each man was over-come by instant, nauseating horror.

The lower half of the casket was empty. The bottom of Borley's torso was twisted, torn flesh; a pale, broken spine jutting out from the raw meat. Thin leather straps held the torso in place deceptively. The tranquillity of Borley's final expression was a shocking mockery of whatever power had ruthlessly, and savagely, disposed of his lower half.

Above, the Sergeant lunged away from the grave with a deep, raspy cough, followed by the sound of acidic vomit gurgling up and splashing on the ground. The stranger eyed the macabre display with a firm lip of contempt. All blood drained from his cheeks, Fish was too shocked to fully process the revolting remains. "H…How…How did he die?" Fish stammered, almost child-like.

The stranger lifted his eyes, already lost in a sea of thoughts. He then turned to Fish and gave a lethargic nod. "*Heart failure.*"

<21>

CHAPTER TWO

LIKE AN EXPLOSION of brilliant sunbursts, a flurry of golden autumn leaves glided down and fell upon Asheville. The warm breeze lifted them in near-weightless swirls and either soared them to the ground, or dropped them gently, twirling downwards as though a feather upon a sigh. The urban population was abundant on such dreamy days. Both tourists and longtime residents were drawn to the enchanting outdoors. The dark, vast mountains, splashed with the bright colors of fall, were a spellbinding backdrop to the honorable structures in their foreground. The courthouse and city building, towering gems of intricate architecture, stood as icons of the city to travelers from afar. The Vance Monument, like a miniature Washington Monument of gray stone, soared upwards in Pack Square, the center of Asheville, like an elegant, dignified projectile, ready to launch deeply into the sparkling azure sky.

Though the town was speckled with those wishing to breathe in the rich scenery, it was not the beauty of the area which interested the stranger. He passed amongst the sightseers, heading somewhere with intent, as usual, viewed as nothing more than another eccentric element of a place renown for artistic genius. On speedy foot, he made his way down Haywood Street, not far from the masterfully-constructed Basilica of St. Lawrence, and veered to a right, then sharp left, finding the brief and narrow Wall Street. Wall Street was cobblestone, and on each of its sides an array of warm and intriguing shops and restaurants could be found.

<22>

There was an overwhelming sense of old-fashioned peace and comfort on Wall Street. As the stranger trekked along its timeless path, he felt transported to the era of Riverside Cemetery. It was a sentiment shared by all on the street. The filling aroma of delicious foods wafted in the breeze, intermingled with the sounds of delicate music occasionally escaping from an open doorway. The signs of shops sometimes hung ornately above their doors, written and constructed with the taste and care of antiquated times.

A little girl with long blond hair, and wearing a neat blue dress, bubbled with excitement after reaching and jumping to snag a falling leaf from the sky. It had evaded her, dodging in and out erratically on its smooth descent. Once in her grasp, she held it tight and pulled it close to her body, hunching slightly to guard it. Closing her eyes, she made a wish. When she opened them, the blinding sun was blotted out by the form of the stranger. She inhaled suddenly at his huge presence which casually swept around her to enter a shop behind. With wide eyes, she raced to her nearby mother.

The shop which the stranger entered smelled like a pungent mixture of incense and candles. The tinkling of a bubbling miniature fountain dribbled in the air. Placed in the corner, it was a skull, with water which should have presumably been dyed red, pouring from its crown to a bed of rocks below. Dream catchers, tarot cards, bongs, fantasy artwork, occult books, and other items of controversy and intrigue were arranged around the shop. There were no customers inside, but a female clerk sat alone at the counter. With long, black hair, and a right ear lined with silver piercings, she relaxed beside a box of arrowheads, reading a copy of *Haunted Asheville*. Upon his entry, she lifted her eyes from the page, and smiled tenderly, crookedly. "Hi."

"Hello," he replied.

"Can I help you?"

"I'm looking for Kinner," he said, leaning in close to the counter.

<23>

"Okay," she turned her head towards a doorway behind her, blocked off by worn, puke-green curtains. "He's in the back. Hold on just a sec."

In a graceful, feminine way, she disappeared behind the curtains. Left alone, the stranger eyed the peculiar items in the shop as though calculating their presence into some grand, self-absorbing equation. In a few moments, the girl returned. At her side was a ruffled, scrawny spectacle of a merchant.

He had salt and pepper hair, slightly stringy and dull. It was a modest length on the sides, yet long enough to reach his shoulders in the back. Despite his uneven complexion, scruffy face, and near lack of lips, his most bizarre characteristic was a wandering right eye. A bright and unique shade of hazel, it stared obliviously into what might have been another eerie dimension. And though his left eye did not compensate with the most direct stare, it at least focused acutely. Altogether, his unbalanced features and scraggly burlap shirt, made him look something akin to the subject of a cubist nightmare.

"You need me?" Kinner asked raspily.

"Yes," the stranger answered. "I'd like to speak with you alone."

The good eye brightened and flashed with bewilderment. The other remained the same. "What's the problem?"

"There's no problem. I just need to speak with you alone."

"Alright," Kinner said. "Come on back here." He motioned to the area behind the curtains.

The small back room was cluttered and dusty. It was packed with a wealth of obscure, occult paraphernalia. An oak ouija board, built on a lavishly carved stand, set near the wall. The crystal pointer magnified a mythical, boisterous image of the moon. A collection of pendulums dangled from pegs on the wall. Some were as simple as cheap rings tied to the end of threads; others were sparkling, balanced tips, hanging from the end of a taut silver or gold chain. A bookshelf held an array of old and mystic titles, from *The Necronomicon* to the *Holy Bible*. There

<24>

were rows of ceremoniously arranged candles, and gothic sculptures of gargoyles, wizards, and the grim reaper.

Closing the curtain behind them, Kinner spun around to meet the stranger. "So what's goin' on?" He leaned on a messy metal cabinet which was hidden under flattened, stained piles of bills, statements, and invoices. The stranger crossed his arms and pressed his chest forward with swollen virility.

"Tell me about Borley's Castle."

Kinner's level of attention immediately dissipated. "I don't know anything about Borley's Castle," he said, displaying a touch of premature exasperation.

The stranger reached into his pants pocket withdrawing a neatly-folded fifty dollar bill. He laid it on the cabinet beside the merchant. Kinner rolled his good eye. "Listen," he said, his voice uneasy, "I don't know anything—I've heard it's haunted, that's all I know."

"Oh really?" The stranger's expression hardened confrontationally. "It's funny you can tell all the teenage boys on this side of town, but you can't tell me."

"Are you a cop?"

The stranger smirked. "Cops don't pay for information."

The merchant subconsciously took a slight step back, withdrawing from his visitor. "Are you one of them?"

"Them?"

"The Borleys…Are you with the Borleys?"

"No," the stranger reassured him. "I'm not with the Borleys, nor do I sympathize with them."

Kinner glanced down to the fifty dollar bill. It was obvious he needed the money. "I…," he paused, "Why should I tell you anything?"

The stranger was losing patience. "You can either take the fifty dollars and tell me, or I can use other means of extraction. It's your decision."

<25>

Kinner looked down, mulling the predicament over in his mind. On the verge of complying, a new thought sprang into his head. "Who are you anyway?"

The stranger, inhospitable, ignored the stall. "This is the last time I'm going to ask you civilly," he threatened, "Tell me about Borley's Castle."

"Alright, alright," Kinner submitted, his palms already sweating. "Look, I don't have all the answers. All I know is, there's something evil inside that castle."

"Evil?"

"Yes. The Horror—that's what they call it. They say it stays locked in a room at the end of the hall on the fourth floor." Kinner's throat was dry, and his manner was jittery.

"Yes?"

"It's such an evil room that you can't sit with your back next to the wall in the room beside it. It feels like wicked eyes are looking over your shoulder, and the hair on your neck tingles with electric fear—like it's watching and breathing behind you."

"What is it?" the stranger asked intensely.

"I don't know. Nobody knows. Everyone who has ever stayed in that room leaves dead or insane, and lots of them die of fright." Kinner shot his eyes around the room, then leaned closer to the stranger. "*Do you realize how many people have died in that castle?*"

"How do you know this?" the stranger inquired.

"I've lived here for a long time," Kinner nodded. "People talk. You hear things, you know—stories. Some true, some BS, but there's somethin' goin' on."

"Have you ever been inside the castle?"

Kinner grinned with a half-shake of his head. "Borley won't let anybody inside that castle."

"I heard you'd been there," said the stranger, lowering his brow.

There was a shift in the merchant's nature. He looked down, as though a somewhat sensitive subject had surfaced. After a moment of

<26>

mental preparation, he looked back up. "I've never been *inside* the castle," he said. "Sometimes I tell the kids that just to scare 'em. But I *have* been on the property."

"When was this?"

"That was a long time ago," Kinner reflected. "I was barely a teenager. Me and some o' my friends thought we'd sneak into the castle to see if the stories were true. We didn't make it that far across the fence, though. Some o' Borley's guys got ahold of us." He stopped, looking down at the floor wearily.

"What happened?" asked the stranger.

Internally, Kinner was obviously struggling with what to say. "They uh…they just roughed us up a little, that's all." The stranger could sense that Kinner was holding back, but felt no need to press the issue. Kinner looked back up, having moved to a new thought. "They say there's a lot of devil worship on that mountain, but nobody talks about it."

"I need to get inside that castle," said the stranger. "Do you have a layout of the place?"

"Hell no," Kinner answered, as though the question was absurd. "The Borleys keep that stuff secret. But I tell ya though, if you want some real information, there's a guy you need to talk to."

"Who?"

"He's a reporter with the *Citizen-Times*—"

"No," the stranger abruptly cut him off. "I don't talk to reporters."

"But this guy ain't like that," Kinner said. "He's been researching the Borleys for years, but not for the paper. He does it on his own time. Here," searching speedily, he found an old business card and, grabbing a pen, flipped it over to write. "His name's Wilson Benedict." Kinner scrawled the name. "I don't have his number, but you can call the paper."

The stranger took the card with little enthusiasm, and slipped it into his coat pocket. "What else can you tell me about the castle?" asked the stranger.

"That's all I know," he replied. "I swear."

<27>

The stranger stood for a few moments of silence, staring deeply in the merchant's good eye, as though to detect deceit. When satisfied, he nodded his head, and lowered his confrontational stance. Disappointed, yet sated, he turned to leave. Then suddenly, he stopped and looked back to Kinner. "By the way," he said, "what happened to your eye?"

Kinner was taken aback by such a personal question. "I…I was born this way," he said. The stranger's gaze wandered into space for a moment, obviously thinking; then returning, he nodded his head and passed through the curtains.

Kinner stood by himself in the stuffy room, pondering over the stranger's questions. Picking up the fifty and cramming it in his pocket, he heard the stranger mutter a courtesy to the girl outside and then exit the shop. He scanned the row of books on a nearby shelf. At the end was a black and white photograph of a beaming, delightful little boy in a silver frame. The child's eyes were bright, and his gaze was healthy, firm and straight.

*   *   *

Like a dark, everpresent storm cloud, Borley's Castle was planted majestically on a steep mountain, the city of Asheville sprawling at its base. It towered so high above that most never lifted their eyes far enough to see its rocky, gothic form looming. And yet, there was always a feeling of being watched as you strolled down the streets of Asheville. Contrived of worn, gray stone, the wicked structure sat quietly and firmly like a massive beast, breathing slower and deeper than the eye could detect. It had been seated on the mountain so long the two had merged, making the castle look rugged and natural, and the mountain look hewn and sculpted. There was, and had always been, a gloomy, drawing energy about the location itself, and the melancholy mountain had most certainly called to the builder of the tremendous stronghold.

<28>

Besides speculation based upon its leering silhouette, no one seemed to know how the grounds or interior of the structure appeared. There were rumors, of course, about fantastic statues, mystic ponds, and overwhelming feats of architecture; but no one really knew. Asheville was full of castles and mansions. There was a time when it was fashionable for its wealthy residents to compete by constructing monumental homes. All of them were marvels, yet none cast the intrigue of Borley's Castle. It was certainly the most sinister, and the one which the public could never see. Though there were other homes on the mountain, Borley's Castle clearly dominated the range. It projected somber, subtle power—old, strong, and bitter. The power could be lucidly observed not only by its location, age, and design, but also its entrance.

Not visible from the winding, near-vertical roadway leading up the mountain, the castle was hidden at the end of a moderately long drive. On its opposite side, the mountain dropped off in a treacherous slope that flowed into a secluded cove, another mountain, much lower, rising on the opposite side. The black entrance gates were tall, iron, and immovable. They held no lavish designs or insignias of their owner. Instead they were made of straight, solid lines, conveying their cold intolerance for the uninvited. Massive, square, stone columns rose on each side of the gates. They gave birth to an imposing wall of granite, perhaps ten feet high, which convexed from each side, forming a circle around the estate, partially alongside the mountain road, as though holding each ounce of its sacred soil in place. Along its top, upheld by outward-bent metal poles, ran several strands of electrified barbed wire. Looking through the gates, one could see a small, stony shed set a short distance back in the middle of the drive. Presumably, it housed a gatekeeper.

Due to the lush, green growth surrounding the fortress, it was nearly camouflaged in the searing heat of summer. But in the fall, the carcass of colored leaves dropped from their ancient branches, peeling away the blanket of foliage, and revealing the lair within. The castle was particularly impressive at night as devilish yellow light poured from the veiled

<29>

windows. One could scarcely fathom how majestic Asheville would look from the castle's highest windows. In the midst of a black night, the city below was surely a dazzling pattern of easing illumination.

With the exception of the portion which paralleled the roadway, Borley's estate was enclosed by desolate forest. It was in the thick timbers, just outside the eastern portion of the acreage, that the stranger observed the stone wall carefully. After hiking a short, secluded distance, he had found the immovable barrier, standing as though the sentinel of a hideous concentration camp. Walking alongside it, dodging sharp branches and stinging, untamed undergrowth, he studied it for weaknesses. Surely, within a structure of such age, and some neglect, there was a point of penetration—something overlooked by the Borleys' grounds staff. At last, he found it.

A thick, knobby branch reached across the top of the fence from Borley's side. Though visibly stout, it was so long and heavy that it drooped slightly, its center bowing just enough to make the tip accessible from the ground. It was an obvious bridge to the other side.

A rush of excitement, laced with aching nervousness, filled the stranger's bowels upon finding a plausible entrance to the enigmatic property. Removing a brush snag from the tail of his coat, he approached the limb, examining it thoroughly for signs of infirmity. Reaching up a foot or so, he gave the tip of the limb a tug. He was surprised at its firmness. Lifting his other arm, he interlocked both hands around the limb and lifted his feet. The branch lowered only slightly. After planting his feet on the ground again to prepare his muscles, he took a deep, hard breath, then jumped to grab the limb once more; this time carrying the speed and momentum of his vault into a smooth ascent. With what looked to be surprisingly little effort, he completed a few twists and turns to find himself sitting on the branch. He relaxed a few moments, breathing a bit heavier, and gaining better stabilization.

Upon standing, and using a shorter branch to help him keep balance, an astonishing sight emerged. Though a collage of trees and bright

<30>

leaves expanded before him, square, gray towers sprouted from the woodland a short distance away. The cool blue sky shined behind them. An autumn breeze rushed through, rustling the trees and spilling showers of orange, red, and yellow leaves across the land. The cool fingers of the wind slid across the stranger's scalp, slightly whirling his hair.

The stranger squatted close to the branch to prevent detection, though he hadn't seen a soul, and half-waddled across. With each step, the limb bounced gently. He lifted his coat, passing over the electrified barbed wire lining the top of the wall. His head and vision swirled drowsily as he looked past the razor sharp wire to the forest floor far below. Though unsure, he thought he could hear a soft, nearly benevolent, hum drifting from the wires. The sound of the delicate buzz was suddenly dwarfed by a sharp and mighty noise in front of the stranger. He could nearly feel the explosive shock of the fracture when the firm support of the limb beneath him gave way.

The forest was a blur. Flailing wildly for some scrap of stability, he descended with the limb. Radiating with adrenalin, and unable to process the situation quickly enough, he had no idea how he violently stopped in mid-fall, slamming his shoulder against the unflinching stone wall. His arms were wrapped around the limb on which he'd been standing, his body hanging from it vertically. Apparently, the broken limb was hung on the barbed wire atop the fence. The stranger glanced beneath to find another five feet below him. Lowering a foot more, he released the limb, bending his knees with the fall, and slamming, hunched, on the leaf-covered ground. He instantly sprang forward to avoid the heavy branch which might be falling a split second thereafter.

Once a safe distance away, he stopped and turned around to find the limb, perhaps his only bridge to the other side, broken off and still hanging on the barbed wire. It gave him chills to realize he had barely cleared the devastating wire on his way down. Breathing hard, and attempting to recover his shattered nerves, he assessed the bleak situation. He could only hope that no one had heard the thick limb break.

<31>

Using the rustling of the breeze-swept leaves to mask his steps, he walked softly into the woods. After only a few paces though, he heard the leaves crunching to his left, growing louder quickly, as though something was swiftly approaching. He froze, scanning the direction of the sound, but unable to see through the brambles and undergrowth. The sound of movement swishing in the leaves stopped abruptly several feet away. Holding his breath, beads of sweat rolling down his steamy brow, he continued to search the growth for a glimpse of the clandestine visitor. Then, in an instant, he focused on a dark, low-lying form in the near distance. The muscular shape of a sleek, black Rottweiler was poised, frozen, eyeing him intensely. As soon as he saw it, their eyes locked. Both stood quiet and tense, shocked by the sight of the other; waiting, like gunslingers, to see who would twitch first. The stranger could not suppress his inner twinge of fear, and the animal sensed it immediately. That was all it took.

An ear shattering bark, hellish and deep-chested, filled the forest. The beast snarled, its ears laid back, as a barrage of other barks joined in from the surrounding growth. There must have been a pack of them in the woods. The Rottweiler in sight lunged forward, and the stranger took off like a rocket.

Limbs poked his face, and briars tugged at his coat. His feet ripped through vines, and his heart pounded madly as he raced, blinded with fear and more adrenalin. The air behind him roared with the guttural barks of the vicious, destructive dogs. With the creatures trailing at his heels, he knew it was impossible to outrun them. Once they grabbed him, they would rip him apart mercilessly, each dog competing for the greatest chunk of flesh. Their teeth were large and sharp, designed to destroy meat, and once their powerful jaws clamped deeply onto his body, they would not release. There was no way to reason with this situation. He felt their torrid, aggressive bodies only inches behind him, and so he did the only thing he could. The stranger leapt with all his strength to grab a tree branch. The dogs leapt as well.

<32>

Using every ounce of power in his frame, he forced his body onto the limb. A dog grabbed his hanging coat, nearly jerking him down. He held tight to the branch, resisting the pull, and ripping a portion of his coat from the Rottweiler's mouth. Laying on the limb, he looked down to see four dogs struggling madly to climb the tree. One of them jumped hard, his form zooming upwards, and snapped his teeth only inches from the stranger's face. The dog's breath was hot and rank. The stranger rushed to ascend higher in the tree, the dogs clawing the bark below, growing more and more aggravated at their inability to apprehend the intruder. Finding a suitable resting place, he settled in the tree, clenching the branches around him tightly, and gazing wearily below at the mad pack of canines.

Though overcome by the instant relief of his temporary escape, he knew his troubles were far from over. He had ignored a deep pang in his gut which told him crossing onto Borley property was a mistake, but it was too late. He was trapped. Like a hunted raccoon, all he could do was sit and wait for the dread that was surely on its way. Soon, he heard the footsteps.

With a crash of leaves, a group of men raced up behind the dogs. Their eyes were wide with excitement. Each man wore a light blue shirt—some with jackets, some with caps—and each man carried a rifle. A man up front, with a dusty beard and dark blue cap, appeared to be the leader.

"Back! Back!" the leader commanded the dogs. Two other men rushed to grab the dogs' collars. Though clearly disciplined, the animals still pulled, with moderate force, in the direction of the tree. Their barks stopped, yet throaty growls of dissatisfaction rumbled from within each one. The animals' shiny, black eyes leered at the stranger as though he had personally provoked them by crossing the border.

"Back!" the leader yelled again. This time, the animals quietened and sat still, internally impatient for the opportunity to attack again. The sudden calmness was eerie and dreadful, as the dreamy serenity of a

<33>

sunny, breezy day appeared once more. The leader walked cautiously towards the tree, his rifle pointed at the stranger, and his finger planted firmly on the trigger. Once directly under the tree, his eyes looked upwards with utter suspicion and mistrust.

"Come on down," said the man.

The stranger examined the situation closely. He knew that once on the ground, the dogs could be set upon him, or he could meet a worse fate at the hands of Borely's men. There was, however, no choice. Carefully, he navigated his way down through the branches. He slid unexpectedly here and there, scraping his side on the rough bark. Each man on the ground held his firearm defensively, barrels directed on the descending stranger, waiting to fill him with holes if he moved the least bit erratically.

After leaping to the ground, the stranger stood before the militia, a defeated, yet defiant look upon his face. The dogs snarled again. "Do you know this is private property?" asked the leader, matter-of-factly.

"Yes," the stranger answered respectively.

"Then what are you doin' here?"

"I heard there was a castle or somethin' up here," the stranger replied, his insincerity beaming. Though he knew who had the upper hand, he couldn't stand the thought of being in the weak position. In his disgust, he would only allow himself to be cooperative to a certain point—he loathed giving them the dignity of making him justify his presence.

"What's your name?" the man asked, lowering his rifle a bit, yet certainly willing to fire it in a blink.

"What's *your* name?" the stranger asked with a newfound dignity. His arrogance was immediately detested by the man.

"Alright, grab him and search him."

Three men from the group swiftly took their places on each side of the stranger, all other guns still trained on him. Never breaking eye contact with the leader, the stranger lifted his arms as the dutiful guards patted him down.

<34>

"He's clean."

The leader mumbled something into a radio he took from his belt. "Okay," he said with a nod, "let's go."

Two men took the stranger's arms, one on each side. Their grips were firm, yet absent of emotion or genuine aggression. It seemed obvious they were merely grunts, hired to do a mechanical, technical job. Chances were, they knew nothing about the more private elements of Borley's Castle; they themselves denied access to much of it. They were surely the outermost circle of the estate's henchmen. Those close to Borley however, were probably quite different.

Trailing through the woods at gunpoint, headed towards the rocky fortress, the stranger felt like the prisoner of another era. There was something so medieval, perhaps Draconian, about the scenario. These men were not policemen. They were not taking him to see a public judge; to read him his rights and follow due process. There was no constitution there, or lawyer to guide one through the loopholes. There was simply a great sinister lair, housing a force of malevolence and vice. No one knew where he was, and no one could hear him cry for help. Even if they could, it would do no good. He had crossed the great stone wall. In this land, the rest of the world did not exist.

Breaking through the trees, the stranger was overwhelmed by the structure that towered before him. Gothic and European, the castle stood hard like the gaunt face of intimidation itself. At its entrance, two lofty statues guarded, mounted on blocks of stone. Though much larger, they resembled those at Crawford Borley's funeral. One was a hunched wolf, its ears laid back aggressively, fangs bared, and eyes leering. Its muscles rippled under a thick coat of sculpted hair. The other was an owl, its wings spread wide and chest puffed forth. Its eyes were closed introspectively as it displayed the glory of its size.

"Good God," the stranger mumbled upon realizing the indentation around the castle was a swift moat. No one had ever mentioned such a marvel. Its deep waters rushed around the fortress with the strength

<35>

and current of an ocean. Whatever powers propelled it seemed driven by the well of domination from which the entire area drew its energy. A genuine drawbridge, connected by burly black chains like those from a shipyard, proved the only link between the shadowy lair and the dazzling world outside.

The men dragged the stranger routinely, though he stared awestruck at the dominating place, as climactic as the height of a brooding symphony. Passing the large statues, chilling in their resemblance to flesh, they walked onto the drawbridge. It was solid and unyielding, yet it still echoed hollowly with each step. The water rushing below seemed to sweep away the stranger's last inklings of hope as he left the world of his understanding behind.

The temperature immediately dropped a few degrees when they passed beneath the blackness of a huge stone arch. Clammy and bleak, it created a deep corridor, at least fifteen feet high and ten feet long. At its end, they were greeted by two towering doors, shaped like an arch split down the middle. Its outer ridge was studded with bolts, and two bulky metal rings, as large as steering wheels, hung stiffly as colossal handles. One man grabbed each, and then leaning his weight back, proceeded to slowly open the mammoth entry with a rumble as depthless and yawning as the earth itself.

The doors parted to reveal four new men in black suits. One with a mustache grabbed the stranger's arm aggressively. "We've got him," he said. Another man took his opposite side. Their grips were tight and agitated. It was obvious that these were the real men. While the other two men held pistols drawn, the group that had dropped him off closed the doors behind him. The faint remnant of sunlight seeping across the floor narrowed as the entrance closed, and then disappeared completely just before a lock clicked somewhere deep inside them.

The hugeness of the room was astounding, and the stranger strained his neck to observe the sweeping magnitude of the place. The stone walls climbed endlessly to meet a ceiling so far above it nearly felt as if

<36>

they stood outside on a still night. Two wide, ornate staircases curled lavishly, joining into a landing at the middle, and then splitting again as they approached the floor. Between them was a majestic life-size statue of Crawford Borley, lit divinely by a soft floodlight shining upon it from below. Voluminous shafts of white light poured in from spacious, beveled windows, silvery particles of glittering dust floating in their thick beams. Long, intricate tapestries flowed from the walls, and a slightly tarnished suit of armor stood by a doorway, holding a shiny, wide-bladed axe in its cold grip. The room was round, with many doorways leading from it, and on the stone floor was printed the black design of an antiquated compass face. There was a skylight in the center of the ceiling, and a circular beam of light that streamed from it illuminated a fountain in the very center of the floor. It shot forth a gleaming jet of water that cascaded terraced stones to meet a deep pool below. Man-sized torches, unlit, jutted from the walls at an angle, and an incredible chandelier hung halfway from the ceiling, its center an open ring so the skylight could function in the day.

"You got him?" a pre-masculine voice called almost rhetorically. Brock lumbered into the room with his radio in his hand.

"Yes sir."

Brock strolled up to the stranger with a smirk spread across his face. He stood for a moment, nodding his head slowly, and looking the stranger up and down demeaningly. "I knew you were up to no good," he said, lifting his chin satisfactorily.

The stranger stood stern and silent.

"So who are you?" Brock demanded.

The stranger gave no response.

"Did you hear me?" Brock spat, leaning his bulky face, slightly sweaty, a few inches from the stranger's. "I said what's your name?"

"I'm not talking to you," the stranger replied.

<37>

Brock leaned back. His smirk, which had quickly disappeared, took form again. "Oh. All right, I see," he said. "Well that's okay, because after Mr. Borley speaks with you, *I'm gonna speak with you again.*"

The stranger stared undauntedly. Brock glanced at the other men and snickered. They returned one of their own. After a few more moments of eyeballing the stranger, he finally spun around with a smile. "Okay, bring him on in," he said.

The procession of men walked across the shiny, clean floor towards the doorway guarded by the knight's armor. Passing through, they entered what appeared to be some sort of study. Thick, opaque curtains were pulled across the windows, and amber incandescent light illuminated the room. It was brown and old fashioned—different from the entrance hall. Woodwork was prominent and rich. Smelly, old books lined several shelves around the room, and a massive, tan globe took residence near the corner. There was a desk in front of the far wall, and in the middle of the room a coffee table was positioned. A leather couch sat along its side, and two armchairs, one green and one black, were planted at either end.

The stranger was seated in the green armchair, obviously less expensive than the black one which faced it on the opposite side of the table. Brock leaned down to him with an index finger extended.

"You stay put, you understand?" The stranger did not respond. Brock looked to the two men handling the captive. "Stay right here with him," he ordered, "Mr. Borley will be down momentarily." With that, he walked away gloating and huge.

Save the bubbling of the fountain in the adjoining room, and the ticking of a grandfather clock, the castle was silent. Not one word was spoken between the stranger and his guards. He sat relaxed in the chair, sliding his eyes subtly in his sockets to view the room. On the wall, above a fireplace, was an illustrious portrait that seized his attention. It was a lovely young woman, her long curls of hair a rich brown, her face delicate and light. A warmth radiated from her, yet her dark eyes and

<38>

fine lips carried a sadness typical of such portraits. There seemed an unbridled depth in her unfocused gaze, and the stranger wondered what qualities had earned her a place on Borley's wall.

Below the portrait, on a lavishly carved stand, appeared to be a unique, wooden ouija board. With two seats at either end, the board and stand had been constructed as one piece. It looked old and mystical, as though it had divined knowledge for centuries long past. Its surface was polished and smooth, and a shiny copper pointer rested in the middle of the board, awaiting the inspiration of an unseen oracle.

The grandfather clock rested venerably in a corner. Its tall, thin form, shapely in its composition, bestowed a sense of wisdom on the antique. Like an elder statesman, frail yet knowing, it granted the room its approval—lending experience and taste, and reminding all the while that each moment is sacred. Its sharp ticking became more and more prominent as time passed with no sign of Borley. Minute after minute floated away swiftly and obliviously. Soon, he had been waiting for nearly two hours.

The stranger's head was bowed, and his mind had provided an escape, when the sound of footsteps echoed through a doorway across the room. The stranger could see a tiled floor outside the door. Evidently a staircase led to it, and the sound of approaching footsteps grew more prominent, as though the stairs were being descended. The steps came at a leisurely, almost slow pace, and there was no particular rhythm or stride to which they adhered. The stranger lifted his brow, his eyes shining beneath. The footsteps came deliberately and suspensefully. When they reached the bottom, they stopped.

The stranger stared at the doorway attentively, awaiting a glance of the visitor. There was nothing, only silence. Then, smoothly, inaudibly, a large, dark form emerged. J.C. Borley leaned against the doorway. A bit disheveled, he wore a dark gray suit vest without tie, and his sleeves were rolled midway up his forearms. A wisp of his wavy black hair, parted down the middle, nearly blocked his right eye.

<39>

There was a crystal drinking glass in his right hand, filled with an amber beverage that cast a soft aura when hit by the light. His pupils locked with the stranger's, and he stood a moment, just looking. He was completely relaxed, even taking a sip from his drink, never breaking eye contact. After a few moments, he strolled across the room.

Though an uncanny judge of character and mood, the stranger could not read Borley as he approached. He moved in a slightly sluggish manner, lacking the precision he had demonstrated at the funeral. The ice cubes in his beverage softly knocked against each other with each step. Borley stopped when he reached the black, cushioned armchair across from the stranger. He stood by it, sipping his drink again, and still making no effort to communicate. Breaking his gaze from the stranger, he looked at the two guards standing on either side of the stranger's chair. They both nodded respectively. With that, Borley lowered himself into the chair.

A ghost of a smirk appeared on Borley's face, and for the first time, the stranger could see that his black eyes were slightly bloodshot and glassy. His preternaturally direct stare was so dull and unwavering that he seemed to look eerily deep into the stranger, perhaps even past his soul. His eye contact was strong and intentional, and the master of the castle would not look away, waiting instead for the eyes into which he peered to submit and turn away from his own. The tension in the room was so thick and unsettling that everyone, except Borely, was visibly disturbed. Borley took another gulp of his drink, a bit larger than his others, then set the glass down on the coffee table, right next to a shiny, mahogany box. Having observed the box earlier, the stranger wondered what it contained.

There was an intricate, golden latch on the box, and training his attention on the item, Borley flipped up the latch that clicked with a tiny sigh of release. He opened the box smoothly to reveal several rows of cigarettes, unmarked and surely expensive. Taking one delicately between his

<40>

right thumb and index finger, he closed the box, and then tapped the smoke lightly on the wooden top, packing the rich tobacco inside.

Beside the box set a compact object of golden metal. Its durable, mechanical design looked unfamiliar to the stranger. Canister shaped, it had a long lever at the top, and several bolts jutting from its angular design. Solid and heavy, Borley picked it up and forced down the lever, conjuring a narrow, symmetrical six-inch flame. His cigarette between his thick lips, he stuck the end into the flame, and inhaled the fire which bent submissively to disappear into the cigarette's tip. Releasing a cloud of thick, gray smoke, he liberated the lever to instantly extinguish the flame. Placing the lighter back on the table, he took his first good drag from the cigarette and, squinting as in thought, looked to the stranger once again.

The stranger had observed each of Borley's motions with care and suppressed anxiety. He anticipated that Borely might withdraw a weapon, or some other symbol of intimidation, to bolster the domineering atmosphere in the room. Borley lowered his cigarette, and then switched it to his left hand. With that, he leaned forward a bit, took a deep breath, and extended his hand.

"J.C. Borley," he announced with a devilish grin. Hesitating a bit, the stranger took his hand for a long, firm shake. "How do you do?"

"Oh, very well," the stranger replied, the sarcasm in his voice hardly masked. Borley leaned back into the comfort of his seat.

"So what's *your* name?"

"My name?" the stranger responded. "My name is Kane."

Borley nodded. "What's your last name?"

"That *is* my last name."

"Then what's your *first name*?"

The stranger hesitated for a moment, then gave Borley a penetrating look. "Mister," he said.

"Oh, I see," Borley smiled and nodded. He slightly curled his bottom lip. "Well, Mr. Kane, in that case, I suppose you can call me *Mr.* Borley."

<41>

Borley motioned to the guards still standing dutifully at Kane's sides. They both walked away, one of them disappearing through the main hall, and the other retiring to stand post at the doorway.

"I don't think they're necessary, do you?" Borely asked.

"No," said Kane, "not at all."

Borley took another drag off his cigarette. "You know," he said, "my father made just about everybody call him Mr. Borley all the time—even me sometimes!" He chuckled. "Yeah…he tried to de-personalize himself as much as possible—hiding away in this castle; not letting anyone address him by first name. He called it the *Oz Factor*." Borley paused to flick his ashes into a large, glass ashtray next to the table lighter.

For the first time, Kane noticed that Borley's speech was slightly slurred. "The Oz Factor?" he inquired.

"Yeah," Borley confirmed, "the Oz Factor. He said it was like *The Wizard of Oz*. He said 'never show them the man behind the curtain, because he's never as big as the smoke and lights.' He always figured people would imagine him larger and more powerful than he could ever really be, and it became a self-fulfilling prophecy. If they think you're big, they treat you like you're big—even if you're not. And after a while, before you know it, you really are. They make you into what you pretend to be. It's all a big mind game."

Kane was unnerved by Borley's aloof, talkative persona. It didn't seem natural. It wasn't the sort of thing he'd expected from Borley. Though he knew that alcohol was probably doing most of the talking, he didn't know whether to fear or welcome Borley's impaired judgment. And then again, maybe it was all a "mind game."

"Yes, he was a peculiar man, my father," Borley reflected. "I never really knew him." The rich man suddenly detected Kane's growing discomfort. He twisted his black eyebrows as if surprised. "Why Mr. Kane, are you all right?"

"Oh yes," he replied, "I'm dandy." He forced an absurd smile.

<42>

Borley eyed him with great seriousness and respect, then tilting his head, a mischievous smile blossomed. "*Welcome to my parlor said the spider to the fly.*" His words trailed into an exaggerated chuckle of wickedness. Kane halfheartedly chuckled with him.

Borley suddenly whipped his head around the room. "William?" he said. "William!" There was no sign of anyone new around. "Where is that son-of-a-bitch?" Borley mumbled. "William!"

An older gentlemen with graying hair, obviously a butler in tuxedo, zipped through the doorway from which Borley had come.

"Yes sir?" he responded in a shaky tone, speeding up to Borley.

"I want some shots of whisky," Borley said. He looked to Kane. "And how about you, friend? What would you like?"

"I'm fine," Kane assured him.

"Oh hogwash!" Borley cried. "You'll have some shots with me won't you?"

"No thank you," Kane reiterated.

"Well fine then," Borley said, half-playfully. "Screw you." He turned back to William. "Bring some whisky and a shot glass in for me."

"Yes, Mr. Borley," answered the butler. With that, he sped off.

Borley turned back to Kane. "So," he said, "I understand you were trespassing on my property. Is that right?"

Kane grinned. "It would certainly appear so, wouldn't it?"

Borley looked to the floor and shook his head. "How did you get on my property?"

Kane smiled and lifted his hands. "I just...climbed over the fence."

"You just climbed right over the fence, huh?" There were gears turning in Borley's head, but he simply accepted what Kane told him. He ashed his cigarette and took a drag. "Well that happens from time to time. So you're a—what a 'sightseer'—right?"

Kane nodded affirmatively. "I just wanted to see the big castle everybody talks about."

<43>

"Oh yeah," Borley said nonchalantly. "We get people tryin' to snoop around up here quite a bit. It's usually teenagers though. They get bored cruisin' Patton Avenue and decide they wanna come check out the *haunted* castle, you know."

"Haunted?" Kane acted surprised.

"Yeah, there's all kinds o' little stories about this place," Borley said, waving his hand as though exasperated. "None of 'em true."

"What kind of stories?" Kane inquired.

Borley frowned, grinding his cigarette into the ashtray. "There's one about my father having a lover he turned away, and she got depressed and killed herself in here. Then there's one about a maid who fell down the steps. And there's one about a worker who got killed when my father was buildin' the place—all a bunch o' bull, though. No one's ever died in this castle…except my father, of course."

William, tall and sullen, walked back into the room carrying a silver tray. Atop it set a sparkling crystal whisky container. A clear shot glass was on the side. Running alongside him was a small, hairless cat. Thin and wrinkly, its skin was a translucent light pink. A fine network of spindly purple veins could be seen reaching across some parts of its body, especially in its pointed, sprightly ears. The feline, pathetic in appearance, seemed full of energy. When its nearly white eyes made contact with Kane, however, it froze immediately and stared. The gaze was blank and lifeless, like the eyes of a phantom.

"Here you are sir," William announced, straining lightly to pull out the stopper on the whiskey and preparing to pour a shot for Borley. The cat re-animated and softly pranced over to stand beside Borley's chair. Its small mouth parted and a shrill "meow" escaped. Borley patted his lap and the cat sprang onto it.

"Yes," said Borley, scratching its cool, bald head, its soft, loose flesh sliding across its tiny skull. "*What do you want Angel?*" he said in an exaggerated baby tone. "*Have you missed me?*" Purring loudly, the cat wallowed in his lap, soaking up the affection greedily.

<44>

"Your shot, sir," said the butler, presenting the glass patiently before his master. Borley's attention snapped to the waiting drink. Reaching for it with his right hand, he lifted the cat with his left. Though it was still cozy in his grip, he slung it carelessly aside. "Get outta here. Shoo!" he scolded. The feline soared through the air and landed on the hardwood floor, flailing for its balance, claws sliding in all directions. Regaining its posture, the sinister little creature held its head high and walked away calmly.

Taking the glass, Borley threw back his head and downed the shot without hesitation. Cringing a bit, and twisting his head to the side, he slammed the glass down on the table. "Ahhh…" he groaned, as though having sated a torturous thirst. Then, systematically, he held it up for a refill, looking not to his servant but instead to the stranger. There was a glow about him, as if he felt somewhat proud of killing the whisky. William carefully, but quickly, filled it once again. The stranger observed without comment or expression, unwilling to give Borley any clues as to his mood or thoughts.

"You're absolutely certain you won't have a shot?" Borley reconfirmed.

"I'm absolutely certain," Kane answered.

Borley lifted his eyebrows, as if implying it to be the stranger's loss. Then, he destroyed the shot again, this time coughing a bit on its way down. He squinted and rolled his tongue in his mouth, seeming as though the hot, overpowering alcohol had not missed his taste buds completely enough. William prepared to pour another shot when Borley held up the glass again.

"No, no," said Borley, shaking his head. "That'll be all, William."

"Yes sir." William took the shot glass, set it upon his tray, and after turning around in one fluid motion, paced swiftly away.

Borley sat quietly for a moment. A contained grin bulged on his face, and he looked aimlessly above eye level, savoring his expectation of the coming sensations. A couple of subtle chuckles rolled up from his

<45>

throat, and he returned his gaze to the stranger. "You know," he said, "I could've sworn I saw you at my father's funeral."

Kane looked down to the coffee table. He thought skillfully about the dialogue as though a witness on the stand in court. Looking back up, he nodded. "You did," he confessed. "I was there."

There was a wooden chest on the right side of Borely's chair. Upon it sat a large, silver bowl. A metal cap, engraven with intricacies, was seated on the bowl, rising in a cone shape, with a small opening at the top. On the front of the chest were four drawers. Borley leaned down, as if having suddenly entertained an additional thought, and started digging through a bottom drawer.

"Oh," he replied, his voice muffled from the position. "You knew my father?"

"Everyone in Asheville knew your father," Kane stated calmly.

Leaning back up, Borley held a blue pouch in hand. His attention was focused on opening it carefully. "But I thought you're a tourist," he said.

"I am."

The pouch was open, and Borley reached two fingers and a thumb inside slowly. "Then where are you from?" he asked.

The stranger watched Borley's meticulous hand, wondering what oddity he might produce. Then, lifting his eyes to observe his host's reaction, he responded. "*Elsewhere.*"

Borley's motion stopped instantly. His eyes met Kane's once again. They stared for a moment, and then a smile popped up on the rich man's face. "Well," he said, resuming his activity, "I suppose that's as good a place as any."

Borley withdrew his fingers. He held a fat, green, dry, bud of marijuana in between. Bringing it to his nose, he flared his nostrils, closed his eyes, and breathed in deep of its filling aroma. He grinned and licked his thick lips wetly and deliciously. "Damn that's good weed," he said, holding it out for Kane to smell. "Imported."

<46>

Kane lifted his hand like a symbolic barrier. "I don't mess with that," he said.

Borley withdrew his hand suddenly, his eyes large and his face spread wide with theatrical shock. "Good Lord, Mr. Kane," he exclaimed. "I *do believe* you're 'bout the boringest sumbitch I've ever had in this castle!"

Shaking his head, Borley stuffed the crunchy clump of herb into the top opening of the gleaming bowl's cap. "How do you like this water bong?" he asked proudly. "I bought this in China."

"Yes, it's very beautiful."

Turning to use his left hand, Borley reached behind the bowl and pulled out a clear hose. Holding its silver tip ready at his near-pursing lips, he lifted the gold lighter from the table with his right hand. Producing a flame, he held the lighter over the waiting plant and popped the hose into his anxious mouth; quickly moving his left hand to cover a small hole on the side of the tureen. With a powerful draw, a frenzy of bubbles echoed from the bowl, and the flame arched forcefully into the arid plant, hissing as it swiftly burned its way through. A thick column of gray smoke jettisoned through the s-curve of the hose, feeding Borley's swollen lungs. He engulfed even greater as he removed his hand from the hole on the instrument's side. Sucking profusely, he cleared the hose, and quickly snapped his head to the side, removing it from his mouth. His eyes bugged, and his face bulged red as he strained to hold the tainted cloud inside. At last, when his tight, clenched lips could no longer withhold the pressure, he released. A gush of bitter, leaden smoke shot forth in a three-foot stream, dispersing leisurely into the air.

Borley's face was relaxed completely, and his eyelids rested half-open in their large sockets. The stranger had watched him intensely, and sat stern as always, unsure of how to interpret the rich man's blatant excess. Borley gave him a warm smile.

"This is expensive stuff, my friend," he said. "Not the kind o' junk you'll find downtown. You should really try some." Kane shook his head

<47>

negatively. With that, Borley shrugged and repeated the entire process two more times.

Once finished, he set down the lighter, and slumped comfortably into the soft, black chair. His eyes were glazed and bloodshot; his pupils dilated. There was a euphoria about him as he gazed blankly, happily, into his own wistful thoughts, far away from the castle and riches surrounding him. He looked to Kane and tilted his head a bit.

"Yes, my father was quite a man…quite a powerful, powerful man." A new thought hit him and he looked Kane more directly in the eye. "Are you sorry he's gone?"

Again, the stranger explored the question and its implications thoroughly. "You have my condolences," he said quietly.

Borley nodded with a satisfied smile. "Yes. He was a man of greatness. With greatness he lived, and with greatness he died—and with greatness he shall always be remembered."

The two shared a moment of silence.

"You know what?" The words sprang from Borley's lips. "Some sorry bastard tried to rob his grave. Did you know that?"

An immediate tension gripped the room. Kane furrowed his brow, trying to conceal a rising emptiness inside. "Why no," he said.

"Yeah," Borley suddenly perked up from his relaxed slouch. "Dug all the way down and broke his coffin right open." Kane forced a concerned look. "They tried to cover it back up, but hell—it was pretty obvious. What a lousy, lousy bastard it takes to desecrate a man's grave like that. Don't you think?"

"Yes," Kane agreed, his heart beginning to race.

Borley looked down to the floor, slowly shaking his head; an aura of controlled rage seeping from him. "Oh I'd love to catch him," he mumbled. "Oh the things I would do to that filthy, filthy bastard." Twisting his fingers into claws, he clenched his fist before his face, leering at it ruthlessly. "The things I would do with my own hand."

<48>

Squeezing his fist till the knuckles turned white, he suddenly stopped, relaxed, and raised his dark eyes to the stranger's. They possessed a look of wonder, of depth, of revelation. Then, he spoke. "You like opera?"

Kane, frozen, cleared his throat subtly. "I beg your pardon?"

"Opera. You like opera?"

"Um…yes. Yes, I do like opera."

"Look at this," Borley said, his mood completely changed. He turned to a wooden box on a stand to the left side of his chair. "Are you familiar with the Victrola?"

"I don't believe so," Kane replied.

Borley opened the hinged top half of the box to reveal the general innards of a phonograph. "This," he said, "is the forerunner of the electric record player. It's a mechanical record player—the kind they used back in the old days."

"I see."

Borley lifted up a thick, black disk already positioned in the player. He flipped it over and held it up for the stranger to see. The bottom side was smooth. "Back then, they only recorded on one side. See?"

Kane nodded.

Borley gently placed the disk back onto the turntable. A black, angular crank jutted from the side of the player, and wrapping his fingers around it, Borley wound it enthusiastically. Upon reaching the proper point of tension, he lifted the elegant arm containing needle, and set its honed point precisely into the record's first narrow groove. Given the millionaire's intoxication, the stranger was surprised by the accuracy of Borley's fluid, near effortless motions. Borley returned his attention to Kane.

"Now keep in mind that there is absolutely nothing electrical about this device whatsoever. Understand?" The stranger acknowledged.

Just behind the turntable, a hole spanned the width of the player, apparently leading to an acoustic chamber below the record. Propped

<49>

above it, the inside of the top lid was a smooth, glossy wood, angled towards the front of the device. Borley pointed to the shadowy chamber.

"You see," he said, "the crank turns the spring that turns the record. Then the sound comes out of this hole, bounces off the top lid, and comes out the front towards the listener." The stranger nodded. "All right then," Borley continued, a note of excitement growing in his voice, "listen."

Borley flipped a small switch beside the turntable, and the mechanism came to life. Music—beautiful and haunting—rose like a waken specter from the depths of the wireless box. The scratchy voice of a woman, long since dead, filled the room like an Italian spell. The orchestra behind her rolled as if an ocean tide, its momentum timeless, her voice hovering above. The stranger's mind bridged the boundless gap of time, and he imagined the singer and musicians, now tokens of an extinct age, sitting in a room and performing into a funnel; a needle carving their art into a brittle disk in search of immortality.

Borley sank into the black chair, his eyes closed, his ears and soul savoring the tones like a lost redemption. For a moment, it was as if the rich man had forgotten the presence of his guest, and was absorbed completely by the vibrations that poured from this simple marvel of man's past. It gave him comfort to hear the sounds from those humans long gone. It was a reminder of man's transience—that life is a fleeting illusion to be taken lightly—that men are delivered from all deeds, good and bad, by the great escape of death.

Borley opened his eyes slowly, the music still soothing him. "Someday," he spoke softly, "you and I will be nothing more than a collection of moments—some remembered, most forgotten." He looked deeply, disturbingly, into Kane. Unmoving, his dull eyes glistened. The rest of his face was blank and inanimate. He looked as though he might have peacefully died, but the stranger could still feel the life force beaming from him. He sat like that, unflinching, for at least a minute. Kane stared intensely, trying to see within the dark well of his host's black eyes; trying to read his submerged thoughts. Then, just as the music

<50>

grated to a stop, sharp high heels clicked ferociously across the floor in the entrance chamber.

Both men jumped a bit, startled, and whipped around their heads to see Eileen, Borley's wife, march into the room. Her lip was stiff, her gaze aggressive, and her gait dominating. She stormed up to the table and exchanged a brazen glance with the stranger.

"What's going on here?" she demanded. "I heard we had an intruder." Borley grinned and, with a low brow, rolled his eyes at the stranger.

"Eileen, this is Mr. Kane. Mr. Kane, this is Eileen, my wife. She's usually gone."

"You were trespassing?" Eileen's words darted from her mouth.

Borley held up a hand. "Mr. Kane is a tourist, my dear. He wanted to see our lovely home."

Eileen looked at Borley, stooped a bit, and glared. "J.C., have you…have you been drinking again?"

Borley snickered. "Why darling," he slurred, "you know I never touch the stuff."

Eileen snapped erect once again, her face twisted with outrage. "By God J.C.," she bit her lip to contain a fiery tongue. Casting a final leer at the stranger, she whirled around and stomped off.

Borley cocked an eyebrow at the stranger, reaching over to close up the Victrola. "Say, you're not married are you Mr. Kane?"

The stranger glanced down at his naked left ring finger. "No."

"Good," Borley nodded with tortured experience. "Don't be."

Kane was growing tired with Borley's seemingly idle conversation. Either the rich man was stalling—feeling him out—or the drugs in his system had brought his need for a new conversation mate to a desperate height. The windows, once aglow with golden sunlight, had vanished behind thick, velvet curtains. The great shadow of evening had swallowed up the mountain, and the room looked more harsh. Objects inside appeared starker and more foreign, their lines defined more deeply. The darkness outside, and the evergrowing hardness of

<51>

his surroundings, made the stranger feel as if his isolation was reaching a level of hopeless suffocation.

Still unsure of his fate, the stranger suddenly seized control of the conversation. "So, aren't you going to call the authorities?" he almost snapped, eager to end the small talk.

Borley was taken aback slightly by the stranger's rash affirmation. His mouth curled in a near-admirable smile. "Call the authorities?" Borley said in an affectionate, yet patronizing tone. "Why, the authorities call *me*."

With such a simple statement, the direction of the night was solidified. The stranger sat as a pawn before a self-proclaimed monarch. Borley alone held Kane's fate in his hands. The rich man could render life or death. In his castle, he was God. To give life is a powerful thing. To take life is a powerful thing. But there is no power greater than that which toys with life—and Borley was surely in need of entertainment.

Realizing his visitor's need to change the setting, a new spark of mirth fired in the rich man's eyes. "Mr. Kane," he grinned, "as you can see, I, like my father, am an admirer of the old ways. The new ways are sometimes boring to a man like me. You see, if you have enough money, you can buy any *new* thing you want. However, finding the old things can be a challenge beyond the reach of one's wealth. That is why the old ways interest me more. Understand?"

"Yes," the stranger replied.

"I have traveled the world. And, like many a wealthy traveler of the past, I have adhered to a tradition all but forgotten by today's men of prestige. You know what that is?"

"No," the stranger said a bit impatiently.

"My friend," Borley continued, "I am a collector of bizarre things— oddities from around the world. I procure what some might call cabinets of curiosity. Are you familiar with the concept?"

"Sure," Kane replied. "Conversation pieces."

<52>

"Yes, yes indeed," Borley squinted with self-admiration. "Reminders of life's unwillingness to behave. I am especially fond of biological aberrations."

The stranger's interest was newly piqued.

"I have things which most people never get to see. But you—well, you are a man who can appreciate the bizarre, right?"

The stranger nodded halfheartedly. "I suppose."

"Well then," Borley roared, rising abruptly from his seat, "come! Come and I shall show you my collection!"

Just then, William glided dutifully into the room. "Excuse me, sir," he said, mindful of his interruption, "but you have a phone call."

"A call?" exclaimed Borley, whipping his head around to meet his servant. "From whom?"

"It's Dr. Jensen, sir. He sounds rather persistent."

"Jensen!" Borley scoffed. "Tell that bastard I'll call *him* when I want to speak with him!"

"Yes sir," answered William, accepting the matter as closed. With that, he turned and disappeared as quickly as he'd come.

Returning instantly to his prior enthusiasm, Borley motioned for Kane to rise. "Yes, my collection! My collection indeed!" he nearly sang, indulging freely in a dreamlike euphoria. Kane rose and stretched, his long coat wrinkled warmly by the seat.

"But first," Borley suddenly halted, a finger lifted majestically, "we should retire to the bathroom. I dare say you're in need of some relief, eh?"

"Yes," the stranger agreed. "Thank you."

Observing the world through a swirling fish-eye, and overcome by the primal glee of a reckless school boy, Borley hummed to himself, features inwardly illuminated, and traipsed through the doorway from which he had come. The stranger followed, slightly amused and somewhat unsettled, by his host's uncharacteristic display of lightheartedness. Though a drug-induced joy emanated from the large man, the darkness of his soul,

<53>

great and lurking, waited patiently below the surface, easily accessed by a misplaced look or thoughtless word.

The bathroom, located on the left upon passing through the doorway, was as impressive as Kane had expected. A stone arch formed the entrance, and a barren ten-foot corridor led to the golden toilet. A bright and crisp mirror hung on the wall above it, providing an illusionary sense of added depth.

When the stranger exited the bathroom, Borley, having gone before him, waited outside. Smoke swirled about his head from a freshly lit cigarette in his mouth. Borley's eyebrows popped up when he saw the stranger had returned. Lifting his right index and middle finger, cigarette stuck between, he motioned like a Caesar for Kane to follow him towards another doorway that led from the room. Two jets of smoke shot from his flared nostrils as he passed into the room, reaching to flip a switch on the wall.

A series of strangely positioned lights brought the room to life. Placed either extremely high or low, and most always indirect, the lights cast a puzzle of shadows that reached across the spacious chamber. Like the previous sitting room, it was brown and old. It reeked of exploration and swelled with mystery. Display cases, maps, cabinets, and books were arranged too widely to perceive at once, and though the room was strongly flavored with antiquity, the stranger knew he was about to see things anew to his experience. For there is only one thing more marvelous than an innovation: something old, rare, and forgotten, revisited once more.

The stranger's eyes explored the vast surroundings. A condor, eyes ablaze and wings spread devilishly, stood mounted on a top shelf across the room. Subconsciously, he wandered slightly in its direction, and felt the side of his lengthy coat brush against something unstable. His eyes shot down with the urgency of having bumped a shelf in a china store. Just below waist level was a chess set wobbling a bit from the contact. Rather plain, seemingly heavy, and a bit unbalanced on its stand, he

<54>

quickly steadied it with his hand before the dull pieces escaped the boundaries of their spaces.

"Careful," said Borley nonchalantly, as he opened a long cabinet door near the wall. "That belonged to Hitler."

Kane's eyes widened a bit and he looked at the set again, inwardly relieved. Suddenly overcome by an unexplainable kinship with history, he reached down and delicately stroked the ivory king.

"Before we venture into the past," Borley said, his back turned to the stranger, "we're going to need a little mood music." Kane turned to see that Borley was fiddling with a complex, black stereo in the cabinet. It was riddled with knobs, dials, and illuminated equalizer bars. The technologically modern device clashed bitterly with the atmosphere of the room, and the stranger found bewilderment in its irony.

Suddenly music, in clear and sparkling stereo, encircled the room from hidden speakers. It was a selection not altogether tasteful, and yet eerie and surreal. An xylophone, slow, weird, and darkly magical, thumped out resonant notes, an orchestra creeping behind it. Though very simple, there was something almost innocently perverse about the tune; and its tone was psychologically escapeful, imaginary, and freakish.

Borley turned back to face his guest. The right corner of his mouth curled in a self-serving sneer. The host absorbed the music, matching its darkness with his own. It seemed as if the piece instantly transformed him, placing him in a cinematic world of illusion. He stood as though posing for a shot in a sweeping, gothic thriller, replacing the scope of his own being with that of a character larger than life—yet the sight was not unbelievable.

"Now, my dear Mr. Kane, we shall begin our voyage."

Borley swaggered to the right side of the room, Kane following behind. Next to the wall stood a shiny brass tripod, reaching the waist of the two men. Seated solidly within three spindly prongs at its top, was a black crystal ball. The instant Kane's eyes made contact with its polished, flawless surface, a jolt of unsettlement landed deep inside him. The

<55>

ebony orb sucked his gaze, nearly involuntarily, far within the depths of its infinite core. He felt at once violated and overpowered; besides his peering into the ocean of blackness restrained by the spheroid of glass, he knew that the boundless blackness peered deeply into him.

"Yes," Borley grinned, seeing the flash of discomfort in Kane's eyes. "Remarkable isn't it? A tiny glance at this ancient marvel, and you can see things both foreign and familiar at once."

"Familiar?" Kane whispered, breaking visual contact with the globe and replacing it with Borley.

"Of course," Borley responded. "The secret of the crystal ball is that it possesses no power at all. It's simply a powerful mirror, concentrating whatever energy is cast upon it, and reflecting it back into the eyes of the observer. You can learn a great many things from such a device, and yet the device itself yields nothing at all. The divination of greater knowledge comes not from such an object, but from its ability to open a clearer window into ourselves."

The stranger looked back to the ball, observing the same sensation, yet this time prepared.

"Ahh, you see," Borley affirmed. "You're learning to control it already."

The stranger squinted slightly. "Where did this come from?"

"I purchased this in France," Borley said. "It is perhaps eons old, but in the early 1500s, it belonged to Nostradamus."

With a chill on his flesh, the stranger turned away. Satisfied, Borley motioned a few feet away to a narrow, gray pedestal, highlighted by a searing spotlight focused from above. The two positioned themselves around it.

Atop the pedestal was the massive formation of an upper and lower jawbone. It bore a clean tone of yellow, with long, sharp teeth lining the bone, packed tightly together and curving slightly backwards, towards the vacant throat of the creature. The two incisors were several times larger and longer than the rest, poised as sinister fangs. Each jawbone spanned at least a foot in length.

<56>

"Guess the creature," Borley challenged pridefully.

The stranger examined it a few moments, then spoke confidently. "Some kind of cat."

"Nope," Borley shook his head, then puffed his cigarette. "Good guess though. These, my friend, are the jaws of a prehistoric serpent."

"A snake?"

"Yes, a snake. A big son-of-a-bitch, too."

"I never realized a snake could have a mouth like that," the stranger said.

"You see those teeth?" Borley pointed. "They're shaped like hooks. When they sink into you, you can't pull away, especially if they lodge into the bone. Go ahead, feel how sharp they are."

Kane lightly touched the tips of the teeth. Their points were as hard as diamonds, and sharp as razors.

"Fortunately for us, this monster has been extinct for quite a while, but scientists believe he was quite a killer in his day. You see, unlike today's serpents, this one probably didn't swallow its food whole. It probably ripped off one chunk at a time, gulping down each slab of meat into its long, thick body."

"Was it poisonous?" asked the stranger.

"Doubtful," Borley replied. "This was probably before the evolution of poison. That's why it was necessary to ravage the food one piece at a time. Without poison to paralyze or kill the meal, it wasn't so easy to swallow it all at once."

Kane nodded thoughtfully. "Where is this from?"

"South America," Borley answered. "It was found near the Amazon."

"Very interesting specimen," the stranger said.

Through sparkling, glassy eyes, Borley looked at Kane a moment, then cocked his head to the side with a slight grin. "I see it's going to take more than that to shock you isn't it Mr. Kane?"

The stranger smiled. "Oh I'm quite impressed."

<57>

"*Impressed!*" roared Borley, snapping erect again. "Well we will certainly have to do better than that!" He motioned to a doorway behind him, evidently the passage to more oddities. "This way, Mr. Kane. This way."

Like the patron of a twisted theme park, the stranger followed the instructions of his guide, leading him to the following display. There was a hint of mischief in Borley's demeanor, and he himself seemed anxious to present the next item.

In the middle of the next room, a black cloth covered a rectangular case beneath. Its stark simplicity seemed nearly ceremonial—like a quiet alter seated peacefully in its own chamber.

Borley approached the veiled marvel, his face almost bubbling with delight. Kane stood tensely at his side, internally fearful of what oddity might bring his host such excitement. Borley turned to the stranger, his chest pressed forth as if a bold speech might emerge. And then he halted, with dramatic purpose, and flashed a cheshire grin.

"My friend," he bellowed from within his mighty chest, "I present"—he tugged at the corner of the drape—"the bog man!" The cloth was gone in a flash.

Sealed within a glass case was a human body. It was curled in a fetal position, knees drawn pathetically to the chest. It was a man, plain and real; and yet there was something unreal about the body. Its flesh was a rich and leathery brown, so dark and aged that it absorbed the light completely. The face was that of a middle-aged peasant, worn and weathered, a woven cap upon the skull. Each wrinkle was defined and smooth, and each whisker of the scruffy visage stiff and prickly. The eyes were closed softly, painfully, and the expression of final release was molded and captured in the swarthy flesh. A monument of death, it seethed of freshness and antiquity at once.

"Good God," the stranger nearly gasped. Borley, now leaning on the corner of the glass, watched his guest with bright eyes and a winning smile.

"The man before you died *three thousand* years ago," he said. "Mummified by nature."

<58>

Kane, clearly in awe, leaned to examine the form more closely.

"Amazing isn't it?" continued Borley. "He looks just as fresh as the day he died. You can even see the hairs on his face."

"Where did this come from?" Kane whispered.

"My friend, this exhibit is from the peat bogs of Europe. You see, the ancient Europeans believed they must sacrifice humans to appease the gods." As Borley spoke, the brightness of his eyes dwindled, hidden by half-shut lids. The exhaustion of the drugs was beginning to set in, and with each word, he moved his head with exaggeration, like an actor on a stage. His long, black bangs brushed back and forth across his wide forehead. "They would take an unfortunate peasant, like our rosy friend here, and kill him by bludgeoning, stabbing, or strangling. Sometimes all. And when they were dead, they threw them into the bogs." A new though hit him. "By the way, did you notice his hands?"

The body's hands were behind its back. A well-preserved rope bound them firmly together.

"See, they tied him then killed him. Anyway, they'd throw them in the bogs. But the bogs were full of peat moss, and peat moss creates an acid in the water that mummifies flesh. So instead of rotting away, the body was perfectly preserved. Well, almost perfectly."

The bog man's arms, hips, and legs were deeply sunken. The bones jutted gruesomely from within the drawn skin. Kane studied them carefully.

"So I say to hell with Egyptian mummies! They're all rotted and dry and crumbly. This one's thick and fleshy and durable. He's never going to rot. Not any faster than a leather saddle anyway!"

The stranger stood erect, apparently done with his examination. "A truly pitiful creature," he said, "curled up like a baby."

"Pitiful perhaps," Borley agreed, "but enviably immortalized by his condition."

"Well," frowned the stranger, "it's certainly one of the eeriest things I've seen in a while."

Borley sniggered. "I sure as hell hope so!" he exclaimed.

<59>

The two men shared a customary chuckle and then Borley paused, closed his eyes, and waved his head a bit to the music of the room. When he opened his eyes again, he stared at Kane intensely and shook his head. "My, my, Mr. Kane. You are a tough one. I can see that I have thoroughly fascinated you, but you are not yet shocked."

"Oh I don't know about that," Kane responded, returning his attention to the mummy, "that's pretty shocking."

"No, no, no," Borley shook his head wildly. "You only think you're shocked. Very well, very well. I accept the challenge. Come this way." He motioned to another room that adjoined the bog man's chamber.

This room was filled with cabinets and shelves. Some wooden, and others stone, it was an unbalanced mixture of the ingredients—uneasy on the eye. The ceiling of the room swept upwards into a miniature dome, a light affixed directly in its apex. A ghastly radiance spilled down the bowl of the design, raining about the room and glancing off each item with a hazy glow. The focus of the area was certainly one grand cabinet placed firmly against the wall. It was several feet taller than each of the men, and wider than a single person's arm span. Constructed of dark and heavy wood, deep and laborious carvings embellished the piece with baroque nobility. A human skull rested wearily on its top, and urns and candles joined it on either side.

"Now this…" Borley shook his head, snorting a single gush of ominous laughter, "This you will most definitely enjoy." He led them to the large cabinet.

Arms crossed solidly, the stranger stood in quiet observance of the coming feature.

"This I call the jar room," said Borley, keenly watching the stranger's expression, expecting it to melt and mingle with his own delight. "For of all the monstrosities that wealthy men such as myself may sometimes keep, the most interesting always seem to come in jars. And so I present to you the first and goodliest of my jar collections. I call it," he paused

<60>

with true showmanship, placing his hands on the knobs of the great cabinet's doors, "my gallery of beastly babies!"

With the force of his enthusiasm, he flung open the thick doors. Instantly, they revealed a chilling sight. Row after row of shelves was filled with the pale and bloated bodies of deformed infants in liquid-filled jars. In many cases, the babies appeared too large for the containers, and so their fat, twisted bodies had been stuffed into the jars, filling them completely. The soft and tiny bodies were cold and long-absent of life, some casting forth a pinkish aura, others a purplish blue, and still some a blank and snowy white. Their faces, or the closest facsimile, were grim and forsaken, their squinty eyes closed tight in a hopeless agony. Packed side by side, the basins were as uniform and compact as a display of pickles in a supermarket aisle. A wall of nauseating misery, the knobby, mangled limbs and heads were a shrine to God's most revolting and pathetic mistakes.

Kane turned to Borley with glistening, distant eyes, and a dreary disenchantment on his stiff face.

"All of them genuine, mind you," Borley glowed. "Many of them from Asheville even."

The stranger once again turned to face the livid shadow that fell from the sickening cabinet.

"Look at their little tortured faces," Borley dwelled. "Some were born dead, and others alive. But it's plain to see that whatever moments they spent in this horrid life were filled with sheer torment. Sometimes, late at night, when I come to watch them, I swear I can hear their shrill little voices wailing. It bubbles from the water and echoes hollowly from within the glass."

Kane stood nearly frozen, lost in the horrible display. Sensing his host's amusement, it then occurred to him that Borley hadn't the faintest emotion for the dark exhibition. Borley did not keep such abominations for his own entertainment. Instead, he found his delight in the eyes of those who viewed it. The babies, the bog man,

<61>

the aberrations were not the true displays. Instead, it was he himself that was the show—reacting to the abhorrent scene to feed Borley's knotted psyche.

"So tell me, Mr. Kane, what do you think?"

Slowly, barrenly, the stranger turned to Borley. With that, his cheeks released a sudden, sparkling smile. "Lovely."

Borley exploded with laughter, bending forward and then springing upright to slap the stranger heartily on the back. "Now! Now I have shocked you!" he guffawed. Slapping his hands together and shaking his head, Borley rejoiced in the feeling of newfound release that expanded in the room. The stranger looked onward, his grin glued artificially to his face.

"Very well, very well," continued Borley. "If you like those little jewels, then you're sure to like this one as well." Borley leaned down to a smaller door within the cabinet. It opened with a "pop," and he reached deep inside to withdraw another heavy jar. Taking the weighty container in both hands, he lifted it with a graceful swing to meet the stranger's eyes.

Inside the jar was the swollen head of a black man, submerged, like the babies, in a cloudy liquid. His face forlorn and his features bulbous from saturation, his thick, ebony hair trailed down his temples to form a kinky beard.

"How do you like that?" Borley beamed. "This is the head of a slave. This poor bastard tried to escape down in a South Carolina plantation. As you can see, he didn't get very far."

Kane looked closer to examine a lesion above the slave's left eye. It ran deep and broad, penetrating through the flesh and into the skull.

"I guarantee you they beat the hell outta him," Borley said knowingly, his arms already tiring from holding the jar so high. "Here," he barked, unexpectedly plopping the jar into Kane's hands. The stranger reacted to it like a disease, cradling it firmly at his waist, but unwilling to glance down at it for a moment.

<62>

"Go on, check it out," Borley said. "Poor son-of-a-bitch never had a chance. He was a slave in life, and now he is a slave in death—*a slave to me.*"

Overcoming his aversion, the stranger slowly lifted the head to eye level. It bobbed gently in the container, the chocolate-brown flesh waving thinly.

"So how does it feel to hold a head in your hands Mr. Kane?" Borley patronized.

"Here," said the stranger, holding it out, "put it back."

"Already?"

"Yes. Here."

Sighing and shaking his head disappointingly, Borley retrieved the prize and leaned down to return it to its sanctuary. After sealing it away, Borley stood, leaned against the cabinet, and rested his left index finger on his cheek. He stared somewhat affectionately at the stranger.

"What's the matter, Mr. Kane? Too disturbing for you?"

Kane, at last unable to further conceal his disgust, looked at Borley a moment. His face dripped with discontent. "I simply think I've seen enough, that's all."

Borley bowed his head a bit, his eyes retaining contact from beneath a furrowed brow. "Oh come on now, Mr. Kane. Tell me honestly, what do you think of my little collection?"

Kane looked down for a moment, inwardly struggling for his response. And then, something inside him gave way. He locked eyes with his host once again. "You've asked for an honest response," he said, "and so I shall give one. *I think it's the most vulgar, perverse, maniacal thing I have ever seen.*"

A fire flashed in Borley's eyes. "Perverse!? Maniacal!? What the hell do you mean!?" Suddenly, the large man was expanded like a wild creature primed for combat. His charm had vanished, and the room was stiff and cold.

<63>

"It is nothing more than a psychotic exploitation of suffering and death," the stranger expelled, unleashing his pent aggression from the night.

With that, Borely stopped. His brow was strained, and he froze in place. A moment of silence gripped the room, and the two realized for the first time that the music was no longer playing. Gradually, Borley began to gently deflate, his temper cooling slowly. Intellect grasped emotion once again.

"Mr. Kane," Borley spoke in a quieter tone. "A man of your intelligence...naive in the ways of death?"

"What?" the stranger asked cautiously, now suddenly aware of his mistake.

Borley closed his eyes, shook his head, and grinned. Turning away, he mumbled something to himself, and then quickly turned back to face Kane again.

"Look at this," Borley said, holding up his right hand. "Do you see this hand?"

"Yes."

"Someday this hand—*this hand*—will be withered and sunken and rotted. And there is nothing I can do about it. Nothing. No matter how much money, or power, or prestige I possess can I prevent this flesh from decomposing and dropping from the bone. Never again will this hand be like it is tonight. Tomorrow it will be different. Maybe I won't be able to see the difference tomorrow, but it will be there. It will be older—deader. What you see tonight, no matter how much you love it or hate it, is only an illusion. Do you understand?"

"Yes."

"And so what value should it place with me? What value should it place with you? Each and every one of us will end up like the bog man, or the babies, or the slave—the most beautiful amongst us and the ugliest. So why must we treat it like something sacred? Why must we treat it like something to be pitied? Pity yourself! Pity this wretched, horrid

<64>

world—this cruel unsavory illusion—this unmasterable game we call life. Search this universe far and wide and you shall find nothing so vulgar, so perverse, so maniacal as the fleshy infant, destined for decay the moment it emerges from its mother's womb."

"But these things, these articles of death, they represent memories," said the stranger. "If we dishonor them, then we dishonor the memories of those they represent."

"Nothing can represent a memory," Borley hissed, uplifting his right index finger intently. "Memories do not wither and die like the flesh. If the flesh was a representation, then the memories would deteriorate along with it. The flesh means nothing to me."

The two men stood solemnly in a moment of quiet contemplation. The stranger looked down with a river of thoughts surging in his brain. He then gave Borley a look of intensity, clean, pure, and honest. "What exactly do you want from life?" he asked.

Borley tasted the question, and savored its sweetness on his tongue. "*Immortality*," he answered.

There was a thickness of aged understanding and pained experience that wafted throughout the room. Each man was quiet. Borley held longingly to the remnants of his thoughts, and the stranger tightened with the new awkwardness sealing the men together. He knew that any moment might be his last. Once Borley was done "playing" he might exterminate his toy. Nonetheless, overcome with endless curiosity, he asked a question further.

"Sure. Life can seem miserable. But isn't there anything about it that brings you joy?"

"Joy?" asked Borley, his large eyes dropping in their dark sockets. "Oh yes, there is joy." He seemed tired and spent, his last reserve of dynamic energy expended. "There is joy like a square pat of melting butter sliding across a fresh batch of hot corn bread. Or the stinging smell of a woman's perfumed neck as the sun goes down. But even those things

<65>

are now only memories for me. The curse of supreme intelligence is to know your own mortality intimately, excruciatingly."

The stranger watched him fading, a part of Borley slipping like a wilting flower, greeting a foreboding shadow unseen to the outside eye.

"But enough of that!" Borley exclaimed, having tapped into a new and unexpected vein of energy. "It's too bad," he said, awakening again, but still with less power than he before had emitted. "It's too bad you cannot appreciate my little collection. However, it's plain to see you have a good and worthy heart—an admirable quality in a man—therefore I have saved some redemption for myself."

"Redemption?"

"Oh yes, I think you will certainly appreciate, perhaps applaud even, the final exhibition I will show to you."

A surly smile on his face, Borley motioned and walked a few steps to the left of the cabinet. He stopped, gazing fondly at a heavy shelf mounted on the wall. It was lined with empty jars—a peaceful, yet peculiar contrast to the atmosphere of the chamber. Borley reached to bring down the farthest jar on the right.

"This," he said, "will be my most prized possession of all." He handed it to Kane, who peered deeply inside to confirm its devoidness.

"Oh," responded the stranger obligingly, "and what is that?"

"This jar will hold the genitals of the man who tried to rob my father's grave."

A bolt of frigid shock surged in the stranger's veins. His eyes shot to Borley's. The rich man's face was bold and contemptuous—his gaze like a vile doom. Their spirits clenched dreadfully for a single moment longer than the stare of an innocent conscience.

"Here," said Kane, firmly handing it back.

Borley took the jar, his face unchanging, and his eyes never leaving their mark.

<66>

"It's going to feel so good," he growled. "I'm going to remove them with my own hand." He lifted his large paw and clenched it dramatically, violently, in the air.

With the guarded face of a man on trial, the stranger curled his bottom lip and nodded his head in three swift jerks. "And I suppose those jars are for the rest of his body parts," he said, waving his hand towards the waiting jars on the shelf. Borley glanced back, and then turned to face the stranger with a wicked smile.

"Oh heavens no," he said. "I wouldn't do a thing like that…Those jars are for the genitals of his family."

An instant, final coldness dropped inside the stranger, and he stood silent and accepting. He was partially glad the game was coming to an end. Borley searched him visually, the wide black eyes boring deep inside him. Then, without warning, Borley slammed the jar back on the shelf, turned with a gaping grin and slapped Kane on the back. "Come my friend!" he cried. "Let's have a drink!"

On the backside of the castle was a large, open patio. Lanterns illuminated the area, and a tall, majestic fountain rained down in its center. As Borley and Kane passed through the massive glass door leading to the veranda, six security guards, including Brock, were poised at various points of the area. When they saw the entrants, each man stiffened royally. A flash of glances darted between them, as if each had been waiting—discussing even—the arrival of the two. An unfeeling and foreboding air of duty surrounded each man. The stranger could sense a dark, unspoken communication amongst everyone but himself, and he felt his deliverance unto the "spider's parlor" was surely at hand.

Brock, an impudent pallor on his face, came pacing swiftly forward. The stranger looked at Borley to find a blissful smile still affixed to his rosy visage.

"How are things going, Mr. Borley?" Brock asked, hatred burning in his eyes.

<67>

"Oh just fine Brock," Borley replied, barely completing the thought before lurching around to explore the door behind him. "Williaaaaam! William! Come here man!"

Brock and the stranger exchanged the usual predatory stare. By this time, the other guards had gradually closed in more, their muscles tight like a cat about to pounce. Borley withdrew a case of cigarettes from his pocket and lit one up dashingly.

"Yes sir?" said William, rushing through the door breathlessly.

"Amaretto Sour."

"Yes sir."

"And for you?" inquired Borley, turning to the stranger.

Kane's attention shot back from the impending danger. "Oh uh—no thank you. I don't believe I'll have anything."

Borley arched his eyebrows, as if nearly insulted by the response. "Oh come now. You're not going to make me drink alone are you?" He appeared oblivious to the tension encircling the men.

"I'm sorry," said Kane. "I have other affairs tonight to which alcohol may prove a hindrance."

With that, Borley gave a quick shrug and repeated his command to William, this time a bit softer: "Amaretto sour, William."

"Coming right up, sir." He spun traditionally to glide away again.

"Oh and William!"

He screeched to a halt. "Yes sir?"

"Double shot of Amaretto."

"Indeed, sir." He was gone.

Turning around again, Borley closed his eyes, leaned back his head, stretched out his arms and yawned like a bear. He half-opened them again, still seeming oblivious to the anxious men around him, apparently eager for his command. He slid his large hand into his left pants pocket, withdrawing a sparkling, gold watch. Holding it out a bit, lifting his nose, and concentrating intensely on the face, his eyebrows suddenly bounced upwards. "My goodness. It's getting late isn't it, Mr. Kane?"

<68>

"I should say so," the stranger replied.

"Very well. It'd be unfair for me to keep you any longer."

The guards shifted, as if having entered the final phase of preparation. Their hammers cocked, each clung to their master's every subtle move. Having placed the watch back in his pocket, Borley looked to the stranger with a grin and extended his hand to offer a shake. The stranger took it, and the shake was firm, mighty, and swift.

"It's been a charming evening," Borley said with gleaming eyes.

The stranger nodded.

"So now you have seen Borley's Castle, my dear tourist. I feel assured you will enjoy the rest of our scenic town equally."

"Thank you," responded the stranger, completely uncertain of what would take place next.

"Brock," Borley said, making his first true eye contact with the guard, "please have Mr. Kane shown out."

There was an instant of aggressive motion in Brock's lumbering frame, then he halted suddenly. "I beg your pardon, sir?"

"I said, please have Mr. Kane shown the way out." It was plain that Borley didn't like repeating himself.

Still unmoving, one could nearly see the bulky gears turning behind Brock's bulging eyes. He searched Borley's face for an ulterior meaning in his command—but he found none. "But—I mean," he stammered. "Well—you mean you'd like me to have a *talk* with him first though, right?"

His nostrils flared, Borley was clearly displeased. "I said," he raised his voice, "*you will have Mr. Kane shown off the estate now, and in good condition.* Do you understand?"

"Yes sir," said Brock, immediately embarrassed. His face blossoming a warm shade of cherry, he turned to face two of the equally confused guards on the veranda. "Robert, Chip," he motioned, "come on."

For the first time, Brock avoided eye contact with the stranger, and the guards quickly took their places at Kane's sides. "This way," said

<69>

Brock, standing in the doorway behind the stranger. Before turning to leave, Kane gave Borley a final nod of acknowledgment.

Borley's cigarette smoldered between his fingers. "Adieu Mr. Kane," he said dreamily as the stranger started walking away, a smirk half-hidden on his thick lips. "Adieu."

Once inside the castle, Brock looked to his guards, still uncertain of his orders. "I tell you guys what," he said, ignoring Kane's presence, "take him on out. I need to talk to Mr. Borley about somethin'." He strode off while the two guards in suits led the stranger silently towards the castle's entrance.

Halfway through the castle, the three men heard a shrill voice behind them. "Hey! Hold on a minute!" They each turned to see Eileen, Borley's wife, racing towards them, her heels clicking dominantly on the stone floor. Almost panicky, she rushed up to the stranger, her eyes wide and direct.

"Sir," she said, "before you go, there is something you should know about me and my husband." She touched the stranger lightly on his shoulder as she talked, emphasizing each word physically. "My husband and I are born-again Christians. Just because we live in a big castle, and my husband has some unique collections, does not mean we are bad people. My husband is just going through a very difficult time right now. He just lost his father, you know."

"Yes," Kane assured her, "I know."

"He doesn't usually drink like that, but it's just been so hard on him…"

"Yes ma'am, I understand," said the stranger.

Suddenly, her demeanor turned more aggressive. "But don't judge us, sir. *Do not judge us*. We are good Christian people, and we're doing the best we can."

The stranger looked down, and then raised his head thoughtfully. "I assure you Mrs. Borley, I am not here to judge. I'm only here to see your beautiful home."

<70>

"Well good. Good," she said, shaking her head satisfactorily, and yet somehow nervously. "You have a nice evening then." With that, she walked away again.

"This way," said one of the guards, and the three men resumed their walk.

On the veranda, by the peaceful hiss of the cascading fountain, Borley smoked another cigarette and leisurely sipped his Amaretto Sour. Brock sat with him, engaged in conversation.

"But I don't understand, I thought your policy with intruders was—"

"Brock," Borley interrupted. "I do not pay you to understand. I pay you to do as I say."

"What if he's seen things that—?"

"Brock." Again, Borley interrupted. "Some men are more valuable dead, and others more valuable alive. You cannot squeeze blood from a stone. And I assure you, Mr. Kane is a stone."

"Do you have any idea who he could be?"

"Perhaps," said Borley, his gaze lost deep in the shining liquid of his tart drink. "Follow him. Watch his every move and find out exactly who he is."

"Do you think he's a cop?" glared Brock.

"No, no, no. He's too smart for a cop."

"A P.I.?"

"Ummm—possibly, but I doubt it."

"Do you have any idea who he could be?" Brock exhaled with exasperation.

"I have my suspicions," answered Borley.

"Then what else could he be?"

"More than he appears my good fellow. More than he appears."

<71>

CHAPTER THREE

WILSON BENEDICT WAS slight and intense. Just approaching middle-age, he had worked for the newspaper long enough to be broken, and yet not so long that he'd lost the fire for his job. Both serious and good-natured, he was a peculiar sight—his chestnut hair meticulously groomed, his features solid and well-formed—and yet he seemed out of place in his environment. Wiry and energetic, he dashed about the clamor of the newspaper office with precision that housed no impatience, but bore a hint of unprovoked excitement. The others in his office, seated lazily in the routine of their jobs, viewed him as eccentric. He wasn't strange in a propensity for the insane, however. Instead, he was strange in a propensity for the extremely sane. He was painfully conscious of his articulations, his manners, and his knowledge of customs. He spoke like a well-written article, and carried himself like a humble compendium of all mankind's civility.

Benedict's gaze was solid, yet his eyes were often searching. His attention to detail was unparalleled, and his memory was a delicate system of intricate files. Though most of the newspaper staff respected the work from his carefully chosen assignments, they couldn't entirely relate to him. He communicated with a level of thought and acuteness intimidating, or at least awkward, for some. But his greatest departure from the standard news writer was his personal insight of the subjects about which he wrote. He stuck to the facts, like a good reporter is so often trained, and yet he arranged them, charged them, colored them with purpose that made them dramatic and meaningful. He had difficulty

<72>

entirely separating his ethics and philosophy from his work, and he often teetered on the edge of subjectivity.

As he rattled away at his keyboard, the telephone rang. Unlike his counterparts, he disliked the notion of voice mail substituting for a personal greeting. And so, even though the heat of a deadline hovered at his neck, he chose to answer.

"Wilson Benedict." His voice was soft-spoken and considerate. The voice on the other line was low and mysterious.

"*I understand you know a bit about Borley's Castle*," the stranger said.

Benedict furrowed his brow, immediately drawing a mental image of the owner of the voice.

"Yes, a bit," he answered.

"When can we meet?" Benedict was understandably taken aback.

"Meet? Who am I speaking with?"

"That's not important," was the reply.

Being knowledgeable of society's multitude of unstable minds, Benedict was immediately wary. It was an especially valuable trait for one involved with the media.

"Is this about the death of Crawford Borley?" the reporter asked.

"Ummm...," the stranger hesitated, "you might say that."

"Do you have some new information?" There were a few moments of silence on the line.

"Let me ask you a question, Mr. Benedict."

"Yes?"

"Do you know what the inside of Borley's Castle looks like?"

"No."

"Would you like to?"

"Um, well yes."

"I've been there."

Benedict immediately grabbed his pad and pencil, always waiting patiently beside his phone.

<73>

"You've been *inside* the castle?" Benedict asked, a detectable, hopeful excitement in his voice.

"Yes," the stranger answered, "I've been *inside* the castle."

"When?"

"When can we meet?" The stranger was firm and insistent.

"Uh, let me see." Benedict rustled through some pages to locate his planner. "It looks like—oh, like you could drop by here tomorrow afternoon—"

"No, no, no," the stranger interrupted. "I'm not coming there. This isn't newspaper business."

"I see," replied Benedict, mentally struggling with the question of his own submission. "Then, where would you like to meet?"

"The Grove Park Inn," the stranger said.

"Um, okay," Benedict agreed, satisfied with the idea of a public place.

"How 'bout tomorrow evening?" asked the stranger. "Are you free about seven?"

"Seven, seven—yes, seven will be fine." Benedict began scrawling. "In the Great Hall, I suppose."

"No," said the dark voice, "in the boiler room. You know where the boiler room is?"

"The boiler room?" The reporter stopped writing, his mind racing to process the request. "But the boiler room is off limits to the public."

"No one will bother us," the stranger assured him. "Do you know where it is?"

"Yes," answered Benedict, "I used to do some work in the hotel."

"Very well. See you tomorrow night at seven. Goodbye."

"Wait!" Benedict exclaimed.

"Yes?"

"You said you've been in the castle."

"Yes."

"I've heard there's something special right in the middle of the entrance chamber."

<74>

"What? The fountain?"

Benedict exhaled with a laugh and smacked his desk. "I knew it!" he said. "I knew there was a fountain in that castle!"

"See you tomorrow night," the stranger said. Then, with a click, the line was dead.

*   *   *

The Grove Park Inn was a man-made mountain. It was a block of granite, mammoth and grand, timeless and complex. It was designed to overwhelm the senses and shield its inhabitants with strength and wisdom. Its rocky walls were so firm and mighty, one could imagine them sinking deep into the earth, and joining with pillars that sustain continents. It looked as if it had emerged from the earth itself, a studded outpost of a world buried far below. Like Borley's Castle, its energy was dominant and uncompromising; so much in fact, the two could have been old and bitter rivals. Venerable, arcane, and luxurious, it was the perfect backdrop for a meeting with the stranger.

The evening air was cool, but tolerable as Wilson Benedict passed beneath the covered entrance of the hotel. The building loomed like a poker-face, the terra-cotta tiles of its sloping, shapely roof bulging with the forces they contained. The windows on its face glowed with golden insight, and peered suspiciously upon the outside world.

The reporter, anxiety stirring in his abdomen, navigated the wealthy, beaming crowds that flowed down each hall. They were the same halls frequented by presidents like Franklin D. Roosevelt and Richard Nixon, celebrities like Houdini, Edison, and F. Scott Fitzgerald, and one could still feel the weight of their spirits lingering. The air tasted like champagne and smelled like wood smoke, and the pleasurable sting of success nipped at every corner. The hotel swallowed him hungrily as he

<75>

worked his way, level by level, to the secluded section of the Vanderbilt Wing that led to the boiler room.

Once he found the door, marked for staff entrance, he examined a twinge of doubt circling in his brain. His slender fingers upon the cold, smooth knob, he halted and shifted his gaze around the space behind him: A glass elevator shaft, an unused registration room, staircases and levels—and not a single soul in sight. Benedict's thick tufts of eyebrow were tiny shelves of brown hair, jutting slightly from his forehead. He lowered these awnings until they guarded a portion of his eyes, and then studied the environment, searching for traces of the unordinary. His brain filing the scene like a computer, he gave in with satisfaction and turned the knob.

Benedict welcomed the warm, toasty breeze that met his face upon entering the boiler room. Metallic, dusty, and industrial, the room clashed with the polished hotel outside. The audible rumble of the machinery was a comforting filter against unwanted eavesdropping. Two large tanks were positioned on the floor, and across the room a short, steep framework of steps led to a higher concrete level. This level joined a hallway, off to the right and out of sight. There was no sign of the stranger.

Benedict glanced at his wrist watch: "6:59." In the instant his attention was focused downwards, a flash of dark motion passed in his peripheries. Shooting his face up, he saw a fleeting image disappear towards the unseen hallway on the upper level—black attire, and a bald head.

"Hello?" he called. "*Hello?* Is someone there?" No response. "Is someone there?" Slowly, cautiously, he took a few steps forward, listening intently but hearing nothing. He locked his eyes on the spot, anxious for a glimpse of flesh or moving shadows. Quiet, still, and tense, he watched. Suddenly, a large firm hand touched his right shoulder. With a yelp, he spun around.

Startled, Benedict shot back from Kane standing solemn before him. Kane himself was unnerved by such a greeting. The shot of terror still

<76>

lingering in the reporter's eyes, he exhaled, yet looked unsurely upon the stranger.

"Mr. Benedict?" asked the stranger.

"Yes, yes," the reporter caught his breath. "That's me."

"What's wrong?"

Though his lips stretched to form a word, Benedict was speechless for a moment. "I was just startled, that's all. There's someone else up there," he pointed towards the upper level, "and I thought it was you."

Immediately, a flash of concern animated the stranger's steely features. Without a sound, he dashed across the room, up the steps, and disappeared down the hallway to the right. It was all a confusing display to Benedict, and had it not been for his insatiable curiosity, he would have bolted out the door and relieved himself of the imposing scene. Instead, he stood wide-eyed and bewildered, awaiting the stranger's return.

In a few moments Kane reappeared, his jolt of urgency dissipated, treading steadily down the steps. His face tightened with uncertainty as he made his way back. "There's no one up there," he said flatly.

"Well, isn't there a door up there?" Benedict inquired, his pointing index finger arched back towards the hallway.

Kane shook his head affirmatively. "Yes," he replied. "There's a door at the end of the hallway, but it's locked—from *this* side."

The enigma hit Benedict like a projectile, and his face crinkled sourly. "But…I could've sworn I saw a man up there. Are you sure there's no other door?"

"If there is, it's hidden."

"That's so peculiar." Benedict's senses were keen, and so his mind raced for explanations.

"What did he look like?" asked the stranger, now standing before the reporter in the usual intimidating way, arms crossed and features stern.

"Well I only got a glance. But it looked like he was wearing dark clothes, and he was bald. That's all I could tell."

<77>

Immediately a brisk new energy possessed Kane's face. Its hardness gave way to involuntary wonder, but he instantly tried to conceal the change. To Benedict's attentive eyes, it was clear that the description had meaning to the stranger. "Bald? With dark clothes?"

"Yes," answered Benedict. "Does that sound familiar?"

Kane gazed to the floor thoughtfully, and then lifted his eyes. "No," he said.

Benedict knew better, but stayed silent just the same. The connection between the two had not yet solidified. Even though the stranger looked at the reporter, there was a blankness behind his eyes for a few moments. It was obvious that his mind was elsewhere, while his body carried on automatically.

Eager to refresh the awkward atmosphere, Benedict smiled. "Well," he said, "perhaps it was one of the Grove Park's famous ghosts!"

"Ghosts?" the stranger frowned.

"Why yes," returned Benedict. "You've never heard of the Pink Lady?"

"No."

"She's a young woman who died in the hotel in the 1920s. She supposedly haunts the place in a long pink gown."

"Is she bald?" asked the stranger with a sudden snicker.

The reporter chuckled. "No, no. She's a blonde with long hair. But I hear she's not alone. Maybe that was her boyfriend." The two shared a courteous laugh.

"Wilson Benedict," said the reporter, extending his hand elegantly.

"I'm Kane," said the stranger as they shook.

"Kane who?"

"Just Kane."

"Ah, very well," said Benedict. His curiosity was further piqued.

"Thank you for coming," said the stranger. "But before we talk, you should realize that what we discuss is confidential."

"I understand."

<78>

"And you should also understand I mean what I say," stressed the stranger. "To be quite honest, I don't like reporters. And if any of this ends up in the paper, there are going to be consequences."

Benedict shifted his gaze down for a moment, reflecting on the best way to address the issue. "I understand we're going to be discussing the Borleys?"

"Yes."

"Well, I don't know if you're aware of this, but J.C. Borley owns a good chunk of the paper. Therefore, it would be personally counterproductive for me to print anything detrimental, or even controversial, about the Borleys."

"Are you sympathetic to the Borleys?" Kane interrogated.

Benedict thought about the question carefully. "No," he replied.

"Good," Kane nodded, "then you and I will get along just fine."

Off to the side of the machinery were two salvaged chairs, rickety but sufficient for use. "Here," motioned Kane, "let's have ourselves a seat." Each man planted himself in the imitation leather padding, sparsely attached to a metal framework. Benedict had a thousand questions on his mind, yet he calmly waited for the stranger's words.

"What do you know about Borley's Castle?" asked Kane, leaning forward, hands clasped and bony elbows founded on his knees.

Benedict searched the stranger's eyes and curled his bottom lip. "Are you with law enforcement?"

"No," replied the stranger.

"Then why are you interested in the Borleys?"

Each man possibly possessed knowledge desired by the other; and each understood that such knowledge was the only form of power he controlled. An inevitable teetering of carefully-worded phrases ensued. Unsure of each other's interest in the Borleys, digging into the meat of the subject was a diplomatic venture.

"My interest in the Borleys is a private matter," said Kane. "I represent no one but myself."

<79>

"I see."

"And I shall pose that question to you as well. Why are you interested in the Borleys?"

"Well—likewise," answered Benedict. "It's a private interest. Since I moved to Asheville fifteen years ago, I've found them an intriguing lot."

"What do you think goes on in that castle?" posed the stranger.

"I suppose I should ask you that question. You've been inside, right?"

"Yes, I've been inside. But I need to get *back* inside."

"How did you manage to get in to begin with?"

"I was escorted into the castle by thugs," said Kane, contributing the first bit of substantive information. "I broke into the estate, was captured, was taken to Borley, had a long discussion with him, looked at his collections of weird things, and was released. That's my story. Now what's yours."

Benedict's eyes were sparkling. "What's it like in there?"

"It's amazing," replied the stranger. "A moat, huge fountains, skylights, rare antiques. It's an impressive place."

"You must tell me all about it," the reporter glowed.

"Cigarette?" asked the stranger, withdrawing a pack from his coat pocket. Benedict took one gratefully, then lit up at the hand of the stranger. Taking a drag himself, the stranger leaned back, more relaxed than before.

"Mr. Benedict," he said, "why are you interested in the Borleys?"

Benedict took a deep breath. "In my line of work, I come in contact with a lot of people. Subsequently, I hear a lot of things. I was employed by the *Times* shortly after moving here, and quickly began hearing stories about the Borleys."

"What kind of stories?"

"Just speculation, that's all. Speculation that there may be some…perhaps unsavory business being handled in the castle. I started researching the history of Crawford Borley and the estate and have

<80>

since compiled a file. However, I know very little more than I did fifteen years ago."

Each man had warily tread into unstable territory. Neither had solid grounds for divulging to the other, and yet they trusted their instincts, slowly giving the other the benefit of the doubt. Besides, each recognized the uniqueness of the other. Though Borley conversation commonly peppered after-dinner conversations among Asheville's elite, it was unusual to find someone admitting to being a serious researcher. Because of this, they each shared an instant masculine respect for the other.

"Do you know how Crawford Borley amassed his empire?" asked Kane.

"Yes. It started with real estate investments and branched out from there."

"And the Borleys have succeeded with amazingly little conflict from the outside world, wouldn't you say?"

Benedict scratched his head furiously, still struggling with the inherent tendency to contain information. A part of him began to break down. "I suppose you're familiar with the pattern—?" His tongue chopped off the sentence, and he raised his eyebrows, signaling he had submitted a clue.

"Of deaths?" the stranger picked up.

Instantly relieved, Benedict gave a satisfied nod.

"Yes," said the stranger. "It's a bit much. You don't have to be a genius to figure it out. That's what's so puzzling. No one is surrounded by that much death. Every time the Borleys run up against competition, people end up dead. Everyone seems to know, but no one does a damn thing about it."

"Look," said Benedict, uncomfortable with the extent of the conversation, "what can I do for you?"

"I need a map of the castle," Kane replied. "Some sort of a layout of its design."

Though uncharacteristic of him, Benedict released a chuckle. "Kane," he said, almost as though addressing a child, "for fifteen years I have

<81>

searched for any indication of the castle's interior. *It does not exist*—at least not outside of Borley's office. Aside from rumors, I have no idea how the inside looks. You're the first person I've ever talked to who claims to have been there. That's why I'm so eager to hear about it."

Kane's brow grew stern, and he resumed his hardness. "*No one* else has been in there?" he asked rhetorically.

Sensing that he had offended the stranger, Benedict spoke more courteously. "I once tried to interview a retired woman who worked as the Borleys' maid for years. However, her husband wouldn't allow it. That's the closest I've come."

"Well then," said the stranger, rising abruptly and dropping his smoldering cigarette, grinding it into the hard concrete floor with his thick-heeled boot. "I suppose there's nothing you can do for me. Thank you for your time."

"Wait!" exclaimed Benedict, jetting to his feet as well. "Are you really going to break into Borley's Castle?"

Kane stood silent a moment, questioning whether further conversation was necessary. "I intend to find The Horror," he said. "And I intend to destroy it."

"The Horror?"

"Yes."

"The ghost story?" said Benedict, shaking his head with a smile. "That's what you're interested in? *All* spooky places in Asheville have a great ghost story."

"Ghost stories don't rip people in half," the stranger replied, his eyes intense with the power of his words.

Benedict crinkled his brow, visibly confused by the statement. "What are you talking about?"

"I'm talking about Crawford Borley," Kane said, raising his voice with self-assurance.

Benedict, bewildered, looked at him for a moment. "What do you mean?" he inquired.

<82>

"I *mean* I saw the corpse of Crawford Borley, and he didn't die of heart failure. He died of having his lower body torn off."

Benedict depressed his jutting eyebrows, exploring the stranger's face to confirm the seriousness of his words. "Do you mean that Crawford Borley—"

"Yes," interjected the stranger. "He was ripped in half. I'm no doctor, but generally speaking heart failure doesn't destroy the lower half of the body."

Benedict was quiet for a moment, allowing Kane's words to sink in fully. "Do you suggest that something in the castle physically tore him apart?"

"All I know is that he didn't die of heart failure, and J.C. Borley knows that. Wouldn't that constitute foul play?"

The question lingered in the air for a moment, and each man thought about it carefully. Extremely aware of the question's implications, they felt suspicious towards each other again.

"Listen," said Benedict, "I haven't put much time into researching the Borleys for years. It seemed like a dead end. But if you're serious about this, I can help you."

"Help me?" Kane nearly scoffed. "And why would you want to do that?"

"Because if it's true—if people really are dying—it's time someone stopped it."

"No thank you," replied the stranger. "It doesn't appear you could be of any benefit at all." With that, Kane turned and took a few steps in the direction of the exit.

"What if I *could* get you a layout of the castle?" Benedict called from behind.

The stranger halted, then spun back around, his heels hissing on the dusty concrete. "What do you mean?"

Benedict walked towards him slowly. "I have a friend," he said, "who pilots a hot air balloon."

"Yes."

"A good friend. The kind you can trust."

"Yes?"

<83>

Benedict hesitated a moment as if entertaining a variety of thoughts. "What about aerial photographs of the castle? I've thought about the possibility for a while, but never acted on it."

A new light illuminated the stranger's eyes. "Yes. Aerial photographs would be of great assistance."

Benedict nodded affirmatively. "It would cost money though. It's not cheap to run a balloon. But he'd be more than willing to work with us."

"Money is not a factor," said Kane. "How soon could we fly?"

"I'm not sure, but I could find out tomorrow."

A new connection solidified between the two. "Do that," said the stranger. "Do that as soon as possible and let me know."

"How can I get in touch with you?" asked the reporter.

Kane slid his hand into his left coat pocket and withdrew a small pad. From his right pocket he produced a ball-point pen. Holding the pad on his open left palm, he scribbled forcefully on a page, then ripped it away. "Here," he said, handing it to Benedict. "Call this number and you'll get voice mail. Leave a message and I'll call you back."

Benedict peered at the paper. The number was written elegantly, spiderly. He folded it cleanly in half, stashed it in his pocket, and withdrew his hand with a business card. "Here's my card," he said. The stranger stuffed it in his coat without a glance.

Kane took Benedict's hand again, giving it a strong, hurried shake. "Nice to meet you," he said.

"Kane," said Benedict, a yet unspoken thought breaking through the surface. "Asheville isn't like it used to be."

"What do you mean?"

"Asheville is changing. The population is growing and more diverse people are coming here."

"Yes?" The stranger was uncertain of Benedict's point.

"The Borleys may be the last remnants of Asheville's past—Asheville's glory days. Of that time when honor and secrecy were embraced. When loyalty and old values ruled supreme. It's always been

<84>

a tight community—ruled by a few, and often with poor judgement—but set in their ways—agents of the time when honesty and dishonesty were all relevant terms, and a man was judged purely by the money in his bank, and not the deeds that put it there. That's why the Borleys are so protected, but soon, they'll be extinct. Asheville is changing naturally. Are you sure it's right to take it into your own hands? Should you interfere with the natural development—to stir such black and settled waters? Is the timing right?"

The stranger shook his head and scowled. "Today they drive cars instead of carriages," he said, "but Asheville hasn't changed. The people may be changing, but Asheville will never change. Asheville is a city ruled by hindsight. I don't need anyone's approval for my actions. I have my reasons for what I do."

"I hope you're right," said Benedict, drawing his thick eyebrows close together.

"I am," replied the stranger. With that, he was gone.

∗　　　∗　　　∗

Doug Searcy was lean, like a wet muskrat—his bright, beady eyes shining beneath the shadow of his ball cap. He'd flown hot air balloons since just a youth, assisting his father on countless flights. Most of his life had been spent outdoors, and so gradually he'd adopted the outside ways. He could hardly stand to urinate in a toilet, preferring a tree or bush, and his fingernails were lined with black ridges of grease and earthy grunge. But besides his loose and uncouth presentation, he was reasonably smart. He knew the Southeast like the back of his oily hand, and some claimed he was nearly a mechanical genius. He was simply a free spirit, too free to be confined by etiquette and hygiene. But his submission to freedom was no doubt the best thing for him—because of it, he stayed happy, humorous, and confident. In fact, he was rather personable.

<85>

"Can it be done or not?" demanded Kane, squinting his heavy brow in the bright sunlight.

Gawky and baggy, Doug extended his long finger to scratch the tight, sweaty line where his cap met his bushy hair. "Uh, yeah, yeah. I think we can pull that off," he said. He spoke strongly and direct, the clarity of his words muddled in a thick Southern accent.

"Can we get directly over the castle?" chimed in Benedict. "I want to get pictures of it from the top."

"Well, balloonin' ain't an exact science, but I think we may do alright. The way that castle's placed on the mountain, I oughtta be able to catch a roll, and glide with the current right through the cove and out the other side. On a warm, pretty day like this, it's easier to do that sort o' thing."

Benedict tinkered with buttons on a 35mm Pentax hanging from his neck by a broad, red strap. From his arm hung a leather satchel, a variety of lenses and filters tucked firmly inside.

"You sure you know how to use that thing?" questioned the stranger.

"I was a photojournalist for five years," he said. "I'm quite familiar with a camera, and I know the importance of getting a shot when opportunity is limited."

Kane scanned the land around him, watching for the uninvited. They stood in the middle of a field, a ring of tall trees encircling them, secluding them, from the outside. The day was warm, bright, and green, yet all the colors of fall seared in their distinction. The balloon was set up a few feet away. Doug's young assistant, Ray, was tending to it.

In all its inflated glory, the black balloon towered tight and bold. The warm air inside pressed outward with a dense physical strength that had smoothed each crease and wrinkle in its resilient walls. Pinned ropes held its hard basket near the ground, and the swollen balloon strained upwards with such force that the ropes pulled taut, as straight and solid as steel cables. It was like a mighty, bloated beast, holding its breath and pulling towards its home in exasperation; trying desperately to break its

<86>

exhausting leash and escape. It breathed a rumbling, agitating roar as each screaming jet of propane shot deep into its core.

"I've never seen a black hot-air balloon," said Kane.

"Saves on money," Doug replied. "Black absorbs heat, so the sun helps fill the balloon." He cupped his hand over his brow like a visor, and looked into the blinding blue sky. "Ah yeah. Perfect day for flyin'. Clear, warm, and sunny. We're gonna have some hellacious views today."

"How safe are these things anyway?" asked the stranger, studying the balloon, his long coat slung over his right shoulder.

"Why it's the safest aircraft around," Doug proclaimed. "Hell, you got your parachute built right onto the craft."

The stranger looked at Ray. A meek teenager with dark, ruffled hair, he continued pumping fire into the beast. He was a good distance from the others, and his hearing was drowned by the torch.

"By the way," the stranger said to Doug, "I didn't know anything about him coming today. This is confidential business, you know."

Doug brushed the air with his hand. "Oh him? He's just a kid who helps me set things up—he ain't goin' with us. Besides, he ain't gonna say nothin' to nobody. He's been workin' with me 'bout a year now. He's a good kid."

"Yeah, well what if he does go tell somebody."

"Naw, I told him this was private business. I need somebody to help me anyway. It ain't so easy to set one o' these things up."

Clearly unsatisfied, the stranger accepted the situation distastefully.

"Hey," said Doug, "if it makes you feel any better, I don't like those Borley bastards either. So you don't have to worry about me rainin' on your parade."

Kane thought about his words, then gave him a congenial nod.

"Now Kane, I've loaded 200 speed color film," said Benedict. "You did want color, right?"

"Sure, color's fine. As long as we have the shots, that's all that matters."

<87>

"Well gentlemen," said Doug, squinting towards the balloon, "I believe she's ready to fly."

Kane and Benedict exchanged a glance, and then all three men humbly made their way to the majestic balloon.

The basket of the balloon was of heavier, sturdier construction than Kane expected. The interwoven wicker was bound tight and sealed with a thick, clear shellac. Upon their reaching the vessel, Ray fired up the propane for a few seconds, and a searing wave of unmerciful heat reflected from their faces. Up close, the cry of the torch was louder, more aggressive, more sinister than they had imagined. Its destructive hiss violated their eardrums and made the radiating heat seem more fearsome and intense.

Painstakingly, each man stepped over the gondola wall to find himself standing on the wicker floor—soon to be the only barrier between them and a perilous death. Though well-anchored, the basket wobbled a bit as each man settled into place. It was a helpless feeling of insecurity, and Kane began to question his level of comfort.

"Okey-dokes," said Doug, "are we ready?"

Kane and Benedict looked at each other. "You have everything?" asked the stranger.

"Yes," the reporter replied. "I'm ready when you are."

Kane gave the pilot a nod. "Okay!" Doug yelled, "off we go!"

Ray released the lines. Victoriously, the creature shot skyward.

It was magical. The land was a sweeping vision of colors, shapes, and textures. The limitless blue sky welcomed them, and danced with them, from current to current, varying cushions of warm air rolling them on waves across the horizon. The balloon rose higher and higher as Doug tugged steadily at the fuel tank's chain. The hotter the air, the more enthusiastically the beast soared into the heavens.

Kane and Benedict were overcome by the fresh, exhilarating breath of excitement and fear. Despite the stranger's attempt to adhere to stern virility, his eyes sparkled like those of a child on a speeding roller

<88>

coaster, and once he almost smiled. It was triumphant: gazing down at the mighty trees, now dwarfed; the ancient mountains their companions; all life below so vulnerable, slow, and exposed. The ground was like a prison, simple and controlling, but in the air there was freedom and growth. In that instant, both Kane and Benedict looked at Doug and understood.

The balloon worked its way through formations of mountains, carpeted by a patchwork of colors. The ridges were creased so smoothly and softly it appeared the hand of God had reached down from above, the large commanding fingers depressing the landscape, shaping it like dough. They passed over a tiny person in a yard, his neck craned back, waving at them madly. They waved in return, feeling instantly like heroes simply because they dominated the skies. The tops of vehicles on mountain backroads looked so helpless and primitive, their drivers surely oblivious to the glorious structures just over the hill, or across the pasture from them. It was the big picture, epic and moving, and it made the world seem so small—a world that before had been so mammoth and mysterious.

Being overcome and enchanted by the experience, Kane had forgotten the dangers of height. When he remembered again, he looked down at the wicker upon which his weight rested. He imagined the opposite side—how far and lonely a drop was below him—how lengthy a void begged certain death. It was slightly disenchanting but, being a reasonable man, he reckoned his fears would do him no good now. And so he dismissed the feeling and accepted the experience for what it was.

Like Doug, Benedict was completely enthralled. He soaked up every scenic moment, treasuring each breath and vision. A part of him wanted to lift the camera and take some shots of the masterful landscape. However, at the same time, he didn't want to remember the experience through a view finder. And so sacrificing a good physical memento for a breathtaking memory, he filed the scene vividly into the computer of his mind.

<89>

Alas, like a miniature kingdom, the city of Asheville emerged, nestled among the ranges. It was a jewel, sparkling and beautiful, old and new. The buildings, the streets, the structures, were timeless at such a height. There was no past and present, simply a domain, a character, an old friend seated in the shapely ridges and by the glorious, rushing rivers and streams. It looked as though a small, comfortable seat had been dug especially to house the wondrous civilization.

"What a place, eh?!" called Doug over a blast of propane. Kane and Benedict looked to him and nodded gleefully.

Sweeping towards the city of Asheville, they saw Borley's Castle in the distance. It was the first time they felt more powerful than the structure. Clinging to the mountain side, it was a dark and ominous lair, yet even *it* looked somehow contained when viewed from the air. The balloonists watched it grow closer, enlarging with detail, as though watching a movie on a massive, all-encompassing screen. They were subliminally conscious of an eerie mental distinction between the world as they knew it and the world from above. They felt unseen, omniscient, separate from the land, and this loosening of security made them as vulnerable as the minute people below.

"Oh yeah," Doug growled with delight. "We're gonna go right near the castle. You might even get your overhead shot."

Kane looked to Benedict and nodded. "Better go ahead and snap a few shots," he said.

Pressing himself against the basket to help gain stability, the reporter lifted the camera to his face, and began making adjustments. The castle grew nearer at a steady rate, and Benedict readjusted quickly after each photo.

"Can we get a little higher?" asked the stranger.

"Sure," Doug replied, unleashing a long and lengthy flame into the craft.

Benedict zoomed in for some shots of the castle's roof, just coming into view. Through the lens, he scanned the towers of the fortress until an unexpected, blurry shape caught his eye. Focusing in, the shape

<90>

refined into a man standing on the closest tower, leaning between its blocks. His face was hidden behind large, bulky binoculars. Each man gazed at the other through an optical window, then the man on the tower lowered his device. His face was filled with fiery agitation, tension seething all around him. He seized the radio on his side and dashed away frantically, his mouth spewing breathless words into the unit.

"Uh oh," Benedict uttered, injecting immediate bleakness all around him.

"What?" asked the stranger, the thickness of concern in his voice.

"We've been spotted."

"Oh no," the stranger groaned. "Higher! Higher!" he commanded.

Doug laid into the chain, the beast roaring ferociously, the heat nearly overcoming them.

By this time they were close enough to see more tiny figures rushing to the roof of the castle.

"Photograph! Photograph!" Kane exclaimed. Benedict snapped away.

In a matter of seconds, the top of the castle was crawling. It looked like a small ant hill scurrying with a dozen panicked insects—like a boot heel had stomped its middle, and the confused creatures rushed in all directions to organize and retaliate.

"This doesn't look good," said Benedict, continuing his task, his eye pressed into the camera.

"Just keep taking photos," directed the stranger.

Quickly, efficiently, the chaotic figures below fell smoothly into place, bracing themselves in the nooks and crannies of the towers. Their rampant energy was settled and controlled, and they stared up at the balloon about to pass high above. It wasn't directly overhead, but sweeping alongside the cove.

"What's going on?" Kane demanded, squinting down at the gothic structure.

<91>

Benedict zoomed in on the figures. A lean man in a gray suit gave the others a hand signal. Like clockwork, each man produced a rifle, bringing the weapons up from below. The guns were aimed high.

"Oh my God!" exclaimed Benedict, "They're gonna shoot us down!"

"What!?" cried the pilot.

Benedict fell to the floor of the basket, hunching helplessly into a ball. His head was bowed tight, and he squeezed the meat of his biceps firmly around his skull, protecting his face from the bullets that might soon penetrate the brittle wicker.

The stranger's stomach dropped, and terror was smeared across his visage. He remained standing, eyes wild, casting a look of hatred to the figures below. Instead of tiny black ants, they became tiny black spiders, poised wickedly, ready to strike in the span of a breath.

"Are you serious?!" yelled Doug, one step behind the action, and not yet ready to accept the situation.

"For God's sake GET DOWN!" called Benedict. Like the stranger, Doug continued peering below, his lip curled and eyes skeptical.

Then, without warning, gunshots. Thunderous explosions of crackling firepower echoed in the cove. Swiftly and effortlessly, bullets broke through the tight flesh of the balloon, each with a "thwap!"

All three men hunkered in the basket, surrounded by the high-pitched buzzing of whizzing bullets—an unmerciful shower of death. Held high and naked, each waited for a bullet to enter the lightweight basket and lodge deep into his flesh. The projectiles might enter from the side, striking them in the spine or head; or they might enter from below, piercing their genitals. There was nothing they could do except sit and quiver and, perhaps, pray.

Squeezing his ears to shield them from the noise, Doug rattled off a string of curse words as bullets continued riddling his balloon.

His face smooshed against the stiff wicker, the stranger had no concept of orientation. He looked up to stare into the deep belly of the balloon. The thin fabric rippled as each bullet tore through. He wondered if they

<92>

might be falling and, glancing at the dirty floor a few inches from his face, he visualized the ground rushing up on the opposite side.

The firing still above them, Kane jerked Doug's right hand off his ear. "Are we falling!?" he yelled.

"No, no! Little holes!" the pilot responded. "She can take a lot o' little holes!"

The spray of gunshots ceased for a moment. Benedict raised his eyes to meet those of the men crammed next to him. "They're not trying to shoot us," he whispered. "They're just shooting at the balloon."

Doug scoffed. "They don't give a damn! And one o' you better stick your ass in front o' me 'cause if I go, we *all* go."

The hail of gunfire exploded again, this time the sounds of the shots more distant. Each man continued guarding his head, grateful the current was taking them swiftly away. Then, directly above their heads, came a new sound.

It was a single noise—a "*ping!*" that rang with a long, metallic whistle. Instantaneously, a cloud of frigid, blinding propane erupted. The continuing blast of shocking, icy fuel chilled them painfully—the liquid vaporizing as it spewed from a hole in the tank. Like demon breath, it screamed hideously, its enormous pressure squeezing through the puncture.

Yelling from the excruciating cold, each man dashed to the side of the basket farthest from the leak—a vain attempt to escape the stream of fuel. Panicking, their eyes were sealed tight, and their breathing was choked by the burning, putrid fumes. Coughing and scrambling, they scurried to their feet, moving away from the center of the leak, yet being sprayed with propane mist. Within the agonizing shriek of the escaping pressure, they could still hear the "pops" of gunshots being fired.

"We're gonna burn up!" Doug screamed over the whirlwind. "One little spark and we're gone!"

The pressure of the propane was forcing the balloon into wild, erratic patterns. The men dashing about rocked it terribly, and the number of

<93>

gunshots were taking their toll. Without the capability of receiving new hot air, and with the balloon leaking away, their fate was undeniable.

"WE'RE GOIN' DOWN!" Doug cried.

The landscape was a whirling, dizzying confusion—the colors of fall merged into a mockery of hope. The air current had continued whisking them away, even as they descended, and they had no idea where they might touch down. Unable to see or hear effectively, their panic contributed to the disarray of the balloon.

The stranger clung tightly to the frame that extended between the basket and balloon. Livid fear burning in his eyes, he absorbed the glorious land that would take his life. Below he saw only mountains and trees, growing ever closer by the moment. He turned to see Benedict and Doug, but they were lost in the cloud of noisy propane.

"Hold on you sons-of-bitches!" Doug yelled from across the basket.

Falling at an angle, propelled by the current, Kane predicted their destination. They were headed for a patch of bright orange trees on the downside of a mountain. The stranger was completely powerless. He itched with the instinct to pull back, or somehow cushion the impact to come—but it was impossible. The limbs of the tall trees reached skyward like bony, spindly fingers, hard and unforgiving. The world that had minutes before been so distant, so small, so vulnerable, was gone. This one was harsh and strong and destructive. He held his breath, and then—*the impact.*

It was a crash. The limbs popped and cracked and exploded as the basket tore through layer after layer of thick, old wood. They bounced violently down the length of the trees, and the basket split in half. With the sudden jar of a hangman's rope, it stopped, dumping all three men several feet to the hard, leafy forest floor. A crunchy cushion of dry vegetation did little to ease the unforgiving blow.

Horrified, confused, bruised, ragged, and scraped, but otherwise fine, the three men lay still on the ground. Slightly groaning, their heads spun as they stared up at the tattered remains of the great balloon, rav-

<94>

aged and spread throughout the trees. Their ears rang like the haunting last note of a struck anvil, yet the forest was quiet and peaceful. The warm rays of the sun beamed blissfully down on their numb faces. They laid there for a while like that—not moving, not uttering a single word—too stunned to wonder if they were all okay.

The stranger rolled his head over to face Benedict. They looked at each other for a moment.

"Do you have the camera?" Kane asked.

Benedict held it up, apparently in good condition, the strap still around his neck.

"And the pictures. Did you get the shots?"

"I…I think so."

The stranger looked back up to the balloon, the eerie calmness swirling in his head. "Good," he said. "Develop them soon."

<95>

CHAPTER FOUR

IN A SECLUDED room, on one end of the castle, J.C. Borley was planted solidly in a soft, leather chair. Haunting opera, eerily peaceful, drifted in the air. The lights were low, and the orange tongues of a crackling fire lapped at the darkness. The reflection of the flames bowed smoothly around the curved surface of the black, crystal sphere. It sat in front of Borley, possessing him, draining him of life, and yet breathing all its secrets into his abysmal stare.

The ball was a single eye, window, or gateway into realms below the surface of man's superficial existence. Silent and motionless, it projected the force and distinction of a reptilian pupil, eternally on the verge of striking. Borley could lose himself in its power, escaping the unconquerable loneliness that plagued him deeply within.

Each of us is ultimately alone, doomed to know the world only through our five senses. We are prisoners, trapped within our limited, subjective inlets of perception; our attempts to know genuine closeness a cruel and futile experience. Most learn to accept the illusion—to overlook the barrier of flesh that separates man from reality—to help ourselves forget the dire and infinite isolation. But not Borley. His soul was old and sensitive, its layers of separation worn thin. To him, the unconquerable loneliness was huge, voracious, and painful. Neither money, nor influence, nor drugs, nor art, nor humans, could reach it, soothe it, or make it whole. But this crystal ball, black as a churning tempest, could.

<96>

Something at the core of Borley could connect with the sphere. The two wells of darkness could join like a wormhole of unearthly perception. It was a tap to the powers that lay at the pressurized center of this vast, untamable universe; a tap to the powers of creation and destruction, mystery and enlightenment. Forces too ancient and complex for the collective world to comprehend were pulsating in the mind of this great man. He had inherited his father's legacy, but had little regard for the refinement of his estate. To him, it was this power, understanding, and closeness, however dark, in which he invested his fate. The physical world was a toy, filled with marvelous games and distractions, but through this vein of boundless perception, he would find his immortality.

*   *   *

The streets of Asheville were bright and festive outside the murky windows of Brownman's Coffeehouse. The small and cloudy building sat a short distance from the noble Vance Monument, and inside its walls, a dreary atmosphere shunned the lively world outside.

Brownman's was saturated with the morose and rambling energies of amateur downtrodden poets, philosophers, conspiracy theorists, and self-indulgent artists. In most ways, it was a typical beatnik joint, teeming with caffeine-enhanced eccentricity and, sometimes, insanity. However, it possessed a certain unique tension, perhaps the product of Asheville's two long-struggling super powers: the fundamentalist Christian base and the blossoming New Age mecca; each usually as dogmatic and condescending as the other (despite their avid claims to the contrary).

The walls and ceiling were lined with bizarre works of art. Some were flat and visual, and others were as imposing as three-dimensional plastic body parts, sprouting from the ceiling. A moderately large set of bookshelves were stuffed with rare and eclectic titles, and the chess

<97>

board before it displayed pieces halted in mid-game—queerly symbolic of the broken thoughts to which the room bore tribute.

In the dusky corner near the bookshelves, Wilson Benedict rose to greet the stranger. Upon descending the steps to the lower portion of the coffeehouse, where Benedict waited, Kane's eyes expressed uncertainty as he looked around the room. When he reached the grinning Benedict, he shook his hand respectfully.

"This place isn't as private as you said," he remarked.

"Oh we'll be fine," Benedict assured him, taking his seat along with the stranger. "I conduct interviews here sometimes and never have a problem."

It was clear that Kane wasn't thoroughly convinced, but nonetheless Benedict held up a thick packet of pictures, fresh from the photomat.

"Wonderful," said the stranger, his demeanor instantly more positive.

Without so much as a word, and with only a peculiar expression on his face—bright, like that of a person in mid-joke—the reporter handed the packet over to Kane. As though an anxious child on Christmas morning, the stranger wrestled with the flaps and papers, almost tearing his way inside. Benedict sipped a mug of steaming espresso, sweet with a twist of lemon peel, as he watched marvelously. Opening the internal pack, Kane gently withdrew the stack of glossy prints. Mesmerized, he shuffled through each one, slowly at first, and then with growing speed and frustration.

"What is this?" he demanded.

Every single print was snow-white and blank. He slammed down the stack of stiff photographs, the expression on Benedict's face unchanging. "Camera wasn't damaged huh?" Kane barked sarcastically.

Still without speaking, Benedict reached down beside him and brought up an additional pack of photographs. A spark of hopefulness returned to the stranger's face, and he dug in excitedly once again. Reaching the pictures, he was baffled once more: a lamp, a couch, a yard...

"What is this?" he asked, his frustration returning.

<98>

"Those are pictures around my house," Benedict responded. "Taken *after* the roll over Borley's Castle, and with the same camera." The stranger explored Benedict's strangely delightful face, seeking his meaning. "You see," he continued, "the camera's fine."

"Then these are the ones over the castle?" said the stranger, holding up the blank photos, his mind searching for clarification.

"Yes."

"But you've overexposed them all."

Benedict shook his head slowly. "I assure you Kane, those photographs were *not* overexposed by me."

The stranger placed all the pictures on the table, taking a moment to gather his thoughts. "You're saying that these photographs naturally developed this way?"

Benedict lifted his hands into the air with bewilderment. "All I know is that the camera is fine. The film was never exposed outside the camera— let alone the whole roll—and I personally oversaw the development."

"And you're absolutely positive that you didn't accidentally overexpose the film in all the madness that was taking place?"

Benedict nodded affirmatively. "It's possible that some shots were overexposed, of course. But I specifically remember adjusting perfect exposure for some of the shots. I've been taking photographs on a professional level for years, and I have never produced a single shot as badly overexposed as this entire roll appears to be."

Sighing defeatedly, the stranger leaned back, placing his hands behind his head. "Damn," he said. "Damn, damn, damn."

Benedict took the negatives from the blank shots and held them to the light, as he'd done a dozen times before, examining each one.

"All right Mr. Photographic Expert," said Kane, "then what could have caused this?"

"Well," Benedict responded, a note of uncertainty in his voice, "*something* overexposed the film. Film emulsion of course is sensitive to light, and light is a form of electromagnetic radiation. Therefore, if some

<99>

other form of strong electromagnetic radiation was directed at the film, even if it's invisible to the naked eye, it's possible it could overexpose the emulsion. It might be kind of like taking sensitive undeveloped film through a metal detector at the airport. It can imprint the film."

"So you're saying that some kind of energy emanating from the castle could have caused this?" confirmed the stranger.

"Yes," Benedict replied. "I think so."

Kane wasn't entirely buying it. "But then that would mean there'd be no pictures of the castle in existence; but there *are* pictures of the castle. So how do you explain that?"

"Well there are no pictures of the castle from this angle though," said Benedict. "I've never seen a photograph from above the top floor. They're always slightly below the castle, from a distance, and of the sides."

Kane sat silently for a moment and then scratched his head thoughtfully. "I need to find a way into that castle," he said. "I need to know a weakness."

Benedict put the photographs away, leaving Kane to his thoughts. But on the reporter's face, a look of concern was forming, and he planned his dialogue in the usual way.

"Kane," Benedict said. "Can I be frank with you?"

The stranger looked to him with suppressed anticipation. "Sure."

Benedict leaned closer and lowered his voice. "Do you—do you plan to kill Borley?"

"I told you," said the stranger, "all I want to do is destroy that evil thing he keeps in the castle."

Benedict looked unsatisfied. "You really believe there's a monster in there tearing people apart?"

"I don't care if you believe me," Kane responded defiantly. "I'm not trying to convince anyone. I have my own reasons for doing what I do."

"And what are those reasons?" Benedict asked with concern.

"My reasons are *my* reasons," the stranger replied, "and that's all you need to know."

<100>

With that, the stranger rose abruptly. Immediately, Benedict's mind started spinning.

"Well, thanks for all your help," said the stranger. "How much do I owe you?"

"Just a second," said Benedict urgently. "Sit down a minute."

Kane looked around the room, reassuring himself that the sparse inhabitants were oblivious to his conversation. He then took his seat again as quickly as he'd left it. But his posture was firm and temporary.

"To start with," said Benedict, "you don't owe me anything. But secondly, I have a new lead for you."

"What's that?"

"If you'll recall, I told you I once tried to interview an elderly woman who worked for the Borleys during Crawford's heyday, remember?"

"Ummm—yes I think so."

"Well I was never able to do so because her husband wouldn't allow her to speak with me."

"Yes?"

"I did a little phone calling today, and as it turns out, her husband died six months ago."

The stranger caught his drift. "Do you think she'll talk now?" Kane asked.

Benedict smiled. "I'm sure she'll talk now," he said.

"What makes you so sure?"

"Because she said she would."

The tension in the stranger's posture relaxed once again. "When can we meet with her?" he asked.

"How about tomorrow evening?" Benedict responded.

"Good," said the stranger. "That'll be good."

"Can you meet me at Grove Park around five-forty-five?" Benedict asked.

"Sure."

<101>

"Now that's 5:45 p.m.," Benedict smirked, "Not Room 545." He gave a chuckle.

"Huh?"

"Oh, that's where they say the Pink Lady hangs out."

"Oh," said the stranger, disinterested and hardly amused.

"We can take my car," continued Benedict. "Just meet me in the Great Hall."

"Agreed," said the stranger. With another shake, he exited swiftly.

*　　　*　　　*

Perenia Hawly lived on the backside of Sunset Mountain. Her house was quaint and blue. It was a typical elderly home in most respects, with a tidy lawn, complete with somewhat gaudy decorations and remnants of a small, well-kept garden at its side. Even from the outside, the place seemed sterile, yet comfortable. It was a humble place, quiet and low, and it provided a peaceful, isolated atmosphere for the remainder of a fragile life. Delicate wind chimes tinkled on the front porch as Kane and Benedict ascended a few worn steps. Benedict suddenly held Kane back. "Remember," he whispered, "please be sensitive to the fact her husband just died six months ago." Kane nodded, then a sudden thought hit him.

"You sure she's got a good mind?" he asked.

Benedict confirmed. "Oh yes," he said.

They continued to the front door, greeted by a large, green mat at the entrance: "Friends Are Always Welcome." Benedict gave three concise, gentle knocks.

Endlessly wary, Kane scoped out the surroundings. A station wagon pulled into the driveway of the neighbor's house and some children in the back seat waved. The stranger only stared suspiciously.

When the door opened, the petite form of a delicate old woman stood inside. She smiled brightly and warmly, her drawn cheeks bulging and

<102>

her China-blue eyes accented by the long white hair pulled back upon her head. Her features were fine and shapely, and it was immediately obvious that in her younger days, she had been exceptionally beautiful.

"Mrs. Hawley!" Benedict exclaimed, returning her pearly smile and taking her soft, frail hand into two of his own. "It's so nice to meet you at last."

"Oh yes," she spoke tenderly, "it's nice to meet you, too. I read you in the paper every day. You're my favorite one, you know."

"Oh why thank you. That's very kind of you," said Benedict. "And this is my friend Mr. Kane," he said, introducing the stranger. She showed him just as much warmth, and then invited the two inside without hesitation.

The interior of the house smelled like flowers and perfumed lotion. It was old and distinguished, not in a grand way, but in a small and personal way. There were ceramic collectibles strewn about—dogs, kittens, farmers, snow scenes—and regional publications stacked here and there. Newspapers, books, magazines, and fliers: she plainly had an interest in regional literature and events.

Kane and Benedict were seated in a bleak living room, the haunting yellow light from two incandescent lamps their only illumination. They each sat on a squishy, low couch in front of a coffee table. Benedict quickly adapted, sinking into his seat and seeming comfortable and natural, but Kane, his long coat hanging onto the floor, looked awkward and unsettled.

"Can I get you two anything to drink?" the old lady asked. "Coffee? Tea?"

"Oh I'm fine, thank you," Benedict responded, and Kane agreed.

With that, Mrs. Hawley sat down in a chair off to the side of the couch. A bit of small talk ensued—the weather, local politics, etc.—and then the meat of the conversation finally emerged.

"Well you know my husband Charlie recently passed away," said Mrs. Hawley, motioning to a framed picture on a nearby table. The man in the picture looked solid and stern, his head bald and his cranium large.

"Yes, I'm very sorry," said Benedict. Kane nodded respectfully.

<103>

"We were married over fifty years," she said, her eyes falling to her lap. "That's a long time. For him to suddenly be gone after fifty years, well it makes you sort o' lose balance. It makes you lose your sense of purpose, too."

"Oh now, you only lose your sense of purpose when you think you do," Benedict replied, carrying on the delicate conversation. "You still have a lot of wonderful things to do."

She smiled wistfully, her eyes surprisingly clear and lively. "And then it was sad to hear Mr. Borley had passed on," she said. "Those were the two men I'd spent my life with—my husband and Mr. Borley."

"How long did you work for Borley?" asked the stranger, his tone more interrogative than sociable.

"I was his main housekeeper for thirty-eight years," she said.

"And you lived in the castle?" continued the stranger.

"Well Charlie and I had a house, but we often stayed at the castle overnight. You see Charlie did some grounds work for Mr. Borley after he got outta the service."

"Did you enjoy your work on the estate?" Benedict inquired.

"Oh yes," Mrs. Hawley replied. "Most of the time anyway. Lord knows Mr. Borley could be temperamental at times, but all in all he was good to me."

"I suppose you watched J.C. grow up?" said the stranger.

Suddenly, Mrs. Hawley's brow curled, and her thoughts regressed deep into the past.

"Well, you know," she said, "little James—that's what we called him—he wasn't like his daddy."

"How's that?" asked Benedict.

"Well Mr. Borley was always so dignified and quiet; but James was always noisy and sarcastic. He was big for his age, and when he got to be a teenager, sometimes he'd be real mean to the help, and there was nothin' we could do about it."

"Really?" said Benedict, his face expressing motivational interest.

<104>

"I'll tell you a strange story about little James," Mrs. Hawley said. "One time, when he was just a toddler, Mr. Borley bought a bunch of baby ducklings for the pond outside. He told James they were for him to play with. Well one day I went outside and found little James standing by the pond. All around him were the baby ducklings—dead. He'd stomped every one of them to death. I said 'James, why on earth did you kill the little ducks?' And he looked at me with those big, black eyes, and he said, 'They wouldn't be quiet, Mrs. Hawley. I told them to be quiet but they wouldn't, so I taught them a lesson.' He'd stomped *every one* to death, and he didn't give a darn. Right then, I was afraid he was going to grow up bad."

Kane and Benedict looked to each other with knowing eyes.

"You gentlemen should understand something," the old lady said. "Ordinarily I wouldn't talk about such things. If my husband knew I were telling this he'd be very upset. But now that Mr. Borley and Charlie are passed on, I don't suppose it hurts anyone. Besides, I figure I'll be dead soon, and there's no point taking all this stuff to my grave."

"Mrs. Hawley," said the stranger, rising in his sunken seat, "on the ground floor of the castle, in one of the rooms, there is a portrait of a beautiful woman with long brown hair. Do you know who that is?"

"You know," she responded, "one time, when Mr. Borley was having coffee, I asked him who the woman was. He said it was his mother. A few years later I asked him about it again. That time he said he didn't know who the woman was—that the painting had been given to him as a gift. I thought that was very peculiar."

Kane reflected deeply on her words. This being new to Benedict, he made a mental note.

"What happened to Crawford Borley's wife?" Benedict asked.

"From what I understand she died of pneumonia less than a year after little James was born."

"Did you ever notice anything…bizarre taking place in the castle?" the reporter asked.

<105>

"Oh heavens yes," she responded, "strange things were always happening."

"Like what?" Benedict prodded.

"Well I suppose you've heard all the ghost stories, right? About the room at the end of the hall on the fourth floor?"

Kane and Benedict mumbled the beginnings of phrases, but were more or less speechless, afraid to comment on any knowledge since it might restrict the scope of the old woman's stories.

"Well," she continued, "just between the three of us, there was a bit of underhandedness that took place at the castle most times."

"Underhandedness?" questioned Kane.

"Well nothing we knew about exactly," she said. "It was just sort of something we all knew and never talked about. It was kind of understood that Mr. Borley had secrets."

"Secrets?" said Benedict.

"Oh yes. Some shady business deals—but besides that, everyone always passed rumors about that room—where The Horror stayed."

"What *is* the horror?" Kane asked enthusiastically.

"Oh I don't know," she said. "It was just a story as far as we knew. A story to keep people out. But that room—that room at the end of the hall—it always stayed locked. And no one ever went in there except for Mr. Borley sometimes, and maybe James when he got older."

"You have no idea what was inside?" Kane prodded.

"Oh no," said Mrs. Hawley. "But I'll tell you something weird: For about three years Mr. Borley and little James, and his closest staff, went to live in Europe. They left me and my husband at the castle to tend for things—you know, basic upkeep—while they were gone. But each of those three years, in the fall, a man would appear on the doorstep. He said he was sent by Mr. Borley. He wore a dark suit and a black, wide-rimmed hat, and he spoke with a French accent. He had a key to that room on the fourth floor. He would come into the castle and tell me and Charlie to go to the basement—or the dungeon, as some called it. Then, he would literally lock us down there for hours—*Can you*

<106>

believe that?—and then as far as we can figure, he'd go into that room. I guess he was in there for hours and hours, and then finally, he'd come down and let us out. And then he'd leave without a word. We never did know what that was all about."

"What did he look like?" the reporter inquired.

"We never got a good look at him. He would come in the evening, his face obscured by the shadow of his hat; and he was very evasive. Best I could tell, he wore spectacles."

Kane and Benedict were on the edge of their seats.

"Well what kinds of stories did you hear?" Kane asked. "What were the rumors about what was in that room?"

Mrs. Hawley's train of though suddenly broke, and she looked around the room unexpectedly. "You know," she said, "I think I could use a cup of coffee. Would you gentlemen like a cup of coffee?"

It took the pair a moment to break from their rampant thoughts about the old lady's words.

"Oh, um, oh yes, sure," said Benedict. "I'll have a cup."

"And you?" she asked, standing and directing her gaze at the stranger.

"Sure," he responded.

Raising her eyebrows, she pointed her delicate finger at each of them. "Cream and sugar?"

Each man nodded affirmatively.

"I knew it," she said. "I could tell you were each cream and sugar gentlemen." Hunched and slightly wobbling as she walked, she disappeared into the kitchen.

Kane and Benedict looked to each other with wide, vibrant eyes. Each was bursting to discuss her stories, and yet they knew they must maintain themselves. Ever impatient, they sat silently, waiting eagerly for Mrs. Hawley to return.

The old lady came back a few minutes later, carrying a tray of coffees, almost happy to be serving once again. She set the tray on the old table in front of her guests, and passed out the coffees with pride and satis-

<107>

faction. After each dish and mug had been properly placed, she seated herself once again.

"Umm. Wonderful coffee," said Benedict, after sipping the refreshingly hot beverage. Kane nodded in agreement.

"Thank you," said Mrs. Hawley, before sipping some coffee herself. "Oh, now where were we?" she asked.

"Stories, " the stranger quickly chimed. "You were going to tell us some of the rumors about the…'haunted' room, shall we say."

"Ah yes," she resumed. "Well there were lots of stories. Some people said a worker died when he was building that room—that he, you know, fell off the castle; and so he haunts it. And then there was a story that Mr. Borley was involved with a young lady for a while; but he had to cut off the relationship and she killed herself in that room—but that's nonsense. Probably the most interesting story is that Mr. Borley had a brother he kept locked away in there."

"A brother?" Benedict confirmed.

"Yes," she continued. "They say he had a brother who was hideously deformed and somewhat retarded, and so Mr. Borley kept him locked away in there—sort of a family secret. He was supposed to have been real violent, too. So violent you couldn't get near him."

"Do you think that's true?" asked the stranger.

"Well it seems pretty farfetched to me," she replied. "But I tell you, there was a slot on that door at the end of the hall. A slot just wide enough to slide a food tray through. And they claimed that Mr. Borley would feed him through that slot because he was so violent you couldn't get around him."

Kane and Benedict looked at each other again.

"And so there actually is a slot on the door?" asked Kane.

"Oh yes," she replied. "The slot's there."

"And I suppose no one ever spent the night in that room?" added Benedict.

<108>

"Well," said Mrs. Hawley, again reaching far back into the well of her memory, "there was one man who spent the night in there—that I know of, anyway. He was some fellow from Wisconsin that Mr. Borley was doing some business with. He was a real nice man, very articulate and polite. The next morning, one of the maids who worked under me, Mary, she screamed. This fellow was wandering around the castle in his night gown, apparently out of his mind. He was drooling and chattering nonsense about the devil, and when he saw Mary he grabbed onto her. Well Mr. Borley and James had him tied up and taken off—still ranting like a madman. They said they were surprised he was still alive. Last I heard the poor man never got over it. He was put in some asylum up north. One day he was fine, the next day, he was out of his mind."

"And yet no one ever asked Mr. Borley about what was in the room?" asked the reporter.

"Why goodness no!" she exclaimed. "No one dared. Everyone knew that wasn't the sort of thing you bothered Mr. Borley about. In fact, Mr. Borley passed down the word that we were never to discuss that—and so that was never brought up again."

Kane and Benedict quietly, thoughtfully reflected on her words.

"Do you have any idea what that gentleman's name was?" asked the reporter.

"Why no," she replied. "It's been too long. I couldn't remember that for the life o' me."

During the entire time, Benedict had been itching to whip out his pad and jot notes. Fearful of intimidating the old woman, however, he didn't. Instead he took careful notice of each fact, planting it vividly in his mind, sometimes in the form of a visual representation.

"By the way," said Mrs. Hawley, "what did you say this was for again? Some sort of article was it?"

"Oh, no, no," Benedict swiftly replied. "We're not going to print this, we're simply intrigued with Asheville's history; and the death of

<109>

Mr. Borley has generated a good deal of interest about the story behind the castle."

"Well I wouldn't mind if you wanted to print some of it," the old lady said, "but you probably shouldn't print things like the underhandedness I spoke of, or the insane fellow, or perhaps some of the bits about little James."

"Oh that's quite all right," Benedict assured her, "we would never print anything without your consent anyway."

"Mrs. Hawley," said the stranger. "Was there anything especially unusual about Crawford Borley that sticks out in your mind?"

She rubbed her chin for a moment. "Humm. Well, he had a bit of fascination for the other side," she said.

"How so?" asked the stranger.

"Well, he collected Ouija Boards, you know. Ouija Boards, and things of that nature, from across the world. Now as to whether or not he ever used them—well I don't know. But he had quite a few around."

"Anything else?" Kane prodded.

"No, no, not really," she responded. "Mr. Borley was a very private man. He seldom spoke to anyone, let alone his help. If Mr. Borley ever spoke to you, you usually remembered it—his words were scarce and therefore valuable. But, you know, in the thirty-eight years I worked for him, I don't suppose we ever had a single, casual conversation. There might be a line or two here or there, and then you'd get the feeling he didn't wanna talk anymore. And so that was the end of the conversation, you know?"

Kane shook his head, already struggling a bit as to whether he should ask the next question on his mind. Finally, he gave in: "Mrs. Hawley, what would be the easiest way to—to um, break into the castle? I mean, how's the security?"

Benedict shot an icy glance towards Kane, believing the question was too blatant.

<110>

"Oh it would be hard to break into that castle," she responded, seemingly unaffected by the inquiry. "Mr. Borley, and now James—or J.C. as they call him—they're tight when it comes to their privacy. There are all kinds o' guards, and fences, and guns, and dogs. It's really quite intimidating."

"What about electronics?" Kane asked, "Cameras, and infrared beams and such."

"Oh now that's a different story," Mrs. Hawley said, closing her eyes and shaking her head for emphasis. "Mr. Borley did *not* want any of that kind o' stuff around. Especially cameras. He felt that cameras would be a hinderance to *him*. He was real old fashioned about that sort o' thing. There's nothing like that in the castle—unless James has stuck it in since his daddy passed on. But Mr. Borley didn't believe in that stuff. He didn't trust it."

For another two hours, until the liveliness drained from her clear eyes and she began to yawn, Kane and Benedict interrogated Mrs. Hawley. They asked her about little things, like the way Crawford Borley wanted his food prepared, and big things, like the mysterious structure of the castle. Routines, anecdotes, associates: all were game for a barrage of questions. And though her answers were quirky, fascinating, and perhaps insightful, they revealed nothing of major significance. Instead, she served to document the inner fringes of the Borleys' clandestine lives, and the interrogators soon realized that even she, a housekeeper of thirty-eight years, was kept a stranger to Asheville's most enigmatic figure. Crawford Borley had been distrustful of all, and he exercised such inner tightness and self-control that it was impossible to enter the depths of his soul uninvited.

When finally they resolved to leave, thanking the kind old woman and vowing to maintain contact, she suddenly seemed almost excited from something she remembered.

<111>

"You know what?" she said, that brightness returning to her eyes, if but temporarily. "If you gentlemen are serious about getting to know more, there's a man you need to see."

"Oh," said Benedict, his gaze intent. "Who?"

"John Weck."

"The writer?" said Benedict, slightly surprised.

"Yes," replied Mrs. Hawley. "You know him?"

"I thought he was dead," the reporter said, snapping his head towards Kane for an opinion. Kane shrugged, clearly unfamiliar with the name.

"Oh I don't know," the old lady said. "He might be. But I don't think he's that old a fella."

Benedict furrowed his brow and scratched his scalp. "He used to write regional books, correct?"

"Yes, yes," said Mrs. Hawley. "I have several of them."

"And then, didn't he sort of disappear or something? I heard he became very reclusive; living on a mountain somewhere I think."

Mrs. Hawley shook her head unknowingly. "I'm not really sure. Years and years ago, I think he may have gotten put-out with writing or something like that, and so he sort o' dropped outta the public eye."

"Well why should we speak with him?" the reporter asked curiously.

"Oh he was going to write a book about the Borleys a long time ago. I was working at the castle when he started researching. He came there one day and talked to James—that's when James was a young man. Mr. Borley wouldn't see him. I don't know what they talked about, but he didn't seem too happy when he left."

Benedict was fascinated. "Well what was the outcome?"

Mrs. Hawley threw up her arms and frowned. "We just never heard anything else about it. I don't know how much research he did, but in his books he's usually pretty thorough."

Benedict, appearing quite stimulated, cast his gaze to a less enthused Kane.

<112>

"Thank you very much," said Benedict, turning back to Mrs. Hawley. "I'll certainly have to check into that."

"Well good luck," the old lady said, her energy seeping away before their eyes. "Let me know if I can help you anymore."

The two thanked their gracious hostess again, then escaped into the freshness of the chilled night air.

<113>

CHAPTER FIVE

A GHASTLY STREETLIGHT burned bluish-white by the gate to Borley's Castle. It was the only light around, and in the inky darkness of night, it spilled down on the trees, pavement, and roadside bushes, bouncing hazily from their surface. Just past the entrance, the winding mountain road disappeared into a large curve, continuing upwards, and then joining with other mountain ranges. The place was peaceful, still, and silent, stirred only when the blinding headlights of a passing car illuminated the scene and then vanished around the bend.

Fifty feet from the gate, a short distance down the mountain, a dark-blue jeep was nestled in the roadside woods. It was several feet off the pavement, hidden effectively by its inconspicuous position. Lazy, drooping branches and tall, sharp weeds concealed it serenely. Inside, Kane and Benedict sipped coffee.

"Here comes another one," the stranger said, controlled urgency in his voice.

Though the vehicle belonged to Benedict, he sat in the passenger seat to facilitate his job. Fumbling a bit, he quickly placed his styrofoam cup into a holder and lifted his camera just as a car zoomed by. The car continued around the curve and Benedict relaxed, lowering the device. The vehicle having passed in a rumbling blaze, the stillness immediately seeped back into place.

"You're sure it's adjusted right this time?" asked Kane.

"It was adjusted right the first time," Benedict replied, his defensiveness apparent. "I'm not sure how much good this is going to do

<114>

though," he continued. "I could probably guess and tell you the people who go in and out of this place."

"Well we need to know for sure," Kane said. "All we need is one person—one weak person—who knows the castle. Who knows what they could do for us?"

"Willingly?" questioned the reporter.

"That doesn't matter."

Again, headlights glowed faintly from behind them. A vehicle was making its way up the mountain. Benedict poised, but it too passed the entrance without hesitation.

The stranger opened the sleek metallic thermos they'd brought along and poured another portion of steamy, beige coffee into his cup. It was dark inside the vehicle, and the objects, including the two men inside, were charcoal silhouettes, surreal to the eye. Benedict watched the stranger as he refilled, the pouring sound of thick, rich liquid magnified in the confined space.

"So," said Benedict, "what do you do when you're not hunting monsters?"

The surface of the hot coffee puttered as it disappeared between the stranger's tight lips. "I'm sorry," Kane said, taking the cup away from his mouth, "I can't discuss myself."

"So, do you work for someone?"

The stranger smirked. "Just as I can't tell you who I am, I also can't tell you who I am *not*," he said. "Therefore, asking such questions will do you no good."

"Why is it a secret?" persisted the reporter. "Are you protecting yourself or someone else?"

Kane shook his head slowly. "I don't mean to be offensive," he said. "It's nothing personal. But I *do* have my reasons for my silence."

Benedict smiled. "It's all very dramatic, you know."

"Well let me ask you a question," the stranger said.

"Yes?"

<115>

"You don't know me, and you don't know my motives. For all you know I could be a killer. Why do you want to help me? Why are you putting yourself in danger? Even risking your job?"

Bowing his head, Benedict thought about the questions for a moment. He scratched his neck, and then rested his chin on his hand. "Well," he began, "there are a number of reasons. First off—you're right, I don't know you from Adam. And you might be a killer. However, I usually have a gift for reading people, and although I see a great deal of darkness in you, I think your intentions are good. I've trusted my instincts and I'm not dead yet. Secondly, as you know, I've been fascinated by the Borleys for years—long before you ever came along. To me, they represent everything mysterious about Asheville. And third," he hesitated. "Well, I do believe the Borleys are killing people."

The stranger was surprised to hear such a blatant admission.

Benedict continued: "I think they've killed people for many years, apparently for financial gain. But because they've worked their way into the law enforcement and the media, most people don't know. And those who do know don't care. Believe it or not, in this day and age, I actually have morals—unlike a lot of the people I work with, in fact. It really bothers me to think people are, and have been, murdered regularly in that castle, and no one does anything about it."

"And The Horror," said the stranger. "What do you think about The Horror?"

Benedict took a deep breath. "I'm not really sure," he said. "Evidently you know something I don't. But regardless of what method is being used to kill people—supernatural or otherwise—people are dying, that's all I know. And if I can help stop it, even at the cost of my life and job, then I will. I must trust what I feel in my heart is right."

"And so why haven't you acted until now?" asked the stranger. "Why wait until I came along to start doing something about it?"

Benedict retreated inside himself, thinking thoroughly about his reply and wrestling with the submerged truth. "I—well, a part of me

<116>

was afraid. Not only afraid of the physical danger, but afraid that I might be wrong. Afraid that I might be overreacting. But when you came along, I knew instantly that I had been right. You gave me the confirmation I was looking for; the assurance that I wasn't the only one who thought things were so extreme."

Headlights, growing in brightness, were approaching from behind. Again, Benedict raced to lift the camera around his neck. Now beside them, the car engine slowed down and the darkness was pierced by the pulsating light of a red turn signal. Its license tag framed, Benedict's camera fired away repeatedly.

Though nearly impossible to clearly see, the vehicle appeared to be a luxury sedan. It hummed to a crawl outside the Borleys' gate, and after pulling the short distance into the driveway, it stopped. Like a private investigator, Benedict continued taking shots. In a few moments, the gate opened by remote control and the car disappeared inside, rocking a bit as it topped a small bump where the gate had been. As soon as the rear bumper had passed through, the gate began closing again. In less than ten seconds, the exterior boundary to Borley's estate was sealed shut again with an unforgiving "snap."

"Well there's number three," said the stranger. "Did you get some good shots?"

"I'll let you know tomorrow," Benedict replied.

Kane dipped the thermos vertically. The last, narrow stream of coffee poured into Benedict's cup. He shook off a few final drops that landed with a soft "plop;" then the caffeine was gone.

✴   ✴   ✴

Bowed, rickety, and ancient, Helen's Bridge breached a narrow canyon on Beaucatcher Mountain. A cramped lane of road ran beneath, cutting through the walls of dirt that rose to the ravine. The dreary

<117>

bridge was gnarled and somber, nearly a century of tangled vines and undergrowth weighing atop its gristled, stony arch. Once used to drive guests and livestock to the nearby Zealandia Castle, it was now unused, being slowly and naturally buried by the forest that gradually digested it. Once grand, it had been neglected, and now stood, perhaps thirty feet high, as a phantom of a monument, an exhausted reminder of Asheville's illustrious past. Thick, dark beams of splintery wood stood beneath it, bearing its immortal weight, growing more and more tired with the passing of each year. Rushed carvings and faded graffiti were strewn about the weathered posts, bearing witness to a thousand care-free hours spent beneath it—usually telling the ghost story.

It was in the late 1800s or early 1900s that a poor woman, Helen, is said to have lived on the mountain. A meek and quiet woman, she shared a cottage with her beloved pride and joy: her daughter. But a rich, rewarding life was to elude her; it is said that at a young age, her daughter burned to death in a tragic fire while visiting the castle Zealandia. Shocked and distraught, the shadowy embrace of self-destruction pulled her to the bridge with a rope in hand. Cold breath from the black tongue of suicide whispered in her sensitive ear: *"Come. I will rescue you. I will take you to a safe place. A place where your child waits."* Tears streaming, emotionally shattered, she tied a noose around her neck, and with a final burst of pain, flung herself off the looming structure. The next day, the townspeople found her hanging body.

From then it was said the spirit of Helen glided about the mountain, searching for the lost soul of her child. Her pale phantom, in a long, tattered gown, roams the roads and castle asking those she meets if they have seen the girl. Some claim that if you stand beneath the bridge on moonlit nights and call "Helen Come Forth!" three times, she will appear. Many believe the story, and others claim it to be nonsense. But this night, the story seemed chillingly authentic:

In the wee hours of the frigid, foggy morning, a body hanged from Helen's Bridge. It was real. The solid, fleshy form of a man swung limply

<118>

from the rafters. The old beams creaked mournfully with each sway of the corpse. His head was jerked askew, resting heavily on his right shoulder.

It had been a fast death. The neck had cracked as soon as his healthy body had stretched the rope to its maximum potential. Instantly it snapped back, the body still plunging downward, separating the skull from the spine with a "pop." Elastic flesh and a splintery joint of sharded bone was all that held the head in place.

The fog bellowed around him, his shoulders slumped and arms hanging low. The rough, stiff noose gripped his bruised neck so tightly it had nearly torn through the skin. A trickle of bright-red blood ran from his mouth and nostrils. The tickling streams beaded at the corner of his lips and dripped slowly—splashing in a tiny crimson puddle on the secluded roadway below. Had his eyes been open, had he been alive, the expanse below his dangling feet would have horrified him. But in his state, though an expression of pain was molded on his face, he was content.

✳   ✳   ✳

The next day was bright and blustery, and Kane, having closed himself inside a phone booth downtown, dialed the number for the newspaper office. He voiced his extension to the operator.

After a moment, he was connected: "Wilson Benedict."

"It's me," said the stranger.

"Oh hello," the reporter replied nonchalantly, glancing around the office to ensure his privacy.

"Have you developed them yet?"

"No, no," Benedict replied, blissful and artificial. "I've been slammed all day dealing with the hanging."

"The hanging?"

"Yes. Last night a doctor hanged himself from Helen's Bridge. It looks like it was inspired by the ghost story."

<119>

"A doctor?"

"Yes, a dentist. Robert Jensen."

A surge of electric thought rushed through the stranger's brain. "Jensen? Jensen! My God!"

"What?"

"When I—er, I…we have to meet tonight."

"What are you talking about?" Benedict asked excitedly. "Do you know something about this?"

"Listen," Kane said. "*We need to meet tonight.*"

"Okay," Benedict responded. "I need to go to Helen's Bridge tonight for this story I'm working on. You want to come along?"

"Sure, sure," said the stranger.

"Okay, meet me at Grove Park around eight, in the Great Hall. Can you do that?"

"Yeah, that's fine," Kane replied. "And Wilson—"

"Yes?"

"Develop those pictures."

✳   ✳   ✳

That evening, Helen's Bridge was even gloomier than usual. It was the sort of place that soaked up nightfall, taking the darkness and projecting it like a cloak. But its intensity was strengthened by the recent death. The fresh smell of cessation drifted in the stagnant air, and the structure felt like an open tomb.

Kane and Benedict each claimed to have important news to tell the other, and yet each wanted to wait until they reached the bridge. After passing under the bridge, the narrow road forked and the left lane persisted up the mountain. Midway, it passed by the bridge, separated from it by lush growth and a pile of timbers. The barricade was placed there

<120>

by nearby residents to keep ghost hunters from trekking onto its worn, useless top.

The section of the road that passed by the structure was too confined to park a car. Therefore, Kane and Benedict parked a ways down the mountain and hiked up the winding road to the pile of wood that shielded the bridge. It was dark, quiet and chilly. The roadway was enclosed by twisting, untamed forest that reached out like withered, gray specters. The pair were breathing hard by the time they reached the summit of their steep climb, the wood pile guarding diligently, yet ineffectively.

They stopped for a moment to catch their breath, and then each withdrawing flashlights, they tediously worked their way over the jagged timbers. The radiant, confined beams of the lights illuminated each step while burying their surroundings in even thicker darkness.

After navigating the barrier, the ground smoothed out into a strip of land. This was the bridge. Its top was covered with soil, bushes, and even trees. From such an angle, it looked like nothing more than overgrown land.

Once making it onto the bridge, they looked over its low stone wall to see the road below, visible only by a street lamp. Each was surprised by how calm the scene appeared. There was no police tape or regulation, and had it not been for their knowledge and keen intuition, they would have never known that a man had died there the night before. To look over the side filled them each with an ethereal coldness. They could visualize the dead man's body suspended above the dusky, open drop.

Benedict sat on the wall, his back to the expanse, and looked to the stranger staring silently in front of him.

"You know, they're trying to tear this bridge down," the reporter said.

"Who?"

"The City of Asheville. The Public Works Department. They claim it's unsafe—besides people hanging themselves from it. I'd like to see them clean it up and restore it."

<121>

The stranger looked around at the ancient structure. "Seems quite historical to me," he said.

"It *is* historical," replied Benedict, "but Asheville, both privately and publicly, is notorious for tearing down historical structures. There used to be a grand art museum over there." He pointed towards the castle. "But it was destroyed when they blew out the 'open cut'—the section of interstate that goes between Beaucatcher and Town Mountain—with the cliffs on either side."

"I've heard there's a marvelous view up there," said the stranger.

"Oh there is," Benedict said, "but they won't let citizens appreciate it. You're trespassing if you go there to look over. It's probably the best view of Asheville around."

They sat still and quiet for a while, appreciating the dark and heavy atmosphere.

"So tell me your news," the reporter said.

"The doctor's name," began the stranger. "You said it was Jensen, right?"

"That's correct. Robert Jensen."

"And it was supposedly suicide?"

"That's what the police said."

"Well listen to this," the stranger leaned down, drawing his face close to Benedict's. "When I was in the castle talking to Borley, he received a phone call from a 'Dr. Jensen.' He turned it down though; said something like 'I'll call that bastard when I want to talk to *him*.'"

Benedict was smiling the whole time as if the news was not surprising at all. As soon as the last word escaped Kane's mouth, the reporter chimed in. "Well look what I've got."

Benedict reached into his jacket and withdrew a pack of photographs. "These are the pictures from last night."

"Wonderful," said Kane with gleeful eyes.

About to open them, Benedict suddenly stopped. A mischievous grin spread across his face. "Are you sure you want to see these?" he said.

The stranger gave him an absurd look. "Of course," he declared.

<122>

"Are you *really sure?*" Benedict said childishly. "Because if you'd rather wait till some other—"

Kane snatched the pack away impatiently and Benedict chuckled. The stranger tore it open and found beautiful, clear shots of license plates. "Fantastic," he said. "You really can operate a camera."

"That's not all I can do," the reporter said.

"What do you mean?"

"I've already run a check on the plates."

"How?"

"I'm a reporter," he threw up his hands. "I have a 'friend' at the Sheriff's Department."

"And..."

"Two of the plates are registered to James Crawford Borley."

"And the third?" the stranger hovered with anticipation.

"Take a guess," Benedict said devilishly.

"Robert Jensen."

"You got it."

Kane thrust a quick, victorious fist in the air. "I knew it," he said. "I knew Borley was behind this." His mind raced with a new thought. "But what about your 'friend' at the Sheriff's Department? Didn't he think it was suspicious you were running a check on the dead man's license plate?"

"He knows I'm covering the story," Benedict replied with a shrug. "And I didn't tell him how I acquired the tag number. I have him do that kind o' stuff all the time."

"Well do the cops know this?" Kane asked. "Do they know this guy was at Borley's last night?"

Benedict shook his head negatively. "They think he was at home all last night. Then, sometime after midnight, he drove up here and killed himself. They're blaming it on marital difficulties."

Kane took a seat beside Benedict on the hard, cold stone. He privately shuddered to feel the open drop behind his back.

<123>

"Well, are you going to the cops about this?" Kane asked.

"Are you kidding," Benedict replied. "They're gonna want to know how I got the pictures. If I tell them I was scoping out the castle then I'm going to have to tell them about you."

Kane rested his head on his hand, rubbing his forehead as if to stimulate a new thought. "Well what was the relationship between Jensen and Borley?" he said.

"I have no idea," Benedict replied. "That's going to take some research."

"Good God," said the stranger. "Why would Borley have killed him this way?"

Benedict explored the question then surrendered. "I don't know. It seems very uncharacteristic of him."

Kane rubbed his head some more, and then accepted a controversial realization. "We have to let Borley know that *we* know."

"What?" Benedict was obviously surprised.

"We have to let him know that we're on to him."

"I don't know if that's a good idea, Kane," Benedict frowned with hesitation.

"Wilson," Kane said sternly, narrowing his eyes intently, "Borley killed a man last night. *People are dying.* We have to put a stop to it."

"Well, yes but how?"

Kane gazed at Benedict, eager to see his expression change with the coming comment. "You have to print it."

"What!?"

"You have to publish it in the paper."

"Publish what? That Borley is responsible for Jensen's death?"

"No, no," said the stranger. "That Jensen was there last night—at the castle."

Benedict's face twisted painfully and he sat up a bit. "No, I couldn't do that. We should just keep this to ourselves for now."

"Wilson," Kane addressed him with a new, more convincing tone. "It's only a matter of time before Borley will want us dead."

<124>

"Us?" Benedict exclaimed.

"Oh, I'm sure he knows you associate with me. He's probably having me followed."

"What's that got to do with it?"

"This is our chance to do two beneficial things. First, it would make Borley cease killing associates. Secondly, it would prevent him from killing us."

"Prevent?" Benedict was rattled. "You mean provoke!"

"No. If you print something like that, and then you end up dead, everyone will know Borley killed you. He wouldn't do something like that."

"Oh, I think he would," replied the reporter, "I don't think he cares."

Kane stood up briskly and took a pack of smokes from his pocket. Distributing a couple between them, he removed his lighter and lit them up.

"Listen," said the stranger authoritatively, "we have to show Borley we're not scared of him. Right now he has all the cards, but if we show him we have information we're willing to give to the public, we suddenly have some control as well."

"But how is that going to help you get inside the castle?" asked Benedict, an expression of worry now shaping his features.

"Just trust me," Kane replied. "We need to ruffle his feathers a bit."

"But then he's going to be on guard," said Benedict. "We don't want that."

"I'll say this again," the stranger declared. "*People are dying.* If you're truly as moral as you claim, then it's your duty to print it. In doing so you will save lives—possibly our own."

Benedict rose as well, pacing a bit, cigarette in hand, battling with reason. "This just seems very…rash. I don't think we should make rash decisions. I mean he owns part of the paper for goodness sake!"

"What's the deadline tonight?" asked Kane.

"Midnight," the reporter replied. "But I don't think this is a well-thought-out idea. What about…What about going to the federal authorities?"

<125>

The stranger snickered. "You don't understand, Benedict," he said. "They're all a part of the system that people like Borley control. Besides, there are things you don't know—things that are too important to let out of my hands. This needs to stay in our control."

Suddenly, they heard a noise. Each man froze immediately, the thin trail of smoke seeping from their cigarettes was the only sense of motion about them. It was such a small, quick noise, they couldn't tell what it was, or even the direction from which it came. The darkness around them was so dense and cluttered that their eyes searched hopelessly for a clue. Then, there it was again.

This time, they could better tell. The noise was a tiny pop, like the break of a strained twig, followed by a gentle rustling of leaves. It came from ten feet away: the wooded area where the timber pile tapered into the flat ground of the bridge; and it sounded high, like in a tree.

They exchanged a glance, and then shot their eyes upwards to the same spot. A black mass of looming trees towered from the bed of tangled vegetation. Since the giants had been forced to develop in such a cramped, confined, unruly place, their skeletal limbs and decaying leaves were loosely intertwined.

Then the noise came again. This time it wasn't so much a pop as the sound of bark giving slightly, a small creak perhaps. Though their eyes had adjusted to the night, they could see no distinct forms at such a distance. Both men wishfully presumed it was probably an animal, yet their breath swelled in their chests and their stomachs began gradually descending. Each gave a nod and slowly walked in the direction of the trees.

Their flashlights had been turned off for a while, and so as they approached, they strained to see their surroundings against a clouded, deep-blue sky. The stranger took lead a few steps in front of his counterpart, stepping carefully and lightly, yet still unable to completely prevent the crunch of fallen leaves beneath his boots. With Benedict trailing right behind him, he stepped beneath the trees just far enough

<126>

to see around some thick, obscuring branches. Their stomachs dropped with a jolt of clenching shock.

Ten feet above them, on the limb of a tree, sat a monk. A dark cloak was draped around him. His hood was down, but bunched behind his neck and shoulders, revealing a pale, bald head, save a ring of fine hair around his cranium. His thin brow was arched, and his eyes glowed with searing purple light. Imposing and devilish, his teeth were bared perversely, a near-sinister snarl upon his lips. The shadowy reflection of a nightmare, he looked down upon the two like a guardian, the black forest around him mystical. And then, he vanished.

Stunned and panicked, Benedict took a step back, stumbling, falling, and dropping his cigarette. His eyes were wide with terror, his flesh encased in a film of cool sweat. He stuttered incomprehensibly, all the more confused by the stranger whose back was turned to the reporter, still staring at the vacant spot where the monk had been.

"Him! Th...that's him!" Benedict exclaimed. "That's the man I glimpsed the night I met you!"

"I know," the stranger said, surprisingly calm, his back still turned.

Gathering himself, and partially questioning his sanity, Benedict painstakingly made his way back to the side of the stranger. Still having not moved, Kane's face was still and stern, his eyes almost angry and glazed.

"How?!" the reporter, nearly breathless, cried. "What's this all about?" he demanded. He touched Kane's shoulder, bringing the stranger's staunch face to his. Benedict, with open, innocent eyes searched the stranger's steely face. "*Who are you?*" he said.

Kane's eyes were icy and intense. "Print the information," he commanded. "I have my reasons."

<127>

CHAPTER SIX

ONE LINE. IT was one line in an otherwise conventional article: "Sources say Jensen was seen entering the home of Crawford Borley a few hours before the time of his death." Asheville was in an uproar.

The city council, the police, the chamber of commerce, the schools, the churches, the businesses, and the streets were all bubbling with rumors and speculation. "Borley" was not the sort of name one casually dropped in an article. Most articles were built around the name— around the legacy—and "Borley" was a name that no one used in a frivolous way. To publicly imply a connection between "Borley" and unnatural death was profound. It was even more compounded by the recent death of Crawford Borley. The sensitivity of the death still lingered strongly in the minds and mouths of Asheville. It was disrespectful to speak illy of a family in mourning, much less to insinuate their relationship to an already controversial suicide.

In the newspaper office, everyone stayed an even greater distance from Benedict. They were afraid to associate with him, to appear as if they might have some hand, indirectly or otherwise, in his audacious work. Even Benedict's superiors distanced themselves from him. They knew he had crossed a line beyond the range of their reprimand. It was only a matter of time before Borley, himself, requested a meeting with the reporter. In one day, based on one line, his career seemed doomed. And yet, though his logical tendency was to feel dreadful and insecure, he could not escape the tingling excitement of the ordeal. The waters of Asheville were stirring, and he anticipated the forces rearing up from

<128>

the abyss. For better or worse, something extraordinary was about to happen, and he was locked indelibly in the center.

Before the day was over, as Benedict sifted through paperwork at his desk, he received a visitor. A tall, lean man, pockmarked and weasly, showed up at the reporter's desk. He wore a gray suit and carried a briefcase. Upon seeing him, Benedict immediately groaned, assuming an attorney had come to discuss an impending lawsuit.

The man, haughty and swift, had no time for courteous introductions. "Mr. Wilson?" he said.

"Yes?"

"I have here an invitation from Mr. J.C. Borley," he continued, laying a large, expensive envelope on the desk. With that, the peculiar fellow turned and marched away as hastily as he'd come.

The pearly envelope was trimmed in fine gold, and the flap was neatly sealed with a wax stamp "B." Using a letter opener to carefully pry up the stamp, he meticulously opened the enclosure. Inside was a handwritten note:

Dear Mr. Benedict,
I would be honored for you and Mr. Kane to join me tomorrow evening for drinks. Please arrive at the castle at 7:30. I look forward to meeting you in person.

Best Regards,
Signed Borley

Mr. Kane? Immediately, Benedict knew Borley had been keeping tabs on the stranger. He regretted public meetings like those at Brownman's, and wondered how thoroughly Borley knew of their intentions. He picked up the phone at once and called Kane's voice mail.

In a few moments, Kane returned the call.

"I knew it. I knew we were going too far. Borley wants to meet with us tomorrow," Benedict said.

<129>

"You mean both of us?" questioned the stranger.

"Yes, of course. Both of us. His note specifically says Mr. Kane."

"Wonderful, wonderful."

Benedict could visualize the stranger beaming on the other line. "Wonderful?" the reporter said. "What's so wonderful about that? I'm not even sure if I should go."

"What are you talking about?" said the stranger. "Of course you're going to go. You're going to finally see the inside of the castle."

"And what about you?"

"I have my own agenda," the stranger confessed.

"But don't you think it's dangerous?" Benedict insisted.

"Remember, you insured yourself today."

✳   ✳   ✳

Stinging drops of ice-cold rain drizzled from the flustered, ashen clouds, and the hour before sundown was melancholy and bleak. Mud splashed and cars slid smoothly; the muffled impact of rear-end collisions heard regularly throughout the city. An upset sky had spat and misted like an irritated bowel—opening freely for a while to release a steady stream of tension, and then tightening again to restrict the tainted liquid from complete ejection.

The stranger, a wide umbrella bloomed above his head, waited in front of Pack Memorial Library for Benedict. Beside him, a vagabond sat on a bench, drenched in rain much to his own delight, and tossing bread crumbs to invisible pigeons. He looked to the stranger once in a while with a near-intoxicated grin, and then diligently continued his occupation.

His blinker flashing, Benedict's jeep whisked up to the sidewalk, a thin wave of rainwater splashing from his tires. Careful of the slick,

<130>

lubricated concrete, Kane made his way over, fumbled a bit lowering the ribs of his umbrella, and got inside.

"It's about time," the stranger said.

"I'm sorry," the reporter apologized, "but I had some stuff come up at the last minute."

"Why bother?" Kane asked with a smile. "You won't be needing them tomorrow—unless they're your final affairs." Benedict was not amused.

They drove a short distance and pulled off in a parking lot to discuss the evening. Once parked in the far corner, Benedict turned off the engine. The patter of compact raindrops echoed sharply on the jeep as if it was a drum.

Benedict was dressed in an outdated tweed coat with a burgundy tie. "So what's the plan for tonight?" he asked.

Kane reached into his coat pocket to withdraw a plastic grocery bag. Despite its concealment, beads of water glided off it here and there. Opening it carefully, he introduced the coming prize: "You look very professional," he said. "But you forgot one accessory." He took out a small, black box with straps and a coiled loop of wire.

"What is that?" Benedict frowned.

"This is what they call a wire."

"Ha!" Benedict exclaimed. "Are you crazy? Do you think I'm wearing that?"

"I *know* you're wearing it," the stranger insisted.

"No, no," said Benedict. "You've got to be kidding. We *will* get killed if anybody wears that."

"I don't think you understand," a new blackness seethed within the stranger's voice. "You're going to wear this and we're not going to get killed."

"It was crazy enough that I put that line in the article for you! Now you want me walk into the lion's den asking for death?"

The stranger was already out of patience. He cast a fiery leer at the reporter. "Look you son-of-a-bitch," he said. "If you don't wear this then I'll kill you myself."

<131>

The struggle in the air instantly vanished, a hard, uncomfortable, dangerous weight replacing it. The two men looked at each other in silence, Benedict unsure of what he was hearing, and Kane projecting an eternal, predatory coldness. Though he resisted the sensation, Benedict felt sharp, unsettling fear in his stomach. For the first time, he was physically afraid of how the stranger would react, and he instantly questioned his involvement with the tumultuous man.

Deciding it was best to de-escalate the tension, progressing away from aggression towards understanding, he spoke gingerly: "Kane, what's wrong?"

"Nothing's wrong," replied the stranger. "I'm just tired of having to convince you do to what's necessary. Either help me or don't help me. But don't play this childish game."

Benedict, apprehensive, thought about the stranger's words. Then, his shock gave way to emotion as well. "All right. Fine!" he said. "Give it to me." He snatched the device away.

"You reporters are all the same," Kane said. "All piss and wind and no balls."

"I said I'd do it," Benedict snapped, unbuttoning his shirt.

"Okay," the stranger said calmly.

He showed Benedict how to strap the device around his chest, running a tiny microphone up near his collar, and attaching it with a small piece of tape; also taken from the stranger's bag. It contained a minute cassette, capable of recording one hour. A switch on the back would have to be pushed to start the device.

"And what happens when Borley searches us?" Benedict asked, still thoroughly unconvinced of his role.

"Borley won't search you."

"How do you know?"

"Because *I know*."

Benedict shook his head. "What do you expect to achieve with this?"

<132>

"I'm going to get Borley to admit his crimes," the stranger responded. "That way, if I fail in destroying The Horror, you'll still have a way to bring him down. Call it *my insurance*."

It was clear that nothing was going to convince Benedict that the wire was a good idea. "The only reason I'm submitting to this is because I'm already in this too deep…And by the way, I'm very offended that you spoke to me like that."

"Forgive me," said the stranger sarcastically. "But you must realize something."

"What?"

"You have no idea of the seriousness of this matter. There are many things you do not know; things you are not ready to know. And so you shall have to trust me or die."

"You're just as bad as Borley," the reporter declared.

"Well then," responded the stranger, "you're going to die either way. So you may as well listen to me. I doubt Borley will provide a better option."

"Sometimes I think you're a madman," Benedict said, starting up the vehicle.

"I have to be," Kane responded. "Only a madman knows the mind of another one."

✳   ✳   ✳

There was a good deal of silence between the two men as their rugged vehicle trudged up the slick and curvy mountain road. It was a silence borne more of anxiety than any tension between the two.

"You should be happy," said the stranger.

"And why is that?"

"Well you've always wanted to see the inside of Borley's Castle right? I'd think you'd be ecstatic."

<133>

Benedict rolled his eyes. "This is not exactly what I had in mind," he replied. "I feel like I'm heading to an executioner."

"At least you'll see the marvelous castle before you die."

The reporter was not comforted.

When they arrived at Borley's gate it opened majestically, eerily. They drove a short distance inside to find the gate keeper, shielded beneath his umbrella, waiting for them by the small, rock shed. The vehicle crept to a halt at his side. Benedict rolled down the window.

The obscure figure of the guard leaned close, rain pelting the tight fabric of the umbrella. He spoke in a dignified, masculine voice: "Could you please turn your interior light on?"

Benedict complied. "Good evening," the reporter said, further blinded by the pallid incandescence. His mind jumped to the recorder on his torso, and he suddenly projected omniscience onto the guard. After all, this was *Borley's* guard; perhaps he could sense the device with some superhuman intuition. Benedict felt sick.

The watchman produced a photograph, his hand cupped around it, and studied it thoroughly. Kane and Benedict couldn't see its image. He raised his eyes. "Mr. Benedict?" he said.

"Yes," the reporter replied.

The guard's eyes glanced down, then up, again. "And Mr. Kane?"

Kane nodded.

With that, the gate keeper smiled. "You gentlemen have a nice evening," he said, motioning for them to continue.

"Thank you," Benedict grinned, then rolling up his window, they continued along the drive.

Benedict exhaled, a pained look about his face. "Good God, I must be crazy!" he wailed.

"What?" frowned the stranger.

"I'm sorry, I can't do this. I'm taking this wire off."

Kane shook his head with exasperation. "Don't start that again," he said. "In fact, go ahead and turn it on."

<134>

"Why don't you wear this damn thing?" Benedict said, red-faced.

"Because if anyone gets out of here tonight it'll be you," Kane replied. "Now don't argue with me anymore."

Cursing under his breath, Benedict fumbled to find the switch with one hand while navigating the lengthy, wooded drive with the other.

"And remember," continued the stranger, "there's only an hour on that tape. That means I'm going to have to get Borley talking soon."

"You know, there's a fine line between courage and stupidity," Benedict reprimanded.

"Don't worry about a thing Mr. Benedict," the stranger smiled. "You're well taken care of."

When they arrived at the front of the castle, Benedict's eyes sparkled with wonder. The fortress, the statues, the moat were all illuminated from below. The light cast hellish shadows around the harsh and shapely forms, breathing a mythical soul into the stone. Lamps submerged in the moat's swift waters flooded the liquid like a crystal. It gleamed off the frothing surface, reflecting a spectral haze onto the stronghold.

"It's overwhelming," Benedict whispered in awe.

Two men in suits, familiar to Kane, waited in front of the castle. Upon seeing the visitors, one of them mumbled into his radio. Benedict parked his vehicle off to the side and, along with Kane, exited. Astonishment and fear mingled torturously in his chest. He tried to ignore it—tried to forget the abominable instrument concealed just beneath his clothes—but he couldn't. He knew his guilt would show if he stayed cognizant of its presence. Surely his body language would betray him.

As Kane and Benedict approached the castle, each of the escorts appeared to specifically focus on an individual guest, almost as if pre-planned. Kane's escort had a hard face, and squinty, experienced eyes. Benedict's had a softer look, more young and open.

"Right this way gentlemen," said Kane's escort. He stood patiently, his arm outstretched in the direction of the drawbridge.

<135>

"Thank you," said Benedict, the twinge of nervousness in his voice seeming natural. Few entered Borley's Castle without anxiety, and the guards were accustomed to its traits. The reporter walked by them respectfully, but the stranger eyed them confrontationally as he passed.

Benedict was increasingly overcome by the towering structure, looming taller and more potent with each step. It was more magnificent than he had ever imagined, each detail rich with dark fanfare. Upon breaching the entrance corridor, the interior chamber unveiled itself in all its brawny splendor and gothic glory.

Hands folded in front of himself, Brock waited just inside. He greeted Benedict courteously and Kane dutifully. It was clear his distaste for the stranger had not diminished. With the escorts still accompanying them almost ceremoniously, Brock led them to the room where Kane and Borley had first met. Now, however, it was set up to accommodate three people: one chair facing two. When they entered, guards around the room bowed and William stood at attention. He nodded honorably at their presence and motioned for them to take a seat.

The room was uncomfortably silent. Benedict felt compelled to speak, breaking the stillness, and yet he questioned the etiquette in doing so. Far worse than the silence however, was the distinct impression that they were being set up. The room was tense and expectant—more so even than when Kane had broken into the estate. Benedict looked to the stranger who appeared exceptionally calm. Then, he remembered again: the wire.

Benedict could feel the light recorder against his chest. A slight, barely detectable warmth radiated from it, and though he knew it was only his imagination, it seemed he could feel the tiny wheels turning inside. An unarmed spy, he sat amongst the enemy, escape or rescue an absurd hope for deliverance. His sharp eyes circled the room, straining in vain to read the minds of the dozen or so men skillfully positioned around him. They returned his gaze with smug faces. Surely they knew. Surely they were planning something awful.

<136>

Then, grand as always, Borley arrived. He strutted through the same doorway as before, but this time his entry was not preceded by his ghostly footsteps on the stairs. As soon as Kane saw him, a spark of surprise ignited in the stranger's face. He was still the same Borley as before, bold, arrogant, and untrustful; and yet he was different. This Borley was not as sluggish and unfocused. Instead, a fresh and honed clarity emanated from his tall, erect frame. His pace was swifter, more controlled and balanced; his eyes were cold and feline, a confident smirk tugging at his lips. His wavy locks of jet-black hair were combed and oily, his thick mustache artfully trimmed. Even his clothes, from his white, puffy, long-sleeved shirt, to his black slacks, were ironed and neat. Despite his healthy build, the lines of his body were straight, angled, and direct.

"How do you do gentlemen?" he bellowed, stepping around his seat to greet his guests.

The visitors stood. "Very well, thank you," said Benedict shaking his hand. The stranger did the same with a nod. With that, the men seated. Borley relaxed into his chair, resting his elbows on the arms and clasping his hands royally.

"I must say I was very sad to hear about your father," Benedict spoke softly.

"Thank you," replied Borley, a bit mechanically. Though he responded to the reporter, his eyes were trained on Kane. "It's been a very upsetting time for me. First my father, and then yesterday my poor little kitten met with an untimely demise. Oh well," he shrugged, "I suppose death comes in waves. Once someone dies, others start to die. You never know who's going to be next."

Benedict bowed his head a bit, while Kane sat unwavering.

"But enough of that!" Borley exclaimed. "So gentlemen," he spoke humorously with an exaggerated Texas drawl, "*what's yer p'ison?*"

The reporter smiled. "I believe I'd like a martini please."

Borley looked to Kane. "And you?"

<137>

"No thank you," he replied, "I'm fine."

"Three martinis!" Borley roared to William at his side, blatantly ignoring the stranger's response. "*Borley* martinis," he stressed with a grin.

"Yes sir," said the Butler with a bow, then turning to carry out the order.

The master of the castle turned back to his guests smiling, a more recognizable tension in the room. "So," he said. "Let's get right down to it, shall we? I understand you believe Robert Jensen was in my home just prior to his death."

Taking a breath, Benedict opened his mouth to reply, but before a word could escape, the stranger cut him off.

"Well that's when you killed him isn't it?"

A low gasp circled the room, and even Borley drew his head back in surprise. Benedict was horrified, yet Kane didn't flinch, his eyes never leaving the rich man's. The shock settled in for a moment, and then Borley gave an admiring chuckle. He loved a confrontation, and this one was presented in true Borley style.

"Well, what an unpleasant accusation," the host commented, his face and voice light, as if he didn't take the allegation seriously.

Benedict gave Kane an icy glare. "I must apologize for my counterpart," he said, turning back to the rich man, "I don't think he meant to be so offensive. What he meant—"

"Oh I'm sure he did," Borley interrupted. The men in the room, having already been on edge, were now ready to pounce.

"Well, yes…but, but I mean," the reporter stuttered.

"You've certainly gotten braver since the last time I saw you," Borley cut him off again. His words seemed directed solely at Kane, Benedict being a trivial accessory to the line of communication.

"And it appears you've gotten bolder," the stranger replied. "Hanging people off bridges."

At this point, Benedict gave up, lowering his eyes and contributing to the deadly silence of the room.

<138>

Borley shuffled a bit in his seat. "Very well," he said. "Let's toy with your hypothesis, shall we? Let's say I *did* kill Robert Jensen. What do you care? What did he mean to you?"

"He was a human being. And you're a murderer."

"No, no," the rich man briskly shook his head. "I'm not talking about that humanitarian crap. I mean to you *personally*. What did he mean to you? How has his death affected you? Did you know him? Would you have even known about his death if you hadn't read about it in the paper, or if someone hadn't told you? Would you have even known he existed?"

Kane took a deep breath, outwardly hard, but inwardly gleeful. He had hit the right nerve. Borley was already breaking down. "No," he replied. "Probably not."

"Then why do you care?" Borley continued. "Why must you prod in *my* business?"

"Oh come on," Kane provoked him. "You don't really believe that do you?"

Borley's cool exterior was swiftly melting, his dark inner passions gurgling to the surface. Borley wasn't used to curtailing his thoughts, and he wouldn't give his visitors the joy of making him do so. "People like you are a disgusting barnacle on the side of people like me who really make a difference," he said, his agitation growing.

"I think perhaps we should leave now," Benedict interjected. Both Borley and Kane blatantly ignored him, the turmoil of the room irrevocably ignited. However, in the instant the reporter spoke, Kane briefly shot his eyes towards his counterpart. In the split second his gaze was about to turn back to Borley, his brain processed an unexpected image. Returning his attention to Benedict, his insides sank with an inkling of fear.

Apparently unbeknownst to everyone else in the room, a thin, yet visible, loop of black wire peeked out from behind the reporter's tie. Delicately bowed, its circumference expanded and contracted with each slight movement of its carrier. Though the motion was small, it was enough to catch a discriminating eye. The stranger had not planned for

<139>

this. He felt confident he could rile up Borley then de-escalate him again for a safe farewell. But this—well this changed everything. Borley had failed to search them, honoring them as guests, and he would detest his respect being taken for granted, particularly in such a deceitful way. Kane knew it would set him over the edge, possibly to the point of taking their lives—or at least giving them physical "mementos" of the evening. He did the only thing he could do: Carried on as normal, perhaps even a bit wilder, to distract attention from Benedict, despite the fact his concentration was broken.

"Each of us are going to die," Borley progressed, his voice raising. "You're going to die; I'm going to die. Why must we bitch about it so? Who cares when or how? Why do we waste our time romanticizing?"

"You're psychotic," Kane stated bluntly.

"Oh?" Borley crooked his neck and bunched his brow. "A loony? Is that what you think I am? A loony? Let me tell you something Mr. Kane, there is only one problem with loonies, and that's that they usually don't know they're loonies. I, on the other hand, know," he smiled dashingly. "Therefore, I'm quite all right."

In the commotion, no one had noticed William standing patiently at his master's side with a tray of drinks. Upon finishing his last sentence, Borley turned his head to find the faithful servant. "Well what are you waiting on man!" he exclaimed. "Distribute the drinks!"

Taking his own, Borley downed a few gulps effortlessly. William handed one to Benedict, the loop shrinking as he stretched to take it. Kane refused to have his, and so the butler sat it on the table in front of him.

Borley exhaled roughly and slammed his glass down on the table. "How 'bout you reporter?" he said, at last turning his attention to Benedict. "Is that what you think?…that J.C. Borley took a man to Helen's Bridge in the middle of the night and hanged him? Is this what I pay you for?"

<140>

Benedict was rattled, and so was Kane, seeing the conversation turn. "Well sir I never said anything about murder," he weakly replied to Borley, the rich man's intimidation crushing him.

"Yeah, yeah," Borley mocked him. "You reporters never do—you never say anything outright. It's always little insinuations. So and so *allegedly* this, and *sources* say that, and all the rest of your happy horse shit. But its not the news that feeds you, no. Its people like Mr. Kane here—Mr. Sensational. That's all you care about!"

Kane seized the dialogue again: "Its no use Mr. Borley. You can save your breath because we *know*."

"You don't know anything!"

"Have you no heart?" Kane carried on with sympathetic fervor. "Do you care nothing about this man's family?"

Frustrated, Borley wiped his long hand hard across his mouth, almost as if removing an invisible gag. "Let me tell you something," he said lowly and calmly, barely restraining himself. "People like you running around, preaching your filth—you'd like to believe all life is such a precious thing. You'd like to believe it because then *you'd* be precious! But its all Social Darwinism see? It's Survival of the Fittest. If the big fish didn't eat the little ones, you'd have a weak school! If you breed with the retards and misfits and idiots, if you let them integrate based on no merit other than their existence, then you wipe yourselves out! You have a society of idiots. That's what's already wrong with this damn world—we've let the idiots remain. We let them run our businesses and own our land and screw our daughters. We let them sit at the nuclear button. And how dare we! It is our evolutionary *duty* to wipe them out!

"Society, culture, The Bible imposes certain rules on men that make them weak. But an intelligent person, knowledgeable in life's basic truths, can wield society's restrictions like a weapon against them—using them to his own benefit.

"Besides, we all make such a damn fuss over how long we live—*how long we live!*" he slammed down his fist, and the room shook with his

<141>

intensity. "We like to think of life as so many little chapters—so many little pieces. We start here," he motioned to the left arm of his chair, "and we have to end up here," he moved to the right one. "But life isn't a bunch of little pieces—tomorrow's a new day and all that crap. Life is one big, long experience. The sun goes up and the sun goes down and the sun goes up…but it's one continuous deal. You're born and you immediately begin to die. You're moving forward always; always speeding ahead—and that scythe—oh, that scythe is right behind you, swinging for you, in one long, continuous motion—swinging for all of us, trailing at our heels! But the smarter ones, well, they can run a little faster, a little more efficiently perhaps. But it's those fools—it's those fools who get clipped the soonest! And so are we to pity them? The fools? Are we to feel sorry for their foolishness?" He paused dramatically, leaning forward and searching the faces of his guests, his index finger lifted. "Hell no. It's evolution. Survival of the fittest. And I…I am *particularly* fit."

The room was drenched with Borley's dark poetry. Kane and Benedict sat motionless: shocked and speechless; the guards, including Brock, were in awe—never more proud to serve their leader. The walls, the furniture, the air were electrified. Borley had tapped the dam that restrained the endless well of bleak mightiness at his core. His nostrils flared with a powerful inhalation. He had never felt so alive.

There was a good thirty seconds of reflective silence, each man introverting with Borley's words. Kane was amazed. The rich man had volunteered a deeper, more potent and disturbing glimpse into his psyche than the stranger had ever expected. Finally, Benedict broke the near-spiritual stillness.

"Point well taken, Mr. Borley," he said. "I think we'd better leave now."

Borley lifted his glass from the table and took a moderate swig. After rotating his hand in a circle, the drink sloshing lightly in its container, he set it down. "I don't think so," he said. His words and tone carried condemnable gravity.

<142>

Kane and Benedict traded a quick glance. The direness of the situation reflected in their eyes. Borley opened his mahogany box leisurely and chose a cigarette.

"I...beg your pardon?" Benedict said sheepishly.

"You must think I'm a fool," the rich man replied, pausing to light his cigarette with the canister on the table. "I've dealt with your kind before," he exhaled a stream of smoke. "I know what you want."

The two guests sat patiently, anxiously, dreadfully.

Borley leaned forward, the cigarette smoldering between his fingers. A knowing look was in his eyes, and a satisfied smirk was on his face. He lowered his broad, black eyebrows. "You want to see what I have upstairs, don't you?"

Kane and Benedict didn't move or make a sound. Their souls were now twisted with the madman's before them. They could feel the shadow closing in around them; perhaps they would never escape.

"Yes. You want to see what I have upstairs...on the fourth floor...at the end of the hall." A sinister sheen twinkled in his eyes.

Borley had clearly seized total and unconditional control. It was he alone who moved and spoke. The solemnity of the room signified its submission. He ruled omnipotently, like a child in a doll house—the characters around him fearful of his thoughts alone.

"Well you know," he said with a patronizing voice, "usually only very special people get to visit our famous room. But tonight, since you are such valued guests, I think I shall make an exception." He nodded to the two escorts. They moved swiftly into place at the visitors' sides.

Kane was astonished. He had greatly underestimated Borley. For the first time, he realized how completely the rich man would have his way; and the extent to which he would not be intimidated. It was morbidly confirmed: J.C. Borley had lost touch with reality.

"I'm afraid that won't be possible," Kane said matter-of-factly. "We have another appointment to keep tonight," he lied, "and if we don't show up, they're going to come looking for us."

<143>

"Oh I wouldn't worry about that!" the host exclaimed, leaning forward to ash his cigarette with a frown. "I'll take care of it. I'd be more than happy to vouch for you."

"Thanks anyway," Kane snapped to his feet. Reflexively, the muscled escort beside him produced a pistol and pressed it into the stranger's neck. Terror surged through both Kane and Benedict.

Though he couldn't see the gun, the tip of the barrel below Kane's right ear felt like a cold, hard ring against his warm, pliable flesh. The rod of steel was thrust behind the hinge of his jawbone, and a burning needle of barely-tolerable pain shot upwards from the depressed nerve. An aerodynamic bead of lead, seated in an explosive, was poised directly at his head. He could sense the anxious bullet resisting its nature in stillness—begging the escort to set it free; to let it rocket forward and tear a tunnel through its victim. The stranger's fate would be sealed in the flinch of a finger. A slight tightening of one man's grip could displace him from this dimension.

Kane arched back his head, trying in vain to relieve the pressure of the barrel. He clenched his teeth and strained his reddening face, the flesh drawn tight over his angular features. Though he struggled to suppress them, throaty groans forced their way up from his diaphragm.

Borley shook his head disappointingly. "I'm so sorry it's come to this Mr. Kane, but I gave you your chance the first time. I suppose you assumed I was such a generous fellow all the time."

The guard by Benedict took a handful of the demoralized reporter's jacket, and pulled him to his feet, also at gunpoint.

Watching the display, Borley had to chuckle. "I know you gentlemen think terribly of me," he said, "but you must remember a very important thing about living a life of greatness: Goodness and badness are irrelevant. All that matters is having purpose."

Kane's gunman was a stocky man, a good deal shorter than the stranger. Drunk with the power Borley had given him, he enjoyed pushing the barrel farther and farther into Kane's nerve. He angled the gun

<144>

upwards, bringing the tall stranger off his heels, lifting him like a pathetic scarecrow on display. The gunman grinned with pride and cruelty, and the rich man's other thugs were equally amused.

"All right," said Borley, after admiring for a moment, "take them away."

With adolescent glee, the gunman lowered Kane. The pain remained somewhat, even ringing in the stranger's right ear. "Let's go," said the gunman, still training the firearm at his prisoner's head.

Kane, his face hateful, surly and defiant, and Benedict, in nervous shambles, were led away like soulless livestock to slaughter. They passed across the floor, headed through the door to take them back to the entrance chamber. Behind them, Borley called to them madly, "Adieu! Adieu, my friends! Ha! Ha! So nice of you to drop by!" he exclaimed, his wicked voice fading as the prisoners crossed the entrance chamber floor.

Crossing the majestic entrance hall, apparently headed for the lavish staircases leading upwards, Kane glanced all about, soaking in his surroundings. The dismal grandeur of the castle greeted them like a stupendous tomb. Suddenly, the sublime statues, fountains, and tapestries became triumphant markers of death. They bid the prisoners an honorable farewell, and welcomed them, almost arrogantly, into the company of Borley's virulent vault. These superficial prizes were the rich man's only compensation for taking lives—at least it would be done in the presence of glorious opulence.

Approaching the staircases, the life-size statue of Crawford Borley, lit from below, stood angelically, perhaps bestowing his blessing upon the doomed pair. Their insides churning, the prisoners began the ascent of the staircase splayed before them. In only moments, they might be torn apart like the old Borley himself, surely a miserable and horrifying death. Benedict, pale and distant, was in shock. But Kane, on the other hand, was in furious thought, his mind dashing against the clock to decide a course of action.

Higher and higher they silently ascended, pistols trained on them viciously. Time seemed to slow down hauntingly, even more accentuated

<145>

by the marvels they glimpsed at each level. There were enormous works of art and huge mounted beasts, like a thick, wrinkled elephant rearing angrily in the air, and a long, evil shark, perpetually hunting, suspended from the ceiling. On the third level, the twenty-foot skeleton of an imperious dinosaur, apparently similar to a Tyrannosaurus, was the feature. Gleaming silver shields were on the walls, an exquisite billiard table extended on one floor, and priceless documents and collector's items were strewn about, always encased in protective glass, a small spotlight positioned above. The main floor of each chamber always opened into at least four other rooms. It was an impressive and complex network of chambers, surely filled with the finest and most unique items in North Carolina, if not the entire country.

Though the stranger's gunman delighted in bullying his victim, he was also well aware of Kane's strength. His finger stayed tight on the trigger, and his eyes were supremely cognizant of the stranger's smallest actions and expressions. He pushed him from time to time, forcing Kane to flounder and trip a bit on his way up the unyielding, treacherous stairs.

"You believe in God?" Kane's gunman growled.

"I have to," Kane replied. "I'm in the house of the devil."

"Well then you better start prayin', 'cause I've cleaned up some real messes where you're goin'." He chuckled roughly at his own sense of cleverness.

Benedict's gunman was more quiet and reserved. He sensed Benedict's harmlessness, and therefore prodded him quite loosely. Unlike his counterpart, he didn't seem to derive joy from the job. Instead, he treated it with a level of calm routineness that demonstrated his indifference to the duty.

As soon as their feet made contact with the fourth floor, they could feel a change. It was bleaker—more hopeless and melancholy. Surely it was haunted by the tortured spirits of those it had devoured. Though the chamber was as large and epic as the others, it was not dominated by exploited treasures. Instead, it was ruled by broad, raven vacancies of

<146>

light. The greatest spaces of the room could be felt, but not seen—save a glimpse from the electric-blue flash of lighting in a row of distant windows. The darkness pressed uncomfortably, as if it contained a dozen eyes within; like it served as a natural one-way mirror, allowing hidden forces to view the coming subjects in private. In this room, the prisoners were the illuminated marvels.

Being on the top floor of the castle, they walked in the midst of the leering storm outside. Instead of looming above them, the monstrous thunder rumbled around them, its vibrations reaching deep, enveloping their delicate innards. Every part of the place was deathly and uncompromising. Even the gunmen were uneasy, allowing their minds to slip a bit from their prisoners, distracted by the ominous atmosphere. There were no other guards around. Obviously, there was no need.

To its far right, the chamber gave way to a long, suspenseful corridor. Dim and dingy light escaped, projecting a pale bar of color on the floor. Isolated, meager, and understated, the lofty rectangular entrance was disastrous or romantic—but nothing in between. With a sense of enormous and wearily anticipated conclusion, the prisoners, their guards cautiously at side, entered the doorway. At last, they saw it.

The lengthy corridor stretched before them like a vacuum, and it terminated at a humble, wooden door. Partially clad in shadow, it waited quietly, almost peacefully, perhaps like a resting stomach, preparing to accept the morsels traveling down a wide esophagus. It was disturbingly unpretentious, especially when compared to the rest of the castle. Though its visible lines were stark and clean, it was too far away for the prisoners to see its details. For most, this was a one-way lane, and each man, even the guards, had to force one foot in front of the other. Though the hall sucked them in, each person struggled with a nearly overpowering instinct pushing him backwards—away from the room. A primal and animalistic mechanism of survival cried out that humans should not venture there. Each man willfully overcame his "fight or

<147>

flight" instinct, moving closer to the unseen force barely contained behind the heavy door.

"Resist the tendency to flee," said Kane's gunman, his voice wavering a bit. "It's no use."

Hearts pounding, step by step, breath by breath, they surrendered to the hellish power drawing them down the orifice. Together, they witnessed the dismal rectangle at the summit of the passage grow larger and larger—together, they watched the diagonal lines of the hall spread farther and farther apart, as though opening their solemn arms to receive the anxious visitors. The corridor had surely been constructed with the intention of driving painful and gut-wrenching suspense upon its victims, and there was nary a crack, flaw, or line to ease its perilous stiffness.

Halfway to the door, the men could now see its face more clearly. The knob, being a black, wrought iron handle, preserved the door's only trace of luxury, and that being slight. It was long and curved like a backwards "s." Speckled with grain, and undoubtedly icy, it adjoined with a flat, smooth tab, a bit larger than a quarter, by which its latch could be released with a pressing thumb. Just above the tab was a keyhole. It was oddly shaped, and somewhat larger than a standard opening, but its most memorable trait was the design around the receptacle. In thin, shallow lines, a fierce wolf was etched into the metal. The keyhole served as its roaring, open mouth. The only other feature on the door was perhaps most chilling of all: A silvery, tarnished slot was embedded halfway down and in the middle. Long and curved like an awning, a hinged flap fell over it, sealing it loosely, but completely. This slot showed its age, cloudy with neglect. At any other location in Borley's Castle it would have shined and sparkled, but no one cleaned the metal on this door.

Benedict's eyes were empty, his face was drained, and his mind was detached with horror. Though Kane, too, was seduced with terror, his mind and intention were strong and sharp. The forsaken door only ten feet away, the stranger noticed a feature of the corridor previously

<148>

unseen. The vast hallway was blank with one exception: five feet in front of the door, and on the right side of the passage, another doorway, square and primitive, was carved directly into the wall. Being completely flat, it had blended perfectly with the straight wall that housed it. At first it appeared like an open doorway to a room, but in the moments he approached it, Kane realized a greater depth sunk behind it, and then he glimpsed angular stairs descending from it. Bland and functional, it was obviously a narrow, treacherous flight of winding steps, built to provide servants quick access to the ominous room.

Kane's eyes shot to the brawny gunman at his right. The pistol in his left hand, the captor's right hand was buried in his pants pocket, grasping the key to the door as they approached. In that instant, while the gunman's mind focused on discerning the object in his pocket, Kane saw his opportunity. He reached deep inside the well of his hatred, and with all the power, rage, and might he could summon, he turned in a flash, and shoved the gunman violently—his tall, square frame leaning into the motion. His balance instantly destroyed, the gunman had no time to comprehend his state. He felt his shoes separate from the floor, and there was nothing he could do as he sailed through the air, gun flying, and then crashed below onto the narrow granite stairs, his right shoulder blade cracking and releasing upon impact. The momentum of the blow was far from exhausted, and it sent him rocketing, head over heels down the winding steps, bashing each part of his body, until he disappeared around a bend, his cries trailing as he continued to roll into oblivion.

Before he could process the situation, Benedict's stunned gunman found the stranger turned upon him. Eyes enlarged like a deer in headlights, he raised his pistol, but in a swift, fluid motion, Kane seized his wrist and wrenched it mercilessly forward. The pistol sprung forth and landed on the ground without discharging, and the escort shrieked with the pain of his twisted limb. Completing the hold by gripping the gunman's right elbow with his left hand, Kane drove the henchman's

<149>

hunched body forward, and then lifted his thick knee forcefully into his opponent's abdomen. The gunman's eyes bulged like a frog's, and his mouth opened wide, a sickening, breathless rasp of agony escaping. Not yet satisfied, Kane drew back his right fist, as if building tension on a spring, and then released, his arm speeding in an arc, his white knuckles smashing the gunman's nose with a "pop!" A flower of bright, crimson blood exploded from his face, and his head fell backwards, eyes confused and unfocused. The henchman appeared a threat no longer, and yet Kane seized the collar of his coat in one hand, and the back of his belt in the other. Groaning with strength, Kane turned, hurtling the gunman towards the steps as well. However, his aim was askew, and the escort hit the doorway instead with a "*thud*." His forehead bounced off the stone wall, and he dropped to the floor unconscious.

"Good God!" exclaimed Benedict, spattered with blood, life having returned to his face.

Without reflection, or hesitation, Kane swiftly reached down to his ankle, his eyes wild with adrenaline. He arose with a pistol of his own. "All right listen," Kane said, breathing hard but surprisingly calm. "We're gonna get outta here."

"There's, there's too many of them," Benedict stammered. "They'll be here any second. You can't shoot them all."

"Let's go," Kane barked militaristically. "We can't show mercy or we'll die for sure."

Without another word, the stranger glided back down the hallway, Benedict at his side. Neither man thought twice about leaving the sinister room behind them, but they could feel its stare boring into their backs as they escaped. It was surely most displeased.

Frantically, the two men navigated the winding staircases from which they'd previously come. They rushed quickly but quietly, pausing at each turn and corner to look for guards. Surprisingly, at bend after bend, they saw no one. They continued flying downward, the stranger's coat rustling behind him like a cape. Each patter of their shoes echoed

<150>

in the massive chambers, sometimes veiled by the thunderous storm raging outside. Still, they neither saw nor heard a soul.

Nearly blinded by exhilaration, Kane stopped upon reaching the stairs leading to the first floor. On their way up, they had seen at least four stationed guards. But on their way down, they hadn't seen a single person.

"This is fishy," said Kane, gun poised, crammed behind a statue with Benedict at his side.

"A little too fishy," Benedict responded.

They sat quietly for a moment to listen for sounds. Aside from the tumultuous weather, all was quiet.

"Maybe he wants us to escape," the reporter reckoned. Kane didn't look too sure.

"All I know is that the longer we wait, the worse off we are," the stranger whispered. "So here's the plan. We charge across the floor and head for the door. If anyone gets in the way, I'm gonna shoot 'em. If we make it outside, let's hop in the car and haul ass. Agreed?"

"Agreed."

They sat for a moment, mustering the nerve to charge onto the battlefield. The gun was slick in Kane's sweaty right hand, and he switched it to his left for a moment, wiped his sticky palm on his pants, and then transferred the gun back again. "Okay," he whispered. "Let's do it."

Before the last word had completely escaped his lips, Kane, with Benedict behind, was racing down the staircase. As soon as their feet hit the hard first floor, their eyes scanned madly for a human form or sign of motion. It was all a blur, and so not fully comprehending their perceptions, they dashed across the floor anyway, seeing a clear path to the front entrance. Kane slammed his body into the mammoth entrance doors, immediately spinning around with the hammer cocked on his pistol. Benedict squeezed himself against the wall of the entrance corridor. Brushing a cold, tickling bead of sweat from his brow, the stranger saw no one. He looked to Benedict and nodded. Reaching down, he

<151>

took the huge ring of a handle, turned it, and pressed his weight into the door. It opened with a yawn.

They fled unto the black, stiff streaks of rain, burning down from the hostile sky. The cold air met their faces like a salvation, as their splashing footsteps disappeared into the night. The wind howled, drops of pelting rain misting into the entrance of Borley's Castle—and then, J.C. Borley stepped up to the front door and closed it leisurely.

Borley had a fat, potent cigar between his fingers, and a wry smile on his face. Taking a puff off the stogy, Borley turned to see Brock standing in a doorway on the other side of the room, his radio in hand.

"See what I mean?" Borley said. "Just like I knew they would."

"Yeah, you were right, Mr. Borley," Brock replied. "You're always right."

"Is everything set up?" the rich man inquired.

"Yes sir," Brock responded. "Don't you worry about a thing. I'll take care of everything."

Borley's smile widened, and he chuckled a bit to himself. Then, he turned to a window and stared gleefully into the bleak weather. Just as Brock almost exited the room, Borley entertained a new thought.

"Oh and Brock," he called.

"Yes?"

"On your way out, put on some music would you?"

"What would you like, sir?"

"Prokofiev," the rich man replied. "It's going to be *Montagues and Capulets* tonight." The ground outside was alive, squirming with raindrops. Kane and Benedict trudged through puddles, soaked to the bone, speeding toward the jeep still parked in the same spot. Kane flew up to the driver's side. "Here! Give me the keys!" he ordered. "I'll do the driving!"

From the passenger side, Benedict retrieved the keys and tossed them over the vehicle to Kane. Blinded by rain, he couldn't see the objects in time. He raised his hands to catch them, but instead nicked them, sending them flinging onto the dark, wet ground. The stranger fell to his knees, running his fingertips across the rough pavement, exploring the

<152>

frigid half-inch of water standing on the ground. Having nearly rubbed the skin from his fingertips in panic, he finally felt the outline of the keys. After pulling them from the water, he stood and fumbled with the door lock. He could barely see, and so he felt the keyhole with his left index finger and brought the tip of the key to meet it. After flipping it the opposite way, the key finally slid into the lock. It was a relief when the door opened and the pale interior light ignited.

"There they are!" a voice screamed behind them. With a new surge of fear, Kane and Benedict looked up to see a group of ghostly flashlights, fifty feet away, rushing towards them.

"Open my door!" cried Benedict.

Kane jumped inside the vehicle, slammed the door and pressed the lock. He stretched across to unlock the reporter's side. Benedict nearly fell inside, scrambling to close and lock the door behind himself.

His wet fingers shaking, Kane blundered with the keys. They slipped from his hands again, and scooping them up, he flipped through them with mounting confusion. "Which, which one starts the car! Which one's for the car!?" Benedict added his shivering fingers to the Kane's, complicating the mess.

"It's the same key! Same one!" Benedict shouted.

By this time the men, silhouetted in slickers and ponchos, had reached the vehicle. Their blinding flashlight beams, refracted in the rain, filled the jeep, and they pounded on the side chaotically. "Open up right now, or we'll shoot!"

Having found the right key, Kane started up the vehicle, and hit the gas. It spun, spraying water all over the henchmen at its side. Fishtailing, the jeep bawled and hydroplaned along the drive, heading towards the entrance at full speed.

"Slow down!" Benedict yelled. "You're going to lose control!"

Ignoring him, Kane continued speeding towards the front gate. The lubricated roadway sent him sliding in unpredictable directions, but he refused to decelerate.

<153>

"What about the gate?" Benedict said, his voice trembling.

Kane lifted his pistol in the air. "Oh we'll get that damn gate open," he said. "Don't you worry about that."

A constant wall of white raindrops exploded on the windshield as their force and speed met that of the vehicle. They pounded like a sinister death rattle, and gushed down the sides of the frame. The headlights could scarcely penetrate the torrent, reflecting off the shiny lines of liquid battling against them.

With only a second's warning, the gatekeeper's shed took form in front of them. Though a light was on inside the building, the tenant himself could not be seen. Kane slowed a bit, the car sliding forward, squinting to see the gate. Surprisingly, it was open. The stranger cast a startled look to Benedict, then proceeded through, feeling a grave pressure lift from his shoulders upon passing from the property. He took an immediate left, back down the winding mountain road, driving at a much slower rate than before.

"How do you like that?" Kane said, water trickling from his hair and coat. "He was just tryin' to scare us."

"Yeah, well you almost got us killed," Benedict raised his voice. "You're crazy. I can't believe you did that! And what about those guards? You might have killed them!"

"Well we got our tape didn't we?"

"Oh I'll tell ya what we got! We—"

Before the reporter could finish his sentence, the jeep was flooded with light from behind. Kane's eyes leapt to the rear-view mirror to meet the headlights of a monstrous, roaring truck, having sped around a curve, and braking just inches behind his bumper. Its deep, gurgling engine rumbled like a war cry, and it switched its lights from high to low beam repeatedly. Kane instantly hit the accelerator again, despite the downpour and deadly, bending roadway.

"Be careful!" Benedict cried, "you'll slide off the mountain!"

<154>

The truck would rocket forward, then fall back a few feet; sometimes blinking its lights, sometimes keeping them on bright. Then the driver would lay on the horn, releasing a full, piercing shriek, like a trumpeting elephant charging to attack. It swerved daringly from lane to lane, conveying its insane intimidation, always trailing close behind and barely making some of the curves.

Kane was steely and focused as he navigated the sloping road. Traveling far too fast, he almost lost control at several turns, sending a tidal wave of muddy water crashing off the perilous mountainside.

"For God's sake slow down!" the reporter begged, "they want us to wreck! You have to ignore them!" Each muscle in Benedict's body was morbidly rigid, and he pressed hard into his seat, his fingers contorting as they cramped from gripping the cushion.

Then came a thunderous gunshot. Its shockwave shook the back window of the jeep.

"Jesus!" Kane exclaimed, ducking. He pressed the accelerator to the floor as another gunshot erupted. The jeep gained some distance, and Kane knew he must keep a curve between him and his assailants at all times. Unexpectedly, the road cut sharply to the left. Kane stomped the brake, and the vehicle hydroplaned, its wheels dropping off the pavement for a second, but returning in time for the stranger to maintain control. Then, something terrible happened.

In the middle of the bend, as Kane's foot pressed aggressively on the brake, his leg unexpectedly extended a bit, and he suddenly felt a smooth release below the pedal. Its firmness instantly loosened, and its life-saving power drained into impotence. He knew at once that his brakes were gone. "Dammnit!" he screamed. "Our brakes! They cut our brakes!"

The impact of Kane's words immediately took form in Benedict's face. In that moment, it all made sense: Borley had planned to kill them this way; a more inconspicuous way. He knew they would run, and he knew the lethal terrain awaiting them. They had been driving a time bomb.

<155>

All the fear and anxiety of the night reached an awful apex. Even the emergency brake proved useless. The vehicle rushed down the incline, sliding, wobbling and fishtailing, constantly growing with speed. It was like driving a bumper car as the stranger struggled vainly to seize dominance over the erratic machine. Each curve emerged from the abysmal darkness only seconds before the jeep entered it, sailing around each one with a "whish;" the right-side tires dropping an inch or more from the side of the pavement, jarring the passengers destructively. Each time the tires left the road, they stubbornly adhered to the edge, like a toy race car to its track; every pebble and crack bouncing and shaking the vehicle. Alongside the road, the ground disappeared in a black and stormy drop. As they barely soared around each bend, the harrowing chasm would zoom up to their door, like an evil, grinning face, and then withdraw in a flash as they passed it by.

Though his mind was too preoccupied to dwell on it, for an instant Kane remembered Borley's words about the grim reaper constantly chasing us through life; about the "fittest" being able to outrun the weaker. The rich man's words seemed uncannily true, and the dreadful thought occurred to the stranger: *Death is swift on my heels tonight.*

The beastly truck pursued its victims as feverishly as ever, still firing shots in their direction. It was impossible for the jeep to slow down, and so from time to time, Kane purposefully crossed the left-hand lane to ram the vehicle into the bank. Rocks, dirt, bushes, and roots would blast through the air, tearing at the side; and each time the loud collision would slam the passengers forward, jerking their necks painfully. The driver would struggle to control the stubborn steering wheel, then, after the friction had worn down their momentum a bit, Kane would drive the wheel back to the right, opening the opposite lane.

Its shocks creaking with agony, the jeep bounced so severely the stranger could scarcely see for more than a few seconds at a time. Benedict couldn't breathe. A tight knot clenched the middle of his chest, choking off his air. He knew it was only a matter of time before

<156>

they flew off the mountainside, and his fear of death, a fear he'd thought nonexistent before this night, had never been so horrid, so torturous, so blatant. He didn't profess a relationship with God, and yet he mumbled silent prayers.

Just as Kane turned the wheel to collide with the embankment again, his brilliant headlights intercepted those of another car traveling up the mountain in the opposite lane. Having not yet rounded a curve, the coming vehicle was not visible, but its lights swiftly grew with intensity. They were going to meet head-on. Kane would have given his worldly possessions for just a few more seconds of time to think, but that was impossible. There was no time. He fought the instant rigidity that seized his muscles, and tried to process the situation. To his right, there was a darkened drop, its height unknown; to his left, a steel projectile, and innocent life, sped ignorantly towards him. The moment was greater than him, and so he surrendered to some internal, subliminal mechanism that possessed his incapable mind. With a jolt of unexplainable action, he jerked the wheel to the right. Inhaling a stinging, shallow breath, he prepared for a horrendous crash as the jeep bolted off a cliff.

Darkness and thin air swallowed up the vehicle. Save the raindrops pounding from the sky, two seconds of peaceful, ghastly silence sheltered the jeep like an ethereal cushion. The brutal ground was beneath their tires no more: Here they would not hydroplane; here they would not collide with other cars; here, brakes were useless. Here they were vulnerable and invincible at once. Then, they smashed down.

The vehicle landed, all four tires at the same time, and the buckled passengers were thrown forward and back with immortal force, their spines almost ripping through their necks. The drop had only been a few feet, but the ride was not over yet. Internally, each man begged for simple motionless, but it was not to be. The jeep was on an embankment, and it jettisoned forward, fueled by the power of its crash.

Flying down a slick, muddy, leaf-covered hill, they tore through undergrowth and branches. There was no way to control the vehicle,

<157>

and Kane threw his hands in front of his face. Massive trees passed their sides as a mangled blur, and the passengers knew they would most likely hurtle into one at any moment. The sharp end of a stiff, thick limb punctured the windshield with a "POP," and a spider web of cracks exploded. The deafening sounds of metal breaking, bending, stretching, and shredding enveloped them, robbing them of sanity. Each man felt miserably alone as he faced death, incognizant of the other's condition. Their destiny was completely out of their hands, and they knew if this was the end, it could in no way be prevented.

Kane and Benedict plunged haplessly towards death for a brief eternity. And then, as quickly as it had all begun, it stopped with a single enormous jolt. The bottom edge of the vehicle's front end slammed into the drenched ground at an angle. Gobs of thick, liquidy mud sprang in all directions, and showered back down heavily. They were alive. Thank God, they were alive.

Mounted in the dense ooze, the jeep's headlights still shined, unbelievably, and reflected off the untamed forest around them. Unhooking his seat belt frantically, Benedict lurched across Kane's lap and turned off the headlights and ignition. Being completely disoriented, they had no idea if Borley's men could still access them.

"Get out! Get out of the car!" Benedict exclaimed, his voice uncharacteristically monotone from shock. "They might find us!"

Dizzy and emotionally shattered, Kane could barely unhook his seat belt. Once both men busted the crinkled doors open and jumped out, the mud engulfed them up to the ankles. Kane scrambled to scoop his pistol off the floorboard, and then they raced away blindly, their feet being sucked into the squishy ground. After a hundred feet or so, they plopped down in the shelter of a large evergreen. They panted, each staring off into vacant space, rain bouncing off their faces. The experience had been too much to take in at once.

"You...you okay?" Kane asked, his pale face long and weak.

"I think so," Benedict replied.

<158>

Neither man had reconnected with the world, and yet they were forced to assess their condition. Kane looked in the direction of the jeep. The forest was dark and bleak, and he could scarcely see. "I wonder where the hell we are. I guess we came down the last half of the mountain through the woods. I can't believe we didn't hit a tree."

Suddenly, they froze as headlights illuminated the darkness. They grew brighter and brighter, and the two men dashed down onto the ground, nestling tight against the tree. For the first time, they could see their surroundings. They were at the edge of the woods, and a road ran alongside them fifty feet away. The lights were from a passing motorist, and they could see the smashed-up jeep sitting a few feet from the highway. The car blazed by.

"That's the same road we were on," Kane said. "Except now we're at the bottom of the mountain. We just came right down the side."

Benedict's face twisted with concern. "Well then—that means all they have to do is drive right down here. Right?"

No sooner had he spoken than the rumble of the malign truck's engine shook the air. Its bright headlights lit the woods as it crept along the road, the shaft of a flashlight beam exploring the forest.

"There they are!" Kane whispered. "Run!"

Their adrenaline supply spent, they reacted on pure willpower alone. Like hunted animals, they sprinted through the wet, precarious, undergrowth. Once Borley's henchmen found them gone, they would surely search for them. Soaked, leathery leaves smacked their faces, soggy ground tugged at their heels, and sharp, dank sticks and limbs jabbed them as they fled into the night. They held at least one hand in front of their faces to prevent puncturing an eye. To preclude getting separated, they had to stay close to each other at all times, keeping up with one another, and using their sense of hearing to its maximum potential. They ran and ran, until the hot, searing pain in their sides would allow it no more. At last, they collapsed on the ground with severe exhaustion, streaming with sweat, choking and gasping.

<159>

Benedict leaned over and vomited from the sick emptiness in his gut and the instability of his inflamed nerves. Kane drove his face into the wet ground, cherishing the revitalizing coldness of the moisture. Their chests ached and burned with the frigid air filling their lungs, and their muscles were limp, flaccid, and terminated. Though they were alive and functional, they were broken. After a short while, a great, tingling numbness rose and consumed each man, rescuing him into a perfect silence. A blackness deeper than the cloudiest tempest closed in at all sides, and they each slipped away. Giving into their fatigue, they passed out.

*   *   *

J.C. Borley had waited patiently to hear his guests were dead. He sat at a long, antique grand piano, its shiny but aged form spilling before him—reflecting the vast stone ceiling like an ebony pool. For his deed, the rich man paid homage by soulfully fingering Chopin's *Funeral March*. The notes resonated throughout the castle with spectral beauty.

Sheepishly, carefully, Brock stepped into the doorway from which the rich music escaped. The force of his ego was weaker than usual, his mouth dry, and his eyes expectant. Though he disliked the notion of interrupting the piece, Borley had requested a report. Upon a few weary paces into the room, the rich man sensed his presence, and the music stopped. Borley whipped around with a smile.

"Ahh Brock! So tell me, how did things work out?"

Brock's head dipped lower than common as he proceeded, and his master's smile dropped. The rich man knew something had gone awry

"Well," Brock began, "things went very well. Halfway down the mountain they lost their brakes and went off the side."

"Yes?"

"Hal and the boys drove on down and found the jeep wrecked off the side of the road."

<160>

"And the passengers?"

Brock lifted his hands gently, fearfully, and shook his head. "They were, they were gone."

"Gone!"

"Yeah, they were...well they combed the woods but they couldn't find them."

Borley began rubbing his right temple, attempting to soothe the fire rising within. "No, no blood? No signs of bodily damage?"

Brock shook his head negatively.

"Could they have been thrown?"

"I don't think so," Brock said. "The windshield was primarily intact. And actually it didn't damage the vehicle nearly as much as we thought it would."

"How far down did they go off?" Borley demanded.

"Oh, about three-quarters of the way down, I think."

This clearly triggered a volatile reaction. "Three-quarters! Damn you!" Borley slammed his fist on the expensive ivory keys—a smear of rabid, unsettling notes erupted and rang in the air. Brock flinched shamefully. "I told you they should go off high up! High up! Not more than halfway down, I said. You worthless prick, I should throw *you* off the mountain!"

"I'm sorry Mr. Borley," the guard groveled, "we didn't mean for it to take so long. The road was slick, and our guys almost wrecked."

"I don't want to hear it," Borley lifted his hand imperially, and closed his eyes, calmness prevailing once again. "Your excuses mean nothing to me. I wanted them dead, or at least close to it, and it seems they survived unscathed. That gives us a whole new problem." Brock listened intently, grateful for his employer's gentle, yet tense, tone. "Now we have two men running around out there who will tell everyone what transpired tonight. That cannot be."

"I understand, Mr. Borley."

<161>

"I want those men found and taken care of—especially Kane. We still don't know who he is—and he may be more important than we think."

"And how would you like that, sir?" Brock nodded.

"I want it done discreetly. I want them to just disappear."

"It'll be done right this time, Mr. Borley," Brock assured him.

"It better be," Borley returned, "or I'll have your testicles for breakfast."

*   *   *

The stranger opened his eyes. Evidently, the fatigue that led to his unconsciousness had transformed into deep, restful sleep. It was still night, and the torrential rain had ceased; all that remained were the unsettled pops, cracks, and dribbles of orphaned droplets falling from the saturated trees. His bleary vision quickly focused on the shadowy form of Benedict next to him, quiet and still.

"Wilson," he croaked, nudging his counterpart. Startled, the reporter jerked awake with instant terror in his eyes.

"Huh?"

Kane waited until Benedict's bewildered, fearful gaze grasped reality. "Are you okay?"

The reporter sat upright, next to the tree. "Yeah, yeah I think so."

Kane raised up, stretching his stiff back. "Aw!" he yelped, grabbing a muscle under his right shoulder blade. "Oooh, that's sore."

"Just wait'll tomorrow," Benedict replied, his voice hoarse.

They were both frozen, soaked and filthy. Dried and wet mud was caked in patches across their bodies. Kane even had a gob stuck to his left eyebrow.

"How long have we been here?" Benedict asked.

"I have no idea. I just know we can't go back to that jeep tonight."

<162>

Squinting, the reporter suddenly pinched the flesh between his eyes. "Oh God, my jeep," he moaned, as if he'd forgotten about it in his sleep. "I can't believe that. I loved that jeep."

"I don't think it messed it up that badly," Kane said. "Come on, let's be quiet and get outta here."

Staying low to the ground like soldiers in a foreign jungle, they swiftly moved through the trees and growth more precisely than before. Without the rain it was easier to travel. However, the noises of their trudging were also more noticeable without its cloak. The clouds had cleared considerably, and they could see quite efficiently in the hazy moonlight. After traveling ten minutes or so, they exited at a park.

The area was desolate, and the slick, green grass shined beneath streetlights. There were benches, swings, slides and a sand pit—er mud pit, as it was. Being drenched already, they didn't hesitate to plop down on a wet, sticky bench at the area's edge. They could see themselves clearly for the first time.

"Good Lord, we're a mess," Kane said.

Benedict was preoccupied with his mouth, a swirl of concern about his features. "I, I think I must've bit my lip," he said prodding. "Ouch! That hurts."

Kane examined it. It was puffy, and a film of dried blood was smeared across it. "Yep. You must've chomped down on it pretty hard," he said.

"I should be enraged with you," the reporter turned his attention to the stranger. His speech was a bit slurred from his wound. "I should be, but I'm too damn happy to be alive."

"Mad at me?"

"Of course! Look at me! Since I've met you, I've fallen from the sky, almost been fed to a monster, wrecked my jeep, and I'm quite sure my job is done for—not to mention the fact that J.C. Borley wants me dead! And for what?! You were actually *advocating* this tonight!"

<163>

Kane became defensive. "Whoa, whoa, whoa. I didn't ask you to help me. You insisted, remember?"

Benedict calmed down a bit. "All I know is that tomorrow I'm packing my bags, heading to Tennessee, and paying a visit to the federal authorities."

"You'll do no such thing!" Kane bellowed. "Are you out of your mind?"

"J.C. Borley tried to kill us tonight—just like so many others. And we have his incriminating words right here," the reporter tapped his chest. "We've also got my jeep with the brakes cut. Mission accomplished. What more do we need?"

"*Listen to me*," Kane glared, "if you go to the authorities *we'll* be the ones who end up in prison."

"If we don't we'll end up dead!" Benedict retorted. "Borley's not going to give up now. He's going to kill us."

"Law enforcement is not the answer," Kane stressed. "*The system* is not the answer. Borley doesn't play by rules, and so neither can his opposition. Besides, the system never accomplishes anything. It's people who get off their ass and go take care of what needs to be done. Those are the people who bring about change! But you wouldn't know about that, would you? You're one of the people who sit at a cushy desk and expect big brother to look out for you. You have no idea what it's like to plunge your hands into the dirt—to be so devoted to an outcome that you'll break all the faces and wreck all the cars and sacrifice any and everything it takes to get what you want. You've spent your whole life writing about how things should be, but you've always expected someone else to do the work."

"How do you know about me?!" Benedict exclaimed. "I don't even know who you are! I don't even know why I'm here!"

"Because you're meant to be here!" Kane roared. "Because it's your destiny!"

The words sounded uncharacteristically sentimental from Kane, and Benedict paused to reflect on them. "What do you mean?"

<164>

Kane sat quiet a moment, his brow stern. "Look," he said, "Borley is not even my priority; I've told you that. My priority is to destroy that wretched thing…lurking in the castle."

"That thing?…The Horror? And just what do you think The Horror is?"

"The Horror is the key to Borley," Kane replied. "And The Horror is more than Borley."

"No, no, no," the reporter shook his head, "I want a straight answer. What do you think it is?"

Again, the stranger was silent for a moment. "I don't know," he said. "I don't know what it is. But I could feel it. I could feel it breathing and pulsating behind that door. It was so thick with wickedness; so corrupt with dominance. It wanted me. It would have devoured me. Even Borley is weak beside it."

"And how would you destroy it? How would you destroy it if you don't know what it is?"

"That's what I'm searching for," Kane fired his icy eyes deep into Benedict's. "The authorities will only waste time with Borley. But Borley can't be stopped unless *it* is stopped—that thing which rests behind the door—the electric evil that permeates that castle."

Benedict leaned back and scratched his head. "I thought I felt it, too," he said. "At the time, I *knew* I felt it. But maybe it was just our fear we felt. Maybe there's nothing at all behind that door. Perhaps Borley just took us there to scare us. He knew we believed the room was haunted. Or maybe if something *is* in there, it's not supernatural."

The stranger didn't even acknowledge Benedict's words. Instead, he stared off into the sky. "You know," he said, "not everyone who goes into that room is torn to bits. They say some people are pulled out the next day in one piece, their organs in good working order. You'd think they'd died peacefully if it wasn't for one thing: their faces. Their pale, dead faces are twisted in a mangled frown of sheer terror: Their purple lips drawn back, exposing clenched teeth, and their eyes—well, their eyes

<165>

say it all. They bulge and shine with pure horror. That's where it gets its name—*The Horror*. It seems the last thing they saw was something inhuman. Something so unspeakably shocking, that the spark of hellish fear burns in their lifeless eyes long after death. It's so chilling, you can look into the cadaver's pupils and experience a fraction of how awful it must have been. Those people—they say those people die of *fright*."

There were no more words for a while. Kane had stirred up images disturbing to both men—especially considering they came so close to the sinister room.

"Do you have any cigarettes?" Benedict asked a few moments later. Kane dug into his coat and produced a box.

"If they're not soaked," he answered. The cigarettes lit up fine, and each man savored his sedating smoke.

"I don't know your secrets, Kane," said the reporter, "and I don't expect you to tell me. But tell me this: Is it really worth all this? Is your objective important enough to risk our lives. Is it going to make that much of a difference?"

"Yes," the stranger replied. "Yes."

Benedict was a thoughtful man. He took a moment to enjoy his cigarette and reflect on the stranger. Though his mind told him differently, his intuition remained strong and undeniable. "Okay," he said. "I'm going to trust you. But if I die because of your poor judgement, my death will be on your hands. And regardless of what's in that room, I want to see Borley take responsibility for the murders he's initiated."

"He will," said the stranger. "Once I take care of my business, you can go to the authorities if you want."

"And what about my jeep? How am I going to get around?"

"I'll pay for your car if you want," said Kane.

"Are you serious?"

"Of course I'm serious. I told you, I don't think it's that bad off anyway." Benedict experienced a great sense of relief. "Now take off that wire. Let's see how the tape turned out."

<166>

Locking his cigarette lightly between his lips, Benedict unbuttoned his muddy shirt. He fiddled with the strap for a while, then tore the whole unit off. "You oughtta try sleeping with one o' these on," he said.

Kane took the contraption eagerly. He hit rewind and the unit hummed as the tape wound back. "By the way," said the stranger, "your damn cord was hanging out of your shirt."

"No!?"

"Yes, I'm afraid so. I can't believe Borley didn't see it."

The tiny hum increased in pitch until it slammed to a stop. Kane hit the playback button: "*You know, there's a fine line between courage and stupidity,*" snapped from the tiny speaker, against the drone of the jeep engine. Kane smiled. The dialogue continued: "*Don't worry about a thing Mr. Benedict—,*" and then a staticy hiss drowned out the words. Kane looked to the reporter with a frown. The dialogue trailed back faintly after a second, and then washed out again.

"What the hell?" said the stranger. He fast forwarded the tape a bit. When he hit the playback again, it was pure white noise. Kane's pulse began to rise, and he fast forwarded some more. Again, only static. Farther he fast forwarded. Still, the hiss. His heart pounding, he fast forwarded for a long time. The result was still the same. The entire tape was a constant, even sibilance, like a television station off the air.

"Dammnit!" screamed the stranger, flinging the recorder in fury. "Dammnit! Dammnit! Dammnit!"

"See what I mean," said Benedict, unable to conceal the smirk on his face. "Magnetic tape. There's some kind of energy in that castle—the same kind that overexposed the film. Maybe that's the real reason there are no surveillance cameras."

Seething with anger, trying to contain his pent frustration, Kane buried his head in his hands. His breath escaped like steam from a locomotive. "This…This isn't going to be easy," he snarled.

"Of course it isn't," replied the reporter. "We're dealing with the Borleys."

<167>

CHAPTER SEVEN

A BLAZING BUT merciful sun exhaled warm life on the stately Grove Park Inn. These were the kinds of days that tourists cherished most. Clean, healthy, well-dressed patrons, of all ages, shapes, and sizes drifted in and out of the hotel—smiles radiating. Some flowed through the majestic entrance headed for recreation; trails, historic sights, and fine dining. Others sat leisurely in the shade on large, wooden rockers, swaying smoothly to and fro, the breeze playing deftly at their hair. Everyone was somehow absorbed in the pleasurable, easing atmosphere, and none of them noticed the stranger, coat thrown over his shoulder, leaned against a pillar at the edge of the enormous stone entry way.

It had been two days since Borley had tried to kill him, and Kane spied those around him with imposing eyes, always guarding against unwanted presences. He'd been there for several minutes, and already his patience was wearing thin. Just then, a small, blue sporty car zoomed down the drive with Benedict at the wheel. Though at some distance, the reporter saw Kane, grinned, and threw up his hand. The stranger responded with a nod, and then Benedict disappeared down a sloping hill to find a parking space. A few minutes later, he was marching energetically up the hill with a smile, dressed more casually than usual: jeans, a flannel shirt with the sleeves rolled up, and tennis shoes. Upon reaching the stranger, they clasped hands enthusiastically.

"Mr. Kane!" exclaimed the reporter.

"Mr. Benedict," the stranger returned. "You seem quite cheery today. I'm surprised."

<168>

"Well, I'm unemployed for the first time since—aw, I don't remember when." The two started walking, heading towards the inclined path to Macon Avenue, the somewhat secluded road to which the hotel's drive connected. Kane limped a bit, the burning soreness in his muscles far from gone.

"And you're happy about that?"

"Oh, I don't know," Benedict replied nonchalantly. "I didn't think I'd be, but now that I am, well it's sort of uplifting. Kind of a sense of freedom. You know, like nothin' left to lose. Besides I've needed a vacation for a while."

"What are you going to do for money?"

"I've been saving up for a long time, so I have enough in the bank to last a while. But, I suppose I'll have to freelance until I find another job. I've thought about moving to Tennessee for some time. I might check out things over there."

As they strolled alongside a rocky wall, heading towards the privacy of the shady road, Kane removed his pack of cigarettes and they both partook.

"And your new car?"

"Oh," said the reporter, "I'm just renting that until the jeep's fixed. I've got a buddy who owns an auto shop. He's working on it right now. Turns out your were right—most of the damage was cosmetic. Those are tough vehicles."

"I look forward to receiving the bill," Kane murmured sourly.

"And by the way," Benedict raised his eyebrows, "It looks like I'm not going home for a while."

"Why not?"

"Someone has been, and may possibly still be, in my house."

"How do you know that?"

"Well," the reporter took a puff, "when I arrived at my home, I could tell someone had been inside."

"Oh, and how's that?"

<169>

"I could see through the window that the curtain had been moved."

"The curtain had been moved?"

"Yeah. My living room curtain was pulled out a half-an-inch from the edge of the window; like someone had been looking out."

Kane frowned. "You know how your curtain looked when you left?"

Benedict suddenly stopped, and scrunched his brow as if the stranger's question had been absurd. "Of course," he said. "I know *exactly* how my curtain looked when I left the house. And I could tell that someone had definitely moved it."

"Okay," said Kane acceptingly, continuing the walk. "So where are you staying now?"

"Until things simmer down a bit, I'm staying at a friend's house."

Kane stopped again, and his face turned stern. "You have an awful lot of friends, don't you?"

"Well I used to," Benedict half-chuckled, "but they're deteriorating quickly these days."

"And I don't suppose these *friends* know my business do they?"

"Are you kidding? I don't even know your business."

"I'm serious," Kane reiterated, "have you told anyone what's going on?"

"I told the person I'm staying with a bit—"

Kane sighed irritably. "Are you crazy?"

"Well look, Kane," Benedict defended himself, "somebody needs to know what's going on in case we disappear. Have you ever thought of that?"

"Yeah, well we're gonna disappear a lot faster if you don't keep your mouth shut."

Desiring to move on to more productive talk, Benedict shrugged off the stranger's comment and rekindled the walking. Having traveled up the avenue, they had circled from the hotel's exit to its entrance, and continued through.

<170>

"Well," Benedict said transitionally, "*just 'cause I ain't a newsman no more don't mean I don't get the news.*" His face glowed satirically. "And I got some news for you Mr. Kane."

"What's that?"

"I had a little extra time on my hands to do some research, and I think I may have found our next lead. You remember John Weck, the regional author Mrs. Hawley brought up?"

"Yeah."

"Well he's not dead. Or at least he wasn't three years ago."

"What are you talking about?"

"I talked to his publisher," the reporter simpered pridefully. "He spoke with Weck three years ago on the phone. Weck gave him a p.o. box address for his royalty checks—which, by the way, are supposedly quite measly."

"Uh huh," said Kane. "So?"

"Well," Benedict continued, "it seems Mr. Weck may have something in common with us. He probably had to flee into obscurity because Borley wants him dead. It seems to have ruined his career. So now he lives like a hermit in a shack on top of a mountain in Barnardsville."

"Barnardsville?"

"Yeah, it's a rural area about a half hour away, towards Madison County."

"The publisher told you all this?" Kane questioned suspiciously.

"Hey," the reporter opened his arms. "People around here trust Wilson Benedict. They've been reading my articles for years."

The stranger ashed his cigarette, and the thin, gray flakes showered in the breeze. "So you think talking to this guy could help us out?"

"I think so," replied Benedict. "I mean he must know *something*. Why else would he be hiding?"

Having followed a short, alluring trail near the Grove Park's entrance, the two reached a resting area of wooden benches and rails. There were several elderly people relaxing, enjoying drinks and cordial

<171>

conversation. Kane and Benedict acknowledged them courteously, and then nonchalantly turned to walk towards the hotel.

"There's only one thing that might be of concern," said the reporter.

"What's that?"

"Well, because of his situation, he can supposedly be somewhat hostile at times. I mean he's been alone for years. And also, there is some question as to his state of mind."

"Oh great," Kane rolled his eyes. "You mean he's crazy?"

"No, no, not crazy," Benedict quickly clarified. "Just a bit...eccentric."

Kane and Benedict stopped chatting so much as they entered the Grove Park Inn, strolled across the Great Hall and exited onto the airy Sunset Terrace. The two men stopped for a moment and scanned the area before them, cherishing the scenic horizon. The city of Asheville was splayed in the distance. Its enraptured shapes and tones accented the enchanting ridges of earth at timeless rest behind them.

"Quite a view from this place," Kane reflected.

"Oh yes," said the reporter, having fished a tube of oral salve from his pocket. He squirted a line of the warm, yellow ooze on his finger, and delicately dabbed it inside his lip. He couldn't help but cringe at the sting until the anesthetic stole the sensation.

"I bet that *does* hurt like hell," Kane observed, almost as though he himself could feel the pain.

"Uh huh," Benedict slurred.

The stranger returned to the view. "Okay," he said. "Let's go see John Weck."

*　　　*　　　*

Barnardsville captures all those qualities for which Western North Carolina is famous. It is green and rolling, mountainous and isolated, with crisp, shining streams bringing nourishment to the fertile land. It

<172>

has a soft, ancient voice, perilous to those who ignore it, but generous and enriching to those quiet and patient enough to hear it. Its roadsides are adorned with weathered, experienced barns and farmhouses, great sweeping fences, and honest simplicity. Beneath its cool exterior, nestled and hidden within the labyrinths of the land, are secrets, passed down for generations—secret places, secret buildings, secret words. But these secrets compound the purest beauties of the place, supplying the mortar that has bound its soul together for centuries. Despite its seeming separation from "the system" it, like Asheville, is a place of some contradictions. Though light and peaceful, its emotions run strong. In Barnardsville, even the bears in the forest and the cattle in the fields can be far too trusting of men. And yet, their kindness should not be taken for granted. Their venom burns with equal measure.

In deep Barnardsville, not far from the National Forest of the Coleman Boundary, Benedict's car roved up a dirt road. The winding lane crawled and ascended a virile mountain peak, perched above a ripe, lush landscape below. The tires of the car crunched through the unstable gravel beneath, and both passengers were somewhat paranoid. Their disturbing wreck had imprinted their psyches, however unyielding their minds had previously been. The higher they trekked, the less signs of civilization were visible, with the exception of course, of the land far below, speckled spaciously with beacons of well-nourished life.

The higher they traveled, the more sparsely the gravel was spread. Patches of hard, red clay peeked from beneath the gray stones, and the gravel present grew filthier, blending in with the surrounding dirt. Old, deep trenches, carved by many rains past, divided parts of the course, splitting it like a puzzle. Benedict's car moaned and struggled with increasing difficulty, bouncing, shaking, and vibrating. The woods became thicker and uglier, swarms of vines consuming them bit by bit. The higher they got, the more the vehicle strained, and the more conscious the passengers grew of their anxiety. At last, when the pebbles became all but nonexistent, and the roadway was little more than a

<173>

worn pathway, sometimes even sprouting grass, it was too treacherous to continue.

Benedict stopped the car and pulled up the parking brake with a "crinnnnkkk." Their windows were down, and once the engine was turned off, the completeness of nature enclosed them. It seemed like a wondrous, peaceful silence at first, and then, after their ears grew used to it, they realized it wasn't silent at all. The "silence" was a combination of sounds—birds chirping, the wind stroking the mountainside, a tractor somewhere in the distance—and each sound joined into one, uniform tone, both enhancing its elements and cancelling them out. This was the white music of the country.

Each man got out and stretched. When they closed their doors, gravity pulled the heavy metal from their fingertips and slammed them mischievously. The noises echoed in the valley like explosions, shattering the stillness for a moment. The two walked to the side of the mountain, not far from the path, and looked down at the glowing expanse below.

"This is higher than I thought," said Kane.

"Well, if you're looking for privacy, this is certainly the place to come," the reporter squinted into the rays of the falling sun. "And you could see a heck of a sunset here, too."

The stranger examined the trail ahead, disappearing into the timbers. "I just wonder how much farther up this guy lives," he said.

"Only one way to find out," Benedict responded, trudging ahead.

Kane followed. "There's no way to contact this guy other than mail right?"

"That's what the publisher said."

"Well don't you think we should've tried contacting him first?" Kane suggested.

Benedict shrugged. "If he wants us to leave, we'll leave."

"Yeah, but we're liable to get shot. Especially if he thinks someone's out to kill him."

<174>

They hadn't walked far when they had already begun running out of breath. The terrain only grew steeper, and the slanted earth robbed them of their balance. The path deteriorated to a clearing of grass and mud, and, devoid of tracks, it was apparent that no vehicle traveled the road. After a while, they had to stop and catch their breath. Then they continued onward, expecting each bend to be the last, but continually finding another rising stretch of land.

At last, looking ahead, they could see the summit of the mountain clearly. From their vantage point, the growth-encased trail appeared to terminate with the fading open sky. They marched onward, heading towards the opening, but midway there, just below the summit, they peered a shack off the right side of the trail. Kane pointed at the dingy structure, and Benedict nodded in acknowledgement.

Breathless and sweating, they gradually made their way towards the hut. It was a small, deteriorated hovel—hillbilly in every sense. It was capped by a rusty tin roof, and the walls were gray, dilapidated wood. At its front stood a small, warped porch, bowed and sagging in the middle, accessible by a stack of mud-caked cinder block steps. Murky windows were at the front and sides, some intact, and others partially busted out. The whole area was shady and dense, large, dank trees standing around it. One monstrous oak grew directly at the side of the shanty, so large it nearly touched the wall, bulging as if it might break through at any time. Though it was high up, there appeared to be poor drainage in this slightly level spot, and a smell of mustiness and stagnation hovered.

There was not a soul in sight, and Benedict thought it best to call out a greeting. "Hello! Is anyone here?" They stood in front of the porch, partly afraid to step on it; it might surely cave in at any time. There was no response.

"Say, what does this guy look like?" asked Kane.

"Well, in his pictures, he was always quite debonair."

<175>

In a flash, the screen door of the hut flew open with a "smack!" Commanding loud, heavy steps, a haggard man bounded onto the porch, the thin board sinking a bit. "Who are you!" he demanded gruffly.

The man looked akin to a legend. His hair was long and unsightly, and a thick, brown beard hung from his sunken face. He wore a stained t-shirt, dusty denim pants, and scuffed, leather boots. A long, menacing rifle was in his hands, and he stared out with weary, scornful eyes.

Kane and Benedict held up their hands submissively. "My name is Wilson Benedict," the reporter replied calmly, "and this is...this is Mr. Kane."

The man eyed them suspiciously. "Who are you guys?" he questioned, not aggressively, but cautiously.

"We're looking for John Weck," Benedict answered.

"What for?"

"We'd like to talk about some of his...*your* books. You *are* John Weck, aren't you?"

"Who are you with?" the man interrogated.

"We're not with anyone," the reporter assured him.

"Actually," Kane cut in, "we want to kill J.C. Borley, and we're hoping you can help us." Shocked, Benedict shot his eyes to the stranger.

"Well then," said the man, dropping the gun to his side, "in that case, come on in!" He turned and walked back inside. Kane and Benedict looked to each other—the reporter bewildered and the stranger pleased. They dropped their hands.

"After you," said Kane. Benedict navigated the precarious steps and skimmed across the porch as lightly as possible. Kane followed.

The outside of the house was nicer than the inside. A putrid, sweaty smell met them upon entry. And besides a few flimsy pieces of furniture, the area was strewn with books, papers, liquor bottles, and pornographic magazines. Kane and Benedict stood inside the door. The grungy fellow extended a dirty hand.

<176>

"John Weck," he said. His voice was soothing and articulate, in no way matching his appearance or surroundings. As they shook his hand, they noticed he reeked of alcohol and body odor.

Weck plopped down in a wobbly chair by his table, the rifle propped on the wall beside him. He motioned to a rotted couch, loaded with papers. "Just throw that junk on the floor and have a seat," he said.

Grinning politely, Kane and Benedict rounded up the papers on the couch and placed them in stacks on the floor. Beneath several sheets, Kane unearthed a thick, finely-bound book: *Blue Ridge Mysteries* by John Weck. As he moved it, he turned it over. On the back was a black and white photo of a clean-cut man in a suit. His teeth gleamed, and his gaze was pleasant and confident. Indeed, he *did* look debonair. Placing it on the papers, Kane returned his attention to the greasy mountain man before him. The two took a seat, and hard springs pressed uncomfortably from below the flattened, worn cushions.

"Hadn't had visitors in a while," the author said, reaching below the table to retrieve a large plastic jug. He opened the cap and poured a glassful of the clear, still liquid. "You gentlemen care for a drink?"

"What exactly is that?" inquired Benedict.

"What do you think it is?" asked Weck. "What does an old redneck like me drink?"

The reporter smiled. "Moonshine?"

"Damn straight! This white-lightnin' came direct from across the Tennessee line this mornin.'"

"And you're going to drink that straight?" Benedict chuckled.

"Hell, I always drink it straight," he grinned. Suddenly, a wave of excitement hit him. "Here, watch this," he said. He impatiently fumbled with some items on the table and retrieved a spoon underneath. He then poured a shallow measure of the alcohol into the utensil. Holding it with his left hand, he used his right to open a box of matches. Taking one, he struck it alongside the table, lighting it with an inflammatory hiss. "See, watch this," he reiterated, bringing the flickering bud of fire to

<177>

the spoon and holding it just above the surface of the liquid. When he withdrew his hand, a quiet blue flame wavered and sat lowly atop the moonshine. It moved like a fluid animal, feeding patiently off the slowly vanishing liquid.

"My goodness," Benedict contributed to his glee, "that is some potent stuff!"

Weck extinguished the flame with a quick, single puff. Satisfied, he sunk back into his seat and took another swig.

Kane wasn't quite sure what to make of the author yet, and so he sat silently, allowing Benedict to do the talking. "So I take it you like your privacy," the reporter said affably, moving the conversation to the next phase.

Weck scoffed. "Hell no!" he said. "You think I like this? Livin' in this hole like a pig? I used to tell myself I did, but I wish things were how they used to be."

"And how's that?" Benedict asked.

"What do you mean?" the author seemed perplexed. "You don't know? Everyone used to love me! I was on television sometimes, and in the newspaper, my books were huge sellers—and I even knew some movie people; said they wanted to produce some of my stories."

"And…what happened?" Benedict prodded.

Weck took an enormous gulp, and his face grew disgusted. "They did me like Thomas Wolfe, that's what happened. One day Borley didn't like me, and then nobody liked me. As much money as I made that town, and everybody turned their back on me." He thought for a moment, and then his eyes gave way to a vicious spark. "I'm a creator! Do you know what I mean? *I create things*—people, places, stories. God loves people like me. You know why? 'Cause we're creators just like him."

The author was inflated with years of pain, resentment, and humiliation, and once it had surfaced, he welcomed the chance to relieve its pressure in a flood. He used bold, dramatic hand gestures as he spoke. "Yeah, you think people appreciate you," he continued. "But people

<178>

are stupid. They don't know talent when they see it. They gotta wait until you're long gone, rottin' in the coffin before they realize how great you were."

"I know what you mean," Benedict agreed. Barely conscious of his guest's words, the writer continued to rave.

"I mean some people say there's not a use for guys like me—that just because we don't build the houses and harvest the crops that we're nonessential. Well lemmie tell you somethin', there are two types of people in this world: practical people and creative people. Without the practical people we couldn't live, but without the creative people, life wouldn't be worth living. You catch my drift?"

Kane and Benedict nodded in agreement, each a bit intimidated. Their host was similar to Borley in some respects, drunken, idealistic, and preaching with a gun at his side. Perhaps that's why Borley wanted him dead.

Weck paused like he was done, and then his face lit with a new train of thought. "You ever think about how many people, in the history of time, have lived and died before us? Each and every one of them had their own story to tell—and to them, it was the most important story in the world. Learning, love, death, hate, triumph, and defeat—a whole lifetime's worth of tales. And yet how many of them will we never know about? How many have lived, struggled, and died that we will never even know existed? What's it all worth in a million years? I mean *really*—what's it all worth?

"Ol' Thomas Wolfe, yes he and I can relate. You know, when he died he was no big deal. Nobody really cared about him, just like me. But now—oh! Now, it's Thomas Wolfe Auditorium and Thomas Wolfe historical site, and Thomas Wolfe this and that. It's *Look Homeward Angel* the *classic*. Now they're proud of him. Proud they kicked his ass out o' town? Well I tell you one thing, wherever he may be today, heaven, hell or whatever, I hope he's lookin' down on the world like *this*..." He enthusiastically shot out his middle finger. "To hell with all of 'em!"

<179>

They all sat quietly for a bit, the guests assuming their host might continue, and the author submersed in his own grievous thoughts. The sun had sunk below the horizon, and a deep, gray shadow filled the room, continually dimming the light and projecting an eerie optical deformity on the inhabitants of the hovel. Weck reached across the table to access a kerosene lantern. Its stiff, metallic joints creaked, and its glass rattled. He took a moment to light it up, the soft, orange flame swelling to illuminate the surroundings cozily. The entire scene, with exception of Kane and Benedict, looked surprisingly olden, like a lost moment on the early American frontier.

The reporter noticed the vague form of a white, framed paper hanging on the wall across from the couch. It was the only item displayed. "Is that a diploma?" Benedict inquired.

"Hell no!" Weck's emotions were fired again. "That's a writing award. I wouldn't have a diploma. I don't believe in 'em."

"Oh," responded Benedict curiously, "and why's that?"

"There are too many dumbasses running around with 'em," he replied. "They hold no value for me anymore. It doesn't take any talent to get one—they're all educated fools, you know. Now this," he lifted a thick copy of one of his books from the table, "*this* takes talent. How many people do you know with a degree, and how many people do you know who wrote one o' these? If there's value in rarity, then this is definitely worth more than a damned ol' degree."

"I see," Benedict acknowledged, a bit unsurely.

"And you know who it is that tells the whole world you gotta have a degree?" Weck leaned in closer with a squint. "It's the colleges! That's who! They're the ones makin' all the money! Pretty good ploy, huh? It'd be sort o' like me sayin' 'you're a dumbass unless you buy one o' my books!' And the whole world falls for it! How's that for marketing?"

The reporter reflected on his words for a moment. "I see your point," he said. "I can certainly appreciate what it takes to produce voluminous, publishable writing."

<180>

"Ah hell," Weck brushed his hand and lowered his mood again, staring at the lantern. "Don't get me started on that stuff. I could go all night." He briskly raised his eyes to meet the stranger. "So what's this about killing Borley? We talkin' Crawford or J.C.?"

Kane and Benedict looked to each other curiously. "You mean," said the stranger, "you don't know about Crawford Borley?"

"Un uh," the author responded. "What? He dead or somethin'?"

"Yeah," Kane replied. "He died recently. Heart failure."

"Good," said Weck, having some more liquor. "I'll sleep a little better tonight. Wish it had been his bastard son, though."

"I believe we have something in common," the stranger said. "Borley wants both of us dead, just like you. We know he's a murderer, and we've been trying to stop him."

"Ahhh yes, J.C. Borley," Weck smiled. "I was going to tell the whole world the whole story. What a great book it would have been. But I went about it the wrong way. I was too ballsy. I should've been secretive about my work, but I was bold—overconfident. I thought the public would support me, but I was wrong. I marched right up to the Borleys and let them know that *I knew*. That was the mistake. I should've kept my mouth shut until the book had gone to press. But I didn't—and now, well, look where I am…all these years later."

Kane leaned forward intensely, his elbows on his knees, his hands clasped. "The *whole* story?"

"Yes. The whole story."

"And just what is the *whole* story?" Kane implored.

Weck chuckled slightly, fully aware of the worth and implications of his knowledge. "You wouldn't believe me if I told you. You'd say I was insane."

"Oh, and why's that?"

"Because there are things out there that most people don't believe in. Things most people never see. But that's what makes them so dangerous.

<181>

We don't fear the things we don't believe in. We don't guard against them. And by denying their existence, we make ourselves vulnerable to them."

"Mr. Weck," said Kane, calmly, "I would believe anything when it comes to the Borleys. So please, I urge you, tell us the whole story. It appears you have nothing to lose."

The writer leaned his head back, closed his eyes, and sighed euphorically. "If I wasn't drunk I'd tell you guys to go to hell," he said. "But I guess I need the company. Who knows?" he looked back at his guests, "you're probably sent by Borley to kill me at last—maybe you want to see how much I know first; but I don't give a damn. I'll tell you. I'll tell you if you really want to know, but it'll be *your own* death sentence. If Borley really does want you dead, he'll want you dead a lot more after you hear this."

"I'm afraid Borley could never want me gone as badly as I want him gone," Kane assured the writer.

"Very well," said Weck. "I'll tell you the whole story. It was a long time ago, the early 1900s, and it starts as most *whole* stories do…with a woman."

✳   ✳   ✳

The Evil Eye. That's what she had, or at least, that's what they said. And yet, she was still beautiful, a little too beautiful perhaps; too beautiful to be a witch. Witches are supposed to be ugly: gnarled and wicked, with stringy hair, rotten noses, and clubfeet. But she was enchanting. Even her eyes, those dark, evil eyes, sparkled like wanton jewels. She could hypnotize men with them, off the streets and into her bed, or she could cast a glare as salient and scorching as the devil's himself. And with such a leer, they believed she could transfer a curse; that she could visit blights, and sickness, and even death upon those weaker than her—those whose eyes would receive her damnation—those whose eyes were not

<182>

strong enough to deny it. And her hair. She had long curls of chocolate-brown hair that reached fully to her narrow waist. She was petite and shapely, feminine in every way, and magical, like a fairy of the woods.

Her name was Sareth Borley, and she lived in a cabin atop a great mountain, the rustic city of Asheville submitting below. She loved the seclusion of her home; the freedom she felt gazing down upon Asheville, veiled by a twinkling evening sky. But she was not a hermit, and she was rarely fierce at heart. There was a rich joy and depth in her soul, and a reckless, youthful passion in her spirit. She was indeed a practitioner of the black arts, a worshipper of the earth, spirits, and elements. But she reveled in her lifestyle with a giddiness akin to her darkness. On clear nights, she would dance naked in the forests, her flesh shimmering like silver in the moonlight. And on blazing days, she would wade into icy Blue Ridge waterfalls, the frothing liquid engulfing her in its powerful arms and soothing her with its hiss of a whisper.

To the people of Asheville, she was scandalous: a pagan temptress and whore. Though young, she lived in the cabin with her three children, each by a different father, and no regular man as a mate.

Her first child, a boy named Lawrence, was the product of a two-month fling with a young, local man. He was the academic type, of a strong Baptist background, and from a wealthy, high-class Asheville family. When he found out she was pregnant, he moved up north on a whim, never to be seen again. Accepting full responsibility for the child, she never publicized the identity of the father, respecting his family and the disgrace they would endure if their son's deeds were known by the community.

Her second child, a girl named Liza, was the result of a one-night-stand. To afford food for herself and Lawrence, Sareth prostituted herself to a burly, drunken logger in a seedy downtown bar. He was passing through Asheville on his way to a job in Jonesborough, Tennessee. He too was never seen again, but nine months later, the mistress gave birth.

<183>

But it was her third and final child who was borne from the most shocking of circumstances. The Christians of Asheville commonly gossiped about the harlot, and they warned their children to beware of the witch on the mountain. They told of her mating with the devil and worshipping evil beings by bonfire at night. And these rumors, having circulated enough, stirred up a growing frenzy with the "righteous" folks of the city. At such a time, one man decided he should look into the matter. He was a monk, and his name was Odin.

The Catholic population of Asheville had grown immensely when Vanderbilt brought the European architects over to work on his massive French Chateau. Therefore, the Catholic community had a strong support system, especially when compared to other early towns of the Appalachians. And though he was young, Odin was one of the most respected monks in the local church.

Odin was a handsome man, with deep, sculpted features and bright eyes. He was charismatic, idealistic and vigorous; devoted to his faith, and a leader in the service to his fellow man. He worshipped his Lord with unquestioned devotion, and strove to extend the tenderness of Christ to all those he met. After hearing so much about the unclean woman, the lost soul on the mountain, he decided to see her; to introduce her to his faith; to show her the path to salvation and deliver her from her pagan ways.

On a calm, summer day, Odin trekked up the rugged path to her notorious cabin. When he found her, he was immediately overcome by her beauty. And Sareth, too, was attracted to his naivete and optimism. He spoke kindly to her about the Lord, and she humored him playfully, looking through his religious exterior to see the innocent man beneath. She fixed him a hearty supper and he entertained the children with humor and slight of hand. She observed his exotic inner strength and passionate raw potential, and that very night, she privately fell in love with him.

<184>

Odin began visiting frequently, and with each visit, he talked less and less about religion. Instead, they discussed their bare philosophies, stories from their childhood, and their dreams for the future. He would play his hand-carved dulcimer, and they sang about the things they loved about life, and the parts that made them sad and empty. And slowly, though he wouldn't admit it to himself, Odin privately fell in love with Sareth, as well. As time progressed, his growing love led him to inevitable feelings. They were feelings he had never known before—feelings of shame and confusion—desires that he could not control. He was tortured by thoughts that began consuming him each day. He wanted to *know* Sareth—to taste her like other men had tasted her. He sought the scriptures to repress his swelling lust, but they provided little resolve.

At last, Odin decided their visits must end. He traveled to see her a final time, but Sareth knew his thoughts. When he arrived, she embraced him firmly, burying her face into his chest. Then, she professed her love in tearful whispers. Odin could no longer resist. He too spilled forth his inner feelings, and the damn of their passion erupted. She took him inside the cabin, and in an intoxicating frenzy of emotion, they wallowed in carnal exaltation.

From there, a torrid, forbidden love affair began. In secrecy, Odin visited her as often as possible, the rest of the time upholding his stature in the church as usual. Their relationship blossomed. Odin brought her money from the church to support her, and the two would indulge in each other's most intimate fantasies. His mind, once completely devoted to God, was now inundated with thoughts of Sareth. He couldn't wait until his days were done so he could slip away in the evenings and join his love on their secluded mountain.

With the passing of time, his thoughts turned more and more from God to more superficial elements of power and pleasure. Once weak with shame, he eventually became oblivious to his sins. As his thirst to know her grew little by little, he began exploring her culture and beliefs.

<185>

He began joining her on excursions into the forest at night; first clothed, and then later naked himself. He hungered for the freedom and inner control she knew. Sareth and her lifestyle were sensual and gratifying; they fulfilled him in ways that a life built on faith alone could not. And when finally he had accepted her completely, she introduced him to the source of her mystic capabilities.

By a bonfire, in the woods, cloaked by moonless heavens, she chanted and worshipped as Odin observed. She squirmed and wallowed like a submissive beast on the cold ground, and moaned as a presence filled her body. "He is here. The Sate is in me," she whispered, her sultry eyes rolled back in their sockets.

At first, Odin trembled fearfully as he watched the unseen spirit enter her. But eventually, with the passing of months, she convinced him to join. And so together, they worshipped The Sate, and The Sate gave them power. It granted Odin abilities that Christ would not bequeath him. He could see the future through his third eye. He could control the will of others. He could summon inhuman strength when needed, and he could make small objects quiver and move with a stern glare.

Once, deep in meditation, Odin's body lifted from the ground. Startled by the levitation, the monk opened his eyes to see the earth, a blur of color and texture, rolling on its axis beneath him; in fright, he dropped, finding himself far from his origin. Despite such miraculous powers, Odin had never seen The Sate, nor did he know its source. But in honor of the supernatural gifts, he continued to worship.

The monk submersed himself greedily in the dark ways, privately detesting the church, yet holding his post. His life became a joyous indulgence in physical pleasures, drunkenness, and deception, yet he was still an outwardly affable man. And soon thereafter, not surprisingly, Sareth was pregnant with his child. When she gave birth, they named the boy Crawford. It was the name of Sareth's own father.

Crawford was intelligent and soulful. He had an active imagination, and was filled with the depth of his parents. His relationship with his

<186>

father was especially strong. They would often take long walk on trails together, and Odin would teach the boy about science, philosophy, and the nature of man. Crawford absorbed new knowledge with alarming efficiency, asking a plethora of questions, and always drawing elaborate connections between the facts he'd learned. His memory was exceptional, and though Odin would have loved the boy regardless, he knew that little Crawford was especially capable of great things.

Odin's secret life parted from the church, yet he still wanted to celebrate Christmas. When the season visited in the fifth year of Crawford's life, Odin made special preparations. Despite Sareth's disapproval, he arrived at her cabin Christmas evening bearing gifts. The monk was a skillful carver, and he had hewn small idols for each of the children. To Lawrence he gave a tiny totem pole, ghoulish, grinning faces snarling at all sides. To Liza he gave a doll, patterned after her own appearance. But to Crawford, he gave two objects.

"A good, strong man must have two qualities," he said softly, kneeling before the boy. "And each quality must be balanced. He must be quiet, thoughtful, and intelligent like the owl." Odin slipped his hand into a velvet bag and withdrew a stone owl, its eyes closed. "Always introspective—always learning about himself and thinking about his meaning in life. And he must also be fierce, bold, and aggressive like the noble wolf." Again he reached into the bag. This time, a stone wolf, its eyes fiery with rage emerged. "The wolf is a hunter, quick and ferocious. He is also rugged and determined, always protecting those things he values—and at all costs."

Crawford's shiny eyes sparkled as he held the heavy, intricate carvings in his small hands.

"Keep these forever as reminders," said the monk. "You must always balance yourself between these two. If you ever find yourself more like one than the other, you are making a mistake. A good, strong man bears each in his heart." The boy was to never forget.

<187>

As time pressed onward, Odin's bond with Crawford strengthened. However, to an equal degree, his relationship with Sareth began to weaken. Gradually, she became bored with Odin. His presence became routine and familiar, and what was once a daring, adventurous affair lost its thrill. Helpless against her nature, she began longing for new experiences, and a distance developed between the lovers. She would snap at small things and utter cruel insults at him—calling him weak and spineless—unable to confess his true feelings to the world—living like a coward. Warmth was vacant in her touch, and she displayed irritation from his mere presence. He had invested his life and future in her, giving up all direction for which he'd previously lived. He felt helpless and alone by her rejection, unwilling to accept the growing coldness she projected. She observed his closeness to Crawford and began to loathe it as well. Her instincts were restless for a new lover, but Odin would not make way. Even though she gave him strong signals of her feelings, he stayed to share time with the boy.

One evening Odin journeyed to the cabin, a hefty roast for the family slung over his shoulder. But when he arrived he found Sareth engaged with another man. He was at first in shock, and then enraged by the scene. There was a huge, intense, wicked fight. Odin and Sareth screamed and cursed, slinging and bashing objects from wall to wall of the hovel. The other man escaped through a window, fearful for his life, and the three children, awakened, cowered under their beds. The fight roared on for hours, and then, in a burst of black, sinister emotion, Sareth spat forth a lie—a lie of such magnitude that it would strike deep in Odin's spirit. She wanted only to hurt him, and so she screamed that he was not Crawford's father—that the other man, long gone down the mountain, had supplied the seed—that she had seen him all along. The lie did its filthy job, clenching that sacred, vulnerable spot deep inside the lost monk's soul. He was quiet and dazed. His head swirled with a shadow that swallowed him from all sides, and a perfect, sickening

<188>

silence stole away his ears. Odin had broken. He turned and walked away, into the night, the witch left alone, sobbing, ragged on the floor.

Odin retreated into the dark, private chambers of his church. For weeks he fasted and begged God to take his wretched life. His Christian mindset took form again, and he viewed himself with horror. The monk cried and prayed day and night, pounding his fists bloody on the rough stone walls. He scrubbed his body with holy water and recited scripture and Catholic verse incessantly. And then one day, in a single instant, he felt himself cleansed—cleansed and mighty—but different than before. He stood tall and viewed his unkempt visage in a mirror. With a razor, he shaved his face and head clean, and then, after eating a small meal and making a few special preparations for the day, he walked into the sunlight and breathed fresh air. He was a different man.

The hurt, the neglect, the loneliness he'd felt was repressed inside a stone cold exterior. Only one emotion remained at the forefront of his mind: anger. His power and reputation as a man of God was still strong, and so he set forth throughout the city of Asheville, preaching biting words of infectious enthusiasm, his charisma deadly. "There is a harlot on that mountain! A witch! She is a worshipper of Satan and a harbinger of sickness and death upon our good town!"

The long-concealed paranoia of the people broke out in a flood of hysteria. "Let's get her!" was the cry of the citizens. "Let's take her off that damn mountain! Asheville is a God fearing town!" Hordes of men from all walks of life—farmers, barbers, vagabonds, even policemen, joined in the war cries. "Let's get rid o' that damn whore!" Emotion ran rampant and a mob was soon formed. Odin enlisted the assistance of the other monks who admired and trusted him completely. They took their crucifixes and vials of holy water, and stood completely at service by Odin's side. After gathering a few more tools of medieval practice, the mob marched up the trail to Sareth's cabin. Odin, stern and sharp, nostrils flared with vengeance, led them. He carried a tall, ebony staff with a silver crucifix gleaming at the top. With each step, he thrust it

<189>

forward into the soft ground and pulled himself towards it; as if perhaps his Christian duty led him proudly onward.

Clubs and shovels in hand, the group, insane with fury, reached the top of the mountain. They stormed the cabin, their shouts exploding over the valley below. Sareth screamed as a tangle of groping, merciless hands gripped each inch of her body and clothes. Fabric ripped, clumps of hair were torn away, and strong masculine force bent and squeezed her delicate feminine form. An ocean of mad, voracious flesh engulfed her and carried her away, leaving a wrecked, trampled cabin behind.

"Keep the children safe!" Odin ordered the toiling crowd.

Lawrence and Liza had been playing behind the house, and they shrieked, golden tears dripping from their cheeks, to see their mother being carried away. Spotted by members of the group, they too were chased. "Somebody get them babies!" Strong arms swept them effortlessly off the ground and carried them away, writhing and kicking. Crawford watched from a short distance, his face peeking out from behind a large rock.

The boy was deadly still until he saw the chaotic crowd had turned its back. With that, he ran frantically as fast as his feet would carry him. Never looking back, he dashed down the craggy mountainside and followed a rabbit trail towards the cove beside the mountain. He knew there was a cave in the cove—a gaping hole of blackness sheltered by bushes and shelves of protruding outer stone that made it hard to see. His father had taken him there before and told him of how endless were the caves; of the network that webbed deep into the mountain; of how soldiers had hidden there during the Civil War, and how impossible it would be to find someone hiding within. It was there that he'd first seen a bat, and fish as pale as a winter's snowfall.

When he reached the entrance of the cave, open like the crooked, decayed mouth of a secret, he slipped inside. With only a few steps, he was submersed in chilled blackness. Backing up and burrowing himself in behind a jutting edge of stone, he sat quietly, save his own breath.

<190>

Sharp pains split down his chest when he tried to suppress the pumping of his panicked lungs. Faintly, he could still hear the horrid sounds of the mob on the mountain above. The dull murmur of the crowd was pierced by his mother's helpless screams and pleas.

Above, Sareth was lying on the dirt, her hands and feet bound with thick, dry rope. Each turn was pulled fast by several men. With a "crunch," both her wrists had broken instantly when the ropes had tightened around them, her arms twisted behind her back. Beneath the cord, her flesh had been wrenched from the bone by the friction of the prickly strands. She begged for mercy, but those around her only spit on her, kicked her, and threw handfuls of dirt in her splotched face.

After giving certain people secret orders, Odin, accompanied by other men of the cloth, mumbled over scripture ceremoniously. The rest of the mob combed the forest for kindling and firewood. It was a confusing mass of motion and noises, the intense emotion of hatred permeating the entire area. Though there were few women around, one old nanny sat with Lawrence and Liza, hugging them close against her bosom and speaking with soothing tones. "Now don't you worry. We're gonna get you both good parents. Your momma's bad. Real bad. But there are good people who will love you." She planted a slobbery kiss on their flushed cheeks.

Within a short while, a large pile of wood had been gathered. Sareth was barely conscious, drained by mental exhaustion and pain. A long, sturdy stick was slid between her arms and legs, and two brawny men lifted the stick from each end, carrying her like an animal being hauled to slaughter. They stood her up on the firewood, lodged the stick into the crevices of the pyre, and tied her to the stake.

Odin looked to her, his face distant, blank, and determined. The Holy Bible rested in his long, smooth fingers, and he glanced to it, as if acknowledging the authority it placed in him, and returned his eyes to the limp, battered form, bound mercilessly before him. Once, he had loved this flesh, but now, he could scarcely see it as a human life.

<191>

Instead, it was a concept—a sinner—a being of unrighteousness—a worshipper of evil spirits—a deceiver of man. It was the enemy.

"The devil does not come with horns and cloven hooves," Odin announced, the mob suddenly quiet and respectful. "From these things we would run. The devil comes in those forms that appeal to us the most." An ocean of heads nodded, proud and self-assured. "He comes to us with riches and pleasures that are beautiful. We do not catch a fish by placing an unfavorable morsel on the hook. We find those things a fish loves most, and his weakness for the food is what draws him to his death." Again, nods. "The devil tries to draw us all. And sometimes, even the best of us fall victim. However, once we realize there are agents of the devil working to entrap others in his snare, we must rid the world of them. It is our duty to take their lives before they bear the burden of more lost souls on their own judgement day. Take this woman, for example. Though she is unknowing of her own wrongdoing, she has ruined many lives. For her own sake, we must purify her and deliver her unto God. We, as Christians, will not stand for agents of the devil to wander amongst us!"

The crowd cheered gleefully, overjoyed to be good people. Odin flipped a few pages, read some scripture, then continued. "This book—" he held it high, "*This book* was written by God! This book carries God's commands! Each of us shall be accountable, shall reap what we sow, and *you*," he pointed to the suffering woman, "have sowed evil. Your blood surges with unclean wickedness. And I curse it! I curse your unclean blood and the fruit of your evil deeds!" Odin squeezed his eyes closed tightly, clenched his right fist, and a stream of Latin bubbled from his lips. When he opened them again, he screamed, "Today, we cleanse your soul for God!"

Motion stirred at the edge of the crowd, and bodies moved aside to make way for a handful of men parting the group. An animalistic grunting could be heard, and the man up front, apparently a rugged farmer, was tugging something on a leash.

<192>

"We will follow the example set by the Bible in cleansing you witch!" cried Odin. The men having made their way to the monk, it was at last visible: a fat, uncooperative pig was struggling at the other end of the taut leash. It was gray and hairy, thick, shiny mucous oozing at its snout. Fear and cognizance emanated from its stocky body, and it sealed the eerie, primitive, gothic madness in the air.

Odin, his robe flowing majestically, stepped over to the pile of wood, Sareth mounted above. He reached out his milky hand and stroked her chin lovingly. One last time, he felt the tiniest spark of warmth in their touch, and then his fingers elevated, and spreading his hand, he palmed the crown of her head as firmly as he could. His joints quivering from the exuded pressure, he clenched his teeth. His eyes bulged with insanity, and casting them upon the writhing swine, he shouted more Latin. As the volume of his voice grew, so did the discoloration of his squeezing knuckles. It seemed her skull might crush in like a cantaloupe, rescuing her from the torturous death to come.

Beads of sweat formed on Odin's brow, and as he continued chanting the twisted, ancient words, a nearly unbearable heat began to churn in Sareth's chest. She could scarcely breathe at first, and as its intensity grew, whatever wind she had was used for screaming in pain. Her face contorted, her cheeks turned yellow, and she heaved forth a chunky mass of vomit. Still, she strained and groaned, saliva dribbling from the corner of her mouth. She made horrific, inhuman sounds, cold chills passing throughout the mesmerized crowd like an icy breeze. Alas, a long shadow, faint but visible, streamed from her howling mouth; against its will, it followed the line of Odin's pointing index finger, gliding fifteen feet through the air, and slipping into the mouth of the pig like a blacksnake escaping to its burrow. Immediately, the creature reared back in a spasm, squealing and shrieking like a whipped child.

In an instant, the eyes of the swine were wide and human, filled with horror, and with supernatural strength, it bolted. Its owner, firmly grasping the leash, was jerked powerfully forward, his feet flying from

<193>

beneath him and his chin plowing into the dirt. The leather strip burned as it ripped easily from his sprained fingers, and the pig raced away, deep, immortal grumblings escaping its small mouth.

"Capture that pig!" Odin commanded. "I have cast the demon into him!"

A trail of screeching heads popped up among the crowd, marking the path of the fleeing creature through the onlookers. They panicked as the stiff hair and hot breath of the beast rushed past their legs. A group of men flew after him, reacting militaristically to the monk's order. As the pig disappeared into the forest, the men sprinting after it, Odin returned his attention to Sareth.

"I have cleansed your soul," he said, "and now I shall cleanse your unclean body. Do you accept Christ as your savior?" Sareth's brain had been bruised, and Odin's words sounded like a dream. She could not respond. "Very well!" Odin cried. "Light the pyre!"

Within moments, the wood beneath Sareth's feet was crackling with flames. They did not have a flammable liquid, and so the fire burned slowly. It nipped first at the woman's toes, initiating her ear-piercing screams. Her dress was quickly engulfed, and her vocal cords were soon broken by her agonizing cries as the sharp, pitiless flames began feeding on her sensitive flesh. The unimaginable intensity swallowed her in light. Her skin bubbled up with surprising resiliency, rising in large spheres before popping like bubblegum. Her beautiful locks of hair spit sparkles of flame and, swiftly consumed, the hair nearly appeared to melt and drip from the skull, instead of scorch off like strings. The pungent, unique smell of the burning flesh and hair filled the crowd's nostrils, and Sareth was soon a squirming, jerking body of fire. Once her clothes had fallen away, she appeared like a black, bald, emaciated body writhing beneath the inferno. It took longer than they'd expected for her sickening cries to dwindle, and even then the body continued twitching as the blaze fed. They said she couldn't feel it at that point, though. Only nerves.

<194>

The crowd was quiet and entranced by the sight. Many were unexpectedly disturbed: some puked and others left. However, most were righteous and enthusiastic. As they watched the witch burn, they were overcome with a sense of satisfaction and accomplishment. After all, pagan worshippers had been killed in the Bible, their deaths commanded by God himself. Sure, it wasn't a pretty sight, but it was still the wish of the Lord—at least in the Old Testament. Within Odin, there was a great sense of peace.

Even after the body had burned a while, the blaze was still working its way through the crispy corpse. Suddenly, the shrieks of the swine could be heard again. All heads turned to see six brawny men tugging the leash, dragging the animal, kicking and resisting with all its might, to meet Odin. When they arrived, the pig continued to seizure.

"Be still demon, I command you!" the monk raised his hand. The beast stopped, still pulling back on the cord and grunting heavily, its breathless chest pounding. Its glaring pupils, chillingly man-like and intelligent, focused on Odin from the corners of its bloodshot eyes.

"Demons do not die," the monk growled, "but since you are a creature of darkness, in darkness you shall spend eternity." He raised his head high. "Bring forth the box!"

Two other monks marched from behind Odin. Between them they carried the form of a box, perhaps three feet wide and tall, cloaked by a black, draping cloth. They set it gingerly in front of the pig and removed the covering. The container beneath was dull and metallic, solid at all sides except for the front, which was hinged to make a door. On the front there was a crucifix, constructed from holes punched in the metal, and at the edge of the door was a lip through which a lock, of the padlock type, could be easily inserted.

"In the box with him," ordered Odin.

Instantly, the swine exploded in a tormented rage again. Those holding the leash gritted their teeth, biceps bulging, to contain the wild force. They dragged the pig towards the open mouth of the receptacle,

<195>

its stubborn feet digging trenches in the soil. Others positioned the box in front of the animal. The beast flipped erratically from side to side, avoiding its destination and twisting the arms of those attempting to control it. More members of the crowd came to help, some using sticks and shovels to poke and jab the pig, driving it towards the box. The swine's eyes swelled with terror as the cold, sterile opening slid closer and closer. At last, its strained legs gave out, and the creature's plump body hurtled into the small, metallic enclosure, the door slamming behind it with incredible finality.

Odin towered over the box like a staunch statue. In his right fist, he held his long, black staff high, its silver crucifix gleaming at the pinnacle. He cut his eyes to the bulging door, the swine thrusting against it from the inside, and turned his staff upside down. In one last gesture of closure, he spat a furious line of Latin, and then lifted the stick upwards like a weapon. With a mighty burst of emotion, he brought it down like a bolt of lightning; the air shattered by a divine clash of metal; the crucifix jamming into the latch, breaking off from the staff with "snap." The container was locked with a silver crucifix. Try as it may to escape, the delirious animal was sealed inside by the power of God.

The crowd erupted with cheers. The witch had been burned and the demon was captured. It seemed an enormous victory. The triumphant cries of the maddened mob rang out across the land, and hidden in his cave, trembling with fear, young Crawford Borley could hear it, too. When he heard the cheers, he knew his mother was dead.

Pale and entranced by shock, Crawford sat in the bleak cave, once in a while gazing back at the morbid abyss behind him, waiting to hear the noises of the crowd disappear. A long, grievous hour passed, and in the course, the sounds above him dwindled somewhat. And then, new noises took their place—closer ones—the sounds of footsteps coming near the cave. "Here," Odin's faint voice could be heard. "There is a cave back here. Bring it in here."

<196>

The small boy was petrified to see a form break the pale, uneven light pouring in at the mouth of the cavern. It was the silhouette of a man wearing a hat. He stuck his head in, unsure and curious at first, and then motioned behind him. "I'll be," he said with a Southern drawl, "I didn't know there was a cave here." Other figures joined him, and Crawford silently scurried farther back into the moist blackness. Then, Odin's form stepped into view.

"Yes, in here," he said, speaking to those behind him. "This is where I'll seal him away." The boy could hear the muffled grunts and groans of the pig inside the container. Its hooves scraped sharply against the metal floor. Within moments, the opening was crammed with figures clearing a short pathway and hauling the box inside. The container was being carried between three men, and each time it tilted, the body of the pig could be heard sliding across the metal and hitting the side with a "thud."

"Where should we put it Odin?" someone asked.

"That's not important," he replied. "Just set it firmly against the wall, behind those rocks."

As the cave recessed, its floor inclined, and having crawled deeper inside, Crawford watched the dusky action below, far enough away to remain undetected. The images stirring about below him, oblivious to his eyes, seemed unreal. They moved in black and white, busy and intent, disposing of a locked up pig as if it was a monster. It was barbaric and medieval, and it heightened the trauma wrenching the boy's mind.

Once the box was in place, Odin ordered everyone out of the cave. "Now we must seal it up," he said, pointing at the edge of the entrance like an engineer. "We have to make sure no one finds this abomination." Crawford's heart dropped. At first, he wasn't sure he'd understood the monk's words correctly, and so he listened more closely. "That's it," Odin continued, "rocks, logs, vines, whatever will fill this hole—for now, anyway, until we can seal it up better."

The boy wanted to call out to his father—to tell him that he was in the cave. To rush out, tears in his eyes, and bury his head in his father's

<197>

cloak like he had so many times before. But this was not his father—not the one he had known, anyway. This man was cold and harsh. He was a murderer, and a distant spouter of verse, detached from emotion. Crawford wanted to explode with all his heart, but he could not overcome the paralyzing fear. Stunned, he closed his eyes and sat silently, nestling closer to icy stone which shielded him, imagining perhaps it was the warm touch he had once known.

The men went to work, and by the time the sun had disappeared from the sky, the entrance to the cave was nearly sealed. The voices of the men grew fainter and fainter as they added layers upon the tightly packed timbers and brush. The boy watched as the last, hazy strip of light was snuffed away. He was alone in total and complete blackness; the only element of humanity, the fading voices outside.

When finally the murmurs outside were gone, the cave grew eerily silent. Once in a while a grunt echoed slightly, but after a while, even those noises ceased. Crawford, his knees scraped, and his face dusty, sat like a stone himself, the cavern so dark he couldn't see his hand an inch from his face. All he could do was listen. He listened as he breathed the cool air in his nostrils, the blackness weighing upon him like birth and death. Gradually, the silence dissolved into the obscure hush of what may have been water running deep within the abyss, and the sharp resonance of a "drip" would startle him from time to time. These were sounds previously hidden by his thumping heart, but now, they were his only perceptions of the world. He was blind, alone, and cold.

No one knew he was in the cave. His mother was dead. There was no light. And he was hungry. After hours had passed, the boy's sanity was already slipping. He wondered if he might in fact be dead—if perhaps he was in hell. But despite his circumstances, he was gifted with a strong mind. He remembered what his father—the father he had once known—told him: one must be like the owl and the wolf, thoughtful and aggressive. He knew if he was not yet dead, he would be soon. He would have to find his way to the entrance and attempt to dig out.

<198>

Crawford stood up and he heard a few pebbles roll away from his feet. The rock floor was slippery and smooth, and he was almost immediately disoriented. The flat spots of the floor sometimes gave way to sharp, jagged ridges without warning. He dropped down on his hands and sore knees, and inched along like an animal, feeling his way with the tips of his fingers. He thought he could perceive himself traveling down the incline, blood rushing into his swirling head. After thirty minutes, his fingers unexpectedly reached a wall. He had no idea where he was, and so he sat up for a moment, resting, trying to calm his dizziness. Again the silence closed in around him, and he sat there for a long time. Suddenly, the silence was broken.

"*I see you,*" a deep, raspy voice rumbled in the blackness. A painful surge of fright electrified the youth. Then there was breathing. "Where go you boy?" the voice said, "haven't you eyes for the darkness?"

The voice was clear, masculine and evil, and paralyzed, Crawford could not tell if it spoke from in front of him or behind him, and from how far away. Had lights switched on, it may have been inches from his own face.

"Speak young Crawford. There's no reason to fear me. Your father and mother know me." With those words, light appeared in the cave for the first time. Blurry at first from his unadjusted eyes, the boy saw a purple crucifix glowing ten feet away. It was the perforated cross on the door of the box. The light came from within the container and streamed through the holes of the crucifix. Each stone, shape, and crevice of the cavern reflected a ghostly violet lining. "There you are," the voice said. "There is light."

The boy was choked by a knot in his throat, and too horrified to move or breathe. He sat plastered against the wall, tears rising in his eyes, so scared that his fear was a physical pain. The light brought him little peace.

"You had may as well calm yourself," said the voice from the box. "I am your only way out, and I promise I will not hurt you." For half an

<199>

hour Crawford sat silent, struggling to comprehend his state. Finally, he mustered the courage to speak.

"Who are you?"

"I am different things to different people," he answered. "To your mother I was God. To your father I am a demon. Some call me The Sate."

"You…you sound scary," mumbled the boy.

"I am your friend Crawford," the demon replied. "Be fooled not by my voice. I, like you, am a victim of cruelty. Now we are locked away together in this dreadful cave. But if you help me, I shall help you."

Crawford relaxed a bit, staring at the spectral, blazing crucifix. "What do you mean?" he asked.

"I can get us out of here," he said. "But first you must release me."

"You're a monster," said Crawford. "If I let you out you might kill me. I'm digging out myself." The boy crawled speedily over to the entrance of the cave and began scooping out handfuls of debris.

"It doesn't matter," The Sate called from behind. "Even if you get out, your father has cursed you."

Crawford stopped. "What are you talking about?"

"Before he murdered your mother, he cursed her blood. Her blood runs in your veins, does it not?"

"What's a curse?" the boy, ceaselessly curious, asked.

"Sometimes, if you say things, and you mean them enough, they come true," hissed the voice. "Especially in the holy name. Your father uttered a curse, and it will follow you the rest of your life. And if you live to see children, it will follow them. And their children's children. Your brother and sister are doomed, but I can save you."

"What kind of a curse?" Crawford crinkled his brow. "What will happen?"

"Horrible things," answered the demon. "Things that will follow you forever. Things that will take away all you love."

"But, why would he do that?" asked the boy, crawling a bit closer to the box.

<200>

"Because your father harbors hatred, and evil is borne of hatred. He hated your mother, and he hated his sins. And you, little Borley, you are the product of his sins. And so he hates you, too."

Crawford crawled even closer as he spoke. "What if you're lying? What if you just want out so you can do bad things?"

"Lying?" The demon laughed sardonically. "You are locked up with me, and your father has killed your mother. Who should you believe? Me, or him?"

The boy stopped, reflecting on the words, and tears came to his eyes again.

"Little Borley, you are capable of great things. You are just a child, but you know it in your own heart. And I can help you become great. I can make good things happen in your life if you will help me."

"Help you? How?"

"Remove the crucifix from the lock. Free me and I will free you."

"And then what?"

"And then I will make you great. I will build you a castle on this mountain, and bring you wealth if you serve me."

"Serve you?" said the boy. "What do you want?"

"What do I want?" replied the voice. "I want what God wants. I want to be worshipped."

"I'll never worship you," said Crawford.

"But you will bring worshippers to me. And if anyone defies you, I will devour them."

The boy grew close to the box, squinting from the rays of light in his eyes. The silver crucifix, inverted, a fraction of the broken staff still at its top, winked like a jewel. Crawford looked at the mound sealing off the cave, and then back to the box, the voice tempting him like a snake.

"Yes, little Borley, I can make you powerful. I can give you great things. Just remove the crucifix and set me free. Yes, little Borley, we will rule together…"

<201>

The boy wrapped his fingers around the shiny cross, and with all his might, he pulled. In an instant, it broke loose, and the sinister power inside was released.

✳   ✳   ✳

John Weck's glossy eyes were half open, his body slumped, and his empty glass dangling from his fingertips. The lantern light had been slowly dying, and was now a bouncing radiance that lapped gently at the shabby room.

"After Borley let him out," Weck continued, "the demon took him deep inside the caves—raised him. And when he got older, the demon helped make him rich, just like he'd promised. And Borley built his castle on the top of the mountain, where his mother's cabin had been; the townspeople had burned it down." Weck placed his glass on the table, just before it slipped from his grasp. "And he kept the demon locked away in a room in the castle, where Crawford would feed his enemies to it. Anybody who goes in there, other than a Borley, gets killed. They put a slot on the door so the Borleys could stick their fingers in before they entered—to let the demon sniff them so he'd know it was them, and he wouldn't get them when they walked inside."

Kane and Benedict sat transfixed after the long tale. Glued to their sunken seats, hidden in shadow, their minds both crawled and raced with separate thoughts. After a moment of reflection, the stranger spoke. "That's quite a story," he said solemnly. "And you're right. It is hard to believe."

"But now, what's this part about being worshipped?" Benedict asked, a bit more serious about the tale.

"Every successful person in Asheville is tied into Borley money," Weck slurred. "And they pay their dues for it. There's a place called The Devil's Circle, not far from the cave, and everyone from the mayor to

<202>

the chief of police worship The Sate there—or, as some call it today, The Horror. And ya know, these mountains are the best place in the world to worship the devil. Look how nice and secluded it is around here. Ya never know what's just over the next ridge—or maybe down in the narrow bowl between two hills—all covered up with trees and bushes."

Kane glanced to Benedict and rolled his eyes subtly. At this point, Weck seemed little more than a ranting drunk. Benedict ignored the gesture, immensely interested in the writer's story.

"This cave," said the reporter, "can it be accessed today?"

Weck looked down and frowned, seemingly unsure of the best way to answer. "Well," he groaned, "supposedly, a couple days after Odin sealed the cave with debris, he came back with some workers and sealed it properly. He had a metal door installed at the mouth of the cave, sealed around the sides with mortar."

"A door?" said Kane.

"Yeah," responded Weck. "I've seen it myself. It's a metal door with a lock that looks like a wolf. But you can't get it open. Odin was the only one with a key. And, according to legend, he hid the key in the St. Lawrence Catholic Church."

"Basilica of St. Lawrence?" Benedict perked.

"Yeah, yeah," confirmed the writer. "In the tomb with Guastavino." Benedict's eyes lit up.

"Guastavino?" Kane asked, confused.

"Yes," chirped Benedict. "He was the builder of the church. But when he died, he asked to be entombed in its walls." He instantly returned his attention to Weck. "So these caves, where do they lead?"

"Well that's just the thing," answered Weck. "There was a passageway installed from the caves to the dungeon of Borley's Castle. I mean this network of caves runs right underneath it." With that, Kane's eyes lit up as well. "But you can't access the castle through the caves anymore. Back in the 70s, Crawford Borley rerouted some of the springs and flooded the caverns. He was afraid of people entering the castle that way."

<203>

"So they're filled with water," asked Benedict. Weck nodded. "But if you can unlock the door, you could still possibly find a way to get into the castle."

"I suppose," the drunkard sighed. "But you'd have to get that key."

"To hell with a key," Kane sat up. "I can pick a lock."

"No, no," Weck smiled. "You don't understand. It's not that kind of lock. It's the kind of lock without a lock, if that makes any sense."

Kane and Benedict looked to each other with a curled brow. "You see," Weck continued, "it's not mechanical, it's mystical, just like everything else. There's a keyhole but no lock. It's not about the lock. It's about the right key—just like the cage the demon was in."

Neither Benedict nor the stranger completely understood the writer, and by this point, he was almost struggling to speak coherently. "All right," said the reporter, urgency in his voice, "where exactly is this door?"

Weck pointed in the air a few times, "It's uh…uh…in the cove. You know that cove behind the mountain. Down there behind the castle. It's…ah, you'll find it if you look hard enough—unless it's been overgrown or somethin'."

"Look," said Kane authoritatively, rising from his seat, partly stretching, "I can see you're pretty tired, but just let me ask you two more questions. One, if your story is true, why didn't Odin just banish the demon instead of locking it up? And two, why would it kill Crawford Borley?"

"Kill Crawford Borley?" Weck frowned, "What are you talking about?"

"Never mind," said Kane. "So what about the demon?"

"You can't banish a demon," said the writer. "That's all bull. All you can do is lock 'em up like that…" his last word sort of dribbled from his mouth, and his guests knew he was almost gone.

"Was anyone ever tried for murdering the witch?" asked Benedict, springing from his seat, eyes wide.

"Oh there was some interest," Weck replied. "Some law investigated, but nobody was ever charged. Too many were in on it."

<204>

The writer's head fell, and his weighty eyelids slowly, barely opened and closed. Kane and Benedict could see it was time to go. Each looked to the other and gave a nod. The stranger reached into his back pocket and withdrew a thin, leather wallet. He removed a hundred dollar bill and laid it quietly on the table, beside the jug of moonshine.

"Thanks for your time," Kane said.

"Yes," added Benedict. "We certainly appreciate it." Weck's head popped up with a snort, and he smiled, brushing his fingers through the air. The two men turned and, floor creaking disastrously, made their way towards the door. Just as they reached it, Benedict was overcome by one final question. He paused, deciding whether or not to ask, and then zipped back around. "One more thing, Mr. Weck," he raised his finger.

The writer's bloodshot eyes opened wide, and he lifted his head attentively. "Yeah, sure."

"If you don't mind my asking," responded the reporter, "what were you going to call your book?"

"Huh?"

"Your book," stressed Benedict. "You know, the one about the Borleys. What were you going to call it?"

"Oh, oh, Weck regained his train of thought. Well," he said, as if an extra bit of information would prelude his answer, "most people never notice it, but the word 'Asheville' has the word 'evil' right in the middle of it. See," he spelled, "A-S-H-E-V-I-L-L-E. You catch it?"

Benedict shook his head affirmatively. "Huh—how 'bout that? I've never noticed that."

"And so," said Weck, "I was going to call the book, *The Evil in Asheville.* Get it?"

The reporter smiled. "Yes. Clever. Very clever."

"Good night," Kane said to Weck, the writer already slipping away again. With that, Kane and Benedict passed through the door.

The walk back to their car was dark and treacherous, though a wide, country sky, riddled with silver stars, glowed far above them. Benedict

<205>

took his jingling keys from his pocket, and with a delicate squeeze, a vague circle of light emitted from his keychain. "There we are," he said, satisfied by the meager beacon. Once they'd distanced themselves from the shack, they drew closer to each other, whispering their thoughts.

"What do you think?" asked the reporter.

"I don't know about the moonshine," Kane replied, "but that story was about seventy percent alcohol if you ask me."

"You don't believe it?" the reporter said.

"I just think Mr. Weck there has been starved for an audience for a long, long time. Once he had one, he just wanted to do what he does best—tell entertaining stories."

"So you don't think there's anything to it?" Benedict asked, his voice retaining a sense of skepticism about the stranger's viewpoint.

"Well I'm sure there are morsels of fact," said Kane, "but that's all pretty farfetched."

As they approached the car, it looked like a neglected creature, cringing alone on the mountainside. The expanse beside it was an overwhelming display of astronomy. Once securely in the vehicle, Kane checked the back seat thoroughly, making sure a henchman was not lying in wait.

"I think we should at least look for the cave, don't you?" Benedict said, sliding the key into the ignition, but not yet starting the engine.

"Sure," the stranger replied. "I don't suppose we have any better leads."

"But what if they're flooded like Weck says?" the reporter relaxed in his seat, gazing off in thought.

"What's the matter?" asked Kane. "You can swim can't you?"

<206>

CHAPTER EIGHT

KINNER DIDN'T HEAR the dark-clad men come in the front door of his shop just before nine in the evening. Having locked up earlier, he was working late, hunched over a pile of bookkeeping in the back room. His one good eye scanned dates and figures furiously, the other gazing uselessly into the empty coldness of the cluttered room. Despite the absorbing distraction of paper work, his handicap made it even easier for the figures to creep up quietly, seizing him in his chair. Terror clenched the merchant's heart when warm, gloved fingers gripped his mouth, and strong hands held his scrawny arms tight against the back of his rickety chair. A would-be scream was little more than an intense, muffled moan.

Having no right periphery, Kinner strained to force his left eye far into the corner of its socket, struggling in vain for a glimpse of his assailants. At any moment, he nearly expected the icy blade of a knife to slide smoothly, deeply across his throat. Instead, he was spun around effortlessly, to see two other men standing, bundled like gangsters, before him. They each stepped aside, and in the doorway stood the towering form of J.C. Borley.

The rich man was sealed securely in a black, wool trench coat, an equally dark fedora skillfully seated on his large head. His eyebrow was cocked dashingly, and a familiar smirk curled his lip. Silent for a moment, he observed Kinner with humor, though the merchant quivered with the docile fear of a captured hare. Taking a few steps inside, Borley winked to the unseen men behind the victim.

<207>

"I believe that'll do," Borley remarked casually. The men released their hold. Breathing deeply with a half-hearted sense of relief, Kinner sat frozen, his good eye bulging with bewilderment and fright. For the first time, he saw the men who had been behind him. Brock and a burly assistant walked around to face the seated merchant. They smiled cynically at him, as if condescending on his level of fear—chuckling in a bullying sort of way.

"Mr. Kinner!" Borley exclaimed jovially, "I do hope you'll forgive this unexpected intrusion. Sorry to grab you in such a way, but we feared you might keep a gun handy."

Though the room was full of smiles, Kinner eyed everyone with dire uncertainty, perceptive enough to sense impending doom. Nonetheless, he forced a smile. "Why, why Mr. Borley. I, I haven't seen you in…"

"Yes, yes, I know," Borley cut him off, plopping down heartily in a nearby chair. "By the way, how's that eye?"

Kinner looked down for a moment. "Well, it's, uh—"

"Ah," said Borley, opening his own gloved hands, "I know. Forgive me. What kind of a question is that?" Pathetically, Kinner dropped his head again. The rich man watched him quietly, sarcastic in his artificial sympathy. Finger by finger, Borley tugged at his snug gloves, removing them in a very deliberate way. "If you don't mind my saying, you've certainly aged my friend."

"Yes," Kinner replied. "Times have been tough."

"Oh, I'm sorry to hear that," Borley responded. "Age has done me well though. I've settled down a good deal in my maturity. I'm not nearly so vicious as I once was. I'm sure you're glad to hear that." Borley's gloves were off, and he wringed them firmly in his hands.

"Yes, yes," replied Kinner, his speech infirm, "that is good to hear."

"Well," said Borley, still twisting the gloves, a silver ring on his right hand catching the light, "I wish I could say this was a friendly visit. However, I can see you're a busy man, so I'll get right to the point."

The merchant nodded.

<208>

"It seems we have a mutual friend," the rich man bellowed. "A certain Mr. Kane. Ring a bell?"

Kinner thought for a second. "No."

Without hesitation, almost expectant of the answer, Borley gave a quick nod. Immediately, Brock grabbed Kinner's right wrist, twisting it back painfully. As the merchant yelped, Brock slid a chair beneath himself, not loosening the grip at all, and sat down. He stared at Kinner wickedly, relaxed in his seat as if intending to stay for a while.

"Now Kinner," Borley leaned forward, his voice almost scolding, "I, like you, am also a very busy man. So I'd certainly appreciate your complete honesty in this matter. It'll make things better for the both of us."

"But I swear! I don't remember!" Kinner's true emotions burst forth.

Borley erected an intolerable forefinger. "Un, un, uh," he shook his head from side to side. "Now see. There you go wasting a bit more of my precious time. Each time deceitful words come out of your mouth, you've wasted time—for both of us. And in order to show you that Mr. Borley is not here to play, I'm going to have to help you tell the truth." Again, he gave a motion to Brock.

Gleefully, the thug reached into his coat pocket and produced a large pair of toenail clippers. Reveling the instrument, he snapped them twice. The thin, metal jaws clicked like the tiny teeth of a sinister mammal. Kinner's face was ghastly.

"What's the matter?" Borley patronized. "Scared? You think that's scary? A simple pair of clippers?" He laughed to himself. "That's not scary, my friend. I'll tell ya what's scary: What's scary is waking up in the middle of the night to see flames. Now, *that's* scary; right Brock?"

His fat face red, Brock chortled goofily and acquiesced.

"Okay, okay," Kinner said, his speech barely able to clear the knot in his throat. "Uh, Kane. Right. What does he look like?"

Smiling with disappointment, Borley looked to Brock and shook his head. Immediately, violently, the thug's grip tightened on Kinner's wrist, and he lifted the hand. "No!" screamed Kinner. The merchant's

<209>

right thumbnail was a bit long. With one quick, indecisive action, Brock clipped off the excess nail. The thick, dirty crescent of keratin flipped outward, disappearing amongst the disarray. Kinner could hardly look down; and found himself in enormous relief to see the nail cut only to the tip of the finger.

"There you are," said Borley. "Looking much cleaner already." He examined his own fingers, stroking the wrinkles of one hand with the other. "I myself can't stand to have long fingernails. There's something feminine about it, don't you think?"

Breathing heavily, Kinner agreed.

"You see," continued Borley, "I've been trying to track down this friend of ours—Mr. Kane. But I've been having an awful time making any progress. Then, earlier today, a little birdie told me he'd been here. That he spoke with you about my home. And I though, voila! There we go. Surely Kinner must know where he is; I mean, being that you two are such good friends and all."

"Oh, oh!" Kinner glowed with delight. "Yes! I know who you're talking about. That guy, sure he came in here a while back."

"Oh," Borley said, "you remember now. How wonderful."

"Yes," Kinner continued breathlessly. "But he never told me his name. He just came in here and asked what I knew about Borley's Castle. I told him I didn't know nothin'. I'd just heard it was haunted. And he gave me fifty bucks and left. That's all I know."

"That's all you know?" Borley lowered his brow suspiciously.

"Yes sir. That's every bit of it."

Borley didn't flinch. "Brock," he commanded.

Without hesitation, Brock lifted Kinner's hand again. "What're you doin!" the merchant cried, jerking back. The other thug rushed in to hold him from behind once more. "No! Wait a minute!" Brock crammed the cold, unforgiving steel of the clippers deep under the thumb nail. He pressed the handles, and with a "pop," the top half of the nail was gone.

<210>

Kinner shrieked. He could feel the air pressing down on the sensitive, exposed flesh. Crimson blood oozed to the torn surface, and his entire thumb immediately began to throb. "Aw Jesus!" the merchant yelled, squeezing his eyelids together, unwilling to look at the deep-cut nail.

"Calm down, calm down," ordered Borley. "Looks like Brock made a little mistake. Oh well, worse things have happened you know. You'll surely recover."

Panicking, and in shock, Kinner could barely hear the rich man's words. "If you're gonna kill me, kill me!" he shouted. "But not this…"

"Kill?" replied Borley. "Who said anything about killing?" he scoffed. "Listen to this," he eyed those around him, "a man begging for death over something so simple. You're quite the baby, Kinner, you know that? Why you don't even know what you're asking for—wanting to die like that. What do you know about death anyway?"

Kinner had quietened, trying to regain his senses.

"Me, on the other hand," Borley continued, "I'm quite the expert when it comes to death. I know all about it. And death is not such a pretty thing. Everyone thinks, 'oh, when I die it will all be over.' That death is the great release and all that—that it doesn't hurt to die. What let me tell you something: I happen to know for a fact that medical science is wrong about death. They think you die when your bodily functions cease, but they're wrong. You see, believe it or not, when you die, you're still conscious. Yes, that's right. You're just lying there, unable to move. You can hear everything around you, you can think clearly, but you just can't move the body. If your eyes are open you can see—you just can't focus them, that's all. And when they toss you in the coffin, you're just lying there, all alone, waiting for your brain to deteriorate. That's when it's really over, when that fleshy mess in your skull rots away. And then, you exist no more. Does that sound like a nice release?"

<211>

Kinner stared blankly at the rich man, unsure of how to take his words. The boundaries between serious and absurd were leisurely crossed by J.C. Borley. It was his entertainment.

"Now, if you're lucky," Borley rambled on, "someone might bash your brain in to begin with. That would save you from all that lying around, waiting to waste away." He paused, looked out as if a new thought hit him, then carried on: "But even if I'm wrong. Even if death is some great spiritual release, have you ever really thought about that? Have you ever considered how it will feel when your soul leaves your body? That can't be a pleasant thing—surely frightful. But oh well, whatever the case, we all must face it. Each and every one of us must reach that wretched phase. And we must do it all alone. No matter how close and dependent we are on other humans, we must each face death utterly alone—just as we face our dreams at night. What do you think about it all Kinner?"

Kinner licked his lips and scanned the room. He took a deep, calming breath, and clarified his frantic thoughts. "Mr. Borley," he spoke calmly, "I swear to God, I'm telling you the truth. I don't want to die, and I don't want any of this. I would tell you what you wanted to know if I knew it. *I swear to God* I would."

Borley just looked at the pleading man, a great, flat indifference in his black eyes. His stare latched onto the askew visage across from him, and he studied it quietly. "Mr. Kinner," he said at last. "I believe you're lying to me."

"No!" the merchant screamed, as Brock again shoved the clippers under the remaining thumbnail. With greater force, he pressed the handles, and the nail snapped just above the cuticle. However, the cut was not clean, and so Brock wrenched the instrument in the soft, bloody flesh, cutting again and again, until the nail fell away. Still engulfed in his passionate brutality, Brock grabbed the thumb and forced it back. The springy tension of the socket fought hard to save the digit, but the henchman's power was too great. With a "snap," like the break of a stiff

<212>

green bean, the joint broke, and the resistance gave way—the limp thumb, ajar in its socket, disconnected beneath the skin. The pain was vile and intolerable, and Kinner felt himself growing faint.

Borley stood up and stretched, looking away from Kinner with disappointment. "You know," he said, gazing around the room as he talked, "you could avoid all of this by just telling me what I want to know. And so this will be the last time I ask you. *Who is Mr. Kane?*"

Tickling streams of blood were running down Kinner's wrist, and his thumb was covered with a scarlet mess. Barely retaining consciousness, a warm peace suddenly overcame him. It was almost like an escape from the agony. The villains around him were nearly unreal, and a deep, powerful, angry force seeped to the surface of his shattered emotions. In an instant, he found a strength inside that Borley had stolen long ago. And seizing that moment—tapping that prideful energy, however fleeting, he looked into the deep, dark eyes boring down on him, and spoke two words that J.C. Borley had never received: "*Fuck you.*"

It was a moment frozen in time. The entire room fell silent, and each man, save the merchant, braced himself for the tempest he knew would erupt. It was inconceivable, classic perhaps, in a twisted way, that such words would be spoken. And Borley, more icon than man, was solid and perplexed. A dullness in his eyes gave way to a glint—a light of bewilderment and rage. But, ever the winner, the rich man contained it. He didn't alter a muscle on his commanding body. Instead, his thick lips parted, and he spoke softly. "Bash his brains in."

Immediately, the room was alive with motion. Being an extension of Borley's power, each man took the insult personally. They were upon Kinner, who was now silent with shock, and dragging him away sloppily towards the back door. Each man punched and kicked at the withdrawn victim as they hauled him off. Just as they reached the door, Borley suddenly stopped them.

<213>

"Wait," said the rich man, lighting up a cigarette. He placed the golden lighter back in his pocket and exhaled. "Don't bash his brains in," Borley said, seemingly having come to a more rational thought. "Let him live. But put his other eye out."

"Nooooooo!" was the merchant's sickening cry.

✳   ✳   ✳

Kane and Benedict trudged within the dark gulf of shadow nestled in the cove behind Borley's Castle. Though the sun had long since faded, and the sky was rich with blackness, the stretch of forest where the mountain met the valley was completely void of light; it was darker and bleaker than the evening around it. Silently, they had parked their vehicle off the side of a dirt road. The area around the lane was speckled with dreary homes, and a worn roadway sign proclaimed the community's title with little fanfare: Covenwood.

The weight of the mountain's shadow—a somber, arcane power—pressed upon the trespassers as they navigated thick trees and unforgiving brush. From time to time the soaring wail of a canine would take flight in the distance, and the two would halt rigidly, wondering if the beast could sense them so far away.

"Say," Kane whispered, turning off his dim flashlight as he spoke, "whose property is this anyway? Is this Borley's?"

Squinting in thought, Benedict surveyed the woods in vain. "I'm not really sure," he said. "I don't think so. I believe the Borley line comes down the backside of the mountain and terminates around a creek. So, in that case, we're on someone else's property now, until we cross the creek."

"Then if this cave is at the base of the mountain, it's probably around the creek. Right?"

<214>

"I would say so," the reporter responded. "That may partially account for the water used to fill its chambers—if in fact that's true."

The pair continued onward, following no set course, simply heading in the direction of the mountain's rise. Soon enough, the clean sound of rushing water teased them through the trees. In their hurry to reach the site, they didn't notice a twisting, rusted strand of barbed wire stretched low to the ground, its wooden posts having long since rotted and fallen. Leading the way, Benedict was thrown face-first, his flashlight hurtling, when the filthy, metal claws gripped his right shoe. In a crash of broken twigs and crushed weeds, he flailed for stability on the ground.

"Good Lord, man!" Kane exclaimed, "Are you all right?" He reached down and took the startled reporter's arm, hoisting him to his feet.

"Yeah, yeah, I'm fine," Benedict assured him, brushing his clothes and composing himself with slight embarrassment.

"Did it stick you?" Kane asked, shining his light onto the devilish wire waiting patiently for its next victim.

"I don't think so," Benedict replied. "I don't think it penetrated my shoe."

"If it did, I hope you've had your tetanus shot."

"Oh yes," Benedict fished for his flashlight. "I get my shots regularly."

Without further thought on the matter, Kane pressed onward, Benedict happy to let him lead. Within twenty feet, they encountered the creek.

Kane and Benedict panned the water with their flashlights. Though difficult to see in the darkness, the stream was about ten feet wide. It ran swift and smooth, the light bouncing magically from its surface. There was a high, rugged bank on the opposite side, and it terraced into the walls of earth that ascended to form a mountain. As Kane and Benedict examined the area, their flashlights circled the banks like threatening prison searchlights. Suddenly, a beam landed on an unexpected scene.

Like a stunned muskrat, eyes aglow, a black man stood frozen on a sandbar. A raggedy, wide-brimmed hat was pulled low on his head, and

<215>

a gray beard hugged his aged face. At his feet, partially submerged in mud, was a large, black gold pan, and in his arms he clenched a shotgun, aimed perilously at the sources of the lights.

"Gawd damn!" he cried, "You caught me!"

"Whoa! Whoa!" Benedict exclaimed, "Don't shoot!" Both the reporter and the stranger held their hands up, displaying nothing but their flashlights. The man didn't budge.

"Are we trespassing?" Kane asked.

"Are *you* trespassin'?" the man called out. "What—who are you?"

"We're just lookin' for somethin'," Kane said.

"You mean," the man sounded puzzled, "you ain't one o' them Borlers?"

"Borlers?" Benedict responded.

"Yeah, yeah," the man spoke with frustration, "from the castle."

"You mean Borleys?" the reporter said.

"Yeah, that's what I said!"

"No, no," Kane and Benedict both assured him. "We're not with anybody."

"You ain't poe-lice or nothin'?"

"No," the reporter said. "We're not here to bother anybody."

The man lowered his weapon, and suspiciously lumbered through the water, his knee-high rubber boots splashing, and came ashore.

"Who are you?" asked Kane, positioning his light to illuminate the man, yet not shine directly in his face.

"Who am I?" he replied. "Everbody calls me Papa."

"Hello," the reporter extended a hand, a bit over-congenially. "I'm Wilson Benedict, and this is my friend Kane." They all shook.

"So what are you doin' out here?" Kane asked, keeping his keen eyes on the gun.

"Oh me," Papa brushed his hand nonchalantly. "I just like to come down here and—you know, just hang out."

Benedict looked back to the sand bar. "Is that a gold pan over there?" he asked.

<216>

"Ah, yeah, yeah," Papa smiled. "I do a little pannin' down here sometimes, but it ain't no good." He sounded phony.

"So you're pannin' someone else's property, huh?" Kane announced
boldly. "And we thought *we'd* been caught."

Papa scratched his forehead, leaving behind a grainy streak of mud.
"What are ya'll doin' out here?"

"Well, actually, you might be able to help us with that," said Benedict.
"You know this place pretty well?"

"What?" said Papa. "You mean this here area?" He pointed
around himself.

"Yes," replied the reporter. "You come here often?"

"Oh, once in a while."

"Well," Benedict continued, "do you know where a cave might be
around here?"

"A cave?" Papa responded. "Uh, you mean with like a door on it?"

The stranger's eyes lit up. "Yes, yes," he said. "That's the one."

"Oh yeah," Papa nodded. "I know where that is."

"Can you take us there?" asked the stranger.

"Yeah, sure," the old man said. "But now, wait a minute." Kane and
Benedict reserved their excitement. "This cave here—this is what you
guys wanna see?"

"Yes," the investigators replied.

"Well then, uh…I can show you the cave, but, ya'll'll have to do me a
little favor."

"Yes?"

"You gotta promise you ain't gonna tell nobody you seen me here."

"No problem," said Kane nobly. "You have our word."

"And also," Papa continued, "you gotta promise you ain't gonna—well,
you know—come here and, well…," he searched for the right words.

"Pan the water, right?" Benedict filled in.

"Yeah! Yeah! That's right. I mean it's kind o' like—well, even though I
ain't supposed to be here—it's kind o' like it's my place, ya know?"

"We promise," Benedict assured him. "All we want is to see the cave. And we won't tell anyone you were here if you don't tell anyone we were here."

"Okay, okay," Papa nodded his head with satisfaction, shaking hands with the searchers once again. "Well then it's right this way, gentlemen."

The old man led the pair down a winding length of creek. The banks and shores dipped in and out, curving around mounds of soft dirt, peppered with shiny, shapely pebbles. Small craters here and there surely led to an underground world of delicate amphibious life, and an occasional silver glint would prove to be a sparkle of mica, or perhaps an orphaned bottle cap. Tiny mammalian footprints, soft and delicate of toe, riddled the water's edge, bearing transient tribute to thirsts quenched earlier in the day.

A veritable cornucopia of healthy vegetation—mosses, algae, weeds, and trees—drew strength from the rushing vein of life, enclosing the creek in a hallowed shrine of botanical peace. Like seasoned explorers, the three men dodged vines, mud pools, and crumbling shelves of bank as they prodded onward through the increasingly wild underwood. Upon rounding a bend, a section of the stream widened into a calm pool. On the opposite side of the bank, an enormous tree emerged from the water's edge, its crooked, exposed roots bent outward like decrepit fingers. Beneath the arched awning of each root, a pitch-black hole bored deep into the earth, perhaps leading into a miniature cavern of turtles, crawfish, salamanders and the like. When he saw the tree, Papa nodded his head.

"Here we go," the old man said. "We cross over here."

The three men scanned the banks, hunting for a spot where the waterway was narrow enough to leap across. When they found such a spot, where the weeded banks pinched the creek closer together, each bound across, mindful of the slick landing.

"It's just a li'l ways up here," Papa pointed deeper into the woods. They continued marching across the ever-treacherous land, finally

<218>

reaching a spot where low granite cliffs, mostly hidden by brush, formed coves and crevices at the base of the towering mountain. He led the men through an obstacle course of large, broken boulders and fallen trees, until they saw the shadow of a deep and narrow hollow in the cliff. "Here we are," said the guide. "It's back up in here."

When they reached the mouth of the hollow, their flashlight beams fell on the cold and eerie sight: A rusty metal door, looking terribly out of place, was deeply set into the stone around it. Straining their eyes for details, the men enthusiastically approached the anomaly.

The door was about four-and-a-half feet tall, and perhaps three feet wide. It looked thick, heavy, and worn—and by a mere glance one could see it had remained immortally closed for generations. There were no visible hinges, and the area directly around the portal was smeared with a rock-hard grayish paste, speckled with black fungus. In the area in front of the door, aged cigarette butts, a couple of faded beer cans, and a shoestring were remnants of casual sightseers of the past.

Fascinated, Benedict examined the metal with his flashlight, bringing his face close to the brown, pockmarked ore. Midway down, on the right side, he gasped. "Kane," he said. "Look at this."

Around a large keyhole was a wolf, etched thinly, barely visible, into the metal. The keyhole was placed directly at its roaring mouth. "Good Lord," whispered Kane. "Just like the room in the castle."

Kane dropped to his knees and brought his right eye mystically close to the keyhole. He held his flashlight a few inches from it, attempting to cast a beam onto the other side of the door. The meager light entered the hole, yet it displayed nothing. There was only a deep, impenetrable void, like a dark eye leering back into Kane's. The stranger pressed his ear against it, the rough, rusty metal icy against his cheek. There was only silence. He shoved his weight against it, but it was as solid and firm as the granite cliffs.

"What do you know about this door?" Kane glanced back to Papa, watching quietly in the background.

<219>

The old man shook his head. "I don't know a thing," he said. "I seen it back here before, and ever once in a while some teenagers'll come out here to hang out. But I don't reckon nobody knows jus' what it is. I guess it was a minin' shaft at one time. Do you fellers know?"

The stranger and the reporter looked at each other with intense eyes. They knew next what they had to do.

*   *   *

A looming reminder of divine power, the Roman Catholic Basilica of St. Lawrence kept constant watch on the city of Asheville. A timeless structure, it sat across from the civic center, a stone's throw from Pack Memorial Library. It was a hulking building, with two illustrious Spanish towers and a sound, stone entry way. Between the towers, on the main facade, St. Lawrence, poised as a sentry, spied outward. In one stony hand, he grasped a palm frond, and in the other, he clenched a gridiron, the merciless instrument of his torture. But the outside of the church was far inferior to the inside, almost masking the glorious interior like a well-kept secret.

Through its doors, a breathtaking chamber emerged. The ceiling soared into a colossal, free-standing dome, the largest in North America. It had been the prize of its builder, constructed with a cryptic technique known only to the architect. So valuable was the method that when observers came to awe at his feverish work, he would go home for the day, rather than allow his process to be known.

The gray tiles of the dome rose and capped the shrine like the global ceiling of the heavens themselves, raining down at the sides into lavish and painstaking lanterns and carvings. The saints, three-dimensionally engraven in stone, surrounded the circular chamber. Saints Margaret, Lucia, Cecilia, Catherine of Alexandria, Barbara, Agnes, Agatha, Rose of Lima: Each stood guard, positioned high upon the walls, their eyes

<220>

bright as if peering into the spiritual realms. Dark, stained glass glowed mystically from the burning sun outside, the rays themselves dissipated by the force of consecrated ground. Miniature domed rooms were spread about the structure, each containing its own ghostly lighting, biblical scenes, alters, rosaries, candles, bowls of holy water and oils. But the centerpiece of the church was placed mystically behind, and askew from, the pulpit: it was a grand and eerie statue of Christ, his limp figure hanging heavily from the cross. The softness of tortured flesh emanated from the sculpted form, commanding a rare sense of life granted and coaxed by the artist.

Weighty, bold, and dark, the basilica was as overwhelming as rapture, yet as bleak and gothic as a tomb. The force of greater power pressed firmly on the shoulders of those inside, and resounded with the dominance of the lofty pipe organ encased at the building's rear. The place was magnificent and cold, mysterious and deadly quiet. It smelled like an old book, and touched the flesh like a tingling storm cloud. But the greatest chill of all was the body enshrined in its wall—the body of its builder—Guastavino.

In the back room of the church, a place that only clergy usually get to see, Kane and Benedict sat quiescent before Monsignor Federico. The Monsignor was a thin, dignified man, with swarthy flesh, affable features, and a thick head of shiny, salt-and-pepper hair. His brown eyes were calm and intense, and his voice was soothing and well-paced, a subtle Latin accent playing at each word. There was a great peace and warmth about him, and his thoughts were clear and educated.

"He said you would come someday," said the cleric with a smile. "He was right as usual."

"Oh," said Kane, his brow curled, "and who did he say I was?" Benedict leaned forward expectantly.

"He didn't tell me," said the Monsignor. "But I'm sure he knew. He could see things sometimes—things in the future. And he was usually right."

"Then just what did he say?" prodded the stranger.

<221>

"He said a man would come—a tall man—and he would want the key. And he said that you should have it."

"So, you knew Odin?" asked Benedict, his mind eager to piece the puzzle together.

The cleric nodded, his eyes closed thoughtfully. "I knew him about as well as anyone alive, and even that isn't saying much. He was a very…complicated man. But he was my mentor and friend. I came here as a young man, and I watched him grow old. And when he died, I was at his bedside."

"If you don't mind my asking," said Benedict, "what were his last words?"

The Monsignor's mind drifted back to the moment, and he smiled again, fondly. "I don't know," he said. "I couldn't understand them."

Kane shifted a bit in his seat. "And the story, about the demon, is there truth to it?"

The Monsignor tilted his head to the side. "Well, yes, but it's a very difficult subject. Father Odin was an exceptionally private man. He never told me the entire story at once, but in many different pieces throughout the years. You see, he kept up with the progress of Crawford, even though he never saw him. And sometimes he would have enormous feelings to get off his chest, so he would tell me."

"So," said the reporter, "he knew that Crawford was…I suppose, enlisting the help of the demon?"

The cleric rubbed his eyebrows as if deciding how to proceed. "Well, you see," he said, "the church does not become involved in demonic activity like the movies would have you believe. You hear stories, but it's not the kind of thing that we usually do—nor, in most cases, are qualified to do. Father Odin made a mistake as a young, naive man—a mistake he paid for the rest of his life. If there was indeed a demon, it should have been banished, but instead he allowed it to remain on this plane."

"Banished?" said Kane.

<222>

"Yes," confirmed the Monsignor. "You cannot kill a demon per say. A demon is a spiritual being, and can only be destroyed by God. However, you can, by proper rite, banish a demon from the physical realm, enlisting the authority of the Lord. But, Father Odin did not banish the demon as he should have."

"And why is that?" asked Benedict, lowering his thick eyebrows.

The cleric frowned. "Well, that is one of the great shames of Father Odin. It seems he was drawing some nature of…supernatural power from this being. And he knew that if it was banished, his powers would cease. Instead, he chose to lock it up—maintaining its influence on the physical realm for his own good—and yet preventing it from tainting others. He had no intention of ever releasing it, and when he discovered what Crawford had done, he at last fully realized the error of his ways."

"What do you mean?" asked the stranger.

"Well, he felt genuine guilt over his deeds, and yet he maintained his position—a very respected one, I might add—in the church. But, for the rest of his life, till the day he died, he never quite knew if he had truly reconciled with God. You see, as a man grows older, he begins to become more and more afraid. He realizes that the physical world will soon be of no value, and so all he is left with is his inner self. And even if he believes he is right with God, there is always a fear of those dark, repressed sections of the mind and heart, those places each man knows he has, but does not want to face. And he wonders if those secret desires, thoughts, and doubts should be there. Even if he pretends as if they are not—even if he proclaims his soul to God each day—deep inside he is afraid of those sinful parts of himself that he wishes were not there. And Father Odin struggled with those black little sections of his heart and mind each day."

"How do you mean?" the reporter motioned for him to continue.

"Well," the cleric exhaled, "life in the church is very difficult. There is great isolation and great introspection. You spend your entire life speaking to invisible powers that usually never speak back. And so

<223>

you're never quite sure if you're doing a good job. You think you are, but you wonder how you look through the eyes of God. Father Odin knew that his adoring public had no idea of his darker self. And the fact that they respected him so much made him feel even more ashamed. He spent all his time in prayer, and yet he retained his special abilities until he died. He didn't want them, but he couldn't help but use them. Just when he'd think he was a full servant of God again, he would levitate, or hear someone's thoughts. When he died, he was trembling with fear, mortified of meeting the Lord. And he felt that he would surely go to hell, or at best purgatory."

"But, I don't understand," said Benedict. "If he needed to banish the demon, why didn't he go do it?"

"There were two reasons," replied the Monsignor. "Firstly, he didn't want to face it again. He chose to ignore it, hoping it would go away. And secondly, he didn't know for sure if it was necessary. That is why he left behind the key. He felt that if he went to purgatory, the only way he could pass on to the kingdom was if the demon was banished. And so he made preparations for its banishment after his demise."

"Preparations?" asked Kane.

"Yes," said the cleric. "They are included with the key."

Kane and Benedict cast a glance at each other. "And do you think he is in purgatory?" inquired the reporter. The Monsignor puckered his bottom lip, and looked away indecisively.

"Does he haunt you?" asked the stranger.

"I wouldn't quite say that," answered the clergyman. "But sometimes—sometimes I think I sense his presence. You know how that sometimes, for one startling instant, the past can swallow you up completely? How you can sense things that are gone forever? Sometimes a smell, or a piece of music, or a stranger on the side of the road can resurrect a feeling you once had as a child; a feeling you never realized you had until it was gone. Perhaps it's the feeling of someone you used to know, or a place you used to visit, or a perspective you once held of the

<224>

world. And for one more moment, it is resurrected from the past; sometimes with such clarity that a chill crosses your flesh, or tears well up in your eyes. And often I sense him that way. Often I feel as though he's here again, and then I realize, almost surprised, that he is gone."

The three men were silent for a moment, an homage to the power of the Monsignor's memories. And then Kane spoke: "Monsignor, did Odin ever tell anyone else about his involvement with the demon?"

The cleric rubbed his chin. "There is only one possibility. A long time ago, Father Odin befriended a writer. He was an historian, and was very interested in the execution of Sareth Borley. The event had been all but forgotten in history, and this writer wanted to record it properly. He and Father Odin had many long, private conversations, but I don't know what was said, and I felt it improper to ask. Unfortunately, I don't remember the man's name. Whatever the case, as far as I know, nothing came of it."

Again, a knowing look passed between Kane and Benedict.

"Well," said the Monsignor transitionally, leaning forward and placing his hands on his knees. "I'm afraid I have nothing more to tell you. Father Odin was too secretive. However, he prophesied your coming. And though I don't know who you are, and I don't expect you'll tell me, I feel assured that the key is meant for you." He looked at Kane with a smile. The clergyman's eyes locked with the stranger's, and he stared at him for a moment, a subtle sparkle of fascination in his pupils. "Funny," he said to the stranger. "You somehow remind me of him." Kane looked away.

The cleric rose, a new solemnity about him, and spectrally motioned towards the door with his left hand. "Shall we?" Kane and Benedict stood, and after passing through the mammoth oak portal, they ceremoniously followed the Monsignor to the crypt of Signor Rafael Guastavino.

The great architect's tomb was nestled unpretentiously in the shadows at the front, left corner of the church. There was the tall, arched door, set against a wall of sculpted castles and crowned, raging lions.

<225>

The face of the entry was grayish-green tiles, in backdrop to a large, thick crucifix, a flower in its center, and its edge lined with symbols shaped liked penetrating eyeballs. Two scrolls were molded on the door: one bearing "AD # 1908," and the other, below it, inscripted simply with "R. Guastavino." On its left side, midway down, was a black keyhole.

The three men stood before the chamber suspensefully, their eyes falling on its somber face with graveness. His eyes closed, the Monsignor extended his left hand and dipped his fingers in a small bowl of holy water hanging from the wall to the right of the crypt. There was a barely audible sound of their divine immersion, and then he withdrew them, glistening, and formed the four points of the crucifix about his head and chest. Finishing with a swift kiss of his thumb and index finger, held to form a cross, he opened his eyes again. His hand slipped into the neat, ironed pocket of his black pants, and then reappeared with a wrought iron key. Without hesitation, the key was inserted into the lock, and with a counter-clockwise twist of the wrist, a "click" was released inside the mechanism. The clergyman pulled back on the lodged key, and silently, heavily, smoothly, the door opened.

Directly inside the tomb, only inches from the door, was a long, gray, stone sarcophagus. Resting parallel to the floor, and vertical to the entryway, it was wedged between two close walls, its upper end at the door. Above it, and below it, were stark, blank, and empty spaces. Only one section of the coffin, that above the crown of the head inside, faced outward, and on it was hewn a design. Against a rough and broken pattern, perhaps like pieces of a puzzle, was a circular seal. Three fat cherubs grasped the plate, one on each side, and one at the top, a crucifix hanging from the top one's neck. It was intricately inscribed with Latin text. Though surely enormously heavy, the vast, deep spaces below and above the coffin almost made it seem light and weightless—as if it might be floating effortlessly on a dank and stale cushion of air.

The Monsignor cut his eyes to Kane. "Here, in eternal and immortal slumber, lies the body of the father of this church," he said. "It is the

<226>

most secret and sacred place in this basilica—and perhaps this entire city—and that is why Father Odin hid the key here."

Kane nodded in understanding, and the clergyman unexpectedly stooped, half his body disappearing beneath the hovering stone casket. A slight, metallic scrape echoed from beneath the box, and the Monsignor stood again, a long device similar to a crowbar in his hands. "Are you ready?" he questioned.

"Yes," replied the stranger.

"Give me a hand," said the cleric, turning to grind the lower end of the bar beneath the smooth, dense slab enclosing the remains. The stranger joined him, and the two worked skillfully to pry the lid. The leery reporter watched from behind, imagining the form of the dead body inches below their fingers.

With a strained heave, the slab rose significantly, and Kane lowered his body, driving the metal bar upwards. A dry, musty odor escaped and lingered. The Monsignor pushed with both his hands, and the lid rose nearly a foot, a rough, chalky growl of friction resounding in the narrow tomb. "Here," the cleric rasped, "there's a depression under here somewhere."

"I found it," said Kane, slipping the upper end of the bar into a groove on the underside of the slab, and propping the two-pronged lower end on the ridge of the box below. Each man exhaled with the immediate release of pressure, the tool now absorbing the weight. For the first time, the stranger's eyes glanced into the box, but he could see nothing; it was filled with darkness.

The Monsignor turned to Benedict. "Would you grab a candle please?" he asked.

"Sure," the reporter responded, snapping from a trance-like state. He turned and grabbed a short, white candle, just within his reach. "There you are," he spun around, handing it off to the cleric.

Seeming surprisingly calm, the Monsignor bent over and led the dancing, orange flame into the darkness, his face following close

<227>

behind. Kane lifted himself a bit, peering over the cleric's head to see. As soon as the illumination cleared the coffin wall, the eerie contents were visible.

The candlelight adhered softly to the head of a decrepit corpse. Its nose was sunken and its closed eyelids were shriveled, and yet it looked better preserved than they'd expected. A thin, tan, barely-existent film of flesh was stretched tight across the skull. Below the rotted cavity where a nose had once been, a thick, dull mustache, curled at the ends, was still in place. Beneath it, the phantom of barely-visible lips partially covered the teeth; drawn back in decomposition so that the yellowed teeth appeared bared in anguish. His receding head of hair looked just as natural as the day he'd died, but at one spot, just above his left eye, a small patch of flesh was gone, exposing bone. He wore a dark suit, and his hands were folded across his chest, the fingers seeming quite skeletal. But most importantly, around his neck was a silver chain, and from it hung a small, wooden box, a silver crucifix mounted on its lid.

The reporter's head was crammed into the tight squeeze of the doorway, and all three men marveled at the legendary cadaver. "This is incredible," Benedict marveled. "I can't believe I'm looking at Rafael Guastavino."

"You mean what's left of him," Kane replied.

"And that should contain your key," the Monsignor said, reaching his hand into the casket. As soon as his hand passed over the skull, he could feel the vacuum of death emanating into the corpse's lifeless flesh; it tugged ever so slightly at the hair on his arm, and goosebumps erupted on his skin. Overcoming the reaction by his will, he continued reaching until his hand was just above the box. Then, in an instant, a half-inch spark of blue static electricity snapped from the metal crucifix to the tip of the cleric's index finger. Reflexively, his fist flung back, banging his knuckles on the underside of the propped-open slab. "Aw!" he yelped. "It shocked me."

<228>

The Monsignor looked at Kane as if a new realization had formed. "Perhaps you had better be the one to take it," he said. The stranger shook his head knowingly.

The clergyman drew back and gave Kane the room to maneuver into the box. The stranger cast a stern, apparently unemotional glance at the corpse, and reached dutifully inside, planting his fingers on the box quickly. He moved almost as if trying to outrun any counterproductive emotional response he might have, his face indifferent in carrying out the task. With just as much composure, but a bit more care, he lifted the chain from around Guastavino's neck. However, the chain barely caught on the architect's left ear, and with the most insignificant of pressure, the ear fell off like a shaped clump of dirt.

"Oh, Good Lord forgive us!" whispered the Monsignor in horror. "You have desecrated the corpse."

"What are you talking about?" said Kane rigidly, having cleared the wooden box and chain of the sarcophagus. "I didn't desecrate anything. God's the one who's making him fall apart."

Without another thought on the matter, the stranger examined the box closely. It appeared quite ordinary on the outside. It was no more than six inches tall and three inches wide; and aside from the silver cross, there were no other decorations. Completely absorbed with the object, Kane opened the lid. The eyes of all three men were locked on the interior.

Resting inside the container, where they had been safely sealed for an unknown span of time, was a key, a glass vial of liquid, and a small scroll. Kane reached inside, taking the key marvelously between his thumb and index finger. It was silver, thick, and heavy, and at its top was engraved the intricate form of a puffed owl, its wings spread, and eyes closed. His eyes then shifted to the vial. Delicate and clear, it was a simple piece, shaped nearly like a bottle. A stump of cork sealed its narrow opening. The stranger lifted it as well, but almost as soon as it left the box, he returned it, eager to explore the scroll.

<229>

Only slightly yellowed, and of a very thick paper, the scroll was rolled tightly, a green string tied in a bow at its center. Kane took it into his hands, and with one tug of the string, the roll of paper expanded with a small, but long-pent release. The Monsignor and Benedict stood back, unsure of whether its words should be kept confidential for the stranger. Each eagerly awaited his invitation for them to observe, but it never came. Instead, he unrolled the note and read, and within a few moments, the impact of its words reflected in his eyes like a searing ember of joy and tragedy combined. He lifted his glowing pupils.

"This is it. This is what I've wanted for years," the stranger said, his words flowing swifter than usual.

Benedict couldn't stand it. "May I see?" he asked. Instantly, Kane's fist tightened on the scroll, the paper crunching lightly.

"Some day you can see," the stranger replied. He locked eyes with the clergyman, and a half-smile curled his lips. "Thank you, Monsignor," Kane bowed gratefully. "Thank you so much." He took the cleric's hand and shook it soulfully. The Monsignor smiled in return, his calmness everpresent.

"You are welcome."

Without another word, Kane swept away, his coat flowing behind him. "But Kane," said Benedict, not expecting such a hasty departure. The reporter turned to the Monsignor. "Yes, thank you, thank you," he said, already beginning to jog after the stranger. "Kane?" Benedict called, trying to catch up.

Behind them the cleric stood with a satisfied grin. And then he turned to see the crypt still open. "*Wait...*" he halfheartedly yapped, realizing he would need help to close it up again. But it was no use, the pair were already gone.

<230>

CHAPTER NINE

A GRUELLING WIND pressed against the backs of Kane and Benedict as they stood before the bold entrance to the caves. The door appeared exactly as it had before—old, rugged, unforgiving and stubbornly sealed. But the mere notion that it may soon be open made it seem different to the two as they hesitated, for a reason neither could quite grasp, to open it. Now, it seemed as if the entrance welcomed them somehow; as if it wanted to be open, as if it was exhausted from the secrets it had so long concealed.

Kane stepped forth, the silver key wielded like an omnipotent weapon. The pale circle of illumination from his flashlight highlighted the keyhole—the target. He extended his arm, the key slipping carefully, slowly, into the hole. And then, it was as if some powerful unseen force sucked the tip, and the key darted easily from the stranger's fingers, like iron to a huge magnet. Instantaneously, it locked securely into place, the impact of the connection resounding in the metal frame.

Kane shot his eyes to the reporter's, attempting to confirm what he had seen. Benedict had seen it all too well, and with his gaze, he communicated his wonder. Silent, the stranger returned to the door and, unsure of its operation, rested the tips of his fingers on its surface. Effortlessly, it creaked open an inch. A frigid breeze streamed from the black crack like a released apparition.

With that, Kane gave the door a quick, controlled shove, and it submitted, swinging inwardly, moaning on its way. The rusty square swung until almost completely open, and then ground to a stop, as if a mound of dirt

<231>

had risen in its path. Kane shined his flashlight inside. Aside from cob-webs and spider eggs around the frame, all they could see were rugged, rock walls—a dusky chamber of stone—continuing off to the left.

"I'll be damned," said Kane, turning back to his counterpart, "here they are. Caves." He began trudging through the doorway.

"Wait a second!" exclaimed the reporter.

"What?"

"Well, I don't know if we should just walk right in here like that. I mean, what if this door gets shut and locked behind us? A lot of people die from being trapped in caves."

"Here," said Kane, already just inside the entrance, having stooped to get through the door. He pushed the door back as far as it would go, grinding it deeper into the rise of soil below it that held it firmly in place. "This thing isn't going anywhere."

"But what if someone closes it behind us?"

"Look," said Kane in frustration, "if you don't want to go in, don't go. Just wait here. I, on the other hand, am going in now." The stranger dis-appeared inside. Casting away his fears, Benedict followed.

The chamber just inside the doorway was a bit tight—low ceilings and cramped spaces. But it almost immediately expanded into large caverns. The caves appeared to be massive black holes, spacious voids through which the two passed. Only through the circular beacons of their flashlights could they glimpse the features of their surroundings: gray and brown walls, tall, lumpy and smooth, ancient stalactites and stalagmites dripping in cones from the ceiling or rising from the floor like saliva-gushing teeth, and the sandy, pebbly ground crunching below their feet with each step. The air was cold and wet, and fresh trickles of mineral-bearing liquid dropped here and there, beginning a journey that would sweep them to the salty oceans. All around were the grooves and patterns meticulously sculpted by eons of leaking streams and condensation runoff.

<232>

"My God," said Benedict, his voice echoing softly and his flashlight falling on a scene perhaps fifteen feet inside the entrance. "Look."

Nestled in a crib of rock, off to the side of the cavern, was a tarnished, metal box. Having sat undisturbed for decades, its hinged door was partly open, the black dots of a perforated crucifix showing valiantly. It seemed to cringe, shunning the light that burned its long-darkened exterior.

Kane marched over and stooped beside it, his brow intense with fascination. With one finger, he opened the door farther, its decrepit hinges whining. He shined his beam inside and then jumped a bit, startled by what he found. What had at first seemed a creature resting inside was actually the gray skeleton of a pig. The skull bore an ominous, tortured look; the sockets wide, and the jagged teeth gnarled. It was a haunting display.

"I'll be damned," said the stranger, turning back to Benedict, "it's true after all."

Benedict stooped beside him. "These bones...these bones once housed a demon."

"It doesn't make sense though," Kane replied. "Why would they still be here? If the demon left, why didn't the pig run away?"

"I don't know. Perhaps the demon killed it. One might venture to say it was dead the moment it became possessed. Perhaps the evil spirit was mistaken for life."

They turned to see a mound of treacherous rocks overlooking their position. "There," said the reporter, "that must be where young Crawford Borley hid, watching himself being buried inside this dungeon." Benedict turned out his flashlight. "Go ahead," he said to Kane, "turn yours off, too."

The stranger complied, and the rich impenetrable blackness fell instantly upon them. They sat quiet for a bit...listening. The sounds of dripping wetness echoed from time to time, but after a minute, when

<233>

their ears were even more receptive, they could hear the faint rush of water in the distance. They turned on the flashlights.

"Can you imagine that?" said Benedict. "Can you imagine what that must have done to a child? To hear your mother murdered, and to be sealed inside this cave; a demon speaking with you from the darkness? No wonder he became what he was."

Kane stood, oblivious to the reporter's words, and continued trekking through the cavern. The two ascended the inclining floor, rising to a higher level of walkway. As they made their way deeper and deeper into the heart of the tunnels, bizarre formations of rocks and minerals emerged at each bend. There were places where columns of flowing stone rose twenty feet high, raining down like a frozen river of mud, and others where the ceiling dropped so low, the explorers would have to crouch to pass through. There were enormous cliffs, vanishing into a bottomless abyss that ran alongside parts of the pathway; and crevices lined with the plump bodies of sleeping bats, hanging upside-down like sinister little umbrellas.

"Look," Kane pointed to the creatures. "This place has other access to the outside world."

Though several narrow paths were always networking into other parts of the cavern, it seemed obvious that a primary walkway, perhaps once carved by water, was leading them in the best direction. All the while, as they continued, the sounds of water grew stronger until, at last, they rounded a rugged bend to find the stream. Wide and strong, it swept through the gray walls with the icy freshness of a virgin snowfall. Stepping up to its edge, the pair marveled at the crystalline clarity of the liquid.

"Magnificent, isn't it?" the reporter observed. "Sort of like the Linville Caverns."

"Yes," Kane replied halfheartedly, his eyes trained on the ceiling. "So you suppose Borley's Castle is somewhere above us?"

<234>

Benedict's gaze shot upward. "Probably. At least his property, anyway. I'm not sure if we're deep enough to be under the castle, though. It's difficult to tell. This cave is so disorienting."

"Ah ha!" Kane exclaimed, having spotted something anew by the water. Benedict turned to find the stranger's light shining on a small, flat-bottomed boat sitting at the water's edge. Though it wasn't tied, it seemed caught in some curious, isolated current, bouncing lightly about on the hard bank. The two sped over.

"Isn't that strange?" the reporter puzzled. "First off, why would a boat be here? And secondly, isn't it odd how it doesn't float away?"

Kane aimed his flashlight downstream. The light dissipated in the darkness, showing only what appeared to be the tunnel continuing ahead. "Well," he said, "we're going to answer one of those questions right now." Careful to keep his balance, Kane stepped onto the boat; it wobbled from side to side with his weight and, jarred from the current, began drifting.

"Wait a minute!" exclaimed the reporter. "What are you doing?"

"Better hurry and hop on!" Kane grinned. "There's no stopping her now!"

Without time for a better decision, Benedict leapt onto the craft, almost flipping it when he landed. The two men scrambled to regain control, cold water sloshing at the sides, and then they settled into place, the swift current carrying them into unknown terrain.

"Don't you ever take more than five seconds to think about things!" Benedict scolded, trying to regain his posture.

"Oh, I take all the time I need," Kane responded. "I just don't tell anyone about it."

There were paddles on the floor of the boat, but the stranger left them laying, preferring instead to let the wild waters lead the boat away. The cave swallowed them like the broken throat of a serpent, the water gliding smoothly towards it stomach. They only sat still, their eyes focused on the deep void before them, waiting both hopefully and

<235>

dreadfully for a new form to materialize. The cool breeze of the under-world flowed around them as a tender rumble.

"What if there's a waterfall or something up here?" the reporter said, a stiff paranoia in his voice.

"Well then we'll hear it coming," replied Kane.

"Yes. And?"

"Will you be quiet?" Kane insisted. "We'll never hear anything if you talk."

The rocky ceiling lowered and rose as they flowed beneath it, some-times dodging stalactites. As they proceeded, the stream would change directions, bending sharply to the right or left, and sometimes the water would pick up speed on a slope. It would feel as though the stream bed had disappeared for a moment, and then they would go flying down an incline, icy, frothing bubbles slinging at their sides. For a few seconds the boat would feel out of control, dropping into the unknown dark-ness, and then the disciplined current would grab them again, pulling them firmly along.

At one point, the stranger's light fell on a large, plump fish a foot below the surface. Its skin was a milky albino, and its large pink eyes were surely vacant of sight. It remained motionless, hovering softly, and then it disappeared into the darkness behind them.

"Kane," said Benedict, his eyes exploring the ever-emerging folds of cavern. "Don't you think it's time you told me who you are?"

"Look!" the stranger exclaimed, pointing ahead.

Protruding from the water was a magnificent stalagmite. It stood like a majestic shark fin, and the water gurgled around it. Fortunately, their craft was not heading for it.

"Isn't that peculiar?" said Benedict.

"You know what that means?" said Kane.

"What?"

"That means this portion of the cave hasn't been covered in water long—otherwise, that would be worn away."

<236>

"So," the reporter said, his gears turning, "that must mean that Crawford Borley took the natural stream and rerouted it here. We're coming into the area he intentionally flooded."

A row of several other stalagmites, of various shapes and heights, lined a portion of the stream. Their boat passed them closely, and Kane extended his arm, rubbing their smooth, slick surfaces as they passed by. Shortly thereafter, the waterway doubled in size and calmed greatly. The two shined their flashlights into the water, but the bottom could not be seen. What was once clear now reflected with a translucent greenish color.

"There's no telling how deep this water is getting," Kane said. "There's surely something under here that Borley wanted to hide." They each peered into the milky liquid in vain.

"I can't believe how unclear it is here," said the reporter. "It was completely transparent where we started."

Kane shined his light in front of them again, and was startled at what he saw. Straight ahead of them was a solid rock face. He moved the illumination to the right and saw that the stream continued—however, it channeled through a tunnel in the rock wall, its ceiling only a few inches above the water. He shined his light to the left: Again, another tunnel, its ceiling also only inches from the water, carried the stream away. Just when they were about to panic, they realized there was a pebbly shore off to the right side, and that shore continued upward, over the rock wall and down the other side.

"I believe it's time for us to dock," said Kane, reaching for the paddles in the floor of the craft. He dipped one into the water, and the stream instantly tugged at the flat wooden face. "Here, grab the other one," he ordered Benedict. The reporter took charge of the second paddle, and they began working the water at the sides of the boat. It was awkward at first, their motions out of sync, and then slowly the craft, ever drifting forward, meandered towards the shore.

<237>

Within a few moments, the rough, grainy dirt was scraping at the bottom of the vessel. Kane hopped out, bracing himself, and then pulling the boat to dock. Once Benedict stood on land, they shined their lights around, surveying the surroundings. Aside from the waterway forking into the separate caves, there appeared no obvious means of exit. Their strip of shore ascended over the rock face as a flat walkway, the ending wall of the cave rising at its side. Aside from the crevices formed by rock folding in upon itself, it appeared they had reached a dead end.

"Oh no," the reporter groaned. "*Oh no*, we might be trapped here!"

"Just hold on," Kane said, his voice calm and fatherly, let's look around and see what we can find. There has to be a way out. Otherwise, that boat wouldn't be there."

"Hey, look at that!" Benedict exclaimed. His flashlight illuminated a large torch on the wall, held in place by a thick, metal ring. It was attached to the cave at the top of the rock face. The two rushed up the inclining pathway. When they reached the summit, perhaps twenty feet high, they peered over the side, viewing the water on which they had traveled and seeing their boat on the shore below. The view was enchanting.

"This has been burned recently," Kane said, rubbing soot on his fingers from the torch's blackened tip.

"Then perhaps we should burn it now," the reporter replied, exploring his pocket for a cigarette lighter. When he retrieved it, he pushed on the flint, a small, yellow flame appearing, and then held it to the torch. It was quickly engulfed in fire, and a new, orange light spread warmth across the glacial stone. They turned to view the cavern anew.

What had been mostly black and white now had colors. The rocks emanated a browness, the water reflected a deep green sheen, and veins of various minerals reflected a variety of subtle colors in the cavern walls. What had seemed so primitive only moments before, now appeared much more civilized, accented only by the wide beam of a

<238>

crackling torch. Other torches, unlit, hung on the walls as well, but less light was better for remaining inconspicuous.

"Isn't this wondrous," marveled the reporter. "Who would have ever thought all this was below the mountain?"

"Look at the water down there," Kane said, his eyes focused below. "Do you see what I see?"

Kane leaned over the side of the cliff a bit, examining below. "Oh yes," he said, "I hadn't noticed that until just now."

The currents of the running water were much more visible at their height. It appeared as though the waterway separated, two distinct streams running towards their prospective caves. But in the middle, between the two, the water swirled slowly, spinning widely in a clockwise direction.

"It looks almost like a weak whirlpool," the reporter commented. "It must be created by the stream breaking into two different directions."

"No," Kane shook his head. "That's too distinct. I know what that is. That means there's another cave down there—another hole. And I'll bet you anything that it leads into Borley's Castle."

"You think the entrance is under there? Under the whirlpool?" asked Benedict, a hint of worry in his words.

"Yes," Kane answered confidently. "You see, before any of that water was down there—before this area was flooded—I'm sure it was simply another level of the cavern. For example, it's like we're standing on the third or fourth floor of a building, at the edge of the staircase. That entire expanse below us was probably another level, or levels, of the cave. It appears as if we're standing on the first level, but only because the water is so high. I'm sure that if we dove under that water, we would find another segment of the caves: the segment we're looking for."

"Yes," answered the reporter, nodding agreeably. "But…well, I mean, there's no way to get there though. We have to…dive." He looked at Kane pathetically.

<239>

"Damnit!" shouted the stranger, motion catching the corner of his eye. The boat had somehow dislodged from the shore and was at the mercy of the water. It was quickly caught up in the whirlpool, took a few spins, and then was slung into the straight current on the left side of the stream. Speedily, it glided away into the darkness of the left hole.

Kane sighed. "There went our boat," he said.

"Kane," Benedict spoke thoughtfully, "I'll bet these waterways somehow make a big circle. I'll bet that boat will end up back at the entrance, just like we found it."

"I don't know," the stranger answered. "But I know one thing—these kinds of currents don't occur naturally. They occur when things that aren't meant to be under water get covered with water. All these cracks and holes, and God knows what all else is under there, are channeling the water in bizarre, confusing ways. And you're probably right. It probably is somewhat cyclical."

Benedict looked around himself. "I think we'd best find a way out of here now," he said, "before this torch burns away."

"Start searching the walls for openings," Kane said. "There must be a way out of here."

"Kane," called the reporter, turning to search, "did I mention what a horrible death it is to be lost in a cave?"

"Yeah, yeah," scoffed the stranger, "just keep lookin'."

Each man explored the numerous facets of the rock walls. Every few feet, a tall black shadow stood stark against the stone, and anyone might contain an unseen crevice; an opening to another area. Kane viewed one side and Benedict the other; shining their lights into the umbras. Again and again, each cleft terminated a few feet into the wall.

"Hey Kane," Benedict summoned, "look what I've found."

Expecting an opening, Kane paced over to find the reporter inspecting a mark on the wall. In the tradition of cave art, the stenciled form of a spread hand was painted on a bulging lump of stone. The image of the

<240>

hand itself was the naked surface, but outlining it was a dark auburn mist of color.

"I wonder how old that is?" said the stranger. "It might be the hand of a Neanderthal."

"Fascinating," the reporter awed. "I wonder if there's other art?"

"I donno," Kane remarked, "but we can find out on our next trip. For now, let's get the hell outta here."

They again continued their search, examining each aspect of their surroundings for an egress. As time passed, as each fold of earth proved fruitless, a growing, dreadful panic began to rise in their stomachs. The stranger even climbed a jagged tier of rocks, seeking an unseen opening, but it was not to be found.

Their blood pressure rose and their breathing quickened. Soon, beads of sweat were forming at their brows. But just as their heightened alarm was about to cloud their minds, the reporter spotted another uncanny sight.

"What the…?" Benedict frowned.

Striking against the dingy interior of the cave, was the motion of a small, white object. Kane spotted it too, and both men scrambled to place a beam of light on it. Benedict's hit it first, and in the bright orb of radiance sat a meek, fragile cat, its eyes reflecting like diamonds.

"It's…" Kane paused with wonder, "I think it's—is that Angel?"

The two walked swiftly over, but the feline immediately raced away, heading towards the downside of the pathway, opposite the side they'd first come up. Then it disappeared into a shadow, shaped like an upside-down "v".

"Where's he going?" exclaimed the stranger, fast on the creature's heels. When they arrived at the crevice, they found it extended about ten feet into the cave's side, terminating with another wall. And there, at the bottom, right corner, sat the cat, calmly. It wailed forth a shrill "meow."

"Hello kitty," the reporter spoke childishly. "Kitty, kitty. I thought you were dead."

<241>

The cat meowed again, and then spun around in a flash, disappearing through a tiny hole hidden by its body. The gap was irregular in shape, as if having been broken out, and the bony little mammal squeezed through with ease, its loose flesh sliding back as it passed through.

Benedict immediately rushed up to the spot, kneeling down to the rough hole. "Look at this, Kane," he said, holding his sensitive fingers near the gap. "I—I can feel a draft here. This leads somewhere."

The stranger took a few steps forward, facing the narrow wall. He scanned its length up and down with his calculating eyes, and then, as if skilled in the action, he placed his hand on the right side of the surface. With a steady push, the wall gave way, turning counter-clockwise, as if rotating on a central pivot. The panel spun slowly with a primordial groan, displaying a dark opening at each side; a comforting blast of air rumbling quietly in the explorers' ears.

Kane and Benedict looked at each other, a glow of enlightenment in their gazes. They knew they had surely found a way into Borley's Castle. Quickly, each man squeezed through the spaces, prepared to journey into the great fortress. As soon as they passed through, they could feel a drastic change in their surroundings—a weight lifted from them, and wherever they were was large and spacious. They shined their lights all around, and then were suddenly taken aback. They were outside. Stars speckled the sky above.

"What?" Kane exclaimed. "Damn! I thought we'd found a way into the castle!"

"Well at least we're out of the cave," Benedict replied, his voice almost cheery. "That's not such a bad thing, now is it?"

"Where are we?" Kane mumbled, peering around himself. Two faint, ocherous shafts of light poured from the panel from where they had come, the torch still burning on the opposite side. From their perspective, the secret portal appeared like nothing more than a portion of a tawny wall of granite. Kane's flashlight beam followed the wall to find that it curved, circling around them. He panned the other direction to

<242>

find the same. The were standing inside a small canyon shaped like a crescent, its walls fifteen feet high. "What is this?" the stranger continued to perplex.

"Kane," the reporter said flatly, "look at this."

On the cleared ground inside the canyon, a large pentagram was thickly etched with white powder. Benedict cut his eyes to the stranger. "This is it. Remember what Weck said? This must be The Devil's Circle, where they come to worship."

"Ceremonial grounds," Kane stated. "Hence the secret passage to the caves. Before they were flooded, they probably traveled from the castle through the caves to this place."

Each man stood solid, somehow fearful of where to move or step, their minds soaking in the eerie display before them.

"Wait a minute," said the reporter. "I've heard stories about this place. I want to see if they're true." He reached down and carefully picked up a pebble from the ground beside his shoe. "They say no plants ever grow in this circle, but I've also heard another tale." He tossed the pebble. It soared in a gentle arc, patting down in the middle of the pentagram. But when it landed, it seemed as if the momentum of the toss, though it had been slight, continued to carry. The pebble kept rolling and rolling, perhaps as though propelled by an unseen hand. It rolled ten feet, until it cleared the pentagram, and then it came to a wobbly rest at the edge.

The reporter nodded his head. "No unceremonial object will stay at its center. They say the force of the Devil pushes it aside."

Slowly, they each walked around the occult emblem, minding their steps like men at the edge of a crater. "You suppose this place was man-made?" Kane asked. "It looks unnatural—almost like it was carved out of a cliff intentionally."

"No," Benedict answered. "Places like this predate man."

Kane suddenly stooped. He found a scattered clump of feathers near the canyon wall, each of them snow white. They reeked of violence.

<243>

"Say," the reporter entertained a new thought, "where did the kitten go?" They each looked around, but there wasn't a creature in sight.

Having both navigated half the circumference, Kane and Benedict met at the opening of the crescent. To better view their location, they stepped outside the circle. A dreary, depressing crawl of energy slipped from their skin when they crossed its boundary. They hadn't realized how uncomfortable they felt until the circle was behind them. They appeared to be surrounded by thick, untamed forest.

"We've just come out somewhere else on the mountain," Benedict said. "Somewhere halfway up the cove, I guess." From the outside, The Devil's Circle looked like a mere break in a cliff behind them: a break that opened into the circular design.

"What a strange formation," Kane observed. "I never knew the land around here could be so bizarre."

They stood for a moment, feasting their eyes upon the unsettling sight. Then, the reporter withdrew his pack of cigarettes. They each took one, lit up, and then exhaled the smoke like a burden let loose. "So what do you suppose we should do?" Benedict said.

Kane looked down in thought for a moment, and then lifted his eyes again to the ominous scene. "I'll tell ya what I think we should do," he said. "I think we should go back in there, put out that torch, close up that passage, and then find our way back down this mountain. And then tomorrow night, we should come back, perhaps with assistance, dive into that deep section of the water, and find the entrance to the castle that's been flooded."

"Whoa, whoa, whoa," the reporter held up a hand. "Dive? Where the whirlpool is?"

"It's not a whirlpool," Kane rolled his eyes. "The water's just swirling a bit. That indicates an underwater tunnel."

"Dive? What—how are we going to dive?"

Kane grinned. "Self-contained underwater breathing apparatus."

<244>

"SCUBA?" the reporter furrowed his brow ridiculously. "You can't be serious. SCUBA dive in those waters? I'm not even certified!"

The stranger took another drag from his smoke. "Tomorrow night you will be," he said.

*　　　*　　　*

The following evening, Kane and Benedict were gliding on foot down the refreshingly cool streets of Asheville. In the stranger's eyes, there shone a hardened glaze of determination. To an equal extent, such a glaze coated the reporter's eyes, yet his was borne of uncertainty.

"Where exactly are we going?" Benedict asked, barely keeping up with Kane's brisk pace, dodging between buildings and careening down narrow walkways.

"We'll need some extra help tonight," Kane answered. "Carrying SCUBA equipment isn't exactly 'the king's work'. Besides, if we make it into the castle, we may need some extra manpower if worse comes to worse—and I think we just *may* be in the castle tonight."

The reporter was confused. "What? You're involving other people? Who on Earth are they? I didn't think you wanted help!"

Kane didn't answer, but continued prodding forward, apparently quite confident in his destination.

After a rash of twists and turns, the two passed through a dank alley, a section at its end terminating with a chain-link fence. A portion of the fence was ripped from its post and bent backwards in a wave of sharp-pointed wires. It was quite obviously an entrance to the other side, one which invariably finds its place in most chain-link fences futilely placed to prevent passage. Pulling the torn section back more, Kane crouched and squeezed through, the jagged wires scraping his coat lightly. The reporter followed with greater ease, his smaller frame a suitable size.

<245>

Once through the makeshift gateway, they found themselves inside what appeared the mouth of a garage, its length disappearing into darkness. Kane withdrew a flashlight and continued walking, the floor declining with each step.

"Where are we?" Benedict asked.

"We're entering the tunnels," Kane replied.

"Tunnels?"

"Yes," the stranger said. "It's a fact most don't know: Asheville is riddled with underground tunnels—a little secret the authorities keep quiet."

"Oh, I think I've heard of these," Benedict added thoughtfully, "built in the early twentieth century to facilitate maintenance. But I've never been down here."

"Well the first thing you'd better learn is to keep your mouth shut," Kane warned. "You'll find every type of human vermin down here: junkies, whores and thieves. If you appear weak, you may not make it out alive."

The tunnel descended deeper, and Benedict found its strange parallel to the caves under Borley's Castle ironic. This was a manmade cave in essence, and instead of enchanting beauty, it was filled with decadence. Trash and hypodermic needles littered the sides of the walk, and graffiti covered the walls—pathetic and ghostly relics of shattered, hopeless lives. It was gloomy and dark, despite the thin forms of light that would sometimes emanate from cracks and spaces above and from the sides. A short distance within, the first signs of human life emerged.

Stuffed away in each crevice or indentation of the shaft, a huddled form would lounge; sometimes staring back with the frightened or insane eyes of an animal, sometimes with eyelids closed in escapeful slumber. There were men and women, of all races and ages, occupying each corner of the tunnel. Dirty, stinking, and tattered, some were surrounded by small collections of refuse they called possessions—broken sunglasses, used combs, wads of string, styrofoam cups—others sat

<246>

barren, with perhaps a spent bottle of booze nearby. Kane avoided eye contact with them all.

The tunnel commonly branched off into other directions and Kane took a few turns, quickly confusing the reporter's sense of orientation. At one point, a one-armed vagabond crept from a shadow, rasping for change, but the two simply sped up, leaving the unhealthy beggar behind. Benedict was fearful of the place, its thick despair suffocating him. He wasn't sure whether to feel sorry for the beings around him, or to see as them as wild creatures waiting for an opportunity to ravage the intruders like a pack of hungry hyenas.

Just after a plump, gray rat scurried across the walkway, Kane's flashlight fell on two familiar forms. Toking from a glass pipe, behind some boxes, were Sergeant and Fish. At first terrified by the beam, supposing it belonged to a policeman, they were relieved, and then immediately rigid again to find it was the stranger.

"Oh no!" the Sergeant exclaimed, "it's Karloff again!"

"How'd you know where to find us you spooky son-of-a-bitch?" Fish croaked, his eyes squinty and puffy.

"That's not important gentlemen," Kane answered. "But I'm here to offer you another job. Surely your rock supply needs replenishing."

"Oh no," Sergeant shook his head, pressing forth the palm of his right hand. "I ain't diggin' up no more dead bodies. Sorry. I'd rather be beggin' for money."

Benedict appeared both horrified and perplexed.

"No, no, no" Kane assured them, "there are no dead bodies this time, and the money's good. In fact, you'll be right in your environment."

"What's that?" asked Fish, shielding his eyes from the light.

"Tunnels," Kane said.

*   *   *

<247>

...

Kane, Benedict, Sergeant, and Fish stood at the edge of the gently swirling pool, the dim cavern echoing the breathless panting of the bums. Fish and Sergeant had been assigned the duty of hauling two large, metal containers of gear, not to mention four SCUBA tanks. They crouched at the bank, relaxing their tight muscles.

"Christ!" Fish yelped between gasps, "How heavy are those damn things?"

Kane ignored the question, already popping the latches on one case. Benedict hovered at his side, butterflies dancing in his empty stomach. When the stranger opened the container, a glorious array of underwater technology was revealed: regulators, to carry the air from the tanks, BCDs to assist in floatation, weight belts, wet suits, masks, snorkels, fins and the like.

"Goodness," the reporter admired, "this looks expensive. How on earth do you afford all this stuff?"

"I'm an avid hobbyist," Kane replied, diligently engaged in assembling the pieces. As he continued the work, Benedict walked to the edge of the water, peering deeply into its murkiness. He leaned down, dipping his fingers into the stream; the iciness chilled him to the bone.

"I don't know about this," he turned to the stranger, obvious worry in his eyes.

"Yeah, me neither," Sergeant chimed in enthusiastically, dipping his hand into the water as well.

"That pool is freezing," the reporter continued.

"Don't worry," Kane assured them, "that's what wet suits are made for."

Benedict was not satisfied. "And I mean," he said, "*we're going to jump into a whirlpool?* What if we just get sucked down and drown?"

"Yeah!" Sergeant offered more support. "Right on!"

"It's not a whirlpool," Kane replied, annoyance surfacing in his voice, "And you're not going to drown. You'll have an air tank hooked to your back."

"And how long does it last?" Sergeant questioned.

"Long enough," the stranger replied.

<248>

"But how can you be so sure it's not a whirlpool?" the reporter said. "*Something's* sucking the water down."

"Look," Kane halted his action, raising his eyes to meet the men, "I know water. And that is not strong enough to be a problem. In fact, some of you will probably have trouble staying down. If you don't want to go, then don't go. Otherwise, shut your mouths and trust me."

"Well I know one thing," Sergeant resolved, "I think you better be payin' my ass in advance. 'Cause if you get killed down there I still better get my money!"

"You'll be paid when you finish the job," Kane said. "And finish it right."

All were quiet for a bit, reflecting on what they were about to do. Suddenly Fish lifted a fist in the air triumphantly. "Hell I'm all for it!" he cheered. "I always wanted to be like Jacques Cousteau. This is gonna be awesome!"

The torch lit, and battery-powered lanterns about, the cool, mammoth chamber of the cave cast dark, everchanging shadows upon the pool. Benedict shined his flashlight into the water, but its beam only penetrated the milkiness a few feet. He gazed downward as intensely as possible, struggling to see any kind of form below. But there was only the smooth, rich cloudiness radiating a faint green.

"Go ahead and put on your wet suits," Kane ordered, flopping a mass of them out beside him.

"Cool," said Fish, swiping one. "Does it matter which one?"

"Just find one that fits," the stranger replied.

"What do we wear underneath?" Sergeant asked.

"Nothing," said Kane. "At least nothing you don't wanna get wet."

Within a few minutes, the three men were struggling clumsily with their suits. The thick, black, rubbery material was heavy and stiff, adhering hotly to the flesh as they forced their limbs inside.

"I think mine's too small," Fish complained, half-dressed.

"You're fine," said Kane. "They're supposed to be tight."

<249>

Benedict was the first one dressed, the long, bulky zipper trailing down his back still unhooked. "Would you zip me up please?" he asked Sergeant. The bum complied, and with a smooth "buzzzzz," the zipper glided up the reporter's back. As it ascended, the suit engulfed Benedict like second skin, swallowing him, squeezing him snugly from all sides.

One by one, piece by piece, the stranger added accessories to each man. The reporter was the first one, and he nearly fell backwards when the vest holding his tank was secured on his torso; the heavy metal canister tugging backwards with a firm, steady strength. After all three were dressed, with the exception of fins and gloves, Kane advised them to sit while he dressed himself. Each man grew exceedingly anxious, observing his costume and imagining jumping into the cold pool so weighted down.

"I hope you're gonna tell us how to work this shit," Sergeant said, examining his pressure and depth gauges. "I feel like some kind o' astronaut or somethin'."

Once completed with everything but his BCD vest, Kane stood. "All right, gather around everybody. It's time to get certified." The three congregated around him. "This is your air," he continued, holding up the mouthpiece. "You breathe through this." He held up a hose from a BCD. "If you push this button, you float. If you push this button, you sink. Any questions?"

The three men looked at each other dreadfully. "But, but what about getting 'the bends' and all that stuff?" Benedict asked.

"I don't think the water's *that* deep," Kane replied. "But nonetheless, don't ever, ever shoot to the surface. Just come up slowly, no faster than the bubbles floating to the surface from your mouthpiece. If you're real deep and you come up fast, your lungs can burst from the decrease in pressure, or you could get nitrogen bubbles in your bloodstream—'the bends'."

Sergeant shook his head. "But now, wait a minute, wait a minute…what if I get way down there and this thing falls out o' my mouth?"

Kane stared at him for a moment. "Then you put it back in."

<250>

The bum rubbed his forehead in agitation. "And why are we goin' down here again?"

"We're going to explore," Kane answered. "Now look gentlemen, this isn't some deep sea excursion. You'll be fine as long as you stay with me, and don't do *anything* unless I do it first. Remain on my heels at all times. And keep in mind, the number one reason people die diving is because they panic. Regardless of whatever happens, *don't panic.* Stay calm. Just remember, your air is right here in front of you. And one last thing: *this*," he gave a thumb down, "means to descend. And *this*," he gave a thumb up, "means to ascend. Got it?" They all nodded. "Good then, let's go."

After Kane had fully suited up, and the others had slipped on their gloves and fins and received their underwater flashlights, hooked to their vests with a cord, they all waddled to the shore like ducks. "My mask is foggin' up," Sergeant complained.

"Then rub spit in it," Kane replied.

"And what if I have to pee?" Fish inquired with burning concern.

"Then pee," Kane answered.

"Why do we need snorkels when we have air tanks?" Benedict questioned.

"Because if you're resting at the surface, but your mouth is below water, you can use it to breathe—saving the air in your tank."

Sickly nervous, the three men gazed into the cavern water about to receive them, Kane's demeanor cool and nonchalant. "Go ahead and fill up your BCD with air," the stranger said. "That way you'll float when you first jump in."

The three complied, their vests bulging and swelling around them, hugging them even tighter. "And if I do *this*," Kane gave an "okay" sign with his right hand, "that means I'm asking if everything's all right. To answer, you give me the same sign."

All men stood with their mouthpieces locked in place—their quickening breaths echoing mechanically off the cavern walls. Kane nodded to

<251>

Benedict. The reporter returned a perplexed look and removed his mouthpiece. "You want me to get in first?" he asked, his stomach sinking.

Kane removed his regulator. "Yes."

"But, but how? Just jump in?"

"That's right, just jump in."

"Okay," said the reporter, replacing his air supply. He stood over the murkiness for a few seconds, and then with a burst of adrenaline, jumped forward wildly.

The pool was shattered by the massive splash—a shower of white water raining down all around. Amidst the aquatic chaos, Benedict, his eyes aglow with terror behind the glass mask, flailed and bobbed, grasping for nonexistent support around him. He was already drifting slowly downstream and the stranger called to him.

"Grab those rocks!" Kane yelled, pointing to a small group of stalagmite tips peeking from the water near the shore. Benedict quickly secured himself on the points and, having spat out his mouthpiece, the first words escaped his lips.

"God! Oh God! It's cold!" he quivered.

"Don't worry, you'll warm up," the stranger grinned. "Now put your regulator back in." The reporter nodded his head and complied with a cough.

"Next," said Kane.

One by one, the others plunged into the frigid water, their bodies immediately shocked by the violent clash of blood-chilling temperature, their lungs collapsing morbidly as they sucked a deep, involuntary breath. Fish and Sergeant each wanted to spout profanities, but they were afraid to release their teeth from their mouthpieces. From the water, the others watched Kane jump in beside them, the force of his immersion blowing past them in a wave. Once everyone seemed stable, the stranger eyed each person, looking for signs of panic or hysteria. He felt confident with what he saw, and so gave the "okay" sign to each one. All returned the sentiment. The stranger looked below himself, seeing

<252>

his body disappear into the dark, endless waters. He looked above himself, observing the dazzling, wavering lines of light reflected from the water onto the ceiling of the cave. And then, with a final look at the pale faces around him, he gave the "thumb down." With the push of a button, the four submerged.

As soon as their heads fell below the surface, the bubbling roar of a silent, watery universe filled their ears. Each looked at the other, a ghastliness emanating from their snowy faces. Below them, they could see nothing but stark blackness. Fat, strong shafts of pallid illumination extended from their flashlights, but they could only permeate a few feet down, quickly neutralized by the thickness of the liquid.

Into the frigid, ravenous unknown, the drone of water vibrating in their heads, the echoes of their own breathing the only intelligent sounds, they descended. Smoothly, they fell into the abyss, all traces of light above their heads quickly gone. The blackness engulfed them entirely—above and below, and on all sides. Though they could not see around them, they could feel the hugeness of their surroundings. Tight knit, like villagers bonding in the night to guard against imposing evil, they were plagued by thoughts of what might lie in wait below.

After dropping a short, quiet distance, Sergeant grasped Kane's arm. The stranger looked to find him shaking his head in pain, pointing to his left ear. Kane pinched his own nostrils and blew through his nose, then winking to the vagabond. Sergeant did the same and his ears popped, an enormous release of pressure snapping away. His eyes projected delight, and he gave the "okay" sign. Every few feet, each diver repeated the procedure on his way down. Sometimes, they could hear the building pressure whine as it forced to seep out.

Kane looked at his depth gauge: 17 feet. Still there was nothing. He had expected to find some traces of bottom by such a depth. Feeling sure it must be close, they continued sinking. Fish fell behind a few feet, and before his eyes, the others disappeared in the inky waters.

<253>

Panicking, he kicked wildly to catch up. As quickly as they'd vanished, the frogmen emerged, and a swell of relief passed through him.

As they continued to fall, their depth accumulating quicker than they realized, Kane caught a glimpse of something in his flashlight. Turning the light back, he saw it was the rocky wall of the abyss. In their descent, they had apparently grown closer to the edge. Just when he was about to look away, another sight took him by surprise. The wall was covered with cave art. Black line drawings of men, animals, and the earth passed by. And then a startling work: a wolf and an owl, side by side in red and black paint. It was in Kane's beam for two seconds, and then he watched it disappear into the darkness above as he sunk below swiftly.

Fearful of jagged rocks, Kane led the men farther away from the wall, again enclosing them in nothingness. He looked at his gauge again: 41 feet. It was much lower than the stranger had planned on going. He looked above, the blackness at his face, and imagined—there were 41 feet between them and life. He wondered whether or not he should take them back up. Peering at each one, they looked surprisingly calm, their eyes trained below, waiting to see their destination. They had no idea how deep they had gone. Determined, Kane was not yet ready to go back up.

The feet passed by more quickly than the eye could detect, and yet there was no trace of existence. Not one fish nor form was to be seen. Deeper and deeper they passed through the muted void: 51 feet...62 feet...71 feet...and then, something happened.

Kane stopped. Something brushed by his leg. It was something firm and large—something moving. Seeing Kane had halted, the men held onto each other, struggling to hover, balancing their flotation with their weight. Unable to communicate verbally, the stranger looked at the others with a frown. Benedict was closest by him, and so he pointed to the reporter then motioned to his leg, attempting to ask if Benedict had brushed against him. The reporter couldn't understand Kane, reflecting expressions of confusion. Suddenly, Benedict jumped, something passing

<254>

by his legs, as well. Instantly responding, he directed his beam down. For half an instant, a segment of a thick, fleshy, serpent-like form shined, and then dropped from the light. It was as fat as a large tree trunk.

The men looked to Kane with sickly horror in their eyes. Again, someone's flashlight caught a fleeting, scaly form, albino white, gliding around them. It was stark and bright against the coal-black waters. Sheer panic was setting in, and Kane raised his hands in a calming gesture. He reached down to his leg and quickly brought up a long, acutely-sharp knife—one side slightly curved outward, the other side serrated.

Instantly, in a violent flash, the broad, flat head of a serpent, as wide as a dinner tray, locked on Sergeant's midsection. It twitched with lightning speed, and a rich cloud of blood burst from around its head. In his brown eyes, the vagabond cast forth a reflection of all those unthinkable things in life—those things too abominable for recognition—those pains unbearable to sense—a glassy supernova of extraordinary life, having broken a threshold of pain previously unknown. In that instant, he gave forth more energy than he had expended in the last two decades of his life. His mouthpiece was blown away, and a tower of bubbles jettisoned from his anguished lips. Despite the weighty thickness of the water, his final scream could be heard by all—a bubbly, guttural high-pitched shriek that hovered throughout the abyss. The serpent chomped again and again, each time, carving its nose deeper into Sergeant's flesh. The bum's face was forlorn and hellish, kicking vainly to relieve his unholy pain. Chunks of flesh fell, a trail of blood, like jet exhaust, following each one. The scene was obscured by a veil of billowing crimson, and then the snake, eating furiously, pulled him away. The black man squirmed in misery, and then disappeared into the cold darkness forever.

It was chaos amongst the others: Benedict and Fish immediately torpedoed for the surface. Kane, struggling to retain his wits, reached up and grabbed the reporter's ankle. Benedict's feet were kicking madly, and Kane wrestled him down, risking being pulled up with him. Once

<255>

they made eye contact, and the stranger projected the direness of the situation into Benedict's eyes, the reporter regained his senses. Indeed they began ascending, but it was a slow process. Fish, however, was already gone.

Insane with fear, Fish was shooting to the surface. His flotation device was full, each seam straightened with inner pressure. With a flick of the wrist, his weight belt dropped from his waist, falling behind him as he rose. All he wanted was land and the sweet, fresh air. Faster and faster he sped, rushing into the darkness like birth and death combined. It seemed to take forever to breach the gulf of poisoned waters that led back to his world. But halfway there, the pains began to nip at him.

They came first in his joints: sharp, burning stings of pain that electrified his muscles. And then, almost exponentially, they multiplied. His entire body, from his toes to his scalp, burned like a stiff cramp. Tight, compact bubbles of nitrogen were lodged in his bloodstream and tissues, and the higher he rose, the larger they became. Paralyzed with torment, his eyes rolled back in their sockets, his arms hanging back on the sides, all he could do was wait for science to deliver him from liquid to gas.

At the same time, an unbearable pressure rose in his chest. He could feel his lungs expanding as if he'd taken a huge breath. But then, they continued to expand. And continued. And continued. His chest puffed forth with crushing intensity, and then he could feel the delicate little split in the soft lining of his right lung—like the hot point of a blade had sliced him inside. Then, the left one. Split after split opened, his lungs rupturing with every foot he rose. His limp, phantasmal form was a speck in the great, dark waters, sweeping upwards towards a salvation that mocked him.

At last, his veiny, purpled head broke the surface of the water. His mouth opened, and a gush of frothy blood was ejected. His blind eyes were also filled with crimson. Unconscious, his body torn apart inwardly, each cell and vessel ruptured, he floated on top of the gentle

<256>

stream. He'd come up right where they had entered the water, where the stream divided into two parts, each traveling into a tunnel of the cavern. And, after bouncing around on the currents a bit, his corpse floated peacefully down the tunnel on the right side, taken deep into an endless maze of tiny caves.

Kane and Benedict were still deep below. The bubbles escaping their regulators dawdled patiently towards the surface, the pair almost out-running them again and again, and then holding back, slowing to travel at their rate. They envied the precious orbs of air, shimmering as they ascended. Benedict clung to Kane's tank, unversed in how to control his own rate of ascent. Around them, their flashlights passed in wild pans and circles, frantically searching for any threatening sign. The stranger's knife was poised high, its blade gleaming when the light passed it. But Kane could only protect in one direction at a time. He couldn't see the reporter well, the bulky equipment restricting his range of motion. At any moment, something could quickly, silently emerge from outside their lines of sight. They had no idea of their depth, having no opportunity to check a gauge. Slowly, painfully, they rose, the bubbles seeming to almost slow more and more the higher they got.

And then, there it was again. The pearly loop of a serpent passed a few feet in front of Kane, its head nowhere in sight. A split second later, Benedict caught two loops. Perhaps there were more than one. The reporter's mask was fogging up—already robbed of hearing, he watched his vision gradually cloud and dwindle as well. Peering down through the last transparent patch of his mask, he saw the form of a snake head flow past his feet; it was a vague form, caught in the half-light from Kane's lantern. Benedict was helpless. Unarmed, all he could was hang on and hope that an attack, if it came, would come from the stranger's side. It did.

Directly in front of Kane, the head of the creature appeared. Wide and heart-shaped, a dull luster glowed from its flesh. But instead of striking directly, the serpent arched its trailing body, lifting its face more

<257>

than an arm's length from the stranger's. Protruding like juicy domes on each side of the visage were two, white eyes. Each was divided down the middle by the pink slit of a pupil. Though creatures in such conditions are usually blind, the snake locked eyes with Kane's, and he could sense the creature's cold, emotionless gaze boring deep into his mind. With an immense, primitive instinct, it explored the strength of its victim, relishing the weaknesses it seemed to find. With that, it lunged.

The serpent spread its jaws wide, rows of razor-sharp teeth curving backwards towards its dark gape of musclely throat. Like an arrow, it shot for the stranger's midsection. In a forceful flash of titanium, Kane stabbed down his blade. Through the handle of the weapon, he could feel the firm impact as it broke through the top of the skull, spearing the snake through the crown of its head. Light-pink fluid exploded in the water. The serpent spasmed violently from side to side, wrenching Kane's wrist which still gripped the dagger tight. The stranger pulled mightily on the handle, but could not dislodge the knife. The creature flipped around furiously, finally breaking Kane's hold on the weapon. Still convulsing, it flopped away, the knife firmly sealed in its cranium.

Weaponless, Kane and Benedict continued rising, the void around them as empty, yet full, as ever. Still, their flashlights circled about—aside from visibility, the lights were perhaps their only instruments of self-defense, useful in bludgeoning, though great force of blow was difficult to manufacture in the water. Benedict was now sightless, his window of vision a steamy translucent film. For a while, there was no sign of danger, but then the sinister head of another serpent appeared near Kane's legs.

The stranger kicked his legs savagely, hoping to keep the snake at bay. In a flash, its jaws closed on the blade of his right fin. A few teeth barely broke through the thick neoprene over his foot, and Kane felt the tips of the fangs like needle points. He continued kicking, bending over to beat the monster with his light. The creature seemed hung on

<258>

the fin, and Kane popped the strap from behind his heel. The fin and the serpent fell away.

The pair continued to gradually ascend, and Kane watched below. Aside from his rubbery boot, his right foot was now naked. It dangled helplessly above the infinite blackness underneath. At any moment, the devilish jaws of a serpent might dart from the darkness, latching onto the foot, grinding it away in a chomp and a gulp. The flesh of his foot was suddenly more sensitive and precious than it had ever been.

In an unexpected burst—they broke through the surface. Like convicts having torn through prison walls, guard dogs on their heels, the two men struggled hysterically to get out of the water. Benedict flung his mask away so he could see. They swam madly towards the nearby shore, Kane still viewing his surroundings through his mask—droplets of water clinging to the glass as if a car windshield after a rainstorm. Frenzied and gasping, their mouthpieces hanging at their sides, they pulled themselves ashore, rolling away from the evil waters that had nearly taken their lives. Peering behind themselves, they saw the long, beefy body of a serpent pass just below the surface. It arched wickedly, and then slipped away—back to the depths of the abyss.

Breathless, shivering, in shock, they laid on the cold, hard floor of the cavern. Their minds were a blur of emotion—confusion, horror, violation—and adrenal intoxication. For perhaps the first time in their lives, they had become a lower part of the food chain. Freezing and taking control of his quivering body, Kane dashed over to one of the equipment cases. He threw pieces aside, retrieving three silver, plastic bags. Ripping them open, he pulled thick, brownish blocks from each one. After throwing them in a pile, he lit them with a barbecue lighter, also in the container. They burst into white-hot flames.

"H—h—here! You'll f—f—freeze. Get a—around the fire!" he ordered Benedict, already rubbing his own hands briskly over the flames. The reporter crawled over, and the two huddled around the glowing, precious heat.

<259>

"Wh—where's that guy—ah—ah, Fish?" Benedict stammered.

"I don't think he m—made it," the stranger replied.

"Oh dear God," Benedict moaned. "Wh—what kind of snakes were th—those? I've never seen s—such a thing."

"That's because th—they've been extinct for m—millions of years," Kane said.

"What?"

"Never mind," Kane grew closer to the fire, soaking it into his numb flesh greedily.

The two sat for a long time, quietly worshipping the radiation. Their minds swirled and raced with maddening thoughts of what had happened; reliving the recent events and wondering if they'd been handled in the most effective, logical ways. They grappled with their body's sense of shock, slowly taking back control of their minds.

After a while, his body warmed, Benedict spoke. "Two men. We killed two men tonight. Oh, oh…two men are dead." He looked at Kane with heavy, guilty eyes. "Two men. Do you realize we've lost *two men*?"

"Not to mention a lot of money," the stranger said, his eyes on the fire.

"What?"

"I said I've also lost a lot of money," Kane reiterated. "That was damn expensive equipment."

Benedict looked at him for a moment. The look of guilt had given way to a blank stare. It became a stare with thoughts behind it; those thoughts eventually making their way into his glossy eyes. "I—I can't believe you just said that."

Kane looked up innocently. "Why?"

Benedict abruptly stood. "Two men are dead. Two men are dead because you took them diving when they had no business diving. And all you can say is that you've lost money? What if it'd been me? Would you treat my life so cavalierly, as well?"

The stranger rolled his eyes. "Wilson," he said, "those men were bums. I gave them the greatest adventures of their lives. If they hadn't

<260>

died tonight, they would have spent another ten years lounging around in the trash getting drunk and high. Then, eventually, they'd freeze to death in some godawful snowstorm—or starve. At least they died doing something productive for a change."

The reporter was shocked. "You know who you sound like? You sound like J.C. Borley, that's who. In fact, sometimes I think you're just as cold as he is."

"Those were capable men," Kane stood, his voice raising. "You saw them. They could've gotten a job anytime they wanted, workin' at the local gas station. But instead, they chose to come here tonight—to dive down there for money. They knew the risks, and they died on the job. I don't feel guilty for that."

"What do you mean, they knew the risks!?" Benedict shouted. "You said it was safe—that we wouldn't be going down that far!"

"I can't help it that snakes were down there," Kane glared. "I could've been killed too, ya know. I almost was. And as far as going deep, that doesn't matter! I said plainly: DO NOT shoot to the surface! *I* didn't shoot to the surface, *you* didn't shoot to the surface—hadn't I saved your life, that is—and we're here. Fish shot to the surface knowing that can kill you. And indeed it probably did! That was HIS stupidity! They weren't children you know!"

"So you feel no sense of responsibility?!" the reporter exclaimed. "I can't believe this! I've been risking my life to help you when you don't even value my safety! I...I..." he searched for words in frustration. "I don't even know you, for God's sake! I don't even know what any of this is really all about! But I know one thing, I'm through!"

"I never asked for your help!" Kane roared. "You volunteered. In fact, sometimes you get on my damn nerves!"

"To hell with you, you...you heartless bastard!" Benedict screamed, storming off towards the exit that opened into the Devil's Circle.

Kane was statuesque, seething. His brow was lowered, and his fists were clenched as he watched the reporter maneuver over rocks. He

<261>

looked down at the stony face of the cavern, then closed his eyes. "Wilson wait!" he said.

"Screw you!" the reporter called back.

Kane took a deep breath. "My name…my name is Kane *Borley*!"

Benedict stopped in his tracks. He stood for a moment, a bitter, unexpected weight dropped on his shoulders. Then he turned around, his eyebrows lowered and his mouth agape. There was a long silence— awkward and intense. The two men who had parted so angrily were now suddenly clashed together again.

Kane was staring at the ground. Inside him, two vast, tumultuous forces swirled and grappled. His dark and secretive self fought to repress the words surfacing. It felt unnatural for him to give in to the release, but he knew it was time. A faint mist of sweat boiled at his brow, and with a grit of his teeth, he allowed the words to pass: "Ever since I was a child," he said, "I've been haunted by the monk." He stopped, reaching deep inside, coaxing the emotionally-charged tale. "I remember waking up in the middle of the night to find him standing over my bed, his eyes glowing. He never spoke though. He just looked at me, grinning. It used to seem like such an evil grin…."

Trance-like, the reporter began slowly walking back. He wanted to say something, but his thoughts were too airy and shocked to materialize. Instead, he absorbed.

"But it wasn't just me," Kane resumed, "it was my whole family." Kane looked Benedict in the eyes morbidly. "You see, I'd heard bits and pieces of the legend my entire life, but I didn't know what to believe: When Odin killed Sareth, Crawford got away. But his brother and sister, Lawrence and Liza did not. They were taken to orphanages and split up, never to see each other again until adulthood. Lawrence was soon adopted by a businessman and his wife, and they took him to Wisconsin to grow up. They wanted to give him their last name, but he insisted on keeping 'Borley.' His adopted father was the wealthy owner of a furniture company, and when Lawrence grew up, he took over—did quite

<262>

well for himself. Later, he got married and had six kids. One of them, the last one, was me.

"Then, the bad things began to happen...When I was only six years old, my brother Carl was killed in a car accident. When I was thirteen, my sister Carol was raped and murdered. My other three siblings, Jack, Robert, and Alice, had kids of their own; but one by one, each of the children met untimely deaths. Sickness, accidents, one tragedy after another. They all died—every one of them. And, in the years since, the rest of my brothers and sisters." Kane rubbed his brow as he talked. The words escaped stubbornly, and they left behind a tartness on his dry tongue as they passed. "When Odin cursed Sareth's blood, it was passed on to her children, and her children's children, and so on. Crawford nearly escaped the curse because of his alliance with the demon."

Kane paused for a moment, as though reflecting. The reporter was numb with awe and confusion. "What, what about your father?" Benedict whispered.

"My father came to see Crawford later in life," Kane returned to his past. "Crawford told everyone he was simply a businessman from Wisconsin. I don't know what happened between my father and Crawford Borley, but my father ended up in that room—on the fourth floor—at the end of the hall. At least that's apparently what happened, based on what Mrs. Hawley said. He didn't die though. He just went crazy—completely insane—and he died a few years later in a hospital."

"And your aunt? Liza?" inquired the reporter.

"I met her when I was a young man, and she told me some about the legend. She sort of kept up with family history, genealogy, that sort of thing. She said she thought our family was cursed. And she told me about Crawford, my rich half-uncle in Asheville, who kept something terrible in his castle. She believed that someday the curse would get Crawford Borley, too—that The Horror would eventually destroy him like everyone else. That's why I suspected foul play when he died. My aunt is dead now, but two of her daughters are still alive."

<263>

"How did she die?"

"She drowned," Kane replied. "And so I, and my two female cousins, are the last ones left. If we ever have children, the curse will be passed on to them. One after the other, everyone has died who came before me. Obviously, I'm next. It could come at any time, in any way. A curse is like a deadly, dormant virus, waiting to strike at the most unpredictable moment. Therefore, I've done what anyone would do—after I inherited my father's money, I began using it to fund my efforts to salvage what's left of a bleak life. If I don't stop the curse, then I will soon be dead, as well as my cousins. And though it has been necessary for you, and the rest of the world, to see me only as a hard, unfeeling shell of a man, inside there burns a desire for life that has tortured me for as long as my memory will serve."

Benedict's mind was flooded with questions. He was looking at the stern figure before him as a new creature—one who had feelings and vulnerabilities like any other. The transformation was so sudden that the reporter felt lost. He opened his mouth, but specific words were difficult to form from massive cloud in his mind. "And Borley? So Borley—J.C. Borley? He's your…your cousin? Half-cousin? And he doesn't even know it?"

"That's right," Kane answered. "Though I hate to say it."

"But how?" Benedict threw up his hands. "How can you stop the curse? What's the answer?"

"The answer is here," the stranger said, turning his attention to a black waterproof sack attached to his side. He unzipped both its linings and withdrew a sealed plastic bag. After opening it, he poured the scroll, vial, and key from Guastavino's tomb onto his left hand. "Odin gave me the answer." He handed the scroll to Benedict.

Almost ceremoniously, the reporter took the yellowed scroll. Its imminence tingled his flesh electrically. The green string was tied gently around it, and Benedict removed it carefully. Upon doing so, he delicately

<264>

unrolled the aged paper, straightening it before himself. Then, with fascination, he read the words lavishly written in fine, black ink:

My Dearest Man,

Though we do not share blood, we both face a complication of my making. If you are reading this, it means I have made a terrible mistake, one that I have feared I made for many years. In the balance now lies your life and my soul. In foolish, sinful passion, I placed a curse upon your lineage. And now, it falls upon you to reverse my wicked actions. There is a great evil in the castle, a demon of incredible power and capable of disastrous manipulation. I should have banished it myself, but I lacked the strength. And since it was I who used its power for a curse, it is I, and only I, who have the power to defeat it. Since I am now gone, I have placed the power in this vial of holy water. It has been prepared with a ritual by my own hands. To banish the demon and release us from our doomed fates, this water needs only make contact with the demon that resides in the great castle. Use this key to enter a passageway below the castle that will take you inside through a series of caves. Surely, I am now tortured by my deplorable acts, but I hope you will forgive me for what I have done in my reckless youth. May God be with you as you undo my evil deeds.

~Odin

Benedict rolled up the scroll and handed it back to Kane. His eyes were melancholy and inept. "I'm sorry," he said.

Kane squeezed the scroll and sighed. "God…I thought we were going to get in there tonight. I thought tonight I would end it all. But now, I don't know what to do. We've followed every lead, and I still am nowhere closer to my goal."

They shared silence for a moment. A wave of hopelessness filled them, and the reporter searched for something positive. "I don't know either," Benedict said. "But at least you've tried…at least you've tried."

"Now do you understand my secrecy?" Kane asked.

<265>

"Yes," there reporter answered. "If anyone knew you were a Borley, they would never help you. But, there's one thing I don't understand. What made you trust me? Why did you let me in?"

Kane looked to the vial in his hand. "I let you in because of what you saw the first time I met you." The reporter seemed confused. "The first time I met you, you saw Odin's ghost, right?"

"Yes," Benedict replied, "at the Grove Park Inn. It was his fleeting form—I thought it was you at first."

"That's why," said Kane.

"I don't understand," the reporter frowned.

"My family has seen the apparition for decades," explained the stranger, "but no one outside the family has ever seen it. That is, except for you." Benedict's face lit up. "I don't know why you saw the phantom," Kane continued, "but I knew immediately that you were meant to help me on my quest. I was right."

The impact of the words settled heavily with the reporter, and a sense of enormous honor overcame him. It was the first time Kane had ever come close to genuinely complimenting him. Basking in the veneration for but an instant, he quickly moved on. "Kane," he said, "are you afraid of it? That *thing* in the castle?"

"I'd like to think I'm not," said the stranger. "But when we walked towards that door, I could sense it on the other side, craving my destruction."

"No, that doesn't make sense," Benedict replied. "Weck said the slot is on the door so the demon will know a Borley is entering—that he wouldn't kill Borleys."

"Then why was Crawford Borley ripped in half?" Kane snapped.

The reporter placed a finger on his chin. "Hummm. I don't know. But still, I get the feeling it wants to feed off you—off your energy. That it would like to see you alive so that you, too, can serve it."

"Perhaps," Kane said. "But it doesn't matter now. I'll never get inside that damn castle."

<266>

Benedict was frozen in reflection, his brain processing the enormous situation. The past, the present, and the many possible futures were complex and intricate. The magnitude of it all was astounding. He looked at Kane with a dire glare. "My God," he said, as if the implications had taken full effect, "*there is a demon in Asheville.*"

The stranger's eyes were dismal and defeated. "Let's get out of here," he replied. Silently, they began to gather the remaining equipment.

<267>

CHAPTER TEN

LIKE UNCERTAIN THIEVES, creeping through the writhing fog to find their mark, Kane and Benedict slinked towards a drowsy, soundless house. Their vehicle was parked a block away, and the pair, poised and edgy, had crossed through backyards, over half-hung fences, and through driveways to conceal their approach. Kane gripped his pistol in a sweaty hand, his eyes exploring the darkness like a cat's.

"Perhaps we should do this tomorrow, when it's daylight," Benedict whispered in the stranger's ear.

"Nonsense," Kane replied. "It's *your* house. You should be able to go there any time you like."

Benedict was quite distraught. "Yes, but my friend doesn't mind if I stay there again tonight, and I just think it'd be better during daylight, when we can see."

"No, no, no," the stranger reiterated. "If *we* can see better, that means *they* can see better, as well. We should use the darkness to our advantage."

They entered the reporter's back yard, adhering as tightly as possible to the long, wide shadows cast by a few old trees. The grass and fallen leaves were slick and shiny with moisture, giving way softly and quietly beneath their feet. From behind a sleeping maple, they examined the house.

Benedict's abode was simple and quaint. It was a boxy house, neat and clean, but devoid of personality. Not one light emanated from the home; it was as dark and still and lifeless as a structure can be. In every way, it seemed utterly empty, like the inhabitants were conspicuously gone on a long trip.

<268>

Kane gave the reporter a questioning look, motioning to the house with his head. Benedict viewed it a long time, watching it closely, but also tapping his intuition, anticipating a feeling of abnormality. Finally, he returned a relaxed nod to the stranger, as if his tests, based on physical and psychic observation, had come back clear.

Nonetheless, the two men dashed across the yard, running low to the ground. Shrubbery surrounded the home and, using it as a shield, they snuck around, peeping into windows and looking for signs of unlawful entry. Again, all seemed clear. With that, feeling quite satisfied, Benedict deftly unlocked the back door. The pair slipped inside, still maintaining the obscurity of special forces agents.

As hushed and elusive as a shadow himself, Kane skulked within the lightless building, checking each room and corner. Having determined the place was indeed vacant, he began flipping on lights. With each newly-lit room, the subtle coziness of the modest house replaced the guilty darkness that had greeted the two.

Once the place was firmly secured, all lights on and all doors and windows locked, Kane plopped down on the spongy, brown couch to relax. Benedict, on the other hand, was busy investigating his curtain, eyeing the way it leaned against the window sill, and the crinkles that sprawled down its length.

"I'm telling you," said the reporter, "somebody moved this curtain. I would have never left the house with the curtain pulled out like this."

"Oh well," said Kane, extending his hands nonchalantly, "at least they're gone now. And at least they didn't break in a window or something."

"I suppose," Benedict replied. "Yet I despise the thought of some thugs trudging and snooping around in here while I'm gone."

Mentally and physically exhausted, Kane stared at a glass ashtray on Benedict's coffee table. There was a golden sparkle at its edge, and the stranger lost himself in it, his worn mind searching to escape his sore body.

"Would you like a drink?" the reporter offered.

"Sure," Kane snapped out of his trance. "What have you got?"

<269>

"Oh…bourbon, vodka, gin…"

"Mix me up somethin' with bourbon," the stranger requested. "I'm not particular."

"Very well," said the reporter, pacing to his makeshift bar in the kitchen.

While Benedict rummaged about, glasses clanking, liquids pouring, swizzle sticks stirring, Kane lost himself again in the singular gold reflection. His mind wandered and his body drifted into drowsiness. Within seconds, he slipped into a peaceful, welcoming sleep. For a short but immeasureable time, he was taken away from harsh reality, his delicate dreams escorting him gently. And then, "Knock! Knock! Knock!"

The vibrations of hard rapping on the front door rattled throughout the house. Instantly rejuvenated, Kane was on his feet, keen awareness in his eyes. Benedict appeared at the kitchen doorway, drinks in hand, his face doused with alarm. The stranger glided to him.

"Who could that be?" Kane hissed. The reporter shook his head in confusion.

Again: "Knock! Knock! Knock!"

"I'll go out the back and sneak around the front," the stranger said. "Wait a few seconds before you open the door." In a flash, he was gone.

Benedict placed the drinks on a nearby table, raising his enlarged pupils to his own foreboding door. "Who is it?" he called, pacing dreadfully towards the entrance. There was no reply. Upon reaching the door, his hand resting unsurely on the knob, he asked again. "Who is it?"

"I'm looking for Wilson Benedict," a muffled voice replied.

"And who are you?" the reporter inquired.

"Are you Mr. Benedict?" the voice came back.

The reporter was flustered. "I said what is *your* name?" he demanded.

"I'd like to speak with you in person," said the voice. "It's a private matter."

"I'm sorry," Benedict stated, "but you'll have to—"

"Slam!" There was a loud, forceful thump on the opposite side, immediately followed by a grunt. Then came the unclear words of the stranger. At last, Benedict opened the door. Pressed against the frame

<270>

was a young man, his face smooshed into the woodwork. Kane clenched him from behind, a pistol crammed into the man's temple.

"This is the last time I'm asking!" Kane shouted. "Who are you!"

"Please, please, don't shoot me," begged the man. "I'm Lee Jenson; Robert Jensen was my father!"

"*Doctor* Robert Jensen?" Benedict questioned.

"Yes, yes, that's right," the man struggled. "Doctor Robert Jensen, who recently died."

Kane and Benedict traded a glance. "Are you alone?" asked the stranger.

"Yes," the man said. "I only want to talk."

The reporter motioned to bring him in, and Kane tossed the visitor inside the house, his gun still trained.

For the first time, they got a good look at the man. He appeared to be in his mid to late twenties. A somewhat fragile person, his hair was neatly cut and combed, and thin-rimmed glasses on his face propelled an air of intellectual distinction. There was a certain awkwardness in his build, and a frightful innocence in his eyes. Dressed in a sweater and slacks, he certainly looked as though the son of a doctor. Completely surprised and mentally off balance, he bore the expression of a captured creature.

Kane closed the door back, latching its deadbolt securely.

"Please," Lee implored, "I haven't come to cause trouble."

"Then why are you here?" Kane barked.

"I'm sorry to come so late, but I saw your lights on for the first time a long while. I've been trying to get in touch with Wilson Benedict. It's very important, and every day and night I've been driving by, trying to see if I can catch him."

"I'm Wilson Benedict," the reporter offered his hand. "I apologize for the rough introduction, but we've had some…unfriendly people after us lately."

"I understand," the young man said. "I've been quite cautious myself. That's why I was hesitant to give you my name."

<271>

"Have a seat," Benedict presented his living room.

"Thank you," Lee replied humbly, seating himself on the couch, the other two settling around him.

"Let me offer my condolences with regard to your father," the reporter said politely. "Now what can I do for you?" Like a guardian, Kane watched quietly, his gun not far away.

"Everyone in town, even the police, insisted my father killed himself," Lee began. "They say he was home all night, and then he went out and hung himself from that bridge. But that's not true. He went to J.C. Borley's house that night. But the only person who said he was at Borley's house was you, in your article. Then that was the last I heard of it. Now, the police aren't even investigating anymore. I tried to get in touch with you right after the article was published, but the paper said you didn't work there anymore. Your house was always empty, and I couldn't find your phone number. That's when I knew that Borley had gotten to you, too."

Benedict was thoroughly intrigued. "What do you know about Borley?" the reporter asked.

There was a ripe answer in the young man's face, but he delayed in his response. "Listen," he said. "I don't mean to be rude, but this is rather personal stuff. I don't feel comfortable talking unless I know who you are." He was looking at the stranger.

The stiffness in Kane's face gave way a bit. "I'm Kane," he said, shaking Lee's hand. "I'm investigating J.C. Borley. That accounts for my secrecy."

"Are you a policeman?" Lee asked.

"No," Kane said. "I'm private."

The young man was perplexed. "Then…who hired you?"

"I'm sorry," the stranger replied, "but I'm not at liberty to say. However, I assure you, I'm on your side."

"You can trust Kane," Benedict vouched. "Borley wants him, too."

Much more at ease, Lee continued. "I'm not sure about my own safety. Therefore, after I say what I've come to say, I'm leaving town. I

<272>

hope you'll forgive my rush. You may find some of this hard to believe, but I give you my word, I speak only the truth."

"Thank you for your honesty," the reporter nodded.

"J.C. Borley," Lee said, "is an…evil, evil man. And it's his cruelty that has given him, and his family, such power. He practices black magic, and he uses it to influence business deals—to win people over and to get rid of others. And his direct link to the other side comes from a devil he keeps in the castle—he calls it The Sate. In order for anyone to succeed in this town—and I mean acquire any measure of wealth or influence, he or she must eventually join Borley's coven, worshipping the demon. The demon gives them Borley's power and protection, and in return, they give a percentage of their earnings to Borley. They also pull favors for each other. And it spans from politicians and law enforcers, right down to teachers, news anchors, and various community professionals."

"So," Benedict interjected, "would you say it's more like a religion, a secret society…a cult?"

"There's little difference between them," the young man answered. "I should point out that to a lot of people, devil worship, sacrifices, cere-monies and that sort of thing, seem too silly to be true. But it's no more strange than what all religions do. Look at some of your typical Christian churches: speaking in tongues, laying on hands, baptism and ceremony. You have the 'eating' of Christ's body and the 'drinking' of Christ's blood. All those things are strange, too. We're simply used to them though. For the most part, the ceremonies of worshippers of the dark side are no different—except in one way, that is: When you wor-ship the dark side, you see immediate results."

"All right," Kane said, eager to get back to the point. "So where does your father's death fit into this thing?"

"I'm not proud to say it," Lee bowed his head, "but my father was a part of Borley's coven. That's how he became such a prestigious doctor in the area. It was with Borley's help. For decades, he was an integral part of The Sate's cult, and he used to tell me about it—in secret of

<273>

course—and how that I, too, might someday have to join. But things changed about a year ago. He started questioning his role in the religion. He began to wonder whether or not it was right. I don't know if he was involved in any of the killings, but he certainly knew they happened. And so, one day he decided he wanted out. But that was a mistake. Once you join, you stay in for life. And so, for a long time, my father and Borley went back and forth. My father said he wanted out, and Borley kept telling him to reconsider. But, my father never would. In fact, my father decided to go public and tell the world what was happening here in Asheville. But, not surprisingly, that was a big mistake. Obviously, Borley decided to kill him. But instead of killing him privately, in the castle—instead of giving him to The Sate—he wanted to make a billboard out of my father—a symbolic display, for all others in Asheville to see what happens when you defy J.C. Borley. And it worked, just like it always works for Borley. He got what he wanted, and he's paid no consequence."

Kane and Benedict lit up a cigarette, thinking intensely about the young man's heartfelt words. The massive scale of the sinister conspiracy chilled them to their aching bones.

"Lee," the reporter exhaled a line of smoke, "Kane and I have been researching J.C. Borley for quite a while. We want to get into the castle, but we can't find a way. Did your father know of a secret way inside?"

"Oh yes," the young man shook his head. "There are caves underneath the castle, and there's a secret passageway that leads inside."

"No, no," Kane frowned, "it's been flooded. We've already tried."

"Flooded?" Lee curled his brow. "No, you're talking about the old passages. There's another one that they use all the time."

"Then where is it?" the stranger threw up his hands.

"Well there's a passage that leads from the caves to The Devil's Circle, where they have ceremonies."

"Yes?"

<274>

"And then there's a passage that leads from the same area which goes *into* the castle—at least that's what my father said."

"Well then," Kane leaned forward, "where, *specifically*, is this passage?"

"Oh, I don't know," Lee brushed the air with his fingers. "But if you hide and watch when they're having their ceremonies, you're sure to see them enter it."

Both Kane's and Benedict's eyebrows popped up, like the proverbial light bulb had switched on within their skulls. Its radiance glowed from their faces in high contrast to the gloom that had previously consumed them.

"When do they have ceremonies?" the reporter asked, anxious for the reply.

"At various times throughout the year," the young man said. "But the largest one is coming up in just a few days, on Halloween night."

"Halloween night?" Kane said, entranced. "How theatrical. Please, tell us more."

"Well, it's all about Samhain," Lee settled a bit in his cushion. "November 1st was the New Year for the ancient Celts, otherwise known as Samhain. The night before, October 31st, belonged to neither the old year, nor the new year. Because it was a moment separate from time, the realms of the past were opened, and the spirits of the dead could roam the earth. Therefore, the druids would perform ceremonies to honor the dead. In the same tradition, though now an evil one, each year Borley's coven joins on the eve of Samhain to honor The Sate, the dark spirit world, and the Lord of the Dead. The high priests meet in Borley's Castle to have a great feast. Then, they dress in ceremonial garb and pass through the castle's dungeon, arriving in the caves. From the caves, they enter The Devil's Circle, perform, and then re-enter the castle through the same passageways. They get dressed then leave—back to their normal lives again."

"And what about Borley?" the reporter asked. "Does he join in the ceremony?"

<275>

"No," the young man replied. "Borley never joins in. He hosts the feast, of course. But that's all."

"My God," Kane said. "I never realized it was so elaborate."

"Oh yes," Lee reassured him. "It's an intricate system of power and organization."

"So if we watch the devil worshippers," Kane said, "we'll be able to see how they enter the castle."

"Certainly," Lee responded. "I don't see why not. If you're there Halloween night, you should get an eyeful. However," he raised a finger, "I should warn you. Whenever a ceremony is being practiced, the worshippers set up three circles of guards around them—boundaries, if you will—each spaced perhaps a few hundred feet apart. These are usually people dressed in ordinary clothing. If you meet the first circle, they will simply tell you to turn around and leave. Most people comply gladly. If you make it to the second circle, you'll be beaten. And if you make it to the third circle, you'll be sacrificed. Sometimes, the third circle will be identified by a carving on a tree—a gruesome face or an inverted pentagram. So, if you do intend to go, please be wary of these obstacles."

"Thank you," said the reporter.

Glancing at his watch, Lee suddenly stood. "I'm afraid I must be going," he said, his voice much calmer than when he'd arrived. "I've done what I wanted to do."

"And what exactly is that?" asked Benedict, standing as well, Kane at his side.

"I've told you the truth," the young man said. "Even if it may be the abridged version. But now you know. And now I trust you'll let the rest of the world know, so that I may have justice for my father's death."

"But I'm not a reporter anymore," Benedict grimaced.

"However," Kane jumped in, "I assure you. Justice will be served."

After walking to the door, Lee once again clasped hands with the two. "I'm heading out of town in the morning," he said. "Borley knows that *I know*. I'll be dead soon if I don't disappear."

<276>

"Thank you so much for coming here," the reporter smiled. "You've been an enormous help."

"Thank you," Lee returned a grin. "Thank you for being bold enough to publish the truth."

In a few minutes, the young man, alone and assailable, was inside his tidy foreign car, sputtering away into the night. Kane and Benedict looked at each other. For the first time, they possessed a buoyant, fortuitous wavering in their guts. Something about the brief meeting felt good.

*   *   *

October 31st. It was like the earth had died for a night, and on its last exhale, as the life slipped away, the darkness of the other world had oozed into the void left behind. Ever so gently, the sun had submerged into the grave of the horizon, leaving behind a cold, blue world to fend for itself. The leaves and trees were dry and crackly, and the air was so thin that it could not restrain the spirits of the dead, unleashing them into the helpless realm of the living. The color black had never looked blacker, and the lustrous moon above, a mangy cat at the side of the road, and the fire in a jack-o-lantern's eyes never looked more sinister. The sky above felt bigger and bleaker than before, its infinite mystery overwhelming; and within each shadow, a spectral predator lurked and waited—watching, always watching.

But amongst the more substantial, underlying malevolence of the night, frivolities danced about its crust. There were rubber bats, flapping from bands of elastic, fabric ghosts hanging from trees, grinning, gap-toothed pumpkins at every doorstep, and the people—ahh, the people. It was like the world had turned inside-out for a night, and all of society filled the streets. Both children and adults were decked in costumes of every kind. Witches, goblins, werewolves, Frankenstein monsters, and grotesque, slashed faces strolled every lane. Plastic caul-

<277>

drons of candy sweets abounded, houses were mummified with soaring rolls of toilet paper, dry ice fog rolled off green fountains of punch, and floating apples were bobbed for from wide, germ-filled vats. In ghoulish garb, storytellers sat around lapping campfires, relating creepy tales of the past: stories of hooks and hitchhikers, spook-infested houses, heads in bags, cold-blooded murders, and pranks gone terribly wrong—all of them true, of course. And at Helen's Bridge, teens gathered to spot the ghostly mistress, perhaps to find her handprint burned permanently into the finish of their cars. At other places, like the secluded, vacant water tower, the "open cut," or Spivey Mountain, some of the more bold searched to find Satanists absorbed in their cursed rites, a human sacrifice splayed before them. Young men, intrepid and dashing in their capes and masks, competed for the favors of young women, dressed seductively in the revealing costumes of morbid temptresses. Smoke, candy, mischief, tales, spirits, ancient evil, and the crisp air. This was Halloween.

Mid-evening in downtown Asheville, the Wiccans had gathered for their annual celebration. Kane and Benedict disappeared into the freakish crowd of curious observers, using the vantage point to view Borley's Castle on the mountain above. Its windows glowed orange from the festive feast inside, a human silhouette passing by from time to time. They had decided to wait until closer to midnight to approach The Devil's Circle.

Deep into the night, when most trick-or-treaters had retired to their homes to indulge, and the only ones about were drunken partiers flowing from the bars, Kane and Benedict drove towards the cove. It was enchanting in the darkness, and the peacefulness of the night made its eeriness all the more complex. Through the windows of the car, they viewed their surroundings like hawks, waiting for the first glimpse of abnormality. Passing the "Covenwood" sign, they turned up the dirt road that led farther into the unruly forest. On the way they passed a small, still pond, seen not for its reflections, but instead its utter lack of them.

<278>

Upon rounding a curve, the rough gravel grinding beneath them, they were startled to see confirmation of their suspicion. Standing in the middle of the road were two men, slightly bundled, with flashlights and rifles in hand. Surely, they were the guardians of the first circle.

Benedict brought the vehicle to a lazy stop, and the bright headlights flooded the men, washing them out like pale corpses. One of the men, the largest one, leisurely approached the driver's side. The other man stood firm, his face edgy and stiff. The reporter rolled down his window.

"Happy Halloween," the man uttered in a gruff voice, leaning down to peer into the vehicle.

"Likewise," Benedict responded with a smile. Kane secretly held a pistol tight beneath his flowing coat.

"What are you boys up to tonight?" the guard said. He had a rugged visage, with a stubbly face and a cap pulled low on his brow.

"Oh we're just taking a shortcut through here," the reporter grinned. "Besides it seems like a spooky place for a drive tonight."

"Yeah," the man chuckled ominously, his eyes sparkling. "Well, this road's closed off for tonight."

"Oh?" Benedict frowned. "Why is that?"

"We've had a few problems with vandals up here on Halloween night. You know, teenagers doin' all that weird stuff—stealin' black pets and raidin' houses and such. There's also a few graves up here, and we don't want no tombstones turned over and that kind o' thing. You know how crazy kids can be Halloween night."

"Oh yes," Benedict agreed. "You hear about it on the news all the time."

"Yeah, it's a shame," the man continued. "Little girl who lives beside me got a razor blade in a cupcake tonight. Sliced her gums wide open. What a crazy damn world it is, huh?"

"Indeed," the reporter nodded, "indeed. Well, we'll just turn around here then."

"All right. Have a good'n," the guard waved with a surreal, plastic smile, strolling back over to take his spot.

<279>

The reporter maneuvered the car around in the narrow roadway, he and Kane maintaining sealed lips and expressionless faces until they were away. Driving in the opposite direction, they saw the guards disappear from their tail lights in the rear-view mirror.

"That was a creepy son-of-a-bitch," Kane said, relaxing a bit.

"Well I suppose the job calls for it," Benedict replied. "And I guarantee you those men wouldn't hesitate to shoot someone."

"Neither would I," Kane murmured.

"So what next?"

"I think we should find a cozy little spot, pull over, hide the car, and go back on foot. If those are the only two guys, we can just walk around them in the woods."

"But what about the other circles?" the reporter said.

Kane lifted his gun. "We'll deal with them when we get there."

"You sure put a lot of faith in your firearm," the reporter remarked.

"Well," said Kane, "there *was* a time when I thought if a .45 couldn't kill it, it didn't exist. But now I'm not so sure."

Just outside the dirt road, they found a worn hollow shielded by brush and hanging limbs, behind which they pulled the car. Jittering a bit from nervousness, Benedict exited the vehicle, deftly closing the door behind him. Kane sat for a moment with his door open, intensely engaged in checking his ammunition and placing his sacred vial in the safety of a cushioned coat pocket. The reporter eyed the morose darkness deeply, feeling terribly inadequate compared to its size and mystery. There were houses scattered about, their porch lamps long since turned off, and Benedict wondered if their lightless windows might shroud spying eyes, eager to alert the coven to the intruders.

"All right," Kane announced, softly closing his door as well, "I'm ready. How 'bout you?"

Benedict hesitated in his answer, still viewing the unyielding night. "I don't have a great feeling about this," he said. "I mean, we don't really have a plan. We're just going to walk through the woods, hope we don't

<280>

run into someone, and then watch the ceremony. But if we do get caught, and shooting erupts, that will probably ruin our chances for the rest of the night."

"Listen," Kane drew his large frame close to Benedict's, punctuating his low words, "as long as we take our time, stay quiet, and circumnavigate the guards as best we can, we'll probably be just fine."

Nodding with approval, the reporter followed Kane, the pair wading off into the ocean of scraggly brush and vines at the woodland's edge. It was ever so difficult for them to walk noiselessly. The dry air had drained the leaves and sticks of moisture, leaving their surroundings brittle and crackly; and the smallest noise was faithfully, sharply carried in the clear night. They sometimes tread on the toes or edges of their feet, reducing the amount of surface contact, pressing their weight into the ground lightly and gradually with each step. Progression was laggard and meticulous, but soon enough they found themselves deep into the soul of the menacing forest.

The dirt road was far off to their right, and when they passed the section where the guards stood, they could hear a faint, garbled mumbling through the trees. With just as much ease, the guards would hear the intruders if the utmost silence was not exercised. Kane and Benedict only took steps when they heard the guards conversing—keeping each sound lower than the sentinels' voices. Steamy and agitated by the slow pace, each man had to reject the tendency to speed up, though it plagued him again and again.

Upon safely passing the "first circle," they stayed closer together, viewing their surroundings with greater discrimination. They were unsure whether or not the "second circle" of guards were also confined to the road, or if they might infiltrate the woods, as well. If such henchmen in fact filled the forest, the outline of any tree might conceal their poised, malign forms.

For a good half-hour, Kane and Benedict trudged forward, neither seeing any sign of more guards. At last, they surmised they'd probably

<281>

passed whatever second boundary might exist, and that the guards were either so quiet on the road they hadn't been noticed, or were so sparsely spread in the timbers that they had been avoided. In order to locate The Devil's Circle, it was necessary to cross the gravel lane and continue up the backside of the ascending mountain. Therefore, the two trespassers began working their way towards the right, their ever-increasing paranoia the greatest asset in remaining undetected.

A rough embankment, tangled with undergrowth, adjoined the road, and when Kane and Benedict reached it, they rigorously navigated the steep wall of dirt. The stranger's gun was drawn, and it proved an inconvenience as he pulled himself through the untamed terrain. At the top of the embankment, the two hesitated before climbing onto the gravel, peeking their heads up to spy. All seeming clear, they topped the slope, finding themselves in the middle of an isolated curve. Swiftly crossing the lane, they disappeared into the brushy rise of land on the opposite side.

Continuing up the mountain, not entirely sure of their orientation to the destination, the area seemed surprisingly uneventful. All was quiet with the exception of their own bodies disturbing the woodland. The melancholy strength of the night, Samhain at its heels, was constantly looming upon them, yet their progress was undeterred. The farther they ventured however, the more helpless they became—losing themselves in the dark, unfamiliar growth. Upon crossing the creek though, the same one near the entrance to the caves, they knew they were on the right track. The Devil's Circle was nearby.

The two stopped to rest for a bit, seating themselves on a great misplaced boulder, breathing in the cool, aquatic air. "So what do you think?" Benedict asked. "Suppose we'll find anything?"

"Oh probably," Kane replied. "Those guards aren't there for nothin'."

After a few minutes of reflection, they began hiking again. Leading down from the secluded section of the mountain where The Devil's Circle was nestled, there were wide, gentle indentions in the land,

<282>

perhaps dried up creek beds or the remnants of old logging roads. Having remembered them from before, the two used the landmarks as guides. The ghostly trails led them higher and higher, towards the familiar jagged terrain that should house the wicked ceremony.

The hikers used their flashlights at an absolute minimum, occasionally blinking them on for a second or two to view the path in front of them, and even then, shielding the bulb with a folded hand. Their eyes had adjusted well to the night, and in most cases, artificial illumination was not necessary. The bent and knotted shapes of the forest could usually be distinguished by comparing shades and contrasts: dark against darker. And with their eyes toiling in such a way, Benedict spotted a sight so pale against its background that it seemed to shine like a lustrous patch of foxfire. He froze.

"What's that?" the reporter whispered.

Without hesitation, Kane turned on his flashlight, spilling detail upon the pallid surface. It was a thick, brown tree, and a large patch of the bark had been removed, exposing the lighter wood like the soft underbelly of a toad. Within the barren patch, deep, broad lines were carved: it was a malevolent face, scowling like the evil spirit of the tree itself . Its eyes were long and slanted, its brow tense and twisted, an intolerant, merciless sneer spread across its hewn mouth. A lone visage amongst the cluttered growth, it stood as an unnerving sign.

Kane looked to the reporter. "Consider yourself warned," he said. "And welcome to the 'third circle.'" Nobly, he trudged forward, not sparing another thought on the omen. About to speak, the reporter swallowed his words and then followed along. Now, they were fair game.

As they continued to climb, Kane's gun drawn at his side, they could sense the land rising to a knoll. Unsure of the mountain's layout, they couldn't tell how close their destination might be. Given the threatening carving however, it was clear they had entered the final boundary. Tense with anxiety, lips sealed in thought and preparation, they proceeded

<283>

diligently—until, at last, a sound, faint but distinct, drifted down the incline. Immediately, they stopped.

It was a lone human voice, masculine, yet bizarre. It shifted unnaturally from deep, chesty tones to high, sharp peaks. Kane and Benedict focused on it, their brains attempting to sort it into recognizable speech. It was soon evident that it spoke in a language unfamiliar to them; drifting eerily from the darkness, wafting from across the knoll. For several minutes they listened, fascinated and disturbed, and then the voice ceased. Next came silence, dead and complete, like a charged calm before a building storm. And then, at once, the mountainside hissed with the chants of a chorus of black tongues.

Kane and Benedict could see the top of the incline, the silhouette of its trees darker than the space behind them. The chanting, gothic and evil, poured down the slope, each stiff leaf vibrating with the sinister waves. The Devil's Circle, alive with ceremony, was surely just over the hill. The reporter looked to Kane with distressed eyes, the sound of the group inciting a tendency to flee in his veins. But the stranger appeared as stern and sharp as flint, his nature undeterred. If anything, there was a trace of excitement in his face. He had found what he sought. Discreetly, he continued towards the top of the mound, Benedict following worriedly.

Each step towards the summit was plagued with emotion. A mixture of fear, hate, and fascination weighed upon the pair. They eagerly anticipated, and ruefully dreaded, whatever sight might lie in wait, shielded only by the earth. The plane of land separating them from the tides of bleak wickedness grew shorter and shorter, until at last, their heads rose above the bluff. A blood-chilling sight emerged.

A few hundred feet away, the walls of the crescent-shaped canyon glowed orange with reflected flames. A bonfire raged like hell itself, and around it, in circular formation, a large group of cloaked worshippers clasped hands. Dark hoods hung from their bowed heads, and druidic robes draped from their bodies. Their faces were phantasmally

<284>

concealed in shadow, and sharp, sinister, ancient words spouted from unseen lips. Aside from the bonfire, torches mounted around the site rendered extra illumination to the nauseating adornments strewn about. There were black pets of most every kind—cats, dogs, a ferret, even a calf—hanging upside-down, crucified on crude, wooden crosses. Disturbing mockeries of Christ, a final grimace of horror was frozen on each creature's meek face. Runes, astrological signs, "666,"and other strange symbols were smeared on the canyon walls in blood, each letter having oozed and dripped delicate streams of liquid life. But weirdest of all was the centerpiece of the event.

In the middle of the bonfire stood a tall, wooden stake. Curiously, though it emerged from the blaze, it did not burn. Upon its top was mounted the bulbous, severed head of a pig. Thick with flesh, its eyes closed tight, the head seemed an ornament of intelligent life. Like a scene from *Lord of the Flies*, it was a grisly display, the patrons apparently concentrating their thoughts and energies on the mounted trophy before them.

Enchanted with terror and disgust, Kane and Benedict silently observed, the firelight playing at their own half-hidden faces. There was a group of partially stacked rocks at the top of the knoll, and they laid upon them, using the stones to shield their bodies from view. The morbid sight appeared unreal, and they were so absorbed in its observance, that it almost seemed like a movie—something from which they could feel disconnected—a reality which their minds did not want to accept. In fact, they mentally displaced themselves from the scene to such an extent that they almost forgot they could be seen.

The monstrous chanting continued, raising in intensity. And though the power of the foreign speech grew stronger, the distinction of the words became increasingly muddled and unclear. At last, the demonic chorus became one uniform tone. The voices harmonized on a low, throaty note, and the vibrations rattled lowly throughout the forest. Kane and Benedict could feel the immense sound waves tingling and

<285>

rippling at their cheeks. The note was held for an inhuman period of time, no additional breaths being taken. The resonance seemed to inspire a growing euphoria in the worshippers, their bodies quivering slightly, a rising orgasmic energy flowing through them.

Smoothly, in one swell of transparent force, the pig's head, solid and heavy with tough meat, slid upwards on the pole. The slight suction of its brain sealed around the stake was breaking, and with its gooey release it moved more easily. As if being lifted by invisible hands, the skull slowly, but proficiently, cleared the post, the head floating on a cushion of malign force. Inch by inch, it rose sacredly into the air, beginning to slowly turn on its ascent, revolving nobly in midair like a globe turning on its stand. The cultists were now entirely absorbed in their combined effort, their attention solely focused on the levitating hunk of flesh.

The hidden observers could scarcely believe their eyes. Before them, physics had seemingly been defied. The joined energy of the worshippers was manipulating the environment; its vibrations reached a paramount of intensity that rattled Kane and Benedict's innards, a sickness rising from their shaken stomachs. The air at their faces was being jarred with such force that it was difficult to suck in, producing a nearly claustrophobic effect on the two.

Supremely involved in their ceremony, the sorcerers appeared oblivious to anything outside The Devil's Circle, their attention powerfully contained within its bounds. The pig's head revolved on its unseen axis, the energy maximizing and momentum growing. The unified voices inflated to a nearly unbearable crescendo. Then, they stopped. The head fell, its weighty form impaling once again with a "plop." It landed somewhat askew, the pointed tip of the stake jutting from the swine's left eye.

Immediately, the tension of the air released; but it was instantly replaced by another tension—a new tension. Each of the cultists were frozen. Though their lips had extinguished the note in the same second, there was no further motion. They stood like stiff medieval displays at a

<286>

wax museum, perhaps as though a source of energy had left them, perhaps as though they momentarily neglected all physical properties of their bodies to concentrate on a sense. The sudden quiet was almost as hard and unbearable as the crushing sound had been; and Kane and Benedict held their breath to prevent making a noise in the uncomfortable, unexpected silence. They observed the worshippers, waiting for them to resume, hoping their new actions would continue to make them oblivious to the spies.

Then, in a singular instant, so quickly and reflexively that the actual motion was not seen, all the heads—*every individual hooded head*—snapped towards Kane and Benedict. Within the shadow beneath each hood, two purple eyes burned like coals. The malevolent pupils glared into the intruders, violating their very souls. As though a hateful evening sky, filled with purple stars, the group collectively concluded that death was imminent.

"Get them!" a hoarse voice ordered.

Barely comprehending the entire group had seen them, Kane and Benedict bolted. A hundred dark forms exploded into chase after them. From there, it was all a blur: limbs and vines and unstable land, weeds and briars and stones. Rushing, panting, the intruders fled desperately, mindless of the battering terrain. There was nary time to glance over a shoulder, but Kane did, nonetheless. The sight reconfirmed the motivation of his terrific flight. More like demons than men, the worshippers weaved through the trees with incredible speed and agility. It almost seemed as if they flew like witches, the ground below them providing little friction. Despite their rapid apprehension, the sounds of undergrowth ripping and tearing at their robes was widespread and distinct.

Kane and Benedict quickly lost track of each other, catching glimpses once in a while, but each more concerned with making the best time himself. The worshippers fast at their heels, the two angled their path of escape from the sloping mountainside to a plateau of woods off to the side. It made running easier for the trespassers, but

<287>

also for their pursuers. The wicked army of dark druids was ardent in its chase, loathing the thought of spies.

Splashing through a shallow creek, stumbling through fallen trees, and lying low through a grassy clearing, Kane and Benedict ran faster and faster, farther and farther, longer and longer. As he fled, his burst of energy dwindling, the stranger began to realize that escape seemed impossible. There were too many cultists, apparently with too many powers at their disposal. The future was looking grim.

After having gained some ground, Kane and Benedict crossed another creek, the reporter slipping on his way, and then encountered another huge row of boulders, bulkily reclining in the hardy earth. Finally giving in, Kane leapt across the rocks, hugging the other side for precious cover. Having seen him, the reporter breathlessly did the same.

With a "click" of miserable finality, Kane cocked his pistol. "This is it!" he exclaimed. "Here's where I kill them or they kill us!"

The reporter raised his fear-inflated eyes above the boulder. The purple flames of light, a few hundred feet away, grew larger with each second. Kane took aim at the closest pair, his sights trembling as he struggled to calm his hand. He took a deep breath, his sweaty finger tense on the trigger. He knew when the tension released, a man would be dead. His brain gave the command to fire—a gurgling cry rang out in the forest, and the purple lights halted.

The stranger was confused. He had not fired his weapon, and yet everything had stopped. Again came the cry, horrid and agonizing. Every robed figure grabbed his throat, their heads lowering as if each was in pain.

"What's going on?" Benedict whispered. Kane shrugged in reply.

Each of the worshippers turned instinctively, walking towards a common destination. On the ground, towards the back of the advancing group, a cloaked cultist wallowed on the ground. The rest congregated around him.

<288>

His hood fallen back, a man, clean-cut and professional, wrenched in the leaves and dirt. A stick, dry and dusty, with jagged broken ends, was stabbed deeply into his throat. His eyes rolling back as if in seizure, his left hand gripped the base of the stick helplessly, his other hand digging into the soft soil. He wailed sickly, the sound breaking away into chokes and gasps and gurgles. Frothing blood, a deep burgundy, oozed from the wound. Sometimes, with a gasp, a few bubbles splashed inches into the air.

"What's happened here?" a robed figure asked.

"He tripped and fell," someone answered. "It went through his throat."

Kane and Benedict watched the event from their shelter. They weren't sure whether to stay or run. The attention of the group was now on their injured, but it might not stay there.

The figure who had asked the question was apparently someone of authority. The others seemed to watch him submissively, waiting for his decision on how to handle the matter. He peered at the dying man, sighing in disappointment at what he saw. Nodding his head conclusively, he motioned to the rest of the group. Each head dropped and every eye closed. The tone, powerful and moving, again filled the air, just as it had before. The others joined in, focusing their energy on the man.

The wounded worshipper rolled about, still convulsing in pain. Suddenly, he stopped, resting on his back. It appeared as though he might have died, or perhaps slipped into unconsciousness. Ceremoniously, as with the pig's head, each voice grew stronger and stronger, their energies expanding in unison. The stick, jutting from the soft throat, began to quiver. It was naturally resistant to whatever forces played upon it—but the energies grew and grew. Slowly, the stick rose from the moist wound. Within seconds, its tip passed from the flesh with a juicy release. Beneath the object was a dark, thick hole, partially exposing the hollow inside of the esophagus. The stick dropped from the air, its energy now having passed to the wound itself. A thin trail of smoke swirled up from the hole, and the flesh began to

<289>

sizzle and bubble. Crawling with power, the skin stretched and moved, sealing itself where the lesion had been. An orangish, healing luminescence glowed subtly at the throat; it wavered upon the spot for a minute or so, and then the voices dwindled.

Like a corpse resurrected, the previously injured man opened his eyes. Apparently drained, the others helped him to his feet, patting his back and wishing him well tenderly. Satisfied, the superior figure turned his head towards the surrounding forests once again. "I'm sure they're long gone by now," he said. "Oh well, probably just kids."

Calmly, the worshippers retreated back into the trees.

Kane lowered his gun. "I don't believe it," he mumbled. "Somebody must be watching out for us tonight."

"I think somebody's been watching out for us for a long time," Benedict replied.

Still catching their breath, the two sat close to the boulder, cherishing their new sense of safety. After having run so hard, their bodies felt weak from the inside out.

"Guess we blew our chance, huh?" the reporter said with defeat.

"Oh no," Kane shook his head. "We're not giving up that easily."

Benedict was surprised. "What do you mean?"

"Well we know they're going back into the castle through a secret passage. All we have to do is hide in the caves and watch them."

The reporter was visibly troubled. "What do you mean? If they catch us, they'll kill us. Especially now."

"That's why we don't get caught," the stranger waved his hand mystically. "There's no way I'm going to wait for this opportunity again. If we hurry, we can surely make it into the caves in time to hide and wait. Once we see how they enter, we'll know how to enter."

"But you're not planning on going into the castle tonight are you? I mean with all those worshippers there. Our chances of not getting caught would be much better some other time."

<290>

"Of course they would," said the stranger. "We'll observe tonight, and then enter the castle when things calm down. Agreed?"

"Agreed."

✴   ✴   ✴

It was chilling to be back inside the caverns again. As soon as Kane and Benedict arrived at the pool, feelings of death and failure resurfaced. They could not forget the lives that had been lost, nor how narrowly they, themselves, had escaped the iciness of dying below the ground. The torches were burning when they arrived, and they quickly surveyed the dripping walls of stone, trying to determine an effective place to remain unseen.

"Here," Kane said, pointing to a lightless crevice, not far from where they had entered the water before. It would put the two below the level where the group should enter, about one hundred feet away. "That's a good spot. Let's hide in there."

The cleft was slightly taller than the stranger, and a few feet wide. Both men slipped into the chasm, careful to avoid jagged fingers of stone that jutted in places from the sides. Once inside, and with Benedict slightly crouched, both could see out. They watched the secret passage that led to The Devil's Circle, waiting impatiently for the panel to open. Once it did, the pair had no idea how the cultists would reenter the castle from below.

"Do you suppose the castle is directly above us?" Benedict said.

"I'd say so," the stranger replied. "But we should know soon enough."

Time passed slowly. It was tiring to wait inside the cleft, unable to comfortably position oneself. And, as they waited, melancholy thoughts gnawed at the occupants' brains. What if they were caught? The worshippers had apparently "sensed" them before. Why could it not happen again? In the caves they were helpless, unable to run away without

<291>

becoming lost in the maze of tunnels. Their physical discomfort compounded their mental agitation. But soon enough, their options were cut short. With a groan, the secret panel opened.

Silently, each dark figure stooped through the passageway, hands folded in front. They entered single file, so theatrically dressed and mannered they seemed like actors entering a stage. Without a word, as if still bound by ceremony, each cloaked patron took his place near the wall of the cave, leaving enough space for the others to file in. The process took several minutes. Though their heads were gothically bent, at one point, a worshipper near the back of the group raised his face as if he had suddenly heard or seen something. His eyes, the purple glow now gone, peered directly into the crevice where the intruders hid. Kane held his breath. After thirty seconds or so, the man lowered his head again. Kane exhaled.

At last, the entire congregation had entered, and the panel to their sacred grounds was closed again. Kane's heart raced as he waited to see what happened next. It might be the answer to his most enduring question. One figure, tall and willowy, stepped out from the group, his face obscured by his hood. Dutifully, he approached the central torch, merrily aflame on the rock face. He wrapped his firm fingers around the metal holder at its base and, leaning into the effort, gave it a steady twist clockwise. The entire apparatus turned soundlessly, stopping at forty-five degrees with a prominent "click." All the others were more or less lined up against the wall, and the tall one then motioned for a couple to step aside. When they moved, a familiar sight was revealed. Behind them was a small bulge of stone, a handprint stenciled on it like cave art. The tall one placed his hand over the print, lining it up, finger for finger. When he pressed, the bulge of stone receded into the wall. The gritty, grinding sound of rock rubbing rock reverberated in the cave as a hinged portion of the wall opened, like a door, beside the hand print. In the shadows, Kane and Benedict cringed at their own stupidity.

<292>

As if entering a shrine, the worshippers solemnly passed through the door, one by one. With the disappearance of each form into the raven passage, the soft patter of fading footsteps, dwindling like those traveling long stairs, floated from the hole. Once the last member passed through the portal, the camouflaged door ground shut again, presumably pushed from the opposite side. As soon as its fine, irregular edges sealed into the genuine stone again, the torch holder instantly snapped upright once more, and the formation beneath the handprint sprang forth into its seemingly natural position. A few seconds later, magically almost, each torch extinguished itself simultaneously, burying the cavern in familiar blackness.

Kane and Benedict did not speak for a while, the fresh rushing of subterranean water the only sound. Once confident that the cultists were permanently gone, the stranger shattered the darkness with a press of his flashlight's switch. The illumination was broken by thousands of chaotic shadows cast by the cave's ancient stone artistry. The two carefully exited their hiding place, and the reporter's light joined Kane's, erasing hundreds of shadows, fleeing like goblins from a sorcerer's spell.

"Good God," Benedict grumbled, "it was right there in front of us the entire time. We dove to the frigid depths of hell, and all we had to do was twist and press. We would have saved lives."

"Don't be so sure about that," Kane remarked, making his way towards the upper level, "we don't yet know what's on the other side of that passageway."

Upon reaching the hidden door, the stranger leaned down, closely examining its edges, running his cold finger along them. They dissolved flawlessly into the natural folds and grain of the cavern wall. It had been constructed with extraordinary skill and ingenuity. The seal was so tight and perfect that he doubted a razor blade would part the cracks. "So what do you suppose is under the water then?" the reporter wondered.

"I'd say it was indeed a tunnel that led into the castle, but it was probably too large and inconvenient to control. Therefore, the area

<293>

was flooded, and this new passageway constructed. As we've seen, it's perfect for the worshippers to travel secretly from the castle to The Devil's Circle."

Benedict, too, marvelled at the secret entry way. Upon brushing his hand from the door to the wall, there was no bump, or differing sensation at all, as he passed from surface to surface. "Well, now we know," he said with a sigh. "So when are we going to come back?"

Kane stood, a prickling euphoria enclosing his cool demeanor. "We're not going to come back," he resolved. "I'm ending this tonight."

"What?" Benedict rose as well. "You want to go in tonight?"

Kane answered with his eyes.

"But, you said we wouldn't do it tonight! We agreed, remember?"

"I know what I said," Kane answered, stiff-lipped, "but I've changed my mind. I can't stand here with it right in front of me and not go in. We might not even be here tomorrow. Borley may have us in the morning for all we know. Besides, time is always of the essence for me; that's why I'm here to begin with."

The reporter frowned. "But even if you destroy The Horror, Borley will still be there tomorrow."

"No," Kane whispered wisely. "Borley is dependant upon The Horror. If I destroy it, Borley will go down as well. He is what he is only through its power. But if I take that power away, his empire is no more. Then...*then* he becomes a part of the system. It is the demon which keeps him unaccountable."

"All right," the reporter acquiesced, "but shouldn't we at least wait until there's a minimal number of people in the castle? Tonight, it's full of druids."

"We'll wait a while—a half-hour or hour—and then proceed. And once inside the castle, everything's done nice and quietly. I'll just sneak to the room and slip in. Once I'm done, I'll slip out. In fact, there's really no reason for you to even come."

<294>

"Are you serious?" Benedict lowered his thick eyebrows. "You think I've come all this way to step aside and usher you alone to your final goal? I want to be a part of this, you know. I'd like to see this Horror for myself."

"I'm sorry," said Kane, "but that cannot be. This is *my* demon, and I have to face it alone. Otherwise, it won't work."

"Why not?"

"Because it knows the smell of a Borley. And I," he hesitated, "am a Borley. It might allow me to enter unharmed, while you it would most certainly kill. But," Kane raised his finger, "but—you may prove quite useful in another capacity. It's possible that I might not make it to The Horror. Along the way, I might be captured by Borley's men. In that case, I would need you to help me escape. But you'd only be able to do so if you yourself stay hidden. Do you think you could remain in the castle undetected while I venture to the room? And if I am caught, you'll need to be clever to save me."

Benedict lowered his head, mulling over the proposition. He closed his eyes and searched deep inside, retreating into his most sacred self. In a few moments, he raised his head high, resolute words at his tongue. "Kane," he said, "since the beginning of this thing I've been the faithful sidekick. Time and time again, I've felt my services to you have been taken for granted. I've lost my job, my social standing, and it would seem, my home. I often become so wrapped up in the mystery of this ordeal—keep in mind that I am the curious reporter-type—that I easily forget my ultimate reason for being involved. And that is, I believe that J.C. Borley, like his deceased father, is a murderer. And I believe that no one else will do anything about it. Certainly, I feel more invigorated by this whole episode than I've felt in years, but I'm here to see Borley put away, and also to help a man in need—you. Therefore, if it genuinely helps bring justice to this criminal, I'll do whatever you need. I'll hide in the shadows, I'll spend my last dime, I'll dance like the court jester while you grind out a tune. But, you had *damn sure* better know what you're doing. Because if you go in there tonight and blow this, everything

<295>

we've worked for will have been in vain. So, I have one question for you: in your heart, in your soul, in the pit of your instinct, do you *know* that tonight is the night to do this?"

The stranger did not hesitate. "Yes."

Benedict nodded. "Then I'm with you."

Kane lifted his hand, and the reporter grasped it. They shook powerfully, unspoken words thick between their minds.

✳   ✳   ✳

A good hour had passed, Kane and Benedict having spent the time slouched in the cool darkness of the cavern, their lack of sight making each concentrate intensely on his thoughts. It was a phase of preparation, mentally and physically, for the challenge which lay ahead. At the proper moment, in the early hours of the morning, the stranger rose. "I believe it's time," he said, turning on his light. The brightness shocked their sensitive eyes.

The reporter stood as well, a nervous quivering in his empty stomach. Following his observation, the stranger twisted the torch holder. It responded just as before, producing the "click" of an unlocked mechanism. He gave a nod to the reporter who stood beside the handprint. Benedict placed his own hand on the chilly lump of rock and pressed. It slid inwards easily, and a release, like that of a weight dropping, could be sensed through the hard panel. As if clockwork, the door yawned open.

Kane paced over briskly, shining his light into the passageway. In the hazy rays, an ascending stone staircase, damp, narrow, and dreary was revealed. At its edges, tangles of filthy, silken spider webs were bunched and twisted. A moldy, stagnant smell rolled out in a dismal wave. With a final nod of confirmation to his counterpart, the stranger entered, Benedict just behind him.

<296>

Kane had to stoop as he made his way up the precarious passage. The air was stifling and claustrophobic, and the sheer steps were barely the length of a foot. It was like entering a poorly kept tomb, or like venturing through the tunnel from hell to heaven—or, in this case, perhaps heaven to hell. It was a rather long way, winding and unpredictable, turning so sharply and steeply as to make one easily lose balance. Neither uttered a word, fearful that the sound might somehow carry into the castle above. Only their footsteps, hard soles against unflinching granite, announced their presence in the shaft. Midway up, a mangy rat, scurrying away in horror, startled them for a breath, but otherwise, there was little sign of life. The higher they ascended, the more they could feel the weight of the castle's morbid energy pressing down on their bones.

Alas, the cramped path terminated in a short, square, black panel. Standing lowly before it, each man's pupils glistened at its sight. "Off," the stranger whispered, and their flashlight beams were gone.

Kane reached his hands into the darkness and felt them contact the apparent door. It was smooth and firm, mysteriously constructed. He could not tell if it was wood, metal or stone. Having no idea how it should be opened, the stranger pressed—lightly at first, and then with more pressure. With little pressure, the panel gave way, opening outwardly. Soundlessly, it moved a few inches and Kane stopped. They could hear a faint sound, and the reporter watched Kane anxiously from behind as the stranger held an ear to the crack. Confidently, Kane pushed it open further, this time far enough to crook his neck around to see. Several feet in front, illumination spilled across the floor, ending in a corner. Above, there was a wide, flat shadow.

Kane turned back to the reporter. "Classical music is playing," he murmured in his comrade's ear. "And it looks like we're underneath a staircase or something, off in a corner." Benedict nodded in acknowledgement.

Turning back to his task, the stranger continued opening the panel, stopping when it was just wide enough for his broad frame to slip

<297>

through. Upon stepping out, he was uncomfortably bent to prevent hitting his head. Having a better look above, he solidified they were indeed below stairs, wide to his left, and narrowing as they descended to his right. Kane moved to the side, allowing Benedict to exit as well. With that, the door was carefully closed again, save a half inch.

They sat under the steps for a while, peering out from the triangular shelter, watching for moving shadows in the light. Despite the romantically haunting music, Bach's *Air On a "G" String*, there was no other sign of activity. Each felt it was terribly late to fill the castle with a melody— but then again, this was a special night: Samhain. The sound was good, though. It would conceal their unwelcome presence in the fortress.

Mustering up a good deal of nerve, Kane crept over to the edge of the staircase and inched his face around. A grand hallway, tapestries streaming down its sides, loomed majestically. Arched doorways down its length led to a network of other chambers. The warm light glowed from a series of lamps and chandeliers. They were certainly in a secluded corner of the structure, a place so dark and submissive as to seem invisible to an observer; especially in contrast to the visual wonders to behold.

"Where is the music coming from?" Benedict uttered.

"I donno," Kane replied. "But it doesn't sound near. I think it's just echoing through the halls."

"And the lights?"

"Borley keeps this place lit up all night," the stranger said, "but that doesn't mean anyone's around."

The reporter slinked from beneath the steps as well, analyzing the environment for himself.

"This should be easy," Kane smirked. "You keep hidden in this area. I'll just sneak up to the room and take care of business. It'll all be over soon."

"How will I know if you're in trouble?" Benedict raised his brow.

The stranger grinned. "If you hear a commotion, I'm probably in trouble."

<298>

"Good luck," wished the reporter. With a last glance of determination, Kane was gone.

Benedict sat for a moment, unsure of what to do. He supposed he would stay there for a while, listening. For all he knew, a virtual cavalcade could be waiting all around him, knowledgeable of the intruders the entire time. Patience and observation were his greatest assets now.

The stranger wasted no time traveling throughout the castle. He had at first skulked up the simple stairway which he had been beneath. But halfway up, he saw the back of a suited guard, standing routinely on the floor above. Submersing himself below the wall alongside the stairs, the steely prowler skimmed back down, this time disappearing through an archway on the first floor. He stayed close to the walls, low to the floor, and as noiseless as possible. The castle's music was everpresent, sometimes muffled by a wall or object, only to find clarity again when Kane took a few steps. He used the music to pace his travel, moving more quickly when it reached peaks and climaxes, and exercising greater care when it lulled soothingly. All the while, his gun was drawn, anxiously anticipating use as a last resort.

The stranger was quite lucky. Once in a while a guard would enter his peripheries, but due to a turn of the watchman's head, or the placement of an antique, or the very layout of a room, Kane was able to flow about secretly. His greatest liability was ignorance of the castle's design. It was a confusing labyrinth of rooms, some huge and overwhelming, others small and well-crafted; each specifically placed to psychologically aid in the perplexity of the structure. We fear those things we cannot know and predict, and so the castle embodied that fear, being too large, varied, and intricate for one inside to feel comfortable.

After a short, but exhausting round, Kane was at once relieved to see a familiar corridor. He didn't know why it was recognizable, but felt it must surely lead him to a place he would remember—a place where could at least solidify his bearings. Once on track, the route to his destination should be easier to find. Still not a great distance from his origin,

<299>

the stranger slipped down the hall and passed through a doorway, instantly amazed to see it expand to a great, familiar room. It was Borley's collection of the bizarre.

Kane's skin crawled upon realizing where he was. Nonetheless, he knew there was a doorway on the other side that would lead him to a servant's staircase; perhaps the same one that crawled upwards to the hellish room. He dashed through the array of nauseating collections, seeing them only as a blur, and then, rounding a corner, he froze.

A blank look on his bulky face, a half-eaten sandwich in his right hand, a cup of coffee in his left, Brock, for a split second, stood like an innocent deer in headlights. It was a timeless moment, neither man completely processing the scene, and then Kane raised his weapon blatantly.

"*Son-of-a-bitch*," Brock muttered.

Kane glared. "Shhhh," he raised a finger to his lips devilishly.

Brock's face blossomed with red anger, the sandwich trembling a bit in his clenching hand. Kane saw the guard's eyes glance to the pistol secured at his side, and the stranger knew what Brock was thinking. With a knowing smile, Kane shook his head "no," as if scolding Brock's very thoughts; he loved having complete control of the brawny buffoon at last.

Helpless, Brock leered loathingly at the stranger, cursing him with his eyes. Watching the henchman with hawk-like intensity, Kane carefully walked over. "Don't let go of that sandwich," the stranger dared him softly. Fully prepared to pull the trigger, though it would instantly blow his cover, Kane stood face to face with his victim, grinning with delight. He reached down and removed Brock's sidearm, tossing it over his shoulder. Next, he took the guard's radio from its holster on his left side, throwing it down as well. Brock seethed with humiliation as his tools were stripped away.

Suddenly, and without warning, the gentle music in the castle blared, as if a favorite piece was being played. It was Verdi's *Anvil Chorus*, and the loud, new notes penetrated the men's ears, shocking them for a second.

<300>

Jumping a bit, Kane's eyes left the guard's, and it was in that instant that Brock saw his opportunity. With desperate speed and force, he slung the warm coffee in the stranger's face, following through with a fat and mighty fist.

Blackness. Stars. The ceiling. Kane was on his back and his hand was empty. Panicked, his eyes shot to Brock, scrambling to retrieve his radio beneath a delicate table. The brown liquid dripping in his eyes, Kane pounced, coming only close enough to grab Brock's shoe, dragging him back. The radio was just beyond the henchman's outstretched fingers, and he saw it shrink swiftly as his body was pulled away.

From there, an epic brawl ensued. Brock kicked Kane in the jaw, again producing sparkles of light in the stranger's dazed brain. But Kane fought through the disorientation, grabbing Brock once more on his way to retrieve the unit. The *Anvil Chorus* pounded the castle's air, masking the ruckus of the struggling men. Somehow, they each made it to their feet, and Kane took the upper hand, walloping the lug to his body again and again, feeling a rib crack and give way beneath one punch.

In his hiding place below the steps, Benedict thought he could hear the sounds of fighting. He cocked his head to the side like a canine, listening intensely. But the music was too bold and calamitous; he could not separate the noises from the rhythmic clash of steel and the roar of a hundred tremendous voices.

Kane crashed through an ostrich skeleton, brittle bones exploding, rattling across the hard floor in all directions. But, determined to not be beaten, he was immediately on his feet, this time wielding an ostrich leg as a weapon. He swung it like a baseball bat, breaking it across Brock's face, a deep cut erupting on the bridge of the guard's nose. Inspired by his football days, Brock lumbered full speed ahead, plowing into Kane, knocking the intruder's breath forcefully from his chest.

Benedict was getting anxious. Though he could not clearly define the dire sounds, he sensed that something had gone awry. It was compounded

<301>

by the loud music. He wondered if the volume had been increased intentionally—if Kane had been ambushed, and the music used to obscure the tactic from him. He himself fought internal conflict. Should he stay? Should he see if something was wrong? How could he know for sure?

Equally battered, Kane and Brock battled ceaselessly. Kane punched to the face, Brock returned to the body. Kane elbowed to the spine, Brock rammed to the legs. The war waged on, until Brock sealed a firm grip around Kane's throat. Suddenly, the conflict was deadly.

The stranger was thrown against a cabinet, choking. His chin pressed down tight, his fingers working at Brock's grip, he could already feel the tunnel vision enclosing at the sides. In desperation, he released the henchman's thick fingers—the grip tightening—and grabbed Brock's hair, wrenching his neck back, simultaneously lifting his knee into the guard's groin.

Unlocking his grip, Brock dropped to the ground, Kane striking him on the way down. Writhing in the sick, searing and ungodly pain that creeps from bludgeoned testicles, the henchman still managed to jerk the stranger's feet from beneath him. On the floor, his legs entangled with Brock, Kane flailed for anything within his reach. His fingers found a cabinet knob, and he jerked it open. Reaching inside, he felt for something large and hard. He found it.

With a gruelling burst of strength, Kane strained to raise his body as high as possible. Simultaneously, he lifted the object far above his head. Powerful with fury, the stranger brought the object down with all the force of gravity and the mammoth, hulking rage in his soul. In an ear-smashing clash, the heavy, liquid-filled jar, the slave's head bobbing inside, shattered thunderously like a bomb on Brock's ruddy cranium. A million white droplets of water exploded atomically, thick razors of glass raining down. The black, severed head, spongy and bloated, eyes puffed shut, rolled down the guard's back, bouncing off the floor, and gyrating to a squeaky halt on the shiny floor. Brock was out cold.

<302>

Even above the tumultuous music, Benedict had heard the crash. That was it. He made up his mind. Speedily, he raced through the rooms, as concealed as possible, heading in the direction of the clamor.

Bleeding, his clothes torn and dirty, Kane rose, satisfied at the sight before him. He knew the uproarious noise would send other guards to the site within seconds, and he wondered what he should do. Breathless, he peered at the doorway, the servant's staircase ascending just on the other side. Time and time again his efforts had been thwarted, and with each time, the more difficult his quest became. He stood inside the castle. The vial, hopefully intact, was within his pocket. In a flash he resolved what he must do. Indignantly determined that his plan would not be foiled, he scooped up his gun and bolted towards the stairs. He knew that time was of the essence. Once the guards found Brock, they would be looking for him. But if he could only destroy the demon, all might be saved. His coat flying behind him like damaged wings, he dashed up the shadowy steps.

No sooner than Kane's form had disappeared, Benedict bound into the room. His eyes ignited with horror when he feasted them upon the scene. Brock was crumpled on the floor, a thick stream of dark, reflective blood flowing from his skull. Not far from him was the decapitated head, and all about was wetness and glass sparkling in the light.

"Hold it!" a voice shouted.

The reporter looked up to find a small team of men at the doorway, their guns trained on him, their radios buzzing with chatter. Benedict lifted his arms submissively. The men rushed in, slinging him to the ground and twisting his arms behind his back.

"Holy hell," one said as they hauled him off, "Mr. Borley's gonna be pissed at this!"

✻   ✻   ✻

<303>

His energy dwindling, yet efficiently motivated by will, Kane climbed the dingy stairs higher and higher through the castle. These steps were perfect for his duty. They had been built to remain inconspicuous, trailing away from the structure's important places, weaving at the edge, the very periphery, of the fortress.

Upon turning one corner, he almost yelped at coming face to face with a huge, mounted gorilla. Muscle-bound and domineering, its swayed frame stood nearly six feet, its face holding as much cognizance and expression as a human's, and as much anger as the day it was murdered. Kane continued onward, praying he would not encounter another guard. All the energy he had left was meant to be spent on the demon which awaited him.

At last, he topped a flight of steps and found himself in the quiet, lonely hallway, the ghastly half-light radiating about. He turned to his right. There it was: the door. The prickly hairs of his neck stood when he saw it. It looked exactly as it had before. Peaceful. Humble. Simple. But its harmless exterior contained a deluge of nefarious power. He could feel it deep in his guts. It was the same feeling he'd known each time another family member died. It was that empty, isolated vulnerability—that swallowing, sinking bleakness—the unknown, looming and grinning down upon him—the kind of helpless faithlessness that only personal tragedy can bring—knowing that things will never be the same again.

Kane closed his eyes and breathed. He explored far and deep into that sanctioned universe inside—the one we know as a frightened child—the one we try to forget as adults. He reached into that place where imagination, hope, creativity, wonder, and mystery resides, and brought forth the power, clarity, and strength to face that evil cloud that had hovered above him so long.

Kane opened his eyes. The door waited before him. He could go to it now, or it would come to him someday, as it had to so many others. Only he could master it, and he would have to do so now. He looked

<304>

behind himself a final time. The long corridor, down which he had walked not long before, was empty and still. The illumination around him ceased halfway down the hall, resulting in a lifeless darkness. He turned back to the door and stepped closer to it. It was old and saga-cious, the wolf snarling at him from the metal keyhole. The stories were no longer stories; it was all before him now. He reached out and raked his fingers down it, not touching the wood, but hovering just above it. A thick, staticy, electric tingle, like a television screen, brushed the surface of his flesh.

Kane reached into his pocket, fished around, and brought out the vial of holy water, potent and intact. He placed it safely back inside. Still holding his pistol, ever cautious, he then slid his hand into another pocket withdrawing the key. It gleamed mystically, the noble owl pro-jecting its wisdom. With a final deep breath, he held it towards the lock, the dark, iron wolf contrasting with its brilliance. Grasping the owl lightly, he directed the key towards the wolf's gaping mouth. Suddenly, as with the entrance to the caves, it was sucked from his fingertips, bringing completion—the owl and the wolf—two halves joined. The door was now unlocked.

His attention then turned to the slot. Tarnished and innocent, it served a dreadful purpose. Beads of cold sweat adhered to the stranger's forehead, and his entire body rejected what he was about to do. He was right-handed, and so choosing the lesser of two evils, he bestowed the burden of sacrifice to his left. Overcoming his physical instinct, he watched his left hand, almost mentally disconnected from it, as it grew closer and closer to the covered opening. When his fingers finally touched the cold metal, they sat there a moment before he could bring himself to lift the hinged covering. He squeezed his eyes closed again, a frigid drop of salty water falling from his brow. With his right hand, he wiped his eyes. Finally, he gave in to faith. With his left hand, he lifted the metal awning. It rose only far enough for his fingers to slip inside. From the opened slot, a cool breeze drifted across his knuckles. He

<305>

looked at his fingers—each wrinkle, hair, and nail—and appreciated them like never before. He knew it might be the last time he saw them. With that, he slid them inside, the edge of the metal scraping his knuckles a bit on their way through.

His hand was more sensitive than ever, and, on the opposite side of the door, there was a coldness like a dry winter night. He stood there, his digits in the slot as though fresh bait, having no idea what vastness lurked on the other side. For a few seconds there was nothing, save the piercing air; and then, out from the coldness, he felt it. It was a sniffing—a hot, steamy sniffing, like a dog. He felt it first on the tip of his index finger, then it moved to the next one, sniffing them each, one after another. The breath tickled his skin as it spurted torridly around his trusting hand. At any moment, the tickling might be instantly replaced by the agony of razor-sharp teeth clamping down and ravaging. It sensed each digit deeply, selectively, inhaling the scent, savoring its aroma. Sniff. Sniff, sniff. Sniff. And then it stopped. SNIFF. Kane flinched as another surge of hot air, harder than the rest, blew across his fingers. And then, coldness once again. He stood for another ten seconds or so waiting for more activity, but there was none. With a sigh, he withdrew his hand. The hinged covering closed with a "snap."

He had passed the test...perhaps. Gathering his emotions together again, gun in one hand, vial in the other, Kane reached out and took the handle. His thumb pressed the tab, and the lock released. Pulling it towards himself, it opened slowly, whining on its way, frosty air gushing out. Upon opening halfway, a faint stream of light poured into the room. For the first time, he could see somewhat inside.

A bed. A rug. A fireplace. Dim and gray, the portion he could see appeared just as ordinary as the outside of the room; so mild in fact, that its simplicity compounded its eeriness. Hesitant to enter, Kane peered deeply into the darkness, waiting for a brush of motion. There was none. He reached into his coat pocket for his flashlight, but found that it was gone—presumably lost in his fight with Brock.

<306>

Leery as a hare, his legs coiled to spring at any instant, he slowly bent his head around the doorway, viewing the spaces at its sides. All seemed perfectly innocent.

Step by step, each foot painstakingly placed in front of the other, the stranger walked into the room, losing himself in the glacial air which permeated his body. From inside, hidden eyes watched his tall silhouette break the light of the doorway. He could feel them boring into his soul and mind—the eyes of a predator.

Directly in front of Kane was the fireplace. Quite basic and empty, it was made of square, gray stone, stoutly built. At his sides was darkness. He was a few feet inside the room, its energy so dense and drawing that he could feel it sucking his steamy breath away, each vile particle squirming inside his body, hungry for his thumping heart. He knew there was intelligence around him, observing his every move. With violent force, the door behind him slammed. Kane froze, impenetrable blackness all around him.

"*Greetings,*" a voice hissed. "*I have waited eons to meet you.*"

✳   ✳   ✳

Benedict was dragged like an animal, the hateful thugs hauling him to their master. His shins bounced across stone steps, intolerable, bruising pains electrifying him with each impact. But he knew the sheer brutality of the hands which gripped him was surely minimal compared to what the rich man himself may do.

Beethoven playing tenderly, they traveled into a moderately-sized chamber, pillows, drapes, and emblems of comfort all around. Sprawled on a couch was J.C. Borley. He looked surprisingly ordinary for a moment. A thick book was tucked in his arm, dainty reading glasses slid halfway down the bridge of his nose. A long, beautiful pipe, as curvaceous as a swan, was clenched in his teeth, soothing smoke spiralling

<307>

upwards. He wore a luxurious silken robe, a scintillating shade of plum. Completely absorbed in the music and the words on the page, he didn't notice the team of men at first. When his jet black eyes finally shot above his lenses, he drew back his head in surprise, leaning to turn down the music at his side.

"Well, well. What have we here?" he lowered the book.

"Mr. Borley," a bald guard spoke up, "we caught this little rat in the castle. And you're going to be very displeased when you hear what he did."

Putting his glasses aside, Borley leisurely stood up, eyeing the reporter from head to toe. "Oh and what's that?"

"He bashed Brock with your slave head."

"Oh dear," the rich man cringed. "I hope it's not broken."

The bald man looked to the floor. "Yes sir, it is. Shattered."

"Oh damn," Borley shook his head mournfully. "Then perhaps I should have a new one. A *white one* this time."

"Uh, yes," the guard replied, "and Brock, of course, is hurt."

"Ah yes," Borley's eyebrows jumped. "How is he, by the way?"

"He's unconscious, sir. Bleeding from the head."

"See that he gets some attention, will you?" Borley motioned to a particular henchman who dashed off.

Two guards restrained the reporter tightly. Benedict's face was stern and his lips were tight; his eyes locked stiffly on the rich man's. Hands stuffed in his pockets, Borley approached the captive, staring at him blankly.

"So, Mr. Benedict," Borley said, "you broke into my home and destroyed a work of art atop my employee's head?"

The reporter snarled defiantly. "That's right."

"Nonsense!" the rich man chuckled. "I've read your articles. You're a pacifist!" He turned to another guard. "Search the castle immediately. I'm sure Mr. Kane is here somewhere." The henchman took off, accompanied by several other guards. Again, Borley's attention was on the reporter. "This has been an action-packed evening for me. First I had

<308>

the Halloween feast, and now this. I'm not usually up at this hour, but I was having some trouble falling asleep. Perhaps *you* can entertain me now. So, what do you have to say for yourself?"

"I came here tonight to ask you a question," Benedict growled, uncharacteristically.

"Fair enough," Borley nodded. "Ask away."

Behind the solid exterior, the reporter's brain churned for words. He knew that Borley liked to talk, and so he asked a question deserving of a laborious answer. "How did your father die?"

The rich man was unfazed by the inquiry. He smirked. "I fed him to the big monster that lives upstairs. Is that all?"

Benedict was shocked. "You…what do you mean?"

"I'll tell you what," Borley said, spinning around. "Bring him into the *game* room," he ordered his men. "We'll continue our conversation there."

Led by the master of the castle, the henchmen shoved the reporter along. They passed through two illustrious rooms and down a short flight of steps, arriving at a massive stone chamber, reminiscent of the Tower of London. Benedict's stomach dropped. The room was filled with items of torture. A rack—a large, wooden table, upon which victims are strapped and stretched until they rip apart—was tilted benevolently in a corner. An iron maiden—a metal coffin shaped like a voluptuous woman, its interior lined with spikes—stood gruesomely by a fireplace. A chair, its seat a cushion of nails, thumbscrews positioned on its armrests, lounged beside a wall of needles. It was a dreary and macabre sight, the unfamiliar stench of prolonged agony hovering.

"Chain him," Borley demanded nonchalantly.

Terror in his pupils, the henchmen drove Benedict to a recess in the wall, about the size and height of an average man. There, two medieval cuffs, joined to the stone by chains, hung heavily. His cranium banged into the rock, the reporter's hands were drawn over his head, the tight cuffs clamped mercilessly around his wrists. Now, it would be torture.

<309>

"You see," Borley said, returning to the earlier train of thought, "my father, in his old age, began to think a lot like you. He had amassed an incredible fortune with the aid of his dark little secret—it was a fortune that I myself, as you can see, would someday own. But, he started feeling guilty later on. He started wondering if he was going to hell when he died! And so he wanted to get rid of the demon—just in time for me to take over." The rich man brought his face inches from Benedict's. "But I couldn't have that. I couldn't have my father throwing away the one thing I needed most. It wasn't fair! He had the demon all those years, but he wanted to rob me of it. And so I told the demon of my father's intentions, and together, we destroyed him; a bit of an exception to the demon's normal behavior. Is that what you wanted to know?"

"How could you do it?" Benedict spat. "How could you kill your own father?"

"I didn't kill him," Borley leered. "*His own demon did.*"

The reporter, disgusted, would not look away, his stare penetrating the abysmal eyes before him.

"And now comes the part where I ask you questions," Borley resumed, now pacing about. "Who is Mr. Kane?"

Though full of fear, Benedict would not give in. "I wish I knew," he said. "But he won't tell me."

Borley rushed up to the reporter, a diabolical flame in his eyes. "Look at you!" he shouted. "Look at you! You're in no position to toy with me. You are an intelligent man—therefore you should know when to save your own ass. It's over for you! You are completely and ultimately under my control. I can do anything I want to you. Anything! Look...I can poke you in the eye if I want!" He lifted his straightened index finger and lightly, but firmly, jabbed Benedict in the right pupil.

"Aughh!" the reporter cried, his eyelid fluttering, tears immediately streaming.

"I can leave you here for days if I want, forcing you to urinate and defecate on yourself; allowing you to die painfully, slowly, of starvation

<310>

or dehydration! Or I can cut off your fingers, or pull out your teeth, or slit your tongue down the middle like a snake! I can do ANYTHING!" He punched the reporter solidly in the stomach. Benedict gasped and choked, his face pallid with pain.

"Let me try this again," Borley spoke into his victim's face, his brackish breath like a bull's. "Who is Mr. Kane?"

"He's..." Benedict choked again, "he's a private investigator."

A calmness dropped like a veil over Borley's face. "You're a liar," he said politely, "and I hate liars."

The rich man took a deep breath, visibly collecting himself. He paced around the room some more, quietly gathering his thoughts. "Mr. Benedict," he finally spoke, "you see around you a collection of torture. As you may or may not know, I am a world traveller. And on my travels, I enjoy acquiring objects of uniqueness. Not surprisingly, instruments of torture qualify. There are plenty of such instruments out there—God knows there has been a great deal of torture in mankind's past—and man has rarely been so creative than when it comes to the task of bringing his fellow man unparalleled misery." He made his way over to the fireplace. "But, in times such as these, despite the intricacy of properly crafted mechanisms of agony, I find, again and again, that few things get results as fast as a good ol' red-hot poker."

He lifted the long, heavy poker from its holder and nodded to the bald guard. "Put this on a flame, will you?" he licked his plump lips perversely. "It's time we give Mr. Wilson Benedict some inspiration."

*   *   *

The room of The Horror was as lightless as the caves had been. Deprived of sight, Kane's other senses maximized, his own pounding breath filling his ears like a tempest. It was a gross, violating nightmare, the pressure of evil and sin enclosing his body from all sides.

<311>

"Who are you?" the stranger demanded, his voice dry and wavering.

"I am who you think I am," replied the darkness, its voice raspy and low.

"I want to see you!" Kane ordered, his gun trembling in his hand. There was silence for a while, the sense of a thinking mind pulsating in the void.

"Very well."

At once, the fireplace at the back of the room was ablaze with tall, yellow, roaring flames. Before it was a silhouette, as black as the rest of the chamber. Crouched and poised, its outline was more creature than human—its head knobby, its shoulders powerful and arms long.

"I want to see all of you," the stranger said, firelight dancing in his eyes.

"This is all you need see of me," the demon responded. "And even *it* is only an illusion. Unlike mortals, I have no body. I have only thought and energy. How your eyes see me, is how your eyes *want* to see me."

Kane squinted at the form, but he could see no further detail. "What do you mean, that you've waited eons to meet me?"

"Time to you is different than time to me," spoke The Sate. "Your mind is restricted to your brain capacity. The life experience is too large for you to perceive at once, and so you see it moment by moment—hence the illusion of passing time. But I am without restrictions. I can see all experience, past and future. To me, it is one. I have always known that we would meet in this year."

"Then why did you have to smell my hand?" Kane patronized him. "If you know so much, you should have known it was me."

"Humans are specific, but neglectful of the broad. I am broad, but neglectful of the specific."

"All right," said Kane, gathering his strength again, "then I suppose you know why I have come here tonight."

The demon laughed, slowly and deeply. "You have come here to banish me. But instead you will serve me."

"No," the stranger snapped. "I will not."

<312>

"Surely you will," said the demon, "or I will kill you."

Kane rolled the vial in his sticky, sweaty hand. He wondered if The Horror knew it was there.

"For many millennia, I have made countless humans great," the demon said. "I have fed off the mortal desire for power and pleasure. I give humans what God will not, and in turn, I only ask to be served—just as I serve the Great Lord of Darkness. I can give you power, too; just like Crawford Borley."

"So many have died," Kane glared. "So many precious people have died because of the curse you inspired in Odin. Your evil has haunted my entire life, and taken away those people I loved the most. You stand for everything I despise, and I will not yield to you."

"Indeed," the Sate agreed, "I am those things that mankind fears. I am rape, I am murder, I am loss, agony and violation. I am spiders and blades and blackness and death itself. But I am also riches, enlightenment, dignity, strength and euphoria. I am the yin and the yang; the circular balance of karma. I can bring wonder or terror—and I offer you the choice."

Something inside Kane moved, and he knew it was time. "I have made my choice," Kane spat angrily, "and here is my decision." Just above the fireplace, a mantle, in the form of a heavy stone ledge, hung. With lightning speed, the stranger drew back his hand, the vial cupped in his palm. With all the force in his body, he threw it. End over end, the tube of glass hurtled through the air, the platinum flames sparkling in its clear, divine liquid. Kane watched it soar with wide eyes, his mind visualizing it shatter against the stone, the water raining down on the malevolent creature.

Almost in slow motion, the container whizzed over the demon, the silhouette of his head snapping back in surprise as it flew above. Even The Sate was helpless as the vial made contact with the ledge. "*Pinngk!*" It struck with intense, concentrated force, and the container, fully intact, bounced remarkably, ricocheting in a towering arc. It hit the

<313>

floor, skipping a bit, then rolled in a large half-circle, coming to a wobbly rest in the back corner of the room.

Kane was horrified. Tense and outraged, the demon stared at the stranger, hatred and rage seething from his devilish form. A depthless, guttural sound emerged from inside the Sate, rising with his anger, swelling like a war cry. All of the blackness in the room seemed to swirl and loop, drawing into the creature as his wrath converged. Howling with fury, the demon rushed through the room towards Kane, his movement ghostly, rippling like a liquid shadow.

An icy shockwave of demonic power blasted the stranger, blowing him backwards, slamming him into the door behind him. He was instantly paralyzed by the energy, holding his back against the wall like a ceaseless gale. The black, devoid face of The Horror was inches from Kane's, and its foul, wintry breath sickened him.

"I can squeeze your brains out your nostrils you impotent fool!" the creature screamed, its voice shattering Kane's eardrums. "How dare you come into my abode and try to banish me! I could have been your savior, but instead, I'll be your executioner!"

Straining, Kane was able to move his eyeballs in their frozen sockets. He glanced at the vial far away in the dark corner. Now, it was lost.

"Do you know what I can do for you!?" the Sate exclaimed. "Have you ever felt such power? Do you realize what power is?! I can make you see the future!"

Instantly, Kane's eyes were shut. But instead of seeing darkness, he saw bright visions—flashing by in an elaborate blur—too fast to completely comprehend.

"I can give you strength and pleasure!" the demon roared.

Kane's eyes opened, but the sick terror in his body had transformed into a feeling of might, dominance, and confidence: feelings he thought he knew, but had never genuinely felt to their fullest. His insides were secure, revered, and stable…careless of others. He felt devoid of worldly distractions, concerned only with pleasuring himself.

<314>

"You could feel this way always!" The Horror raged on, "I can make it happen in the blink of an eye. The world could be your playground if you wanted!"

Kane felt the paralysis release his right hand, holding the firearm. Sensation flowed throughout it once more.

"Look at the gun in your hand," the demon now spoke coaxingly. Kane spread his fingers open, the pistol laying on his palm. "It is a physical object," continued The Sate, "something to which you are helpless. But merely use your mind. Think of its hard metal lifting away."

The stranger could not help but visualize the demon's words, and the gun's feeling of weight dissolved against his flesh. Next, he could feel a smooth, flat layer of air seep between the firearm and his hand. Magically, the object began to rise, turning weightlessly as it hovered in midair. Suddenly, it dropped.

"See!" cried the demon. "See what I could do for you! But instead, you have forced me to kill! Kill! Kill!" Each time he screamed the word, Kane's head banged painfully on the door.

"Forgive me!" the stranger mustered from his numb throat. "Forgive…"

"What?"

The stranger's paralysis vanished, and his body slumped in relaxation. "I'm sorry. I'm so sorry," he panted. "Please…forgive me."

Startled, the dark form before him was quiet. The tumult in the room halted, and confusion was projected by the creature. "What do you mean?" the demon asked

Kane sighed, his eyes falling to the floor. "I never knew," Kane said. "I never knew how it could feel. For the first time, I understand. I've used you as a scapegoat, blaming you for every miserable thing I've ever known. But I was wrong. I *do* want it…I want what J.C. Borley has."

The demon floated quietly before Kane, his outline restless with thought. "Your heart is difficult to read, Kane Borley," he muttered suspiciously. "Perhaps you try to fool me. Perhaps I'll do best to rid myself of you."

<315>

"No," Kane's plea wavered. "I had rather live as your servant than die at your hands tonight. My only quarrel is with Borley."

The Sate shifted with discontent, his powers laboring for clarity of perception. He was quiet and still in the shadows, his thoughts calm. Then, without warning, he leaned down, bringing his raven face inches from the stranger's once again. "Do you accept me as your master?" the rancid breath boiled.

"Yes."

With startling intensity, a column of frigid, lavender energy jetted from the demon's mouth, parting Kane's lips and sliding down his throat. The coldness filled his body completely—a coldness so intense that it transformed into a fiery internal warmth. The stranger could feel the demon's radiant power in every cell of his body.

Once the last photon of energy seeped from The Horror's lips, he glided back a few feet, sinking low to the floor. The creature hung with exhaustion. What was once anger had turned to reflective satisfaction. Admiringly, he stared at his newest creation.

"I will make you *more* powerful than J.C. Borley," uttered The Sate proudly. "You have made a wise choice."

Kane's stern eyes gleamed at the malefactor before him. "Yes," he said. "I have."

In a flash of intent, the stranger's fingers opened on his right hand. He shot his eyes to the vial in the corner. Instantly, it moved. The animated container rolled—so fast as to seem a streak of light—and leapt through the air, landing firmly in Kane's palm. With a burst of desperate, enraged passion, his hand locked down on the vial, crunching it; the thick glass slicing into his flesh with a sting. "Damn you!" screamed the stranger as he flung his palm-full of sacred water onto the dark, bulky figure before him. "Damn you from this earth!"

The liquid cascaded onto the evil creature. As each drop hit him, it electrified his form with searing, purple light, flashing and sizzling

<316>

madly. For the first and only time, in the erupting flashes of purple illumination, Kane glimpsed the face of the demon. It was hideous.

Shrieking in immortal agony, the acidic liquid destroying in a chemical reaction of good and evil, the demon slid backwards like a retreating scorpion. He slipped into the lapping flames of the fireplace, and then vanished, appearing to have fallen through the blaze. The wretched screams of torment then echoed and faded gradually, as if The Sate had indeed plunged down a long shaft.

Once his cries died, Kane stood in the room alone, the fireplace still crackling. Then, out from the silence, a swift "whoosh!" ascended the chasm down which the creature had disappeared, immediately followed by a large, agitated fireball that ejected from the fireplace. It exterminated in a brilliant flash of heat that lit up the room for a half-second, so bright as to be blinding. Again, all was quiet. And then, a rumble.

There was a long, yawning, discontenting groan deep in the earth below the castle. Like a whining upset stomach, it circulated beneath, through each beam and stone and foundation of the great fortress. It was a colossal sound—the kind of sound that continents make when mountains explode and surge up from hellish masses of volcanic upset. It was a moan of shifting and falling, and dire chain reactions rippling through rock. All the while, the rumbling, a tremendous vibration, grew.

Without warning, the hearth began to crumble—a web of thick cracks erupting across its surface. Bricks began dropping off effortlessly, and then, with a deafening crash, the entire structure gave way, collapsing into the chasm that had apparently led to The Horror's lair. Like an expanding tidal wave, the entire floor, from the hearth outward, began falling. A great, black fissure rippled across the chamber towards Kane.

Panicking, the stranger bolted out the door of the cursed room, the void swift at his heels. Blood dripping from his hand, he raced down the long corridor leading from the room, the blackness chasing him like a beast. The entire castle was falling apart on the inside—portions of the top floors hitting the ones at the bottom, making those floors collapse

<317>

as well. Upon exiting the hallway, a light caught Kane's eye to his right. It was a window: the sun was rising.

Seeing it as his last resort, the stranger sped towards the window. His eyes were filled with a wide, scenic view just before he brutally crashed through the glass. His stomach was in his throat as he flailed helplessly. Falling. Falling. "Splash!" Shockingly, refreshingly, Kane's entire body plunged deep below the cold waters of the moat. He jettisoned far under, kicking his feet and pushing down with his arms, pumping his body back up to the surface. Alas, his head broke from the frothy water, and he gasped. Swimming forcefully to the side of the moat, he then realized the liquid was tugging at his heels. A suction was being created by the waterway falling into opened crevices. It pulled harder and harder at the stranger, and he fought despairingly to make it to the shore.

*   *   *

There was a glowing, hot poker a few inches from Wilson Benedict's left ear. J.C. Borley held it loosely in his grasp, seconds away from driving it into the canal. But Borley's mind was elsewhere, as were the minds of his men. Upon perceiving the violent rumbling, the rich man had stopped, turned, and was examining his castle—not only with his eyes and ears, but with his burnished instinct. Each person, including the reporter, wore an expressionless face, their minds at loss to fathom the origin of such chaos in the sound structure.

And then, there it was. In an instant, with a furious sound, the far wall of the torture chamber was gone, the floor dropping away thereafter, speeding towards the master of the castle. It was at that moment that it first *clicked* in Borley's intricate brain: the stranger had won.

There were only a few seconds left in J.C. Borley's dark life. He knew it. And in those last moments, he turned to Wilson Benedict, the man

<318>

whom he was about to torture mercilessly. Borley's black eyes, like depthless pools, looked far into the reporter's. He communicated so many things in that final stare—a million thoughts, ideas, wishes, stories, and concepts that Wilson Benedict would never completely understand. And, dropping the bright poker at his side, Borley lifted both his hands into the air angelically, as if accepting some private and final redemption. As he began to quietly hum a tune that Benedict could not place, there was a trace of a smile on his lips, a sparkle in his eye, and a knowing, affectionate, good-humored sheen about his face. With a tremulous moan, the floor of the room gave way beneath his feet. Dapper, polished, always the rich man...always the winner...J.C. Borley's towering figure dwindled as it dropped, with his men, into an ulcerous abyss that opened below. He was no more.

*   *   *

The newly risen sun cast a crimson lining on the mountains of Asheville. It emerged from the sleeping peaks, as it had for a timeless span. Its golden, life-giving rays were warm and rich, and they reveled in the wafting clouds of dust, billowing from the remains of Borley's Castle. It was now the facade of a castle, its interiors gutted, its doors opening to a crater in the earth. The hollowed mountain below the fortress, riddled with caverns, had given way, and the castle's insides had been built upon them. The interior of the structure was now laying in a mass of rubble at the base of a mound of earth, far, far below. The rumble of the disaster had reverberated throughout the city, regarded as a small earthquake.

Weary and haunting, the walls of Borley's Castle stood silent and looming as they had for so long. But now, they wielded no substance; they were simply a forlorn reminder of what had once been, and what was taken so swiftly, as most great things are—in one fell swoop. They

<319>

stood sadly, meagerly, still with dignity, but nothing more. Around them curled a sloshy trench, all that remained of a moat. A flurry of dark, churning, swollen clouds had rushed into the sky above, grappling to squeeze out the sun, twisting about as though irritated by the malevolence that had dispersed into the atmosphere. The disheartening scene was startling in its appearance—startling for what stood, startling for what was lost. It proved again that basic thought mankind tries so desperately to forget: *all things* must come to an end.

At the cracked entrance of the castle, the two icy statues—snarling wolf and thoughtful owl—guarded the broken grounds. The radiant sting of their realism was somehow gone. Now, they appeared clumsy and inanimate, impotent and didactic. Harsh and gray, they stood as their own grisly tombstones.

Dazed, filthy, wet, and bleeding, Kane staggered towards the empty walls of Borley's Castle, cracks and pops surrounding him as the destruction settled. He was too traumatized to fully comprehend the gravity of what had taken place. His only objective was to find his counterpart.

"Wilson!" he called. "Wilson! Can you hear me?" Nothing. "Wilson?! Wilson!" He paused, thinking he heard a noise. It was a faint, high-pitched noise, but surely a human voice. "Wilson!" he continued calling.

"Help!" a voice trailed faintly from inside the castle.

"Wilson!" Kane sped towards a section of the exterior wall that had fallen away.

The view on the other side of the hole was treacherous. Kane peered through to find the abyss below as gaping as a volcano. Panning his head side to side, he was completely surrounded by a singular wall, soaring high above like the barricade of a fort. On the opposite side, two-thirds of the way up, Wilson Benedict hung weakly to the wall by his thick chains. His feet were wedged into the stones beneath them for more support. When Kane saw him, he sighed.

"Hello there!" the stranger cupped his mouth and yelled. His voice echoed from the walls.

<320>

"What in God's name have you done?!" the distant figure of the reporter exclaimed.

"We'll discuss that after I get you down!"

When the stranger turned, he was startled. One of Borley's outside guards stood, rifle in hand. An older man, he projected a vacant stare. Kane was unsure what to do, his hands in sudden limbo. The guard did not speak. He only stood, looking at Kane, then looking past him at the castle in ruins. There was no sense of emotion or duty in his blue eyes. There wasn't even disbelief. Instead, his spirit was lost—alone— drowned in defeat. Slowly, wistfully, he turned and walked away.

<321>

CHAPTER ELEVEN

THE TOMBSTONE OF Crawford Borley was as tall, shiny, and erect as ever. Even as the mirthful birds chirped, it shone darkly in the sun, always imposing, always carrying the weight of the man beneath it. But it was a monument that marked more than the passing of a man. It marked an era, a time, a way of placing ideas together, and a nobility granted by the people. It would stand there for a long, long time; and someday, no one would remember what it meant. It would only be another headstone, albeit impressive, in a quiet, rolling field of petrified memories. The great, bustling world would tuck it farther and farther away, and someday, when the weather had stolen its luster, someone would strain to read its words. Then, on to the next one.

Well-rested, nourished, and bandaged, Kane and Benedict stood before it. Aside from the peaceful motions of nature, the cemetery was still. They stared at the headstone for a long while, each uncertain of where he stood in the world, still unsure of what he had done.

"Now it's truly over for him," Benedict said, entranced by the alluring obelisk. "Now he and Odin can rest in peace."

Kane nodded his head. "And now, for the first time ever, I can live a life in peace." Benedict looked to him, lowering his chestnut eyebrows.

"What are you going to do now?"

"I'm going home," Kane said. "I'm leaving all this behind me."

Benedict shook his head thoughtfully. "I see," he said.

"So what are *you* going to do?" the stranger inquired.

<322>

The reporter took in a deep breath, his eyes gazing into the distance, then exhaled. "Well," he said, "I thought about moving to Tennessee. But, I've finally come to a conclusion. I've done a good deal of traveling in my time. I've seen a lot of great places. I've seen the Rockies of Colorado, the beautiful coasts of Maine, the expanse of Montana, and the enchantment of Hawaii. I've seen many wonderful things—things I'd like to see again. But, despite all its curiosities—or perhaps, in part, because of them—there is no better place to live than Asheville. So, I'm going to stay right here. I've toyed with the idea of starting my own local newspaper for quite a while. Maybe this is the time to do it." Kane smiled, seeming glad to hear Benedict's plans. "I'm certain you'll do fine," he said.

"Well you know," Benedict replied, "I've been thinking: You and I could do an outstanding job as private investigators, don't you think? Perhaps we should go into business."

The stranger frowned, the breeze licking his hair lightly. "I've done all the investigating I ever want to do," he said. "No thanks."

There were a few more moments of quiet reflection, a relaxing hush of air around them. "Kane," Benedict said, his tone quite serious, "you *do* realize that we've made history here in Asheville, don't you?"

"I suppose," said the stranger. "But I hope it stays a history that only you and I will know about. We'll let the rest of the world keep thinking exactly what they do: that a minor earthquake rattled the foundation of the castle."

"Don't worry," Benedict replied. "Your secret's safe with me."

Kane nodded.

"You know," said the reporter, "it's almost a little bit sad in a way. I mean, the Borleys, and Borley's Castle, were really the final remnants of Asheville's old ways. Now we're moving into new times—the old times forever a thing of the past."

"I donno," the stranger shook his head, "I think some things are so strong that they imprint a place forever."

<323>

Benedict smiled. "Interesting you say that," he noted. "There's actually a quote by Albert Einstein that I enjoy very much. He said, 'the distinction between past, present, and future is only an illusion, however persistent.' That being the case, I suppose you could say that Borley will always be on that mountain, watching Asheville down below him; that in fact, because of its dark history, this place will always be saturated with…*mysterious* energies, shall we say? But now that he's gone, the new Asheville will have to learn how to operate without J.C. Borley. Let's hope things will be better here now."

"I suppose," Kane agreed. "Well," he looked around transitionally, "I should be going. I have to learn how to live again." He looked down at his hands, fidgeting a bit with his fingernails. "Wilson," he said, looking up, "…*thank you*…*thank you* for what you've done. I could never repay you, but I *am* going to try. You'll get a check in the mail next month."

"I appreciate that," the reporter beamed. "But you've certainly given me the most incredible experience of my life—and *that* is invaluable."

Kane extended his hand. Each man shook with honor.

"I don't suppose I'll see you again," the reporter said.

The stranger looked off for a moment, the question stirring in his brain. "I doubt it," he replied, his mind misplaced for a moment, "… but you never know."

Benedict smiled.

"*Adieu*," said the stranger, granting a reverent salute. Then he turned without hesitation and walked away, precious of his privacy to the last.

"Goodbye," the reporter called. "And good luck!"

The stranger wove his path through a maze of tranquil, aged tombstones, his long coat meandering like a cape behind him. As if a ghost dissolving into the wind, he soon vanished into the landscape, his shape another dark and natural form amongst the trees, grass, and rocks. The void left by his presence was filled by a new breeze.

Wilson Benedict stood for a while, gazing at the graves, his mind toiling with inward intensity. He waited for a bit to see if the stranger might

<324>

come back. For the first time, the reporter realized how much he'd enjoyed being wrapped up in the stranger's problems; it gave him a chance to forget about his own. Wilson Benedict was an intelligent man. He had now seen incredible things—things that most never dream possible—things which should bring a more vivid style to life's unanswered questions. Nonetheless, as he retreated introspectively to his car, slowly and gray, he had never been so confused.

<325>

Epilogue

THERE ARE PLACES on this earth that are flat, blank, and shapeless. They are so long and wide and far that even memories escape. Those are the places where the sky meets the horizon with a straight line, and all is honest and plain. They might offer scrubby trees or shrubs for character, but those things are transient. In such places, men are either transparent and good, or twisted by the agony of their exposure. Those places take your soul and propel it upwards, away from the land, away from the endless earth.

The Blue Ridge Mountains hold the spirits of their people. They are forms, worn and weathered, rugged and bold, that soak up energies like plump sponges. The French Broad River is one of the oldest in the world. It parts their solemn ranges, dispersing life to the mounds of continent folded and bunched by the cataclysms of times distant. The river brings life, and the mountains, greedy and hungry, retain it always. The circle of birth and death is a grand process, but those who die in the mountains return in the mountains. The ranges keep their spirits for all time.

*   *   *

From high atop a windy peak, the stranger looked out to bid silent farewell—to see one last glimpse of Asheville, sprawling before him in

<327>

the distance. It shined tastefully, more sophisticated than most lands. He was a small figure as he watched, dwarfed by the glimmering crowns and oceans of earth, as broad and reaching as his own blank future. He could feel the souls around him, brewing and alive, speaking volumes without words.

Asheville was a heavy place, and it would always be. But somehow, today, it was not quite as heavy at it had been before. There was burden, dark and strenuous, that had been lifted from its shoulders. Likewise, a weight was missing from the stranger's back, as well. A bright, indigo sky sheltered the city, downy clouds, a milky white, wisping above. Kane inhaled the scene. The dark, hard somberness in his eyes gave way to a new glint of hope. A light in his soul seeped out for the first time, joining the radiance before him. He had conquered his demon.

To experience beauty and mystery in perfect balance is an overwhelming thing. To the stranger, it was a vast scene, beyond words and explanation. Slowly he turned, the power of the mountains embracing him, drawing him back, as they always do.

Asheville, North Carolina, is a good place for a man to come from— but *he* was from elsewhere. And so he returned.

About the author

JOSHUA P. WARREN was born in Asheville, North Carolina, and has lived in the Blue Ridge Mountains his entire life. At the age of 13, he wrote his first published book. Since then, he has published numerous titles including *Haunted Asheville* and *The Lonely Ameba*, and is the president of his publications and multimedia productions company, Shadowbox Enterprises. His articles have been published internationally, and he has been featured in such mainstream magazines as *Southern Living*, *Delta Sky*, *FATE*, and *New Woman*. A winner of the University of North Carolina Thomas Wolfe Award for Fiction, he wrote columns and articles for the *Asheville Citizen-Times* from 1992 to 1995.

A widely-consulted expert on paranormal research, he was hired by the famous Grove Park Inn to be the first person to officially investigate the Pink Lady apparition in 1995. Such work has earned him appearances on the CNN, ABC, and NBC networks and/or affiliates, and he is frequently asked to be a guest on radio shows across North America (including "The Edge of Reality" on the Talk America Radio Networks). He is the founder and president of L.E.M.U.R., an active paranormal research team based in Asheville.

Warren is also an international award-winning filmmaker, having worked on numerous productions including Warner Brother's *My Fellow Americans*, Universal's *Patch Adams*, *Paradise Falls*, and the comedy *Inbred Rednecks*. For more information, please visit www.ShadowboxENT.com.

<329>

Printed in the United States
59040LVS00003B/49-51

9 780595 122264